WARRIOR'S MARK
DRAGONS
BOOK TWO

MARKED by an OATH

S.E. LOWER

Marked by an Oath
Dragons
SE Lower

Susan Lower Books

Language note: This book uses different Native American words to stand in for the shifters' ancient language, a tribute to the folklore and culture of the fictional people who gain animal spirit guides at their coming-of-age. The end of the book contains a pronunciation guide.

S.E. Lower

www.selower.com

ISBN: 978-945274-16-9

Glossary

Solanu – Mate

Bitatelo - mountain lion

Hehewuti - warrior mother spirit. - One who could hold and bestow a spirit to anyone.

Bodaway Achak - fire making spirit

Unahu - mate

Nimitqwa Ktelo - as you once were and will be again.

Ohunko - guardians whose dark hearts stain their spirits

Wakinyan - thunder/ thunder spirit

Nituwe he - who are you?

Mal'drathir - Shadow snatcher

One

THE FOREST SHADOWS CURLED unnaturally, their silence an uncanny echo.

Conleth entered the tree line. A body lay sprawled on the trail—eyes vacant, jaw slack. No broken branches, scuffed earth, or signs of a stumble.

"Second one this month." Sia stood barefoot in basketball shorts, tension visibly coursing down his arms as if the wolf crouched just beneath his skin. He flicked his gaze toward the body. "I sent for you as soon as we found him."

Four wolf shifters slipped between the trees. They spaced themselves at sharp angles, eyes scanning the shadows. Sia's pack moved like ghosts, cordoning off the area with practiced ease. They exchanged glances between the dark forest and the narrow trail, ready to intercept anyone who strayed too close.

If the tourists discovered what truly prowled in these woods, panic would ripple through the mountain like wildfire.

Conleth's dragon spirit coiled tight in his gut. *The lost touched this one.*

"Someone notify Taran?" His youngest brother probably still flew across the ridge looking for signs of the missing man. Since the thaw, the residents of Sentinel Peak returned in slow waves. Alongside them, thrill seekers and oblivious campers swarmed the mountain trails, deaf to the warning etched deep in the earth.

Taran rebuilt the old ranger station and prepared for humans to return to the mountain despite their oldest brother, Aluk's, attempts to keep them out.

Not one of them.

A hiss slithered from the tree line, sharp and cold as wind over ice. Conleth's dragon bristled. Beside him, Sia tilted his head, catching the same sound. The wolf alpha's jaw clenched, annoyance ghosting across his features.

Ever since Taran's mate, Gwen, arrived on the mountain with her Fae blood and spirit-bound magic, the curse that once threatened the shifters unraveled in loose strands. Lost spirit animals no longer linked to bloodlines came crawling back through the cracks. The mountain's protection dissipated like their ever-growing winter, and the shadow spirits emerged.

The old ones called them *ohunko,* the lost guardians whose souls had become twisted by war and rage remained bound to extinct bloodlines. Among them, the shadow spirits dwelled, not all seeking vengeance, but longing to shift again.

"We need to close off the forest. No more hikers. No more tourists," Sia growled. "The curse doesn't care who they are; the shadow spirits have become desperate."

Beneath it all, the queen beckoned them from the heart of the mountain.

Conleth kneeled beside the fallen hiker and closed the man's eyes with a brush of his fingers. A small mercy since he could do nothing more.

He retrieved an emergency blanket from his satchel. The crinkled foil whispered open, jarring the silence. He draped it over the body.

Futile, maybe, but it kept the body from being recognized when they carried it out.

Shadows watched from the trees. All they needed was a single drop of dormant shifter blood to draw their attention, a beacon to the lost ones.

Their patience had waned with the thaw.

"Aluk has tried reaching out to the state representative," Conleth said, rising and taking a step from the body. "But without a report from the region's shifter agent, they refuse to meet with him."

"They're just going to let the humans invade the mountain and hunt us openly?" Sia huffed. "Where is the shifter agent when you need him? Has anyone actually met the agent?"

"Aluk has," Conleth said.

"They'd speak to the dragon alpha," Sia muttered, scratching his chin. "Perhaps a wolf alpha, too?"

Human officials ignored tribal leaders and shifter council members, bending the truth to suit their political games. The last so-called shifter agent, Cedric McLeod, had weaponized his badge, hunting shifters, and ripping spirit animals from their people.

"Doubtful," Conleth murmured. Beyond the tree line, wisps of movement stirred in the dark. The shadows pulsed in the shade, their presence an icy whisper in the humid air.

He growled low, a rumble that vibrated through the soil and sent warning through the roots. His dragon sight surged, illuminating the forest with the heat signatures of lurking shadow spirits.

Sia let out a bark of dry laughter. "That's one way to keep the lost ones at bay."

Not lost. Waiting. Conleth bit the inside of his cheek. The shadow spirits waited for their bloodlines to return, for old magic to rise. *To reclaim what had been sealed long before he was born.*

"We can't have them attacking anymore humans."

"They're choosy buggers." Sia lifted his chin as his amber eyes darkened to gold. His wolf spirit hovered at the surface. "He wasn't out here alone. There were three of them. The spirits could've taken all of them but lured only one away. You think he might've shared our blood?"

Conleth stared down at the emergency blanket draped over the body. Something unspoken pulled at the base of his spine. "Have him taken to the clinic in town."

Sia frowned. "Not the resort?"

"No." His clinic at the resort served the local village and those at Avalanche Ridge. The resort held no space for a corpse. The clinic, newly remodeled in Sentinel Peak, was a better choice. "I'll run a few tests before you notify the family or file an official report."

Sia rubbed the back of his neck. He stood several inches shorter than Conleth's six-foot-five frame, but no less imposing. The wolf alpha's shoulders stiffened.

"We don't need more trouble from the outside. Looks like an unfortunate hiking accident. Guy separated from his buddies, panicked. Maybe a heart attack."

Conleth grimaced.

Sia's gaze narrowed. "He had a heart attack, right?"

He raised a hand, calling one of the pack enforcers forward.

Sia returned with Conleth to his SUV. He shouted clipped orders to his men while Conleth ran through the story they'd feed the human authorities in his head. He tossed his medical bag onto the seat and dragged both hands down his face. Once they'd settled on the lie, Sia vanished into the trees. Conleth sank into the driver's seat and leaned his head back, closing his eyes.

Another one.

Another one, his dragon spirit confirmed with a low, growling pulse.

Letting the humans in? The council should've known better. Every one of them knew what lived in these woods.

We had no choice.

The council of tribes governed all shifter packs and clans. Aluk, eldest of their bloodline, sat at its head. But human recognition? They all feared more hunters, and another battle gathered on the horizon.

There is no way of telling what Taran and Gwen's mating has evoked.

The lost spirits had risen. The mountain wept above, drenching them in relentless rain. Had the queen stirred within her prison? And what did it mean for them?

As hikers and tourists flooded in, unchecked by government restrictions, residents reclaimed Sentinel Peak. Conleth sensed the old dangers stirring with them.

It took thirty minutes to reach the clinic, an older two-story building on the far edge of town. The exterior gleamed from fresh coats of paint and a new sign, but the shadows in Conleth's mind hadn't cleared.

Outside the glass doors, a woman waited. Pale, silver-haired, and dressed in navy slacks with a lavender blouse, she stood like she owned the space, but it wasn't her posture that made Conleth stumble mid-step.

It was her scent.

Sweet cherries, warm and strange on the mountain air. Not cloying like perfume, but natural. Unusual. He expected rosewater or something floral, something older.

Instead, she smelled like the moment before a storm broke in midsummer.

And something else. Not quite human.

He inhaled again. Not Fae. Not fully. Her scent seemed a little unusual.

He shook it off. Probably half-something, like Gwen.

She stood nearly a foot shorter but carried herself like a general surveying a battlefield. Her jacket draped over one arm, her phone in hand, violet eyes tracked him like a predator.

Not frail. Composed. Dangerous, maybe. He liked that.

He stepped closer, casting a long shadow across the walk. "Can I help you?"

He didn't want to spook her.

Her gaze slid over him. No hint of age touched her face, no crack in the mask she wore. Heat climbed his skin. An invisible tether snapped taut between them.

His dragon spirit strained toward her. *Mate.*

The scent pulled him in, reeking of trouble, not fate.

Still, his dragon insisted on being near her. Choosing.

Conleth kept his face neutral.

"I asked," she said coolly. "Is the clinic always closed midday?"

He ran his tongue over his teeth, a habit of his beast. "Only when something more intriguing presents itself."

She lifted a pale brow. "Shifter, are you? Alpha, perhaps?"

He leaned against the doorframe. "Only one way to find out?"

She brushed past him with the same quiet command in her posture, her scent curling into his lungs like fuel to the flame. His dragon purred in appreciation. *Mate.*

Following behind her, his gaze fixed on the elegant line of her spine and the way her silver hair glinted in the light. Not white. Silver. Sharp cheekbones, and a firm mouth. She didn't flinch, didn't falter.

She has no scent of fear, nor does she reek of lies.

That made her even more dangerous.

She turned once inside. "So, I take it there's no staff here?"

A tug toward her curled hot and dangerous in his gut. *Mate.*

Not a possibility. A certainty.

Her brow spiked higher.

If the curse had broken, it meant the mountain had changed. Everything had.

"You'll be my first." He winked. "Got a name, beautiful?"

"Trinity Oberlin. I'm looking for Dr. Conleth Vasumen. Is that you?"

He leaned against the front counter. "You can drop the doctor part. They don't allow my kind to do residency in a human hospital."

"Ah, so I got the shifter part right. Not a wolf though, perhaps a mountain lion?" she asked.

"Oh, I'm bigger than that," he grinned, and she rolled her eyes.

"Are you always this charming with potential staff?" She kept her arms crossed.

"It relies on the position you had in mind."

She gave a soft, incredulous snort and tucked her tongue in her cheek, and scanned the lobby. Her gaze slid past him to the window, where the sound of tires crunching gravel signaled the ambulance pulling in with the body of the dead hiker.

"Is that a patient? One of the dead tourists found in the forest?" she asked.

Conleth's grin vanished. "How do you know about the bodies?"

He moved down the hall to meet the ambulance at the side entrance, specifically for emergency drop-offs and, in this case, autopsies.

"I'm more interested in what *you know* about the bodies." She followed him, her heels making a clipping sound on the tiled floor.

"I'm afraid you haven't been hired yet, so I'm not privileged to share. However, if you'd like to get together later and discuss a future position here, I'd be more than happy to meet you at, say, five?"

She pinched her lips together.

Conleth swung the door open in time for a set of Sentinel Peak enforcers to wheel the gurney inside.

"Male or female?" Trinity asked.

The body rolled past. Conleth motioned toward the small operating room down the hall.

"Male," one wolf-blooded enforcer said, gray streaking his hair.

"Have they all been male?" she asked, following them into the room.

"Sorry, but you'll need to wait in the lobby." Conleth tried to block her from coming inside the operating room.

She pulled back her shoulders, glaring up at him with a smirk. "You are going to examine the body, correct?"

"I am."

"Then I'll assist you." She shoved her way inside. Three men heading out stepped around her. They looked at her, then at him, and waved in silence as they left.

She put down her jacket and headed for the box of surgical gloves.

"Hold on a minute."

She ignored him. The gloves slid on with practiced ease, like second nature.

A knot tightened in his stomach.

Her focus unsettled him. She moved with intent, and the air thickened around her.

Who was this woman? By the way she dressed and the sudden questions, he took her for a journalist, but her gloved hands said she might be here for the job. He hoped for the latter because they definitely *did not* need this released to the human news outlets.

Footsteps resonated down the corridor. Conleth caught the familiar scent of Rourke, the alpha wolf, and Sentinel Peak's police chief.

Rourke stepped inside the surgical room.

"Ah, Chief Blackwood. It's good to see you again," Trinity said.

"Special Agent Oberlin," Rourke said, smiling. "I see you found the clinic."

Conleth rumbled deep in his chest. Rourke glanced his way and raised his brows as if to say, 'What's up with that dude?' Too bad shifter telekinetic only worked through blood and the mating bond. Otherwise, he'd tell Rourke to back off from his woman.

Conleth stilled. Not his woman. A woman. And until seeing her face, one he thought was older than her face betrayed thanks to her silver hair.

Conleth's internal brakes screeched. "Agent? Her violet eyes twinkled as she watched him.

"Oberlin is with the PPI. She's here to investigate the recent deaths," Rourke said.

Conleth's mind scrambled. "PPI?"

"Paranormal Phenomena Investigations." Her lips twitched into a smirk. "Shifter specialist."

Convenient. Or a complication wrapped in a pair of navy slacks and smelling like trouble.

"What brings you to this part of the mountain?" he asked.

"This case, for starters," she shrugged, "and many others, I presume."

"We're happy to have you here." Rourke's hand landed on her shoulder in that 'welcome to the boy's club' way that made Conleth's dragon growl.

Trinity looked between them and blinked.

"Shall we see about this body, then?" She flexed her gloved fingers.

Conleth didn't move.

She was an outsider, a government agent, and *his mate*.

That presented an even bigger threat than the people who sent her.

Two

The man's body lay under the sheet.

"Heart attack," Conleth said, pulling off his gloves.

Trinity kept her expression neutral, though a knot twisted behind her ribs. Third one in a month. Young. Healthy.

"Preexisting conditions?"

"None known."

She reached out and pulled the sheet back. Pale lips. Skin gone waxy.

The scent hit next. She covered her sensitive nose with a gloved hand. Not smoke, but something rotten and scorched threatened to gag her. Not natural this soon after death.

Her grandfather once called it the stench of a soul burned within. She turned her face away, gulping a breath of air.

Cedric would've filed a report. Would've slammed this case shut with warnings and wards before things got worse. But Cedric disappeared. No message. No body. Nothing to go on.

Now she stood in his place. Someone needed to keep the fragile truce between mountain shifters and the outside world intact.

She suspected something far more sinister than natural ailed the deceased hiker. The same fear crawled across her skin right before receiving this assignment. She didn't find any significant markings or signs, so she covered the body back up.

"This man is too young to have had a heart attack."

Slowly, Conleth's gaze tracked her. A shiver curled under her skin, tightening something behind her ribs, as if he'd already measured the length of her secrets. His eyes turned the color of aged whisky in low light. Beneath those thick hooded lashes, she sensed the predator peering out from within him.

No man should possess such dark, beautiful lashes.

Her pulse jumped, and she wet her lips. Trinity forced her attention back to the body.

Death always had a purpose. This one guarded a secret, but what kind of secret?

Power radiated from him. His presence threatened to crack open a world most humans would never believe. That *she* existed.

His kin had tried to wipe hers out once, long before her time, and that truth alone should have kept her from ever standing here. Her grandfather's vision had driven her up the mountain, and she clung to it now like a lifeline. If she had read it wrong, if she failed, this place would devour her. She needed to believe the mountain could shelter her, that without Conleth beside her, it could still be a refuge. Not another failure. Not another appointment with the potential to end with the agency closing in.

Clearing her throat, Trinity launched into a practiced response, careful to keep a neutral tone. She couldn't reveal her suspicions without blowing her cover.

"Heart attacks are more common than you think in humans between the ages of 25 and 40. Even more so in females. Lack of exercise and poor diet practices can contribute."

"This male appears physically fit."

The lingering scent clinging to the body wasn't from a campfire. What could burn a man's soul? Dragon?

She didn't find any visible burns.

Dragons didn't exist. Her grandfather may have told her stories about them, but something more sinister had stolen this man's life.

She opened her mouth to remark about it when someone said, "I see you found yourself a nurse to help run this place. Good thing we can't afford to lose you at the resort."

Boots struck the tile with deliberate weight, each step radiating confidence that prickled across her skin. The range shirt hugged his torso, broad through the chest, lean through the waist. Power rolled off him, and it wrapped around her, similar but diluted compared to the Conleth.

"Special Agent Oberlin from PPI." She extended her hand. The man's gaze fell to her latex glove, his brow hitching.

Heat pricked her cheeks. She tugged the glove free, crumpling it in her fist before he could comment. Information was what she came for, but here, appearances mattered more. His hand swallowed hers in a firm shake.

"Taran is our chief forest ranger," Conleth said.

Taran scowled.

"Is that like the chief of police?" she asked.

"We work together. While I stick to the woods, the police patrol the town, and we assist each other," Taran said.

"Then it's you I should speak with?" She drew off the other glove and tossed it in a nearby disposable waste bin. Her instincts screamed at her. Both shifters emanated the same powerful vibrations. What were these guys?

She once worked in the shadows, interacting with other paranormal creatures, and having to navigate the bureaucracy of human law enforcement to track down and find her targets.

"Ms. Oberlin is here to investigate the bodies." Conleth stood at the end of the table of the covered body.

"Among other things." She smiled, unable to shake the feeling she knew these men from somewhere before today.

Her grandfather taught her not to fight the visions.

Often, they confused her. More often than not, they came true.

Whatever had summoned her to this forest, this mountain, lay in waiting.

How else could she explain the agency's sudden decision to send her here, of all places?

Taran's hand closed around hers. With his firm grip, the truth lit within her. It wasn't him. Not when Conleth's chest rumbled with the restless growl of his dragon. She shut her eyes for a heartbeat, letting the realization sink into her bones.

What else could ignite that fire in his gaze, if not fate?

No man had ever looked at her twice. The agency director's odd granddaughter. The cursed little girl with hair pale as frost. Names that had clung to her skin like burrs, enough to keep others away.

Heat flared where Taran's palm pressed against her skin, too hot for an ordinary shifter. It burned.

Trinity wrenched her hand back, pulse spiking.

"That's enough hand holding." Conleth motioned them out. "You came for the report?"

Taran grinned. "Keeping it strictly business, brother?"

"Brother?" Ah, it made sense now, looking between the two men. A day's growth on Taran's face and his dark hair gave him a more rugged appearance, whereas Conleth, with the same dark hair, stood an inch or two taller, and his shoulders took up more space. She bit her lip against the quiver of attraction, causing a rush of goosebumps to skate across her skin.

"And we've another," Taran shrugged. "I'm the youngest and handsomest."

"He's also taken." Conleth led past the reception area to an office down the hall. "Where is Gwen?"

"She's on a hike with Arden and the youth. What about that paperwork? Do we have a cause of death?"

"Same as the others." Conleth flipped open an old laptop. It looked ancient compared to the slim government-issued tablet Trinity used.

Taran crossed his arms. "The family?"

"Rourke will have notified them by now. They're most likely tourists," Conleth replied. Their voices dropped low as they discussed the situation between themselves. Trinity patted her arm where her jacket should have been. She glanced toward the exit, then toward the siblings.

"Actually," she interjected, "I think I left my jacket in the examination room. I'll be a minute."

Trinity moved toward the doorway before either brother reacted.

She shut the door behind her. Cabinets lined one wall, and tools glinted beneath the overhead light. Her fingers itched at the sight of her jacket, but the body pulled her forward like a tether. She moved closer to the gurney.

Glancing over her shoulder, she pulled back the sheet. The man's face remained locked in his final moments of terror. The fear remained, etched into the lines of his brow and trapped beneath his skin. Trinity pressed her palm flat over his heart.

Her breath hitched as the man's last memory yanked her inside.

Pain. Breathless panic.

Trees rushed past.

She ran.

Branches scratched her skin.

Heart hammering. Her thoughts scrambled.

Something chased her.

A presence, cold and ancient, moved behind her spine.

The scream wasn't hers, but it vibrated through her bones. It tore through her body and split open her soul.

Trinity gasped, stumbling back.

Light. Room. Gurney.

The scent of smoke and rot filled her once more.

Sweat cooled on her neck.

Her palm tingled where it touched the body.

She curled her fingers into a fist, waiting for the sensation to dissolve.

"Agent Oberlin? Trinity?" Conleth's voice broke through, distant.

Swallowing down the bile rising in her throat, Trinity steadied herself. The vivid terror of the vision clung to her like a shroud, chilling her despite the warm air in the room.

Footsteps.

She willed her racing heart to slow.

The door creaked open.

A tremor ran through her limbs.

Taran stepped into her line of vision. His eyes narrowed.

Conleth followed close behind, his brow tense.

"Agent Oberlin?" Taran asked.

"What are you doing?" Conleth crossed to the gurney.

If either man suspected her gift, she'd lose her cover, and her only shot to stop whatever hunted the humans.

"I... I told you. I needed to get my jacket."

Conleth grabbed the sheet and covered the body again. "I don't remember the jacket being on the body."

"It wasn't." Her eyes lingered on the jacket's fabric. That scream still echoed in her mind. Her fingers twitched, desperate to write something, anything. "I wished only to glance around one final time."

She pulled out her phone stylus. The screen blinked awake, and she scribbled quick notes.

Conleth tilted his head, his pupils narrowing to slits.

She froze. The stylus slipped, dragging a slash across the words

Her pulse stumbled. What kind of beast had eyes like that?

He blinked, and his gaze smoothed back to human. But whatever animal spirit he carried had wanted a look at her.

Her grip tightened around the stylus.

"You may want to hold off on that report," Taran said.

"Another hiker missing?" Conleth circled the gurney, brushing against her heightened senses.

"Another call came in right before I arrived," Taran said.

"What do you mean, *another* hiker missing?"

Trinity put away her phone and gripped her jacket. One more dead, and they'd shut her out. One more body, and someone would bury the truth before she could dig it up.

"One of the other hikers in the group is also missing. In the commotion to find this guy," Taran pointed to the covered body. "No one noticed the other man missing until about an hour ago."

"How many were in this group?" Trinity asked.

"Six, including this guy here," Taran said, cupping the back of his neck. "They broke off in pairs to search when they figured he was lost. One traveled solo; their total was off. The group's turmoil meant it took nearly half an hour for them to realize only four emerged from the forest following the body's discovery.

"I assume a search party is going out?" Trinity's brows furrowed as she imagined them finding another body lost in the wilderness. The mountain didn't take without a reason. This current disappearance fit too well.

"Already forming. Roarke's shorthanded, so we're stepping in. I'll be heading out with a few of the rangers shortly."

"I'll be going too," Conleth said.

"And I." Trinity walked toward Taran. If they were to prevent more deaths from happening, she needed to be a part of the search.

"You should let the locals handle it." Conleth stepped in front of her. "The last thing they need is to search for you, too."

Heat radiated off Conleth, chasing the lingering chill of the search. She refused to welcome it, yet when her gaze caught his, a spark lit the depths of his eyes. She hated how it slipped past her guard before she could shut it out.

The urge to close the space between them pressed hard, and she shoved it down. Any other man this close would have triggered her reflexes, sharp and immediate. With Conleth, her instincts dragged, heavy and unsteady, and it unsettled her more than danger ever had.

She lifted a hand before she could stop herself, fingers brushing the solid warmth of his arm. "I can handle myself."

Unlike Taran, whose touch had burned like fire, Conleth's skin warmed beneath her palm. Heat rippled through her, not searing, but a slow wave that stole her breath. Not a memory. Not an image. A trace, clinging as it had always been there, waiting.

She let her hand linger on his arm longer than she should have, searching for more. Nothing. Only that strange aftertaste, the kind that never fully fades.

Conleth's gaze locked on hers, steady and unflinching. A flutter kicked in her chest, sharp and unwelcome. She might have laughed at herself, even snorted at him, if not for the gravity in his gaze.

"If you're going, I'm coming, too," she said.

"Any help is appreciated. Going out together might work best since Con knows this area. You could scout out by the old youth camp."

Conleth scowled at his brother.

Taran held up his hands. "Or not."

"That's fine." Trinity eased a step back, though the heat of his arm still lingered on her skin. The spark it left behind made her breath catch. She tried to read him, to pin down the type of animal spirit he carried. Nothing. The silence of it sent a chill through her.

"Make sure you take a walkie." Taran tossed one to Conleth.

"Let's hope we find them before dark." Trinity rubbed her palms along her arms as the man's last minutes flashed in her mind. The darkness. The terror.

"It's not the dark you should fear," Conleth murmured. His dark eyes caught her gaze once more, helping her push away the earlier dread of a man's memory.

"What do you mean?" Her fingers curled into fists at her sides. Heat rose in her chest, a steady drum that matched the chaos in her mind.

"I need to check on Gwen before I join the hunt." Taran said, heading out the door.

"Hunt? As in a manhunt?" The casual way Taran phrased it struck her oddly. Conleth's earlier cryptic words about 'not fearing the dark' suddenly took on a new meaning. Shifters wouldn't hunt humans like animals hunting prey in the night. Would they?

"Is that what you shifters refer to as a search party?" She pressed, trying to get him to confess what type of spirit animal he carried. Not many tribes, clans, or packs adhered to the old ways. Wolves hunted, but did the others? What type of creatures prowled these mountains?

Over the years, more shifter-bloods slipped into the world, choosing anonymity over legacy.

They abandoned their heritage, leaving the spirit animals waiting without guardians.

If not for that unraveling, she wouldn't have a role to play.

Only a handful of organizations and humans still knew the truth.

"Yep," Taran backed away and waved. "Channel 2 on the walkie."

Trinity huffed, about to toss her jacket over her shoulder and follow the ranger, when Conleth caught her wrist, startling her.

Her stomach tightened. Nothing but the fleeting sensation of familiarity brushed against her senses.

"Are you alright?" His question, delivered in a low rumble, took her off guard.

Trinity blinked. "Why wouldn't I be?"

"There is darkness in your eyes, Agent," Conleth persisted. "Your pupils are dilated."

Leave it to a medic to notice the lingering effects of casting her gift into the memories of the dead man.

"I'm fine." Her lips curved into a smile, but the edges quivered from the effort. "A man is missing. Every moment counts for us to find him alive."

"I'll grab it. Where are you staying?"

Trinity straightened her spine, a spark of heat climbing her neck. "Why? Do you expect me to invite you in for coffee after those flirtatious statements earlier?"

A smirk lifted the corner of his lips. "You liked that, did you?"

She ran her tongue over the front of her teeth, and his grin broadened.

"Keep your cool, *Unahu*. I asked since you might want to change before hiking out into the woods. Unless you prefer to wear slacks and heels, which I strongly advise against due to the probability of injury."

Her ears burned right up to the tips. *Hold it together, Trinity. You cannot allow him to affect you or get in the way of your investigation.*

"I have a change in my Rover. Shall I meet you out front in five?" She walked out, not giving him the option.

Once out of his sight, she rushed to her Rover. The red sparkled in the sunlight like a ripe cherry parked near the entrance. Her grandfather would no doubt disapprove of her choice of transportation. It drew too much attention. That's probably why she liked it.

Tossing off her heels and grabbing her pack from the back, she glanced around while shedding the government suit and pulled out her tactical pants.

She kept her cellphone, tucking it into one of her leg pockets in case she found a place of service to update her superior, but first, she had a manhunt to join.

Three

Sunlight spilled over her bare skin. Conleth lengthened his stride to block the view of her changing in the parking lot.

When she is ours, we will not permit such acts.

Conleth let out a low laugh. She changed in plain sight, unbothered by the world or who might be watching. The urge to shield her came as easy as breathing.

"Ready?"

She whirled around. "Your approach is quite stealthy for one so large."

"You keep fishing, baby." He gave her room to buckle her tactical belt.

She strapped her gear on with practiced ease. A sidearm, a blade, and pouches packed tight against her belt. Functional and efficient.

A smile pulled at the edges of his mouth before he caught it.

"You could tell me what your spirit animal is, and I wouldn't have to," she said, flashing him a too-bright smile.

"You could tell me what you were really doing with that body."

"Eyes on the prize, shifter. We both know a missing man takes priority over your morbid curiosity." She reached inside her bag for a length of coiled rope and clipped it to the side of her belt.

"Then I suppose we're at an impasse."

"That we are." Her smile twitched.

"SUV's over there," he said, pointing.

"Lead the way." She tossed him a grin and jumped in the driver's seat of her Rover.

Conleth exhaled, half-laughing under his breath, but he couldn't stop the grin pulling at his mouth as he climbed in his own SUV.

Twice in one day, the town fell behind him.

He found the parking area near one of the main trails in the state forest.

She pulled in beside him, taking a moment to scan the area after she parked. Trinity hopped out and walked in front of the vehicle. A truck and another older model Jeep sat parked nearby.

"Strange." She lifted a hand to shade her eyes, glancing about. "Are there not more?"

"They're out searching." Conleth grabbed his medical bag and a couple of water bottles from the back.

Without another word, she grabbed a canteen and moved toward the trail. He jogged to catch up. Seeing the gun on her hip, Conleth said, "You're likely to see wolves, bears, and even mountain lions out here. Don't shoot them."

She gave a sideways glance. "And which one are you?"

"Tell me about the body." He slowed to match her shorter stride.

"Caucasian male. Approximately 24 years old. Five foot eight with light brown hair and an estimated weight of around one hundred and fifty pounds. Scarring on his left-hand knuckles indicated a possible biking or sports accident from childhood, but that's the clinical version."

He kept silent, watching the rhythm of her stride, the way her shoulders tightened as she chewed on her lip.

She whispered after a long stretch of quiet, "His death was not of natural causes." A glance slid toward him. "But you know that, too, don't you? And you know what killed him."

Conleth's gaze stayed fixed on the trees ahead. "Heart issues can get complicated."

The air changed direction. His shoulders drew tight, eyes adjusting as he scanned the trail's edge for movement, for the faintest glint in the fading sunlight. The scent of burned metal and ash still lingered, the aftertaste of shadow.

Ahead, she moved with a quiet intensity, teeth catching her lip again. The gesture stirred the spirit deep in his chest.

"How close are we to where the body was found?"

"A half mile off the trail to the east."

"Show me."

Sia's pack had already scoured the site, yet she still prowled as if some overlooked trace waited for her to discover.

He swept his gaze along the trail. Low oaks, giving way to moss-slick stone.

"As my lady commands." He spotted a gap in the brush and gestured for her to follow. Trinity's eyes narrowed, a glint he couldn't decipher, before she looked away. His fingers twitched in the space left between them.

"If you take my hand," he added, wiggling his fingers. "I promise I won't get us lost."

A half-smile tugging at his mouth.

Trinity shook her head.

Conleth let his hand fall back to his side.

Too much, too soon.

Taran made it look so easy with Gwen.

We are not asking a youngling for advice; his dragon spirit bristled. *We can protect and ensnare our mate.*

They walked in silence, boots sinking in the softened earth. Conleth let the dragon rise behind his eyes, breathing in the faintest trace of shadow, straining past the whisper of wind. When the oaks thickened and the rocks grew slick with moss, he lifted his hand.

"What is it?" she whispered.

Conleth tilted his face to catch the breeze. Nothing stirred. Only damp bark and wet stone filled his senses. His hand lowered. "This is it."

She moved past him, crouching low, fingers brushing the ground with the practiced ease of someone who lived on the hunt for hidden truths.

"The body was found there." He pointed at the spot near the moss rocks and the broken branches. "Face up."

"Strange," she murmured, resting her hand on a flat stone. "The ground is damp here in spots."

She rubbed her fingers together, testing the grit. "Reports mentioned unpredictable weather patterns in the mountains, flash floods at these elevations. Sudden storms."

He cupped the back of his neck to ease the prickle at his nape. "We get heavy snowfall in the colder months, but this season's been too warm. Snow's melting faster than it should."

"That would explain the soft ground." She said more to herself and then pointed ahead. "Did you follow these prints?"

Conleth moved closer to examine the markings she indicated. "It could belong either to the deceased hiker or to someone in the search party."

She stepped forward, eyes tracking each partial print through the undergrowth. "Wolf tracks. Shifters?"

"Like I said, search party."

She moved between the prints with practiced care.

"It might take you in a circle."

Trinity paused, hunched down again to trace the outline of a boot print with her finger. "Look at this," she said, crouching. "These impressions cut deeper into the soil. Whoever made them was heavier. And this set..." She touched the edge of another print. "Wider heel. Different boots."

Conleth crouched beside her, jaw taut, fingers brushing damp earth. The scent of disturbed soil and ash lingered, tugging at his instincts. Tracks lay half-hidden in the shadows. He'd chalked them up to Sia's men, but now, the subtle indications in the earth and the tension in her stance set his senses alight, a warning that gnawed at him deeper than he wanted to admit.

"It's almost as if..." Trinity's eyes narrowed. "Someone dragged something heavy. There are skid marks here."

Conleth's eyes tracked the faint groove slicing through the softened earth, muddied by runoff. His stomach knotted, a low coil of unease winding through him. Fingers itched to touch the soil, to trace the path, but something told him that would only confirm what he dreaded.

"Maybe," he said, clearing his throat. "Or they could have been dragging their walking stick."

"There is only one track." She motioned to it. "Here. It pools with water, but the edge looks cleaner. "This..." She gestured toward a circular imprint a short distance forward, "could be someone's knee."

Conleth inhaled, but the scent of wet earth and rot overpowered anything human. Whatever signs had been left, water had washed most of them away.

"Are you always this thorough? Or just when you're walking through places people die?"

She stood and brushed off her hands. "Do you hunt?"

The corner of his mouth twitched. "What kind of shifter do you take me for?"

"Touché. Maybe I like a good chase too."

Conleth's dragon stirred at the spark in her tone. He watched as she studied the fallen branch, fingers tracing every scrape and torn patch of bark, precise as a wolf following a scent.

She paused before the bend, sweeping her gaze across the slope as if she'd memorized it a hundred times. She skimmed her fingers over the rough bark, almost reverently, and Conleth's dragon spirit shivered at how the mountain responded to her presence. *Fae.*

You're the one who chose her.

"We should start heading back," he said, his gaze lingering on the dark canopy and the way she seemed to hold the forest in her hands.

"We still have a few more hours of light." She stepped over a downed limb. "The trail continues this way."

A low rumble echoed in the trees.

Conleth's head snapped toward the sound. "Trinity—wait."

She continued ahead.

He closed the space between them. The sound had no place in the wind or weather. His dragon pressed outward, coiling beneath his skin, muscles taut with alert.

The air thickened. Shadows waited, stretched between heartbeats.

Conleth sent out a pulse of warning into the dark, pushing back the stirrings that prowled in the gathering dark.

They kept moving, the trail narrowing as the forest closed in around them. Twenty minutes passed. Twisted trunks arched like bodies frozen mid-fall. Water pooled in root hollows, reflecting their prints in quicksilver flashes as the ground soaked every step.

Trinity halted and raised her hand. "Wait. Down there. Near fallen timber… is that cloth?"

The slope dropped off sharply, loose rocks clattering underfoot as she edged toward the log below. Conleth followed, the scent of damp earth and pine filling his nose, the breeze tugging at his hair and clothes. He grabbed her elbow. "Stay here. I'll look."

"I can handle it, but thanks." Trinity moved further down, her foot slipping. Conleth growled low in his throat, fingers around her arm.

"Did you growl at me?"

"Yes, I'll do it again if you insist on going down there alone."

Trinity's violet eyes flared gold. "I've been doing this far longer than you think."

Her foot slid again.

Conleth caught her waist before she pitched forward, the rough bark scraping her palms as he steadied her.

"Not nearly as long as the spirit within me," Conleth said. "I'm coming, but you won't find any humans there."

She paused. "How do you know?"

The trees creaked under a sudden gust. Conleth lifted his face, inhaling. The sharp tang of rot and ash hit like a backhand, curling his stomach. Heat bloomed in his chest as his dragon spirit stirred, muscles twitching beneath his skin.

Trinity squinted at him. "Have you picked up a scent?"

He dropped his gaze to her lips. "Nothing that has a body."

She scanned the slope. "Perhaps we need that scrap, after all. Regardless, most shifters possess the scent abilities of a bloodhound, do they not?" He didn't bother with an answer.

Together, they sloshed down the slope, mud tugging at their boots, sending little sprays each step. The roar of water beneath the log filled the hollow, mingling with the distant snap of branches. Conleth released another pulse of dominance; a silent snarl meant for whatever shadows lingered nearby.

Trinity stopped beside a log.

"It's a shirt." She hooked the fabric with a stick. "Shredded and soaked."

Conleth pulled out a clear bag from his medic pouch. Water dripped from the dark cotton. She slid the shirt inside, her fingers grazing it. A flare of gold highlighted her eyes, then faded.

She lifted her face to the wind. "Can you smell it?"

"I could." But not with her this close. The faint sweetness of wild cherries, the crisp bite of frost, clung to her skin. It twisted through his breath, stirring the dragon just beneath the surface of his control. His senses tangled, pulled in a dozen directions at once.

Shadows circled.

She watched him.

His dragon bristled, tense, unwilling to bend or act like a bloodhound.

She waved toward the bagged shirt. "Well?"

A low growl rolled through his chest, heat coiling beneath his ribs. "Perhaps if you asked nicely?"

She snatched the bag from his hand. "Are you always this difficult?"

Conleth grimaced. The air thickened as the sun dipped lower; golden light dwindled to shadow. He closed his eyes, drawing in a deep breath, sending his senses outward. His dragon sent out a stronger signal while he inhaled deeply. *Search for anything beyond what is here.*

We must protect our female.

He ground his teeth, pulling in a slow, measured breath. The layers of her scent, the river, and the forest all tangled together.

Nothing.

"No scent." His jaw flexed. "We keep moving."

Trinity's mouth tightened. She swept her gaze along the riverbank. When she moved forward, he mirrored her pace, unwilling to let her get too far ahead.

Through the ferns, something pale caught his eye. A single sneaker, half-buried near a tree root, neon pink against the dark green.

Trinity's hand hovered over it.

"Don't touch it."

She froze.

He studied the trees. The last slant of sunlight fractured through the branches; long shadows stretched toward them like fingers.

"Right," she murmured. "We'll look around first."

She pulled out her phone and snapped a few shots before picking her way toward the edge of the trees. The muddy river thundered, swollen from melted snow and recent storms. Water lapped hungrily at the banks, roots exposed like broken ribs, and dragging shattered branches downstream like splintered bones.

Scattered on the muddy ground lay the contents of a hiking pack. A dented water bottle and an unopened protein bar crunched under Conleth's feet, along with ointments and soggy bandages from a first-aid kit.

Conleth pulled out his walkie. Telepathically, he sent the same message to his brothers. "Medic to all search parties." His grip tightened on the communication device. "Pack and clothes near the river. About two miles south of Ash Falls, a mile west of the original site."

His dragon seethed inside him. Shadows.

The walkie crackled. "Wolf team two, on our way."

Conleth spun around. Trinity stood at the river's edge; eyes fixed on the debris caught in the reeds. The current pounded, the air heavy with warning, and the closer they got to nightfall, the more dangerous this part of the forest became.

"Stay back! The bank's not stable—"

The earth beneath gave way beneath her feet with a sickening, wet crack. Her scream split the air, swallowed by the roar of the water as Trinity vanished into the churning current.

"Trinity!"

Conleth bolted toward the river's edge. Mud sucked at his boots, tugging at him, slipping underfoot as fingers dug into wet soil. He couldn't reach her in time. Her pale form twisted downstream, pulled under by the relentless current.

Heat slammed into his chest. His dragon surged, claws raking at the edges of his control. Somewhere distant, wolves howled, their cries slicing through the roar of the river.

He unclipped his medic pack, hurling it clear of the water. The falls loomed ahead, white and violent. He ripped his shirt from his waist; his body betrayed him. Scales erupted, replacing his skin. Bone stretched. Muscle thickened. Pain lanced through him as his body shifted, growing larger by the second.

Powerful wings unfurled with a sharp crackle of thunder.

He launched into the air.

The world snapped into razor-sharp focus. Beneath him, the river became a deafening symphony. The scent of wet earth and churning water burned his nostrils. Trinity's silver hair flashed in the torrent. She fought to reach a branch, barely keeping her head above the rushing water. Too close to the edge.

He tucked his wings and dove.

The branch tore loose, just as he snatched her from the water.

Her body went limp in his hold. He searched for solid ground, wings brushing the mist, and finally touched down, depositing Trinity gently onto the muddy bank.

She rolled onto her side, coughing violently, water pouring from her mouth. Her chest rose and fell in shallow gasps.

His dragon resisted, hovering near her, unwilling to leave

She's safe. Conleth called the dragon back. Wings folded. Scales sank into skin. The shift dragged through him. His breath rasped, muscles twitching as he returned to human. When he looked down, Trinity stared back at him. Her eyes widened. A smudge of river silt rested beneath one eye.

Thirty years of hiding vanished in an instant. His hands trembled as he waited for her to react.

She wheezed, turning her head and vomiting river water all over his feet.

Conleth exhaled. "You're welcome."

Four

TRINITY'S TEETH CHATTERED.

"It's okay, *Unahu*. You're safe now." Conleth pulled her closer. The warmth of his touch seeped through her soaked clothes.

Her gaze traced the hard planes of his chest. Heat flared across her cheeks, not from the cold and perhaps a little from the shock. She hadn't expected him to stand before her undressed.

His eyes, still an unsettling red from his dragon, locked with hers. The fire within him receded, replaced by the familiar dark whiskey she knew.

Not just a man.

A lifetime of her grandfather's stories about majestic creatures soaring through the skies, breathing fire, came to life right before her.

Not just a myth.

Her stomach fluttered, muscles coiling, breath catching as she tried to comprehend what she had seen.

"You're a dragon," she whispered.

Could he be the dragon from her visions, the one her grandfather warned her would someday steal her gift?

Conleth winced at her hoarse accusation.

One moment, she fought against the current, and the next, a dragon plucked her from near death. The indignant roar of the falls rumbled through the forest, angry at the absence of her sacrifice.

He swept his hands down her arms, goosebumps rising along her damp skin, and a strange sense of belonging seeped into her.

His torso gleamed, broad and etched with a dragon tattoo curling across his chest to one shoulder like a brand. His eyes, whiskey brown and too human, held her attention. The beast within him withdrew, leaving the man more dangerous than any creature she'd known.

"As soon as the team arrives, we'll get you out of here and dry."

She reached for his hand, searching for his memories, and found only emptiness.

His fingers closed over hers, a perfect fit. Heat bloomed where their palms met, sliding through her like a slow tide until her breath caught. His warmth rushed inside her, chasing away her gift.

She pulled herself upright, leaning on him, and he rose with her. She should have resisted the pull, the comfort, the heat. But the river's chill clung to her bones.

The sun had turned its back.

Shadows cast in the distance.

And he—he had become the only warmth left.

Her body betrayed her with shivers. Her stomach knotted tight. Shock throbbed in every flutter of her pulse.

A dragon. She never believed her grandfather's stories had any truth.

Until now.

Until the man keeping her from falling on her backside revealed the spirit of one of the most potent and deadliest beasts the Great Hunter could grant.

"Conleth."

A rustle of leaves and the snap of a twig broke the tense silence.

Conleth glanced towards the sound; his expression hardened. "It looks like we have company. We'll talk later."

She scanned the approaching figures. *Pull it together, Trinity. You're a PPI agent. Of course, there are dragons!*

"It's Trace and two others."

She tugged at her wet clothing. "They're part of the search party? Did your brother not send out rangers?" Was his brother soaring above them in his dragon form?

"I'm sure he did. Trace is Rourke's second. More men means we cover more ground. The other patrols might have scattered further to cover more ground."

"Of course." Trinity glanced back again at the dense foliage, where she thought she had seen a glimpse of movement. After battling to keep her head above the current in the river, shock, exhaustion, and adrenaline played a tug of war inside her.

Two men and a wolf approached them. The man in the lead, tall and fit like a seasoned runner, slipped a pack off his shoulders.

"You alright? There are clothes near the riverbank," the front-man said.

"Mine, I'd wager." Conleth put his arm around Trinity. Her shoulders dropped, tension melting from muscles. The ease with which she settled into his embrace made her jaw clench. The man's eyes flicked to the possessive gesture, and he stopped his approach, raising his hands slightly.

Another wolf shifter carried a pair of shredded jeans and held them up. "They won't do you any good in this condition."

Trinity's eyes fixed on the torn fabric. Blood stained the denim in dark patches. Without thinking, she stepped forward and reached.

"They are *not* mine." Conleth's arm dropped from her shoulders and caught her wrist before she touched the jeans. Tingles raced down her arm at his touch.

Her fingers flexed toward the jeans; drawn by the story the stains might tell her. Conleth's grip stopped her cold. Protective or obstructive? In her mind she cataloged the gesture, even as her pulse refused to settle.

"May I?" she asked, ignoring his grip.

"Evidence," Conleth said, waving the shifter back. "We can't contaminate it, wouldn't you agree, Agent?"

"Of course," Trinity yanked free, the title slicing through her like a blade. Agent. Not a woman. Not a witness. Not someone who'd nearly drowned in a river and been pulled from death by a dragon.

"I'll keep these with the rest of the items." Trace folded the jeans, blood blooming dark against the denim.

Her fingers twitched, knowing that evidence could speak and show her its truth.

Conleth stopped her from hearing it. No, she did that herself, not willing to risk exposure.

She watched the blood-stained fabric move further from her grasp.

Dragon, she reminded herself. Not a man. Not safe.

"Ma'am," Trace greeted her with a curt nod. His gaze lingered a beat too long, brow tightening before he looked away. "I'm glad you're both okay."

A rumble came from Conleth's chest that she recognized now came from his dragon.

"You're naked," Trinity said, stepping in front of him, unfazed by his rumbling. She angled her body to block his important bits from view.

"You don't happen to have a spare pair of pants that aren't torn in that pack, do you?" Conleth asked.

Trace grinned. "I might. Are you sure those aren't yours?"

Conleth's grip slid back, tightening around Trinity's shoulder. She curled her fingers into a fist, resisting the urge to place her hand over his when movement caught her eye.

Her gaze drifted towards the trees across the rushing water.

Goosebumps raced up her arms, not as delightful as the warmth Conleth left behind when his hand brushed her back.

She squinted but saw nothing.

Trace dug into the pack and tossed a pair of shorts toward Conleth. "You're on your own for boots. I spotted a pair earlier that looked mostly intact."

"Thanks," Conleth grunted, catching the shorts. Trinity's eyes remained on the river, transfixed by its ripples, though her body leaned slightly toward Conleth. She forced herself to keep her eyes on the water, though the memory of his bare chest lingered. Heat bloomed in her cheeks, quickly extinguished by the memory of her gift's silence around him. She leaned toward him and caught herself. She had to draw a line somewhere.

He belonged to the shifter-bloods. Bad blood had run between their people for centuries.

"We'll keep searching along the river," Trace said, scratching his jaw. "Do you think he shifted?"

"It's likely," Conleth sighed, a gust of air ruffling Trinity's hair. "For how long is the question."

"Shifted?" she echoed. "Are we searching for a shifter? I was under the impression the hikers were human?"

A missing hiker turning into a shifter? If someone was forcing bonds without bloodline inheritance, they would deal with something far worse than a missing person.

"He was. He is." Trace didn't elaborate. He looked at Conleth.

"What?" She blinked, recalibrating. The conversation took a turn. "He's either a shifter or human? Unless you suspect he's a—."

"Come on, Agent. Let's get you back to my clinic in town, and we can sort everything out there." Conleth gently pushed her ahead.

The agency was depending on her to keep humans safe from the things that slipped through the veil, but the humans weren't just exposed this time, they'd been attacked. Changed.

Her chest tightened. That shouldn't be possible. Shifter spirits had to be inherited, bound to bloodlines.

She thought of the laws. The prison terms. The executions. Stealing an animal spirit always meant stealing the life bound to it.

The price was always blood.

As they turned back toward the trees, she cast one last glance at the riverbank. For a heartbeat, she could've sworn something moved in the shadows. Dusk played tricks, she told herself, but the chill in her bones whispered otherwise.

"There is still a man out there. We can't leave until we find him." A missing hiker turned shifter was a potential breach in their code of society, but a wounded shifter left alone, having newly bonded with a spirit animal, created a recipe for disaster.

Trace turned away.

"We can't just abandon him," she said, a knot of dread tightening in her gut.

Conleth pursed his lips.

"If he shifted due to an attack, he could be injured, disoriented, and a danger to himself—or worse, a danger of exposing our people."

"It's a possibility," Conleth admitted, his eyes scanning the darkening forest."

Trinity's teeth chattered as the sun dipped again and a new ripple of chills went down her body.

"We need to get you out of here. It's not safe, and I won't be responsible for you getting hypothermia." Conleth said; his voice deepened. "Trace and the others will keep hunting him. Taran is out searching too. They won't stop until they find the body."

"If-f?" Trinity shot back, not liking the way he said it. Conleth pulled on a boot he retrieved from the mud and didn't notice her reaction.

"Yeah, *if*," he mumbled, yanking on his boot. "A body could turn up, or nothing more than his clothes."

"Find the body? You believe he's dead?"

Conleth stopped searching for his other boot and turned towards her; his face schooled and guarded. He walked toward the trees, one boot thudding against the earth. Finally, he retrieved the other missing boot from the foliage and slipped it on.

"Dead men can't shift," he stated, but there was a glint of red in his eyes, a hint of unease betraying his words.

"No," Trinity agreed slowly. "I don't suppose they can."

A new suspicion curled low in her gut. Was Conleth hiding more than just his spirit animal identity? Could these missing hikers or the shifters be involved with Cedric's disappearance?

She served her organization, but her grandfather's warnings whispered louder now.

She met his gaze squarely and said, "Then let's get back to your clinic. We have a lot to discuss." Her gaze narrowed on him. "Including a certain dragon with black and red scales?"

Conleth's eyes widened, his dragon pupils flashing before they narrowed again. His eyes changed, dark amber to red and back again. Interesting.

He turned back towards the trees. "It'll take us a few hours to hike back from here."

"A few hours, huh?" Trinity echoed, trying to mask a slight groan, glancing down at her wet clothes and her toes sloshing inside her boots. "You won't offer to go dragon and fly me?"

"Are you asking me?" He tilted his head, his dragon eyes flickering with interest.

"No." Trinity walked past him, her clothes sticking to her and sending more chills over her flesh. Her mind whirled with questions. In less than an hour, she'd discovered dragon spirits existed and death nearly claimed her.

Now she owed her life to a dragon.

Her grandfather's stories and warnings echoed in her head, smug and sorrowful.

Teeth chattering, she rubbed her arms.

"My body heat would keep you warm," his voice brushed her spine. The offer curled around her like smoke. Tempting. Dangerous.

She didn't answer. She couldn't trust warmth that came with scales. The price her grandfather warned her about too great.

"Trinity?"

"You're not afraid of being spotted."

Another shiver raked her body. He captured her, yanking her back against him. She gasped, her body going pliant in his arms before her brain could catch up. The heat against her back sent delicious tremors across her flesh, her traitorous muscles ignoring every reason she should struggle.

His hot breath tickled her ear. "Depends. Will you disclose what I am?"

"And if I do?"

His hand splayed across her stomach. Goosebumps ran down her arms.

"Then I'll have to eat you," his voice rumbled like embers beneath stone.

Trinity tensed.

Then snorted.

And broke out into laughter.

"Hey now," Conleth pulled back. "What makes you think I won't?"

He spun her in his arms so quickly that it almost made her dizzy.

Gazing into his dragon's dark, dangerous eyes, she swallowed, placing her hands on his bare arms. She tried to read him. Nothing. Just silence, a void where his memories lived. Yet, the emptiness soothed her, like still water after a storm.

His skin warmed beneath her palms, and she found herself reluctant to let go.

"Because your kind doesn't exist." She looked at the red darkening in his eyes. Her muscles grew tense.

"The most important thing you need to know, Agent Oberlin—"

"Trinity," she whispered.

"Trinity, I will never hurt you."

"And I never lie," she coughed. "I came here for the job."

"You won't include this in your report back to the agency," he kept his grip on her. Their gazes locked in a staring contest. She swallowed; mouth dry the weight of his gaze pressing against her resolve.

He raised an eyebrow. "I'll reserve that until I'm able to do further investigation into the matter." Without proof, her superiors might dismiss her claims or present them as nothing more than a delusion brought on by the trauma of her near-drowning experience. What would her grandfather think? Conleth could face imprisonment, experimentation, or even worse.

She would no longer have a place among her people. This marked her final chance to prove she still belonged.

In less than 24 hours, she learned the secret of the Vasumen brothers. One of them was bound to lead her to find out where Cedric had disappeared. What other secrets did they have locked away that she could discover beyond their dragons?

Trinity giggled. Hypothermia or hysteria, she couldn't tell. Bears. Mountain Lions. Wolves. But a dragon?

Her grandfather's stories held truth.

Now any man with a *bodaway achak* spirit became a threat to her.

Five

OVERHEAD FLUORESCENT LIGHTS GLOWED harsher than usual, throwing sterile white across the pine-paneled walls of Conleth's office back at the Sentinel Peak clinic.

Blanket bundled to her chin. Trinity curled catlike into the corner of his sofa. The fierce glint in her eyes hadn't faded, and her fingers worried the edge of the blanket.

"Squirrels," Conleth repeated.

His hand hovered near the coffee machine, tension knotting between his shoulder blades. His dragon tattoo flared with heat, a warning he couldn't ignore. This whole 'squirrel' explanation was flimsy as a wet tissue, but what else could he say?

She knows the truth.

And yet he kept going.

"Nasty buggers. They can be vicious when they're hungry."

The corner of her mouth twitched. Not quite a smile. More like she was fighting one back.

"Riiight," she said, drawing out the word while tilting her head skeptically. "A hungry squirrel stole your pants."

Her eyes gleamed with amusement, enjoying the tale he spun to explain her rescue from the rushing rapids.

Conleth placed a steaming bowl of soup in front of Trinity. "You scared the living daylights out of me, you know."

A stitch of pain laced through his ribs, tight and unrelenting. Even with her safe, the panic refused to loosen its grip.

He couldn't risk her exposing his family's secret. Not to her agency. Not to the spirit hunters after their abilities. And definitely not the tourists who came seeking mountain air and weekend recreation. Some would carve him open, metaphor or not, just to glimpse the truth beneath his scales.

That kind of truth didn't stay quiet.

The life he'd built, calm and human, would crumble beneath the weight of revelation.

"Here," he muttered, grabbing a set of scrubs he judged closest to her size. "Put these on. Those damp clothes will have you catching a cold."

Pressure used to sharpen him like a scalpel. Now his thoughts scattered, blank as an unwritten prescription, useless in the face of violet eyes and ancient truth.

Too many deaths.

Too many secrets.

Her eyes haunted him. Not just the fear in them, but the way they saw him, truly, for what he was.

Mate. His dragon spirit stirred, possessive in the declaration.

Impossible. The curse... his people. *She's a PPI agent!*

He cleared his throat. "Bathroom is down the hall."

Steam continued to swirl from where she shoved the soup in his hands in exchange for the clothes. He blew on the soup — beef broth, and a few vegetables from the resort kitchen.

Trinity mumbled, 'thanks' as she unfolded herself from the sofa with fluid grace, stretching like the cat she reminded him of before padding toward the hallway.

The bathroom door creaked shut behind her. He drew a slow breath, ripe cherries clinging to the air and to the restless curl of his dragon spirit. His hands clenched into fists. She'd already seen him shift? How much of her PPI training taught her about shifters? Had any of her training manuals explained the mate bond? The primal pull that made his chest tighten every time she moved away from him?

Would his revelation scare her?

The thought made his dragon recoil.

Mate rejection meant death by heartbreak, or by the spirit tearing loose from the soul it once claimed.

The recent disappearance and the escalating shadow spirit attacks all pointed towards the mountain, stirring the dormant shadows trapped to walk these lands for eternity.

Love alone wouldn't protect her. They had to move as a single force against the rising dark. Without that, she was exposed.

Even the hideous wallpaper seemed to sneer, its peeling flowers curling like smirks around the room. Buried under the threat of avalanches and relentless snow, the clinic had waited.

Over the years, residents abandoned Sentinel Peak. They moved north to the resort, and farther still to towns untouched by the mountain's shadows.

Should have taken her to our cave.

Conleth forced a smile as the door creaked open again. "Better?"

Trinity padded back into his clinic, her slender fingers working through her hair in quick, efficient movements as she braided it. His gaze lingered on her silver strands as she twisted them over one shoulder with practiced ease.

"Sorry, the shower is still out. This old place is halfway through renovations." He moved between here and the resort, but the river had carried them miles downstream. Returning here made more sense.

He put the bowl of soup in her hands, steam fading into the cool air.

"It's still hot." Trinity curled onto the worn sofa, tucking her legs beneath her.

"Why wouldn't it be?" He reached for the thick blanket draped over the armrest and unfolded it over her.

"Are we really going to keep dodging the obvious?" she asked, taking a sip.

Steam swirled around her face, briefly obscuring the glint in her violet eyes.

"Or shall we say, the dragon?" She swept her gaze over him.

Conleth rolled back his shoulders and puffed out his chest. The intricate dragon tattoo burned with renewed heat.

"What you saw doesn't leave this mountain."

Trinity leaned back, her fingers drumming a nervous rhythm on the chipped enamel cup in a pattern of index, middle, ring; she seemed unaware of repeating. Her gaze, however, remained fixed on him, a mixture of apprehension and something he couldn't quite decipher flickering in its depths.

"Are you threatening me?"

"No," Conleth countered, leaning forward. The move brought him closer to her than he had intended, and the air between them crackled with a strange tension. "Your job is to protect my people from human knowledge." A hint of a smile played on his lips. "But wouldn't you agree, Agent Oberlin, that perhaps the truth is more nuanced?"

"Oh, I thought it was my job to protect humans from your people." She lifted a brow. Her tone cooled down. Yet, something shimmered in her eyes. Heat? Hesitation? He couldn't tell.

"I need you to forget what you saw. There is more at play than you've seen. Far more. This place holds dangers beyond your understanding."

"More significant than the existence of dragons?"

Conleth held her gaze. Silence thickened between them, charged. His body twitched, his baser instincts demanding he move closer. "Why are you here, Agent Oberlin?"

The dragon pressed upward, heat blooming in his chest like fire seeking breath. His hands clenched into fists, knuckles cracking, fighting the urge to pace.

She took another sip of her soup, her eyes never leaving him. Lavender and gold shimmered in her gaze, hypnotic and unsettling.

Get a grip.

"You haven't been a shifter specialist long, have you?" he asked, distracting the beast within him.

Her eyes narrowed. "I'm not inexperienced."

Conleth forced a smile, hoping it didn't appear too strained. "There's nothing wrong with not knowing everything."

He turned to face her more squarely. "I'm happy to be your informant."

"For a price." She countered, finishing her soup. A shiver racked her body. His nostrils flared to ensure it was just the chill from the river tormenting her body. *She is cold; let us warm her.*

"I can't let you report my family to the PPI. You're here on assignment. The hikers, right?" He ignored the frustrated rumble of his dragon spirit.

"That's right." She leaned forward, plopping the cup into his hands. "My grandfather warned me that the dragon spirits never left this realm."

"What else did your grandfather tell you?"

"Tell me about the hikers?" Trinity said.

Another wave of frustration rose from his dragon spirit.

He rose from the sofa and walked to the coffee cupboard. A jolt of caffeine might coax out the truths her eyes refused to share. Plus, he needed something stronger than silence. Maybe a splash of brandy in his coffee.

He opened the cupboard. A microwave, mini-fridge, and coffeemaker greeted him.

Settling back again, Trinity pulled the blanket up, her eyes drooping as she watched him. "You live here?"

"No. Home is farther up the mountain, but I stay here sometimes when needed." Conleth put his mug aside and grabbed another. "Coffee?"

A yawn escaped her, followed by a slight tremble that ran through her shoulders.

"Perhaps another time. You need to rest."

Another tremor, more pronounced this time, racked her body. Twice now. He didn't want her to grow ill from her dip in the river. She needed a hot shower.

She needs a warm body.

In a swift moment, Conleth slipped in behind her on the sofa, then gently pulled her back against his chest. The warmth of his dragon increased for his mate. It wasn't perfect, but it was better than nothing.

Startled, she went rigid against him. "What are you doing?"

"You're cold," Conleth's dragon rumbled, deepening his voice. "I'm warm." He settled behind her, acutely aware of how small and delicate she felt against him. His arm could easily encircle her twice over, and he had to consciously gentle his touch.

She stiffened further, her voice an octave above a whisper. "Are all dragons this... warm?"

He refrained from nuzzling her neck, his dragon humming at the contact. "We're all hot-blooded."

"So, about those hikers?"

"Since the human tourists have returned to the mountain, it's stirred up some complications."

He inhaled her cherry scent, the lingering beef of her soup broth, and blew out a breath. "The clans, tribes, and packs moved here for protection from the outside world."

"But you weren't the only ones here," she whispered. "You speak of the curse."

"Did this grandfather of yours tell you? Is that how you know about the curse?"

She leaned forward, her back straightened.

His arm tightened around her and froze at the soft tickle of her breath against his throat.

"I may be inexperienced when it comes to shifters, but I'm good at my job. I do my homework, and locating targets is my specialty."

Conleth raised an eyebrow. "You're a tracker. You came all this way and had no clue about dragons."

"I've heard of dragons. They're part of shifter history. So was the Fae and shifter war, but the dragons ceased to exist after. My grandfather used to tell me stories."

Grandfather? Was that a code word? Did she have an informant?

Conleth longed to tell her the truth about the curse, his family, and their dragon spirits, but revealing too much of their secrets could put everyone on the mountain at risk. Not until he believed she was trustworthy.

"Why do you think that is?"

Her weight leaning into him sent a slow-burning ripple through his chest.

"It doesn't matter now that they exist. Did your elders imprison the dragon spirits as they did the Fae into the mountain? How did you escape?"

"We live longer than most people. And when the end comes, our spirits stay. They don't vanish into shadow."

"Why is that?" she asked.

"Part of the curse from the Fae, I believe." His dragon growled. "Does your research tell you how the mountain froze, and our children are no longer born with their animal guide? We wait for them to inherit the lost ones from our bloodlines. And over the years, the spirit hunters have depleted our numbers and stolen our gifts."

"You weren't born shifters?" Her voice lowered, husky and drowsy. "I didn't know that."

So much for her to learn.

"There's plenty you don't know, *Uhana.*" His eyes darkened.

Her organization tried to control his people and hunt them for their gifts.

We must trust her if she is to trust us.

Conleth cleared his throat. "As long as you keep my family secret safe, I will assist you with your search for the missing shifter agent."

Mark her. Seal the deal.

He thought of Aluk. The ache tormented his brother at the loss of his mate. Aluk never marked her.

You will not make the same mistake.

Conleth's tongue heated.

No. He couldn't mark Trinity.

Not with the hikers stirring the shadow spirits.

They'd become more restless since the thaw.

Right now, their top priority was keeping hikers from trespassing into the sacred parts of the forest.

She made a noise. Soft and subtle. He almost didn't catch it. Her head lulled against his shoulder with her lips slightly parted in sleep. Keeping her warm had been a bad idea. He resisted pulling her closer and burying his face in her hair. Gently, he maneuvered her, so there was a sliver of space between them. He reached around her and grasped her coffee cup before it toppled over, the coolness of the ceramic grounding him. He needed to stay clear-headed, but the way she looked right now...

At the risk of waking her, he slipped out from around her, putting more space between them. Conleth tucked in the blanket and allowed his dragon to come forward, to look upon her through his eyes. He tucked a strand of her silky hair out of her eyes.

She was his.

Casting a long glance at her peaceful form before heading out of his office, Conleth headed to perform an autopsy of the body to confirm the hiker's death.

His dragon rumbled in protest, a low growl of displeasure, but if he stayed, he might not be able to resist pulling her back into his arms.

Just need some answers, he assured his dragon. *She needs to rest.*

He paused at the door, glancing back at the room where she lay. His hand hovered on the knob, fingers twitching. Tiny hooks anchored him to stay, but the call of duty pulled harder. He strode toward the makeshift morgue. A body waited for answers.

None of his visions had prepared him for her.

Not the glimpses.

Not the dreams of his future mate.

Nether came close to the woman on his couch.

The connection pulsed beneath his skin.

His dragon spirit had taught him to trust the gifts of his inheritance. Science had taught him to look at the facts. His logic surfaced, steady, and cold.

The dragon quieted.

Inside the dark examination room, Conleth flicked a switch and once more uncovered the body. The scent of decay and mountain lion lingered. "What did you tell her that you're not telling me?"

Six

AN HOUR AFTER LEAVING Conleth's clinic, Trinity stood at the edge of her campsite in Sentinel Peak State Park, drawing a deep breath at the carnage before her. When she'd woken that morning, a note from Conleth waited on the coffee table, asking her to stay for breakfast. He promised to return after nine, but after sleeping on his couch, she didn't want to face him just yet.

Last night felt too dangerously intimate.

She'd slept wrapped in his scent and the quietness of his space. Waking alone, her body caught a chill. She found her Rover parked outside, and she had no time to linger with the hot doctor.

Dragons. Lost Hikers. Shadows in the forest.

Before leaving, she'd searched Conleth's office for clues, but the iPad on his desk mocked her with its password screen. She'd left empty-handed.

Now, she had bigger problems.

A ripped tent lay crumpled on the ground, its contents spilling out like entrails.

A half-eaten granola bar lay abandoned beside a tipped-over water bottle.

Large paw prints marred the dirt, leading into the dense woods.

Trinity pulled out her phone began taking photos.

That's what you get for dumping your stuff and rushing off, she scolded herself.

A heavy silence pressed down, broken by the occasional chirping of unseen birds. The acrid smell of smoke mingled with a metallic tang. The hair on the back of her neck rose.

Walking around the perimeter of the site, she pressed her hand to the large gouges on a tree. Closing her eyes, she inhaled, catching the faint sweetness of decay before something much older and rank teased the back of her throat. Bile rose.

"Speak to me," she whispered, pressing her palms to the rough bark. "Who did this to you?"

Her gift stirred—a slow, serpentine ripple beneath her skin. It thrived on touch, feeding on the lingering essence of life.

A sharp crack of a twig broke the stillness. Trinity spun around, her pulse hammering.

"Nice spot."

Conleth stepped into the clearing, moving with an authority that made silence listen.

She hadn't heard his SUV approach

He closed the distance between them, black jeans molding to the ease of his stride. Static crawled up her arms with every step he took.

He shouldn't have been able to find her. She covered her tracks.

"What are you doing here?" she demanded.

Her fingers curled tighter around the bark, nails scraping against something soft. A tuft of hair, tangled in the tree's wound, pulsed with heat.

Her gift shivered awake. "How did you find me?"

Flashes of power blurred her sight. She blinked hard, struggling to stay present, but the edges of a vision pressed closer, heavy, and dark.

"Trinity."

His voice anchored her.

When had he moved so close?

His hand hovered near her arm, not touching, but close enough for the heat to radiate there.

The vision pulled her senses. Blood boiled beneath her skin.

Her knees buckled.

Conleth caught her by the elbow. "Easy."

His eyes burned like hot embers. "Your scent is different. Your heartbeat..."

He can't know.

"I'm fine," she lied, forcing her breathing to slow. "You drove all the way out here to feed me?"

He studied her, skeptical. "Your scent is returning to normal. What happened?"

"You tell me." She stepped back, rebuilding the wall between them.

"I didn't expect you to take off this early." Conleth said, holding out a small paper bag, "I brought breakfast. Figured we could finish our previous chat." His gaze swept across the campsite. "Where are the others? Are they on their way?"

"What others?" Pressing her curled fist against her heart, she shook her head, trying to fend off the sensations flowing under her skin.

"Your team. Other agents. Backup."

"There is no team."

"You're alone?" He frowned. "They sent you here to investigate missing persons by yourself?"

"I'm capable of handling my assignment." She didn't bother reminding him of her new role as the shifter representative until Cedric returned.

"That's not what I meant. You look pale. Maybe you should have rested longer."

She exhaled, shaking off the lingering haze of the vision. "Nothing a bite won't fix. I've got protein bars in my pack."

Her stomach tilted, a little woozy, probably needing to have more than the cup of coffee she snagged from his office.

"Doesn't sound like a great diet." He dangled the paper bag in front of her. "These are from the bakery in town. I didn't know which you'd like, so I grabbed a banana and a blueberry."

She tucked the tuft of fur into her pocket hoping the imprint didn't grow cold and she'd lose the vision completely.

"I don't need you to feed me."

His eyes swept over her, taking in her fresh pair of cargo pants and long-sleeved T-shirt from the stash of clothes she kept in her Rover.

She planted her hands on her hips, determining what to do next, and how to get rid of him before the window closed for her touch the fur again.

"Are you alright?" He moved between her and the tree line, his fingers curling gently around her wrist. His gaze dropped to her mouth before rising again, dragon fire smoldering in his eyes.

"Mountain Lion?" he murmured, sniffing the trace of the tuft she'd hidden only a moment ago.

"Yes," she replied. "I suspect so."

His touch lingered, a phantom of warmth along her skin.

She snatched the bag of muffins from him before he could pry further.

"I shouldn't have left in a rush. Rourke called about the hiker, and—" She stopped, swallowing guilt. "Sorry if you feel deceived." She hesitated, then added even softer, "If it's any consolation... I imagine most women would be delighted to take the position and work with you."

"I'm not a one-night kind of guy, agent," he winked. "You can't get rid of me that easily. We have a deal, and I need to report this. Your campsite's been vandalized."

"I practically invited whatever did this." She tightened her grip on the bag. "Report it if you wish. I'll just buy a new tent. I'm not a couch-sleeping type of girl."

She opened the bag and inhaled. A blueberry muffin distracted her. She plucked one out, handing the others back to him, trying to focus on something normal.

His amber eyes held her gaze a beat too long. "I'm sure I can arrange for a bed next time, or the hard ground? I'm happy to oblige either way."

Trinity choked on her bite, coughing until he thumped her back. His large hand moved in slow circles between her shoulder blades as her coughing subsided.

"Better?" he asked, sliding his hand against her cheek until she looked up at him. Her breathing hitched, unsure if it was from choking or from the way his thumb brushed across her jawline.

"Fine." She stepped away to regain balance.

"There's more coffee in my SUV," he said.

"How did you even find me?" she asked around a mouthful of muffin. Her pulse quickened before she could stop it. Too soon. She barely knew him, and according to her grandfather, she'd get burned in the end.

"I ran into Rourke at the bakery," he said. "He mentioned the hikers' site was here. I figured you'd be nearby."

She arched a brow. "I didn't tell him where I was staying."

"It's a small town. There aren't many places open to outsiders. This area has been off-limits for years."

"You didn't expect me to camp alone?"

"It's dangerous," he said, scanning the tree line. "If I hadn't found you here, I was going to head to the resort."

"Then why open it back up to outsiders?"

"We didn't. The state did when the thaw happened and no one stood before them to dispute the decision." Conleth's jaw tightened.

"You mean Cedric didn't appear on your behalf as your representative before the state." She licked muffin crumbs from her lips.

"You need to call a meeting and have them close the mountain again."

"I'm afraid it isn't that easy. Now that the floodgates have been opened, it will take a lot more to build the dam again. Cedric will have an easier time of it than I," she said.

A muscle twitched in Conleth's cheek.

"Why do you think the snow melted? A phase of the curse?"

"You know about the curse?"

Only every Fae blood, from the time they came into existence. The history of the Fae and the shifter-bloods became part of their upbringing.

"It's part of our training," she said.

"Then yes." Conleth's eyes glowed red under the canopy of the trees. "At some point we'll have to compare history lessons."

His gaze pinned her. "Have you thought about our conversation?"

A traitorous warmth bloomed in her chest.

His dragon hovered close to the surface.

"You mean regarding your dragon?" she asked.

He lowered his chin, those eyes burning brighter.

Part of her wanted to lean closer, to explore the secrets simmering behind those eyes and draw forth the magnificent creature who saved her from a watery death.

She cleared her throat, suddenly aware of how close they were standing. "Anyway, I'm not reporting back yet. There's more to investigate."

The intensity in his gaze made her pulse quicken, and she desperately needed safer ground. "Please thank whoever brought my Rover back to the clinic," she added, quick to change the subject again. "I apologize if I put you out with my crashing on your sofa."

"It's what it's there for." He circled the site, stopping in front of the same gnarled tree. His nostrils flared, and a glint of red pulsed in his eyes. "Shadows..."

"Wait--don't touch it!" she warned, but his low growl stilled her.

At the campsite to her left sat a pop-up camper with two bicycles propped against its side. The campfire still smoked, a faint thread of gray drifting up from the stone ring, red embers winking like tired eyes. She'd hoped someone there might have seen something.

"Shadows? You sense something?" she asked.

The feeling of being watched from yesterday returned.

"Lost animal spirits," he said grimly.

Great, just what she needed. Lost spirits on top of missing people. She forced a smile, albeit a strained one. "Sounds... festive."

"They're not exactly party animals, Agent Oberlin. When their bloodlines die out, they become tethered to the shadows."

Trinity's smile faded. "Tethered how?"

"They are trapped here. They linger in the deepest parts of the forest, near our sacred burial grounds." He gestured toward the dense woods beyond her campsite.

"And they're dangerous?" The destroyed campsite suddenly took on a new meaning.

"What do you think happened to the hiker yesterday?"

Trinity's throat tightened. "So the hiker--"

Conleth nodded.

"They'll attack anyone who wanders by?" Her stomach turned as she rolled up her ruined bedding.

"The unguarded. The reckless," he said.

"Well, that's... lovely," she muttered. "So, they're hanging around waiting for victims to wander by?"

"You see now why we need to have the state restrict human access to the mountain."

The mountain had remained inaccessible for generations. Locals called it cursed. Officials called it unstable terrain. Trinity knew it as a reservation for those with shifter blood.

"You could have admitted yesterday what really killed that hiker." She tugged at the tent, pulling at the broken poles to add to the trash pile. At his failure to answer, she glanced back over her shoulder. "Is that what you've told all the dead hikers' families?"

"It works." As he pulled her tent stakes from the ground, his arm muscles flexed.

"You could have been honest with me during our initial meeting," she said.

"I could," he agreed, tossing her torn tent aside. "But now we've struck a deal."

"You tell me your secrets; I tell you mine?"

"You keep my family secret from your reports, and I'll help you find your missing agent."

"Cedric Kelly."

Conleth's expression hardened. "What do you know so far?"

"I'm not at liberty to share details."

"Even though I shared mine?"

"You didn't share anything," she countered. "I caught you in the act."

"I saved your life," he reminded her.

"Fair. But no. I know Kelly was monitoring territory borders before the state reopened them. He didn't oppose it."

"There's more your agency hasn't told you," Conleth said quietly.

He loaded her cooler into his SUV, then leaned close. "Find out what's haunting this mountain, but don't come for my people, and don't chase ghosts."

His words chilled her.

"I'm here to find Agent Kelly."

Conleth's eyes flared bright red. "Then you'll want to speak to my brother, Aluk. He's dealt with Kelly before. You can stay at the resort until we arrange it."

The thought of crowds made her chest tighten, but she forced a nod. "And the missing hiker?"

"Still searching," he said. "Follow me."

"First, can you direct me to a place in town to buy fresh supplies?"

"Whatever you need, you'll find at the resort."

"And if I said I was staying here?" she asked.

"It's too dangerous for you to stay here. You'll stay at the resort or with me at the clinic."

"We barely know each other. I can't accept such an offer," she said.

A muscle twitched in Conleth's jaw. "You can't stay here."

"Give me one good reason why not?"

She spent one night with the man. On his couch, no less, and it was platonic at best. Was this a shifter thing? She needed to read up more on shifter behavior characteristics in males. She learned about shifters during training, but nothing about dragons except for what her grandfather shared in his stories.

He opened his mouth, closed it, and growled before he said, "You're right. I intend to change our acquaintance, and as far as reasoning: this place reeks of a shadow spirit. It's not safe for you to stay here."

She crossed her arms. "They're ghosts, aren't they? A ghost could not have ransacked my things."

Her chest tightened, glancing back at the gouged tree.

"If a shadow possessed one of your neighbors over there, it most certainly could. Seems that education of yours is lacking, Agent. You have much to learn."

"They can possess a hiker?"

"Not for long. Not without a trace of shared blood."

"You think the missing hiker is possessed? "She swallowed hard, dread taking shape. "He's dead, isn't he? You never expected to find the hiker alive."

Conleth stayed silent.

"I have to report this." If not, more people could get hurt. "If the state knew what's out here..." Her heart skipped a beat. "They'll shut down the mountain again."

"They'll come for us—try to eliminate the threat. Doing so will only make it worse."

"You *want* them to close off the mountain."

"Yes, but if word gets out about the hikers, the state won't hesitate to eliminate the threat—us included."

Trinity's stomach iced over. "No bloodlines, more shadows, more dangerous. It'll be like..."

She bit her lip. *All those deaths.*

"Are you replacing Kelly?" he asked, frowning.

"I suppose until Cedric returns, I'll be acting on behalf of both the agency and the shifters."

Conleth scratched the side of his face. His knuckles briefly turned white before relaxing. A flicker of suppressed emotion crossed his features before schooling into a mask of indifference. Uncertainty gnawed at her, the silence stretching into an eternity. Conleth's dodge only fueled her to press on. "I understand he's not well-liked in many parts. If there's knowledge that could help me, I ask you to share it. You *did say* you intended to educate me. It's important that I find him and take him back to the agency."

Conleth gestured toward his SUV with a tilt of his head. "Follow me. It's a distance up the mountain to the resort."

Sunlight broke through the canopy of leaves above, sending golden ribbons weaving through the forest. Conleth pressed a hand to her lower back.

A whisper floated in the breeze.

Trinity stiffened. "Did you hear that?"

A door slammed. A man stumbled out of the camper, yawning mid-wave.

"Morning!" he called.

Trinity forced air into her lungs. "Morning," she answered, forcing a smile that wobbled at the edges.

"Let's go," Conleth murmured close to her ear.

She followed him toward her Rover, but the whisper lingered like mist, and she couldn't shake the feeling that somewhere beyond the trees, something watched them leave.

Seven

Conleth led Trinity inside his family's estate, now under his cousin Ben's stewardship. "This land is ours," he said. "When the snow deepened, the tribes and packs gathered here for shelter. It became our home."

Trinity stepped across the threshold, mountain chill lingering on her cheeks before the warmth chased it away. She paused, gaze drifting up to cedar beams dark as old honey. The morning light polished every surface. Pine and old wood scented the air. Sunlight poured through narrow windows and painted long shadows across sturdy leather chairs and carved tables.

"Welcome to Avalanche Ridge Resort," called a man from across the lobby.

"Brother?" Trinity asked, her gaze flicking from Conleth to the stranger.

"Cousin," Conleth said, sliding his arm around her waist, hand settling low on her back. Trinity stiffened. She raised an eyebrow at the possessive gesture. His dragon purred in approval of her warmth and resistance.

Conleth cleared his throat. "Ben."

His cousin grinned, friendly curiosity lighting his eyes.

"Back from town?" Ben called, stepping from behind an oak counter etched with tribal symbols. A stone hearth snapped, scent of baking filling the air.

"And I see you've brought a friend." He extended his hand to Trinity. "Bendis Jones."

A rumble stirred in Conleth's chest.

Trinity shook his hand, offering a crisp professional smile. "Agent Trinity Oberlin with PPI."

His brows shot up. "PPI?"

Ben's gaze darting from Conleth, back to Trinity. "Agent?"

Aluk's out of range. Texted Taran. We need to talk.

"Agent Oberlin is investigating the disappearance of a fellow agent and looking into the recent hiker deaths," Conleth said, his dragon pressing up close. "She needs a place to stay."

Ben crossed to the registration counter. A woman with long braids stepped out of his way, eyes on Trinity. Ben tilted the computer screen.

The woman, a mate of one of the wolf shifters in the village, smiled quietly. Ben's fingers flew over the keys, frown deepening. "No can do."

"Of course not." Trinity's smile was razor-sharp. "I'll pick up fresh supplies and return to my campsite."

The 'I told you so' in her eyes made his lip curl.

"Campsite?" Ben tapped the keyboard again. "Does Taran know she's here?"

Conleth caught Ben's implied warning.

"The ranger?" Trinity asked, an edge sharpening her voice. "Yes, we've met. I hoped to speak with him again today for an update on the missing hiker."

Warmth brushed Conleth's mind. *Aluk is on his way. No word from Taran.* Ben shrugged. "Sia's men are on patrol. Rourke's busy in town."

Ben glanced at Trinity. "Conleth's right. You shouldn't camp alone. Are you by yourself?"

Conleth crossed his arms behind her. "She'll take a single room."

Ben half smiled. "Wish I could help. We're booked. No room at the inn."

Conleth narrowed his eyes. *No room at all?*

Shifters leaving, humans coming. Vacationers. Ben's sly smile stayed. *Convenient, wouldn't you say?*

Trinity shrugged. "All is well. Can you point me to an outfitter so I can replace my gear?" She gave Conleth a level look. "Thanks for the help, but I'm fine. When do I meet your brother?"

Ben's mental voice tightened. *You brought her to meet Aluk?*

Conleth shook his head. "She's my guest. She stays in my suite."

The prospect of having her in his suite sent a wave of satisfaction through his dragon.

Trinity whirled around, her eyes narrowing. "Let me get this straight. No rooms available, but your suite is free?"

He heard her heartbeat quicken.

"My suite or the clinic," Conleth said, allowing his dragon to deepen his command.

"I'm on official business, not a guest. Not staying with you."

She wasn't going back out there. Not while he still breathed.

Trinity's lips thinned. She scanned the lobby, searching for an escape. She didn't like being cornered, but Conleth was willing to risk her anger rather than see her alone in the woods.

"You're staying in the suite?" Ben asked.

"We'll settle you in, then arrange for you to meet Aluk. There's a spa—mud wraps, hot springs." Conleth winked. "Mud suits you."

He needed time to discuss their situation without her stirring up trouble on the mountain for them.

She doesn't look the pampering type. Ben warned.

She likes nature. Have Shania trap her in mud while we talk. Conleth fished in his pocket for his suite key and held it out to her. "Deal?"

"Is that how you do it?" she asked, tilting her head.

"Do what?" Conleth asked.

"Have silent conversations. Telepathy, right? Fascinating."

Ben's glanced at the woman at the counter. She held Trinity's gaze, steady and unreadable.

"Book Agent Oberlin for a spa appointment this afternoon."

"Surely, it's booked, too?" Trinity asked.

Ben grinned. "Nope. Special guest. You get pampered."

Trinity crossed her arms. "Funny how a booked resort finds spa slots for 'special guests'."

Conleth pictured Trinity streaked with mud, tense and alert, caught between irritation and challenge. Maybe hot springs and silence would soften her—if only long enough for him to deal with Aluk.

Ben's customer service smile wobbled. "Agent Oberlin, people come to hike and enjoy the outdoors. I can juggle staff schedules for a spa appointment, but I can't snap my fingers and make another room materialize out of thin air. Unless you have that skill?"

"No," Trinity said, studying the key. "I'm here to work, not lounge. People depend on me for answers."

She was hunting for something bigger than an explanation.

Conleth's gut tightened, dragon stirring.

"You'll get those answers." he assured her, needing them, too.

"Fine." She snatched the key, fingers trembling, scowl fierce. "I assume your brother will be available soon?"

"Shania, please have someone help Agent Oberlin with her bags," Ben instructed, hospitality syrup thick. "And let everyone know—she's a special guest, pays for nothing."

Conleth shot Ben a look. *As if you ever pay, cousin.* That wasn't Conleth's worry.

She's not going to fall for it.

Trinity opened her mouth to protest when Shania stepped around the counter. "Honored to have you, Agent. Follow me. I'll have one of our staff assist you."

Trinity threw invisible daggers his way as she followed Shania.

Conleth watched her stride off, noting how her hips swayed with each determined step, boots tapping softly over the stone floor. The square set of her shoulders and the tilt of her head made something tighten in his chest. She didn't look back, but he wished she would.

Ben nudged his shoulder. "You brought an agent here? Is that our new shifter rep?"

"Worse," Conleth said, pulling out his phone. Since the snow melted, the towers in the area started functioning again, and they had a pinch of reception in the area. "She's Fae, and she's tracking Cedric Kelly."

"Fae?" Ben echoed. "A Fae agent hunting Kelly? Not a coincidence, I take it?"

"No, it's not." Conleth's dragon stirred. The mate issue would have to wait. "We need Aluk. Now."

Coming. Taran responded.

Aluk's growl echoed in his head.

"I'll have Kaya send a meal to the agent's quarters." When Conleth didn't fall for Ben's ploy, his cousin shook his head. "She is yours, isn't she?"

His dragon echoed, *mine*.

Claiming her would complicate her mission and his family's safety.

"On second thought, give me a few minutes. I'll see Trinity is settled first."

Ben lifted a brow. "Should I send one of my staff to keep an eye on her?"

Ben's concern rippled through the bond: *Will she be trouble?*

Oh, she'll find it. His dragon agreed. "It won't take me long."

Eight

"THE SPA WILL BE relaxing. You do know how to relax, don't you, Agent?"

Trinity tilted her head, recalling leaning against him the night before and falling asleep. Heat crept up her neck.

"Of course." She had no intention of relaxing.

A man was missing. Two men—an agent and a hiker. Her grandfather would not approve of spa time while others were in danger.

He led her through frosted glass doors into the reception area. A man with bright white teeth and muscles for miles greeted her with a wry smile, golden eyes bright with curiosity. He kept his long black hair tied in a man bun. "Do you have an appointment?"

Conleth stepped to speak with the man at the desk. Trinity paid no attention to what they said. Instead, she glanced around, searching for ways to escape without drawing too much attention.

Warm, calming air infused with lavender, and lemongrass washed over her. Dim overhead lights cast soft shadows across the polished wood floors. Water trickled from a hidden fountain, its gentle murmur a soothing counterpoint to the cream-colored armchairs and low table crowned with orchids.

Conleth checked her in, then faced her. Behind him, the man waited, his gaze lowered. *Interesting.*

"I'll be back to pick you up for dinner. Shawn will see to you."

Trinity bit her cheek. Her heart kicked up a notch. His eyebrow twitched. She needed to learn to school her reactions better. Remembering shifters had an uncanny ability to hear almost everything.

Conleth leaned close, her breath catching. His warm breath drifted across her ear. "Enjoy."

With a lingering look, he turned and left her with Shawn.

"Would you like a drink? Cucumber water? I'll need a moment to get the mud ready for your wrap," Shawn said, leading her down an ethereal glowing hallway. Bamboo shoots in sleek ceramic vases stood sentinel, leaves rustling softly as they passed. Open doorways revealed rooms promising pampering. He stopped in a dim chamber with a massage table draped in a plush white towel, and the gurgle of a hydrotherapy tub.

"The water is naturally heated from the ground below us. The resort rests atop a hydrothermal spring. A robe and towels are on the bench." He pointed left.

"I'll return in about an hour for your mud wrap. Pull the cord if you need anything." At the door he said, "My family has run the thermal springs for three generations. We know when someone needs healing or space. Take your time." His golden eyes met hers briefly before he left.

As Shawn's footsteps faded, voices drifted through the vents overhead. Trinity caught fragments: "... another missing..." and "... can't let the agent..."

Her pulse quickened. One voice reminded her of Ben, Conleth's cousin. The spa's central location within the resort meant conversations filtered through the ventilation system. "Prevent the agent... what?" She asked, aware nobody would respond.

Calculating swiftly, she knew she could move fast and be back before anyone noticed. Conleth might never know. Two men were dead, one still missing, and for the first time, the ground felt unstable beneath her feet.

Trinity crept toward the door, heart pounding against her ribs. She wasn't a shifter, but years of training sharpened her instincts and taught her to hear beyond noise. No footsteps. Just muffled voices overhead.

This was her chance. Conleth might think a spa day would keep her boxed in, but he didn't know her well. She snorted. He expected her to waste time soaking while people vanished. Cedric could be anywhere, and the clock was ticking. With shifters and outsiders mingling, the resort was a wellspring of information.

She hesitated, hands sweating, planning her escape without alerting the desk staff. Shawn's voice stopped her cold.

"Did you need something?" Shawn asked.

Trinity licked her lips and turned, forcing a smile. She placed her hand on his arm." You offered me cucumber water earlier. I'd like some."

Her palm tingled. After Conleth's blankness, Shawn's memories spilling into her came as a relief. The mountain lion spirit pulsed inside him. Pride swelled inside him for inheriting the last of his family's bloodline. Desperation for a mate filled her. She pulled her hand away. His gaze lingered where she'd touched him. Poor guy. He worked at the spa, wanting to meet women, hoping to find his match.

"If you slip into the tub, I'll bring your water," Shawn promised, hurrying away.

She waited while Shawn fetched her the drink. The whole spa charade was sort of fun. A game she was forced to play to keep Conleth from interfering with her investigation. Helpfully annoying dragon. She didn't need him to follow her everywhere.

Trinity slipped on the robe, then perched near the tub's edge, creating the illusion she'd undressed. Shawn's grimace at finding her not fully submerged made her lips twitch. Let him stew a bit. Conleth's possessiveness was over the top. Flattering, yes, but controlling. With anyone else, one touch would tell her if his protectiveness came from genuine care or possessive dominance. She'd learned to tell the difference, but with Conleth?

She couldn't read him. He left her stumbling around in the dark. She didn't plan to get burned again, but how could she protect herself from a man she couldn't read?

When Shawn left, her doubts circled. Was Conleth's jealousy about care? Or territory? Shifters marked mates in ways she didn't want to contemplate. Rolling her shoulder, she shrugged out of the robe. No one was claiming her. Certainly not with teeth.

She counted to a hundred before peering into the hallway, scanning for cameras. The reception desk was deserted. No Shawn. Heart hammering, she seized the chance to slip through the corridors, nerves buzzing from her near miss. She couldn't afford to get caught.

Around her, the resort sprawled out like a playground for the wealthy. Local artisans offered handcrafted souvenirs and regional delicacies from brightly colored stalls. Children's laughter drew her toward the game room, pulsing with neon lights, games beeping, and parents mingling.

A dark-haired woman cheered for the older kids as they played. The woman's arm cuffs caught Trinity's attention. She recognized the cuffs. They dampened one's Fae abilities. Surely, an ordinary woman wouldn't have worn them for adornment. Was she Fae?

Curious, Trinity threaded through the crowd.

The woman stood beside a boy not yet of high school age. He pumped his fist and danced, landing a Skee-ball in the fifty slot.

The woman gave him a high-five, then her blue eyes locked on Trinity.

"Your turn," the boy challenged, focused on his game. The woman smiled. "I'm not allowed to play anymore."

The boy scowled and restarted the game. "I'm going to get as good as you, then they'll ban me too."

The woman laughed and ruffled his hair. "You do that."

Then she addressed Trinity. "I love your hair. It looks natural. Do you dye it?"

"My hairdresser would love to hear that," Trinity said, but the fine hairs along her neck prickled. Her gaze fell to the cuffs. What kind of dangerous magic demanded restraints like that?

Having cataloged a few of their kinds in the archives at the agency, she needed to ask, "I love your arm cuffs. Did you purchase them here at the resort?"

Gwen crossed her arms. "These were a gift from the council."

"Did they cuff you because of your blood magic?"

Gwen frowned. "You must be Agent Oberlin."

Then it clicked. "You're Taran's mate. Is he here?"

Gwen's lips pressed together. After a pause, she glanced at the boy with blonde hair, worry etched on his face. "Hard to say where he is at this time of day."

"Did they cuff you because you're Fae?" Trinity curled her fingers into fists. She walked a fine line among the shifters. Would they cuff her, too?

"These cuffs are both a blessing and a curse." Gwen's voice dropped. "Without them, touching another person causes me pain." She glanced at the boy.

"Is he yours?" Trinity asked.

The boy's coloring seemed wrong for the offspring of Gwen and Taran. She would have taken the boy for a mountain lion shifter, especially with those honey-gold eyes.

The boy's presence hung like fog. Trinity didn't offer details with him nearby.

"No. I keep an eye on him occasionally," Gwen said, a smile forming.

The boy moved on to another arcade game with the other children. "He seems like a very intelligent young man. Energetic."

Gwen narrowed her eyes further. There was something... off about her. Maybe she was being overly cautious with Trinity questioning the cuffs. Still, caution kept one alive, especially around a dangerous stranger.

"Does Conleth know you're not in the spa?" Gwen asked, crossing her arms.

Trinity flashed her best smile, aiming for charm. "What if he doesn't? I go where I please. New ground is for exploring, not lounging. Spa mud can wait."

"Eww. Mud," the boy called, darting past with the other children and confirming the child possessed the spirit of a mountain lion and very good hearing.

Gwen wrinkled her nose. "I'm with Levi. Mud is overrated. I can't blame you for escaping, although the heated tubs are great after a day on the mountain."

"You've tried them?"

"After hiking all day on the mountain, oh yeah," Gwen said.

Bodies on the trail meant someone missed the signs, but not the guides.

"Know a good guide for the trails?" Trinity kept her tone light. Guides always knew the danger spots.

Gwen smiled. "Ask Conleth. He'd take you whenever he's free."

Trinity's pulse jumped. Conleth. She feigned nonchalance: "True, but I don't want to take up all his time." Despite herself, her gaze locked with Gwen's. "He's the only medic here? No other doctor?"

"No, just Conleth. He wouldn't like you hiking with anyone else." Gwen motioned Trinity down a hall toward more shops.

"Because I'm an outsider?" Trinity pressed.

Gwen stared at her, then sighed "Honestly? There have been incidents. Disappearances in the woods. I'd tell you to stay on marked trails, but even those aren't safe right now. Taran banned me from leading hikes until it's handled."

Disappearances in the woods weren't exactly news to her. She read the silence between trees, the change in wind that didn't belong. With the last hiker's death fresh in her memory.

And Cedric?

He must have uncovered something, making him a target. Was he alive to tell her?

She needed to find Cedric. The local shifters knew about the hiker attacks, and if answers lived anywhere, she'd find them with the pack.

"Conleth will not risk you going out there and putting yourself in danger." Gwen's last words jolted Trinity from her thoughts. Her gaze lingered on Trinity for a beat too long.

Could Conleth actually think she was his mate? The idea sent a flutter through her chest. *No—focus.* Trinity forced her attention back to Gwen's guarded expression. Whatever existed, or didn't, between her and Conleth, people were still missing. Her grandfather gave her one last chance to prove herself as an agent, not to waste it daydreaming about a dragon.

He had always warned her about dragons.

Yet, a thrill coiled in her belly, a delicious mix of danger and forbidden possibility.

She couldn't deny she found him attractive, but memories of her past heartbreak smothered any foolish daydreams of a future with Conleth.

Gwen wasn't offering answers, and the clock pressed in. Trinity moved another step closer. "It's not his choice. I came here to help solve this."

She let the quiet build, then said, "I'm a PPI agent, Mrs. Vasumen. My job is to protect people. Their lives come before mine."

If Gwen knew anything useful, Trinity needed it now. Cooperation mattered more than secrecy.

Gwen's eyes widened. "PPI?" She glanced around furtively, as if afraid someone might be listening. They passed a clothing boutique. "Who sent you?"

Trinity paused, fingers itching to touch Gwen, wanting a vision. Because of the cuffs, she doubted she'd get anything, but the old habit pulled at her. She'd check if Conleth wore something similar, but she'd seen him. *All* of him. He wasn't hiding anything in that department. There had to be a reason behind him blocking her gift.

"I'm a shifter specialist. I've been assigned to the mountain region. What do you know about the hikers?" Her casual facade melted away.

"I can't say I do," Gwen murmured, her face turning pale.

"Is it because you truly don't know, or is it your mate?" Trinity stepped aside, letting two women exit the shop behind them.

"Taran and the police are investigating the incidents. It's not my place to give you information. You should speak to Taran or Sia since you're here at the resort." Gwen stole another glance toward the game room. Sounds of the arcade drifted in the hall.

"I've spoken to Taran and Rourke. Is Sia the law enforcement in this region?"

"Yes, I suppose. He's the beta of the wolf pack here in Avalanche Ridge. I suppose they're what you'd consider the guards and the law enforcers here. You've met Rourke, right? He's the alpha of the Sentinel Peak pack and the chief of police there. But they all answer to Aluk, the alpha of the mountain."

Trinity catalogued the information in her mind. Shifters had clear territorial divisions, but who handled missing person cases that crossed the boundaries? "All good information. Thank you." She paused deliberately. "I still want to know what you can tell me about the missing hiker. Specifically, which pack's land did he vanish from?" Trinity narrowed her gaze at Gwen.

"Why don't we talk somewhere quiet?" Gwen cast a meaningful look at the people surrounding them. A short, blonde hair woman twirled her hair while chatting with a man wrapping a purchase. Her laugh rang loud and free as she flirted.

"There's a coffee shop around the corner. We can chat there. Unless you want to return to the spa?" Gwen said.

Trinity didn't answer right away.

An invitation, maybe. Or a test.

She nodded slowly, noticing the hazy expression in Gwen's eyes.

Gwen remained still. Trinity didn't want to rush her, so she waited. A moment later, Gwen sighed and smiled faintly. "Taran." As if it explained everything.

Confusion must have shown on Trinity's face because Gwen added, "We can converse through the mate bond. Ask Conleth about it. It's best you don't go back to the spa just yet. Though Shawn gives the best deep tissue massages." She bit her lip, pausing for a moment.

"Perhaps it's better you don't go back. Conleth might hurt him if he touches you."

"What do you mean?" Trinity asked, waiting for more.

Gwen's blue eyes paled, and her gaze went blank. Taking it as a sign, Trinity reached out and brushed the woman's arm above the elbow, but only the coolness of her skin met Trinity's palm. "Gwen?"

Nothing.

Gwen shook her head. "Sorry. Taran again."

"Your cuffs don't block you from communicating?"

"No."

"I worked in the artifacts and records department for several years." Trinity gestured towards the cuffs. "It was my job to research such things and ensure they were properly stored. I've seen cuffs like yours, although not so elegantly constructed. You said they enable you to touch others? What is your gift?" she asked, hoping that by sharing her understanding of them, Gwen might open up to her.

Gwen didn't blink. "That's personal, don't you think, Agent?"

"Please call me Trinity." Trinity pointed to the inside of the coffee shop. "Shall we?"

"You'll tell me more about your assignment here?" Gwen got in line at the coffee counter. "And your connection with Conleth?"

A wave of heat flooded Trinity's system. Connection? "What connection?"

The question ignited a storm inside her. She'd known Conleth less than a day, yet already his absence left a hole. Ridiculous. Dangerous.

A secret thrill danced within her, a forbidden tango she shouldn't want to learn.

"I met him yesterday." She focused her attention back on the coffee menu. Avoiding Gwen's gaze proved more difficult than expected.

"He's proved useful in my investigation." Trinity finished lamely; the last part tacked on to mask the unexpected flutter in her chest.

Gwen's eyebrow arched. "Only information?" she asked, her eyes sparkling. "He's gotten under your skin, hasn't he?"

Trinity gritted her teeth and shoved thoughts of Conleth aside. Two men were missing. That's what mattered. Her grandfather's voice shouted in her head. *Let personal feelings cloud your judgment again, and you'll find yourself locked back in the artifacts room.*

This was her last chance.

Her personal feelings didn't matter here. The case was no longer her sole focus. Conleth, with his dragon spirit and unexpected protectiveness, had woven himself into her investigation. Fascinating and potentially dangerous, he posed a promise of her ensured doom. While a part of her mind screamed caution, another, quieter part couldn't ignore the undeniable pull toward the man with the dragon spirit.

"Look," she said, meeting Gwen's gaze. "My personal life is irrelevant."

Trinity turned to the barista, buying herself a moment. "Double pump vanilla in my mocha cappuccino, please." The familiar ritual of ordering coffee helped steady her nerves. Only when they'd moved away from the counter did she continue. "Why target the hikers?"

Gwen ordered after her, sidestepping the question. "I'm surprised they sent you alone. Doesn't the PPI usually work in teams?"

She asked herself the same. After the last time, maybe that was the point. The urge to press for answers nudged at her, but patience had its own strength.

Gwen had every right to be wary. Trinity needed her to open up about the hikers, hoping it might lead her to Cedric. The missing shifter representative wasn't just a coincidence. Had he fallen prey to the shadows like the others? She had wondered about that before. The bigger mystery was why no body had surfaced.

"This is a special assignment," Trinity said.

Her last chance to prove herself.

"You're familiar with the PPI?" she asked.

"The PPI, not so much, but I've heard of shifter agents. My brother used to work for one," Gwen said, sorrow misting in her eyes.

"He was a hunter." Gwen lifted her drink as soon as the barista placed it on the counter.

"A hunter," Trinity murmured. Anticipation's sweetness from her mocha cappuccino soured. "Your brother hunted shifters?"

A hunter's sibling?

This changed everything.

Gwen kept talking, but Trinity missed most of it, too caught up in what she'd just learned.

"He did it to keep me safe." Gwen wrapped both hands around her drink and watched the dark liquid swirl through the transparent container. "A long story for another day."

A hunter's sister, wearing magic-dampening cuffs, and mated to a shifter alpha's brother. Either Gwen was the unlikeliest spy ever, or she told the truth. Her Fae blood might have created a kinship, but those cuffs stood between them. The resentment between shifters and Fae ran far deeper than simple misunderstanding.

Trinity kept a neutral mask, sharing information with care and watching for any tells.

She noticed their drinks came in glass containers with wooden lids and glass straws. Near the exit, a bin stood ready for recycling. She'd seen similar bins around the resort, admiring the local's commitment to protecting the mountain. Shifters held a strong connection to their spirits and nature. Thinking back to the warmth she felt in Taran and

Conleth's hands, she guessed wood, metal, and glass could withstand the heat. It made sense to avoid plastic.

Trinity accepted her order and followed Gwen away from the coffee shop, noting Gwen's guarded body language.

If Gwen knew something about Cedric's disappearance, her reaction would tell Trinity everything. "Do you think he might have known Cedric Kelly?"

Gwen's hand jerked, coffee splashing across her Avalanche Ridge Resort t-shirt. *Bingo.* Gwen jumped, and Trinity went to grab napkins. "Are you all right?"

"Did you say Cedric?" Gwen pulled her shirt away from her chest and groaned.

Trinity took a moment to assess, then shrugged. "He's the shifter agent assigned to this part of the mountain. I'd like to find and have a word with him."

The spilled coffee could have been an accident, but had Cedric's name hit a nerve?

Gwen's eyes glazed, lashes dropping briefly before fluttering open.

"Good luck with that." She held up her drink in salute. "I need to change. Taran and I are meeting Sia and the others by the river."

"Sia is the beta of the pack here at the resort?"

"Avalanche Ridge. You'll learn about pack hierarchy the longer you're here. Trace found shredded clothing near the river last night. He shared the scent with the pack enforcers to see if they could pick up any more leads."

"I'm aware of the clothing," Trinity said.

"I'd invite you, but I believe Conleth has other plans for you. I'd return to the lobby or the spa. Conleth has the entire resort looking for you."

She needed to uncover what was attacking the hikers in hopes it would lead her to Cedric. Had someone discovered his Fae heritage? Was that why Conleth brought her before his alpha? Would they try to cuff her and make her vanish too?

"It's a shifter thing." Gwen blinked. A familiar tingle danced beneath Trinity's skin, a low hum beneath the surface, intensifying at the mere mention of his name. "You're talking with your mate, and he's with Conleth, isn't he?"

Gwen grinned. "There is a lot your agency didn't teach you about shifter men. You know about Conleth and his brothers?"

"I do." No point in hiding it.

"Then you should know, they are not above doing what is necessary to protect their family, and the people on this mountain."

Nine

Conleth paced the length of Aluk's suite inside the Avalanche Ridge Resort.

His dragon grumbled. *When she is ours, we will not permit such acts.*

The growl rumbled deeper than it had in years.

Heat built in his chest, impossible to ignore.

Trinity's scent clung to him like a claim. Each heartbeat sent warmth pulsing outward. His skin tightened as the dragon spirit pressed to break free.

Taran paced near the window.

Across the room, Aluk hadn't moved, hadn't spoken. His fingers remained steepled on the table. Conleth waited, his hands clenched into fists.

He leaned against the back of a large leather sofa, resisting the urge to pace. Usually, he was the voice of reason, keeping his brothers focused.

"She's looking for Cedric," he said.

"Let her search," Taran turned from the window. "What harm does it do if she looks? We all know she won't find him."

"She'll tire eventually and leave," Ben added, "unless Romeo here objects. Then maybe you'll finally figure out what she is."

A tremor ran through Conleth, heat blazing behind his sternum like a struck match waiting to catch. The burn clawed up from his gut, scalding his lungs. He bit down hard, jaw aching, a hiss slipping out like steam from a cracked pipe.

Mine! His dragon roared in his head.

Ben winced. Taran crossed his arms and tilted his head, stretching his neck. "Well, we all know how you feel. What about her?"

His dragon spirit pressed at the edges of Conleth's thoughts; its hunger a steady, insistent thrum. He tried to breathe past it, but doubt coiled tighter. Having been lonely too long, had his beast simply seized on the first human who stirred interest? The dragon bucked harder, restless, heat flaring behind his eyes. Her absence gnawed at him, a low ache rising to a growl. *Mine.*

His mouth parted, the truth burning for release. He caught it and swallowed it back. Silence scraped down his throat. Some things, once spoken, couldn't be taken back.

His hand flattened against his chest, fingers splayed like he could hold himself together. Taran had Gwen, their connection so seamless it made Conleth's pulse spike. His chest tightened. Taran had that. That ease, that certainty. While Conleth stood withempty hands and questions he couldn't answer.

Until this point, Aluk had sat silent, his fingers pressed together at the round table in his kitchenette. His eyes flickered between gold and whiskey brown. "What have you told her?"

Conleth forced himself to take a deep breath, the heat in his chest easing. "She knows we are dragons."

He recalled the way she'd whispered, *You're a dragon*—how she'd met his gaze and refused to look away. Her scent and the rapid drum of her heartbeat told him she feared her own reaction more than him

"She'd have to be blind not to figure it out," Taran said. "Trace said you rescued her from the river."

Aluk sat back, brows knitting. "You shifted in front of her?"

"I didn't have a choice," Conleth grumbled. "My dragon took over when she fell in the river."

Taran pointed at him, grinning. "See? I told you! Now, I'm not the only one."

One wrong move—one flash of scales or ember in his eyes—and she'd run.

First, he needed to show her the truth of their connection. Explaining a bond older than time itself to someone who had so little knowledge about dragons would be no easy task.

Aluk and Ben looked at Taran with hardened expressions. Taran crossed his arms again and leaned back against the tall windows.

"Just wait until it happens to you," Taran said to Aluk.

Taran's arms tightened across his chest.

Ben's shoulders tensed, and Conleth's fingers went still against the sofa leather.

All eyes turned to Taran. His eyes widened, color draining from his skin. They all sucked in a breath as Aluk's eyes flared red at the mention of mates.

Silence pressed against the walls like fog. Taran cleared his throat, the sound brittle in the stillness. No one dared break it, haunted by the memory of those dark months after Aluk lost his mate and his dragon pulled him into a deep hibernation beneath the resort.

Rather than let them dwell there, Ben pressed on. That she knows you're a dragon, she's your mate, and she's still hanging out with you is a good sign," he said, scowling. "But she's a danger to us all."

"We should all get our stories straight, then lead her on a wild-goose chase." Taran strolled to the table and grabbed a sandwich from the platter Ben had brought. "It could be fun," he added with a crooked grin.

Conleth leaned forward slightly, then stopped himself. He missed the easy banter they once shared. The dragon spirit inside him bristled. It coiled tighter, a warning rumble in his chest. She wasn't leverage. Taran didn't understand what this would cost him. Conleth refused to cross that line.

"Stop." Aluk raised a hand. "We expected this to happen, but you need to make sure she discovers the truth about Kelly and his dealings."

If Trinity learned what they'd done to Cedric..." He didn't finish the thought. War. That's what it would mean. Lying to her, watching her search for a man who'd never be found—his gut twisted.

"You can't tell the agent the truth about what happened to him," Ben said, chin lifting, eyes glowing with molten gold. "They'll blame us, and we'll have another war. This time with the humans. In case you haven't noticed, we're outnumbered."

She needs to discover it on her own if she is to believe it, his dragon asserted.

"You don't think I don't know that? Don't know why our ancestors brought us here to protect our people?" Aluk's eyes turned red; his lips turned up in a snarl.

Ben bowed his head and backed away.

"No injuries today." Conleth held up his hands. "I've dealt with enough dead bodies over the past few weeks to last decades."

"Conleth's right. We need to focus if we're going to stop hikers from straying off the trails and popping up off the walking trails on the west side of town. The last thing we need is more dead humans. And the shadows have been restless ever since we opened the portal and shifted the seasons."

"You mean since your mate opened the portal," Ben said, his tone carrying an edge as he settled into a chair opposite them. He leaned forward, gaze tracking between them.

Taran's face turned red, and his dragon shone through his eyes.

"No one is blaming anyone here," Aluk said, rocking back in his chair. "It was the best solution. Taran's mate was the first. Her gift unlocked the door to the garden of the Great Hunter. If this woman is your mate, then what gift does she possess?"

Conleth opened his mouth to deny it, but the word 'human' put a bitter taste on his tongue. It wasn't just the prejudice of the council he worried about. The undeniable pull he had towards her, the primal connection that defied explanation, hummed from his dragon spirit. A human mate?

The repercussions would be devastating should the council object. Would they know? Or had they learned from the past?

They'd caused no issues with Taran and Gwen. Yet.

He settled for a gruff, "She's human."

"That shade of her eyes? I've never seen that shade of lavender on a human, and under the resort lighting, her hair showed those white-violet streaks clear as day. Your mate's part Fae, dude."

Conleth's heart slammed against his ribs. Ben was right. The subtle details clicked into place. Plenty of women dyed their hair and wore contacts to change their eye color, but the way she carried herself, her polished speech, and the way she'd pulled on those gloves insistent on assisting him in the autopsy had all been clues to the obvious.

Her magic could explain the pull.

No. Mate. The word reverberated through him, absolute.

"Fae are notorious for their trickery," he murmured.

"Are her ears pointed?" Taran asked, grabbing a chip from the platter.

Ben chuckled. "She's not an elf, you dolt. She's the real deal. You can't tell me you don't scent it on her. She smells of lilacs and lavender. Two very distinct scents. She's not human."

"You don't know what parts aren't glamour," Aluk said.

Conleth drew in a slow, deliberate breath, like dragging air through a narrow funnel. His chest rose, then stilled. Beneath the surface, the dragon prowled, protective. He recalled the way she'd met his gaze without flinching, even when his eyes glowed from the dragon spirit inside him. The way she'd leaned toward his warmth.

He forced his breathing to steady. Emotion wouldn't help here. Facts. He needed answers like Trinity needed to find Cedric.

If she truly came from the Fae, every step from here they needed to be careful.

Taran grinned. "She could wear a lot of perfume. Women like to smell good."

Conleth lowered his chin in agreement. He didn't trust his voice. The heat in his chest hadn't faded, and Taran's words scraped against it like rough stone. Perfume? That wasn't what had stirred him.

"Not shifter women, Taran," Ben scoffed. "Too sensitive. Fae too, usually, unless one is purposely trying to mask their scent."

"It's not perfume."

A heavy silence descended upon Conleth's words.

Finally, Aluk spoke. "We need a plan. This Agent Oberlin, she'll keep asking questions. We can't simply dismiss her concerns about the missing hikers, but I'm not opposed to sending her on a little scavenger hunt for answers about Cedric Kelly."

"The hikers," Ben muttered, his voice laced with frustration. "They were warned to keep to the trails. Sia sends men out every day to scout them. We have trail leaders to ensure their safety, but they go out on their own and don't listen."

"Trinity mentioned the state opened the borders to the outside because Cedric failed to stop the government from opening the mountain to outsiders."

"We toss the guy into a portal. He cannot sign papers, and here we are," Ben said.

"And the attacks are becoming more frequent from the shadow spirits. We've unlocked a piece of the mountain, and now the shadow spirits have become desperate. They're attacking anything within reach to revive the old bloodlines. They've been dormant for centuries."

"We've unlocked part of the curse. I believe we're in the next stage." Conleth contemplated this ever since the mountain air warmed and the snow melted. It came as no surprise that the shadow spirits became more restless. Bolder.

"How long does this stage last? Don't get me wrong; the snow was great for business, but this endless heat makes you wonder if summer's our new forever season."

Aluk's jaw twitched, eyes darkening. "We can't change what has been set in motion. If the curse truly weakened when Taran's mate arrived, then we'll see what this Agent Oberlin brings. She knows what we are. Make sure she does not leave this mountain. Do what you must to mark her and keep our secret safe."

Ben straightened in his chair. The challenge faded from his expression.

"We need to be transparent with her," Conleth said at last. "Up to a point, of course. She knows the shadows are dangerous, and I've explained the recent deaths as unfortunate encounters with the rogue spirits."

"What about Cedric's disappearance?" Taran asked.

Conleth's spine went rigid, his hands locking behind his back. If she ever discovered they'd essentially sent a federal agent to wander the Great Hunter's Forest for eternity, her law enforcement training would take over. Badge first, mate bond second. That's how she'd see it.

Once she connected the dead hikers, the shadow spirits, and Cedric's disappearance, she'd have the mountain evacuated.

"I'll keep her busy with her investigation. Let her make her own assumptions about where Cedric went," he said finally.

"In the meantime." Aluk said, glancing at Taran. "Keep the human visitors out of our sacred areas of the forest."

"She's Fae. This might be part of a bigger plan," Ben offered.

A murmur of agreement rippled around the table.

Ten

Nestled among the towering pines beyond the resort, a cluster of weather-worn cabins formed a village seemingly untouched by time. Shingle roofs, a soft gray from years of mountain sun and snow, dipped low over walls of rough-hewn logs at the base of the foothills.

Trinity adjusted the strap of her satchel while Conleth strode beside her. His broad shoulders brushed against the canvas awnings as they navigated the narrow plank sidewalks lining the village paths. In the distance, a weathered wooden sign, its paint faded but lettering still clear, proclaimed the village as *Avalanche Ridge*.

"They built wooden sidewalks to keep out the mud from the spring melt. All the snow melting has caused water to flood the mountain."

She flashed him a smile, masking the prickle of wariness of his constant need to explain everything stirred in her. "And we'll see your brother tomorrow?"

Meeting Gwen had only added to her questions. Those armbands marked her as Fae, despite her human appearance. She wanted to meet Gwen's brother, but her bigger concern was with the dragons. Had the shifter council judged a woman for her heritage? And if so, was she next?

"Where did you go?" Conleth asked, catching her hand as she stepped onto the next level of the sidewalk. The warmth of his palm drew her focus, the touch startling in its steadiness. A current danced across her skin, thrumming with attraction. She lowered her gaze briefly, searching for a motive behind the gesture and finding only calm patience.

Porches adorned with brightly colored hanging baskets overflowed with petunias and trailing vines added life to the rustic cabins. Paths wound between wildflowers and grasses, the air humming with soft movement and simple beauty.

"I'm right here." Her stomach twisted recalling Shawn's startled expression when he'd walked in on her in the tub, the blush staining his face, her own nervous laughter. Gratitude for his silence still caught her off guard.

A breeze swept through the pines, carrying the sweet scent of needles, the faint, aroma of wood smoke, and Conleth's scent close beside her.

"In person, but you've been in your mind for several moments," Conleth said, squeezing her hand gently. "I was saying Aluk will see you in the morning. He needed to attend to other matters this evening."

She dug her nails into her palms. "Oh."

A woman with a young girl exited a nearby cabin, a basket full of store goods balanced on her hip. The child clutched a rag doll with black hair and wolf's ears.

"How adorable," Trinity mused. The mother's arm tightened around the girl, her steps quickening until the crowd swallowed them.

"They're still getting used to outsiders here," Conleth said. "Hungry?"

Back at the resort, she'd found an enormous platter with a grilled sandwich and fries inside her room. It may have fed her for a week if not for Conleth returning to his suite and finishing it off for her. It must be nice, she thought, to have the metabolism of a dragon.

His lips curved into the ghost of a smile, amusement dancing in his amber eyes. He couldn't possibly know what she'd been thinking.

They found a quaint bistro tucked away on a side street. A wooden table with log-carved chairs sat on the narrow sidewalk, bathed in the warm glow of a canopy of stringed lights. The rich scent of barbecue and spices drifted through the open doorway wrapping around them.

A weathered wooden sign hung crookedly above the entrance; its surface etched with a swirling script that caught and bent the light.

"What does it mean, *Meetohkah wahkohtah ohtahkah ahtah ohkoh Ahhkaht ohtahkah oohsahkah tahkah ohtahkah?*" She read, stumbling through the words that seemed to roll off her tongue like pebbles on a dusty road.

"The shadows hunt with the Great Hunter. They seek those with long bloodlines who arrive," he said.

Trinity, caught by the gravity in his voice, asked, "It's a warning, isn't it? Why not write it in a language everyone can understand?"

"It is in the language of our ancestors. Until now, there has been no one permitted past our border to interpret it." Conleth said, his tone low, his expression shadowed. "It's a reminder we live each day as a gift. The spirits don't choose all of us. Our women are not blessed with spirits, and when one warrior's bloodline dies out, their gifts and spirit guardians don't move to another family. The spirit stays in the shadows, and over time, it becomes dangerous."

"Then why protect them from the hunters?" Trinity swirled the pink liquid of her raspberry lemonade in her glass, the ice clinking softly against the glass. The logic tangled in her head. If the hunters destroyed the dangerous ones, wasn't that better than letting them fester?

"You approve of hunting down men and killing them for their gifts?" Conleth's growl rolled through the space between them, his eyes reddening.

Her throat tightened. "No. Not when you say it like that." She hesitated, searching his face. "I thought the shadows couldn't reconnect without a blood heir? Do they need one to hold their gifts?" Heat prickled along her neck. She hadn't meant to push him. "I just meant... isn't it better to capture them than to let them harm others?"

"No." He leaned forward, his nostrils flared as the air around him seemed to pulse with restrained energy. "If the hunters get a hold of them, they will corrupt and kill the ones who captured them. It's a far greater evil and better to leave them alone where they may stick to the shadows until the Great Hunter allows them to return to his hunting lands."

"And that would be when?" she asked, even more curious.

"When the curse on the mountain is broken." Conleth leaned back, his shoulders relaxing. "That's why we mark where it's safe for outsiders."

"And this curse?" She knew bits and pieces from her grandfather.

"Our elders opposed pairing with outsiders. Ever since the curse, we've stuck to our own clans and packs." Conleth's fingers tightened around his water glass. "The mountain offered us protection away from the outside world."

He paused, and Trinity leaned forward.

"We weren't the only ones who sought the mountain as a sanctuary. A Fae woman came, and the dragon alpha intended to claim her as his mate." His gaze darkened. "To prevent the union, the shifter council imprisoned her in the mountain."

"The Unseelie queen," Trinity murmured.

"In her rage, she cursed us." Conleth tipped the glass and swirled the water. "She stripped the blessing from receiving our spirits at birth and stole the fertility from our women. The mountain froze over. Our people have suffered for centuries."

The glass cracked under his grip. When he looked up, his eyes flashed red.

"Our numbers dwindled. Those loyal to the queen disappeared. Some claim they went inside the mountain to wait for the curse to end."

Trinity forced herself to breathe evenly. Her grandfather's version painted the natives on the mountain as villains and the Fae queen as the victim. The Fae believed the natives had stolen the animals' spirits from the queen's forest. *A dragon will be your doom, little tracker. They took everything from us.* The shifters' rage had been legendary. They'd demanded the Fae relinquish their hold on the beasts, and battle broke out on the mountain. From there, the details blurred over the generations.

"Is there more?"

Conleth nodded. "The union should have served as a treaty. Once the alpha completed the mate bond, but..." He shook his head. "The specifics get fuzzy over the centuries. What we know is the Fae queen became imprisoned in the mountain, and war erupted between our peoples. Even from her prison, she cursed the dragon alpha and all those with shifter blood, binding our fates together."

"A Fae queen impression, a curse unleashed, and centuries of bloodshed between their peoples. Sounds like a broken fairytale."

"That's the gist of it." His attention returned to the candle burning between them. "Outsiders think it's part of the decor and advertising."

Trinity raised an eyebrow, grateful for the shift to safer ground. "It's only been open to outsiders for a few months. Few humans believe in werewolves and such, but I suppose when you bring cultural heritage into the legends and lore, it makes thrill seekers curious."

"Is that why you became an agent?" Fire glinted in Conleth's eyes. "Are you a thrill seeker, Agent Oberlin?"

Trinity's smile tightened. Memories of a past conversation, a colleague she'd trusted too much, played in her head. It had backfired spectacularly, nearly costing her job. She wasn't eager to repeat that mistake.

"More like truth seeker." She held his gaze. "Why did you become a doctor?"

"Army medic." Conleth shrugged. "To keep our land within the reservation of the mountain and the people within it protected, the government requires us to send men into the military for eight years. I choose to go on behalf of my clan. It gave me the training I couldn't have received here to help my people."

A young woman with ice-blue eyes and jet-black hair set a corn, blueberry, and wild rice salad in front of Trinity and a large rack of ribs for Conleth.

"Did you ever consider not returning?" Trinity asked once their server left. "Not coming back?"

"This is my home. Why would I wish to live anywhere else?" He drained his water, ice clinking against glass. "What of you, Agent? Did you choose to be here?"

"Trinity, please. Enough with the 'Agent' or 'Agent Oberlin'." She stabbed her fork into a blueberry, surprised by her own candor. "I have a feeling I'll be spending an extended amount of time on the mountain until my superiors are pleased with my accomplishments."

"Then I hope they are difficult to please," Conleth said.

Trinity's breath caught. Heat crept up her neck. Gwen's words from earlier echoed in her mind: *Being the dragon shifter's mate was a thrilling, yet terrifying experience.*

She wasn't here for romance. She squashed the flutter in her chest. "You understand our relationship is purely professional?"

"Purely," Conleth picked up a rib, but his eyes never left hers. "I know you met Taran's mate, Gwen, today."

The mention of Taran's mate made Trinity sit up straighter. A faint buzz prickled under her skin, raising a fine sheen of sweat along her arms. She leaned forward. "Taran's mate isn't a shifter, is she?"

She tilted her head, searching for confirmation in his eyes.

Conleth paused, wiping his fingers on a napkin. "No, but you already knew that."

A sliver of hope pierced through her. If he'd accepted a non-shifter mate for his friend, perhaps he might be more accepting of their differences. But what did it matter? The doom her grandfather predicted—perhaps it had nothing to do with her Fae heritage. After all, Taran's mate was Fae too, and she'd survived the bond.

"She's not human either," Trinity said, scratching her left palm as a ripple of power flowed up her arms, chilling her skin.

Conleth's eyes narrowed. Her breath caught. His gaze traveled from her hair, down her face, and landed on her lips.

"Neither are you," he said quietly.

Her hand tightened on her fork. "We're not talking about me."

Her pulse spiked. Perhaps this line of questioning had been a mistake. Getting involved promised her doom. Her grandfather never lied.

"I think we are." His voice dropped, husky and intent. "I want to know everything about you. If you want my help finding Cedric or stopping more hikers from getting hurt, we work together. No secrets between us."

She felt the urge to reach toward him, to reveal everything, but what if it resulted in further betrayal? Another charming face hiding a heart of ice? Alone, she was powerless to stop the disappearances. Time was running out for Cedric, and her grandfather had given her one chance to redeem herself.

Yet, working with Conleth presented another kind of danger. She hadn't known him long enough to feel this way. *He'll be the death of you.*

She searched his eyes, hoping his dragon would reveal what her gift couldn't. When she'd touched him earlier, her gift had yielded nothing. No pulse of memory, no echo of truth. The blankness unsettled her more than anything he'd said.

"You're quite demanding." She gripped her fork like a lifeline, caught between the impulse to push him away and the desire to pull him closer.

"It's my nature." His amber eyes gleamed.

"What did you find out today?"

"I met Gwen today." Trinity searched Conleth's face. If he already knew, if he'd been testing her—.

She pushed back and reached for the doggy bag with what remained of her salad. They walked back the way they'd come, the evening air cooling around them. "Do you know Gwen's brother? I'd like to meet him."

Conleth turned his head, scanning the darkening woods bordering the path. "You can ask Aluk in the morning."

"What is it?"

"Stay close." A frown creased his brow.

Trinity followed his gaze. Dense foliage swayed gently in the breeze. Lights dotted the trail between shops, and voices carried from inside the bistro. Yet, the woods beyond the path held only silence. No rustling. No owl. Even the wind seemed to hold its breath.

She stepped closer to him, squinting into the darkness. Her heart hammered against her ribs. The shadows stilled. The hair on her arms rose.

A low rumble vibrated through Conleth's chest. Trinity pressed her palm against his sternum without thinking, closing her eyes and reaching for a vision. The vibrations beneath her hand offered nothing. No images. No glimpses of truth. Just the steady thrum of his heartbeat.

She opened her eyes and scanned the tree line. "Maybe it was just a deer."

Conleth reached for her doggy bag. His hand brushed hers. Instead of letting go, his fingers curled around hers. Heat spread up her arm.

"Let's head back," he said.

Trinity's stomach dropped. What if he wanted to come in?

"It's getting late," he finished.

A shiver danced down her spine. She glanced back at the darkening woods, skin still prickling. The path behind them lay empty, lights from other cabins casting warm pools along the trail.

She quickened her pace toward the resort. "It's probably beautiful out here when the stars come out."

"Not as beautiful as you." Conleth took her hand.

Heat spread from his fingers, chasing away the chill. Her heart kicked against her ribs. She glanced over, taking in the strong line of his jaw, the way firelight from a distant window caught in his eyes. *He's the one.* Her grandfather's prophecy crashed over her like a wave. *You will find one, my little tracker, and he shall be both doom and great joy to you.*

She told herself there were no dragons left. She'd been wrong.

Trinity had built her walls carefully, brick by brick, after each betrayal. But standing here with Conleth's hand in hers, those walls turned into sand.

Inside the resort, hikers crowded the gathering area near a crackling fireplace. Flushed faces, loud voices, the clink of beer bottles. Trinity wove through them. They didn't know what waited in those woods. Didn't know someone was already missing. Two, counting Cedric.

The elevator doors slid open. Conleth stepped in beside her, close enough that heat radiated from his body. Trinity pressed herself against the far wall, watching the numbers climb. The silence stretched. She could hear him breathing.

When the doors slid open again, Conleth stepped out of the small lobby. His hand moved near the keycard reader of her suite door. Her gaze jumped from his hand to his face. His amber eyes, usually guarded, gleamed. He angled his body toward hers, and for a heart-stopping moment, Trinity thought she saw a spark of gold in their depths.

Every nerve ending sparked to life, tracking his slightest movement. Did he lean in? Was that a ghost of a smile playing on his lips?

Her grandfather's voice sliced through the haze: *He shall be your doom.* The lock clicked open.

Trinity's legs begged to run, but her traitorous mind painted pictures: a warm bed, his presence warding off the dark, one night without her mission pressing against her chest like a stone.

"It's quite early, but it's been a long day," she said too quickly.

Her stomach twisted. Her grandfather's warning. Conleth's dark eyes. The promise of not spending the night alone thrummed through her veins.

"I suppose we should say good night then." She forced the words past the tightness in her throat.

Conleth's mouth curved. "Not quite."

He pushed the door open and stepped aside, gesturing for her to enter first. "I'm coming inside with you."

The line between seeking his help and surrendering to something more blurred. Heat crept up her cheeks. *He's coming in?*

She'd thought about it—hadn't she just thought about it?

That traitorous part of her longed to step into the forbidden.

But darkness crowded at the edges.

What if her doom dragged him down too? What if, by giving in, she condemned him to share whatever fate her grandfather foretold?

The thought of him facing some terrible consequence because of her made her nauseous.

"But I–I didn't think..."

Think what?

Think about him being in your room?

Conleth frowned, brushed past her into the suite.

"I'll sleep on the couch," he said, then turned back to face her. "The bedroom door locks, but you're safe with me, *Unaha*."

Trinity blinked. *Safe?* The word struck like a cruel joke. Her mind spun between the forbidden pull of his presence and the chilling possibility of what might happen.

She could handle whispers. Sideways glances.

But dragging Conleth down with her?

Letting her shadow stain him deeper than the spirits ever had?

Shame rose in her throat, bitter as ash. She'd been there be-fore—each mistake louder than the last, etched in her memory. And now, her weakness would cost them both.

Trinity spun on her heel and fled to the bedroom.

Coward. The voice hissed.

Maybe. But she could shield him from her fate, even if she couldn't give him anything else. She shut the door. Locked it. Slid down until she hit the floor, knees pulled to her chest.

You have a weakness for men, Trinity. Stop.

Have you not brought enough trouble to the mountain?

She pressed her ear to the door and held her breath. How keen was a shifter's hearing? Could he hear the shake in her breathing?

Gwen's voice echoed in her memory: *They are not above doing what is necessary to protect their family and those they love on this mountain.*

Trinity's jaw tightened. *Beautiful?* She was far too smart to fall for that.

Eleven

CONLETH SHIFTED INTO A dragon before daylight and flew Trinity to the shifter prison nestled in the higher elevations of the mountain. She hadn't screamed. Hadn't recoiled when his scales emerged or when his wings caught the wind.

The knot in his chest since breakfast loosened.

Trinity had expected to meet Aluk at the resort. Conleth hadn't liked the plan either, but she wanted to meet Gwen's brother, and Aluk insisted on his domain.

The heavy metal door clanged shut behind them. The sound echoed through the halls.

Trinity flinched.

This is no place to bring her, his dragon grumbled.

Conleth gestured toward a recessed alcove. "Let me get dressed."

Protectiveness tightened in his chest. He walked ahead of her, flickering torchlight casting long shadows across the stonewalls.

At the alcove, he held out his hand. "Here, give me that."

Trinity handed him the pack she'd carried during their flight. He retreated into the shadows and yanked his shirt over his head, cotton clinging to damp skin.

The air hung heavy and stale.

Charm alone wouldn't get them through this visit.

He needed to navigate the treacherous waters of his brother's moods.

When he emerged, Trinity cast a wary glance down the corridor. Her fingers tightened around the strap as she took the bag back. The office door stood open, waiting.

Trap, his dragon whispered.

Maps marking territorial boundaries, incident reports, and government correspondence stacked like burdens on Aluk's desk. Keeping both supernatural secrets and dangerous prisoners kept Aluk from returning to the alpha's lair beneath the resort, where his dragon longed to hibernate. His brother carried responsibilities that would crush most shifters.

"Aluk."

Conleth's eldest brother straightened from behind the large desk in the center of the room.

"You've changed things around since the last time I visited."

"An alpha never positions himself in the back of the room," Aluk said, his gaze sweeping past Conleth with practiced authority before lingering on Trinity. His ancient spirit assessed her, the way a scale decides what must be paid.

A long beat of silence stretched between them.

Conleth's dragon stirred, rising in his chest as Aluk's gaze swept over her.

Mine, a low growl vibrated deep in his chest.

Conleth's jaw tightened, his muscles flexing beneath his shirt.

He forced the surge of anger down, schooling his features into a mask of indifference. A soft push of dominance rolled off Aluk's dragon, nearly provoking a response.

She's unmarked, his dragon reminded him.

This wasn't the time to brawl. Not with Trinity watching. His brother thrived on tension these days, always testing the edge.

"Aluk," Conleth said, getting back to the reason they came.

Aluk's gaze narrowed, pinning Trinity like a butterfly under glass.

She met his stare unflinchingly, a spark of defiance darkening her eyes.

"Alpha Vasumen. I've been looking forward to meeting you." She gave him a head tilt and offered her hand.

A low growl rumbled in Conleth's chest.

Aluk hesitated. *You haven't marked her. I'm not touching her.*

You would insult my mate? Conleth raised an eyebrow.

Aluk's eyes narrowed. His dragon warring with his duty as alpha. Protocol required him to acknowledge Trinity, but touching her before she was marked would provoke Conleth's dragon spirit.

Leadership won.

Aluk reached out and took Trinity's hand.

"Agent Oberlin," he said. "Conleth tells me you're on a manhunt."

A flicker of something unreadable crossed Trinity's face.

She has a strong grip. Her scent is... unique. Aluk smiled smugly. *If she concentrates any harder, she might hurt herself.*

Conleth growled.

Aluk released her hand.

Trinity clasped her hands together, her eyes swimming in tears.

Fae. Aluk looked directly at Conleth. His dragon lurched within him, a low growl rumbling in his chest again as Aluk's amusement vanished.

His brother's gaze snapped back to Conleth, a cold disapproval etching lines across his face. "What can I do for you?"

"Actually," Trinity said, settling into the nearest chair.

Conleth moved behind her, his hand resting lightly on her back.

Aluk's attention lingered for a heartbeat too long on that touch. His shoulders went rigid. His brother turned away, studying the territorial maps on his wall with sudden, unnecessary intensity. The scent of old grief sharpened in the air.

"I am hoping you have information about another agent," Trinity said. "Cederic Kelly. He's the shifter representative for the region."

"I know who Kelly is." Aluk's expression darkened. He rose and circled the desk, each step deliberate. "I have communicated with him in the past."

"When did you see him last?" Trinity asked.

"March. Around the time the hunters attacked one of the Avalanche Ridge pack enforcers."

"What happened to the hunters?"

Conleth growled low, catching the concern in her voice.

Those hunters deserved worse than mountain imprisonment for what they'd stolen from his people.

"I turned them over to the federal agents who arrived after the incident. I assumed Kelly reported it and the feds showed up to handle them," Aluk said.

Let's hope she doesn't discover they're here in your hold, Conleth warned silently, hoping his brother wouldn't push this charade too far too fast.

Aluk paid him no heed. He sauntered over and perched casually on the arm of a separate chair near Trinity.

"There was no report," she said, scowling, her brows drawn together. "You haven't seen him or heard from him since?"

"Not a word," Aluk replied, rolling back his shoulders.

"I assumed you came to introduce yourself as his replacement. After the attack, even the best operatives reconsidered. Some retired, some left, or some were fired."

Aluk's gaze veered to Conleth.

He offered a barely perceptible nod, trusting his brother to handle it best.

"I'll need details about this attack," Trinity said. "Do you think Kelly was the hunters' target?"

Aluk scratched his beard, eyes narrowing. "I've considered a hunter might have slipped through, or someone inside the network turned on him. But why no body? He's missing, right? That's why you're here. You'll replace him until you find him. Unless he disappeared with the rest of the network to lie low, returning later when the air has settled."

"You're implying Agent Kelly was part of the attack?" Disbelief sharpened her voice, edged with barely contained anger.

"Would you believe him?" Conleth asked from behind her.

Trinity tilted her chin to look at Conleth before leveling her gaze on Aluk. "You have proof of this?"

"I think it's time you met Gwen's brother, Peter," Aluk said, keeping his gaze locked on Trinity. "Or should I say, *Asigwani.*"

Heat surged in Conleth's chest. His dragon spirit stirred, coiling low and restless.

Not yet. Not like this.

"Are you sure about this?" The words tasted like ash in his mouth. This wasn't what they agreed on.

Aluk's dragon gleamed in his eyes. Conleth needed to tread navigate his volatile, hotheaded alpha brother and a wary human mate.

Fae. Like Gwen.

Another part of the curse, complicating their lives.

Did she know?

Aluk's eyes flared, burning with dragon fire.

Red like dried blood.

His hand trembled before he clenched it into a fist. *You dare question me?*

She's mine to protect. Conleth didn't blink.

His gaze locked onto Aluk's with the quiet force of a storm held at bay. The air thickened between them, growing heavier with every second he refused to look away.

First clue in the hunt. Aluk's words grated across Conleth's nerves like stone scraping bone.

A growl clawed up his throat, but he swallowed it, forcing calm over instinct.

"Oh good. Conleth mentioned asking you about Peter. Shall we?" Trinity stood and adjusted the strap of her satchel.

"All right, fine," Conleth said, sticking close to her side. "But we need to be careful. I doubt Trinity has ever met one of the *ohunko*."

"It's time she saw the truth, even if it scares her." Aluk turned towards Trinity, a predatory gleam in his eyes. "Ready?"

"Lead the way," Trinity waved Aluk on, then stopped.

Her eyes widened. "I mean... I didn't mean..."

"Don't look him in the eye. Just follow." Conleth murmured and pressed his hand to her back.

Every whisper became a concession feeding Aluk's inflated ego. "This isn't the outside world. Alphas deserve respect."

Aluk chuckled in his mind.

Trinity's muscles tensed beneath his touch, electricity sparking through his fingers.

His dragon spirit hummed.

Conleth forced his hand to relax, easing the persistent tingle.

Mate?

Fae, his dragon concluded.

Conleth stole a glance at her, wishing he could warn her. Aluk's fingers drummed against his thigh. That restlessness told when he had more than one game in play. This wasn't just about Peter. Aluk pushed to see what she'd do.

Down the hall, a heavy iron door, reinforced with rusted bands, creaked open with a rusty groan that reverberated through his bones and made his dragon flinch. The passage beyond breathed dragon fire that licked the walls of the mountainside fortress. Thick, suffocating air pressed against them. His dragon spirit recoiled tight beneath his ribs. He hadn't wanted to expose their mate to this wretched place. Trinity's face drained of color in the dark glow. Her lips pressed together. She swallowed. Again. The metallic tang of fear coated his tongue. Damp earth and the foul stench of unwashed bodies hit them in waves.

Trinity's hand flew to cover her nose and mouth, and his dragon spirit slammed against his control. Each breath clung to her skin, heavy with the scent of the place. It settled in her hair, her clothes, like a stain that wouldn't lift.

Aluk held the thread, and for now, they followed it.

Trinity hesitated on the threshold. With a silent nudge, he urged her to follow Aluk. The warmth of the upper floors gave way to a bone-deep chill that made her shiver.

Heat rolled off him in waves. His dragon spirit pushing against his skin, a furnace Trinity could surely feel even through her clothes. Whatever waited in the depths of this place, he'd burn it to ash before it touched her. His silent vow thrummed through him like a war drum, his spirit's power responding to threat.

Their descent was a slow, winding affair. The rough-hewn stone stairs swallowed the sound of their steps. The further they went down, the wider the staircase became.

"Don't be frightened, Agent," Aluk called from the front. "No one shifts inside these walls. The cuffs handle the rest."

Trinity remained silent. Her back muscles trembled against his palm. Conleth took her elbow as the stairs curved and the stones narrowed. They emerged into a long, dimly lit corridor. Iron bars formed a grim barrier on either side, each one a gateway to a cell. Gaping maws of darkness swallowed any light that dared enter. The occasional water drip punctuated the silence and the distant, muffled snarl that echoed from somewhere deeper in the bowels of this prison level. Conleth's eyes burned with his spirit's shared sight.

Goosebumps raced across her skin under his touch. "We can go back."

"This isn't humane." Her wide eyes reflected the grotesque flames illuminating the passage. He'd scented fear on her before, but never like this. And Aluk's satisfaction? The bastard was practically preening.

"These are not human prisoners," Aluk answered ahead of them. His dominating vibe filled the length of the aisle. Another taunt. Aluk wanted Conleth to challenge him, to break formation and shield Trinity from the cruel spectacle.

Trinity slowed, boots brushing against stone. The corridor narrowed, taking them into the pitch black. "Are all the prisoners... like this?"

Conleth stayed close.

Aluk moved ahead of them.

"Only the special ones. Come, we're almost there," Aluk said.

The further they went, the fewer prisoners inhabited the cells. The guttural snarl of a wolf rippled in the air.

Trinity stopped.

Conleth's hand hovered near hers, not touching.

The iron gate ahead stood silent, but malice bled through the bars.

Aluk stopped in front of a cell. Light flared as Conleth placed a hand on the wall. The stones glowed red, sizzling with heat that burned the dampness from the air. He curled a hand around her waist, grateful when she didn't step away. His dragon spirit settled with her within reach.

The cell matched the others. Stone. Stale air. A cot in the far corner. A privy hole in the other.

A figure shrouded in shadows turned its head.

"Peter, there is someone here to speak with you," Aluk said.

No reply.

"Ohunko," Aluk lifted his chin, his red eyes glowing. "Give me the human, Peter."

"I thought they couldn't shift in here?" Trinity whispered to Conleth.

"The ohunko aren't ordinary shifters. Their spirit can take over while in human form." Conleth moved along with her as she inched closer.

"They were once guardians. The Great Hunter chose one of each type of shifter. The ohunko — the dark-hearted ones. They are the original Sentinels."

"You know your history of our people," a voice said from within the dark. Conleth's chest expanded, his dragon coming to the surface. His spirit tattoo burned against his flesh.

"This isn't Peter," Aluk growled. "Back down, ohunko."

A throaty snarl came from the darkness. A man with mussed hair and gold eyes approached the bars. His skin appeared bronze in the red hue of the glowing stones. A malevolent spirit took control, twisting Peter's soul to host the ancient wolf spirit. The air crackled with dark energy.

"Are you not going to introduce me to this female, Alpha? Did you not bring her here to present her to me?"

"Back off, *ohunko*," Conleth stepped around Trinity. "The lady has some questions for Peter. You'll allow her to speak to him."

"Peter and I are one, dragon. I am he, and he is me." The man, wearing nothing more than a pair of dark pants, grinned at Trinity. "*Nimitqwa Ktelo,*"

"What does that mean?" Trinity asked, keeping her distance. "Are you Peter? Gwen's brother?"

"I am *Asigwani.* The one known as Peter has given in to his destiny."

"That didn't take long," Conleth murmured, glancing at Aluk, who shook his head. *We knew this would happen.*

"*Nimitqwa Ktelo?*" Trinity stepped out from around Conleth.

The man behind the bars grinned. "*As you once were and will be again.* Welcome to the mountain, daughter of the Fae. Your people long warned of your arrival, and now you have come. Soon she will be free."

Twelve

LAUGHTER SPILLED THROUGH THE trees as they stepped into the clearing above the village. Trinity spotted Gwen ducking a bright beanbag, her grin flashing in the sunlight.

"Taran's here."

"You told him?"

Had they spoken without words?

Still, Taran belonged with his mate. Especially now.

She had to be the one to reach Gwen. Trinity didn't trust any of the men to deliver the news.

Conleth's eyes shut, his jaw tightening as the silence thickened between them. Trinity searched the field for Gwen, irritation prickling her skin when he turned to his brother instead of answering. "There she is. Looks like she's having fun." Interrupting their innocent joy. Like stepping onto fresh snow.

"We should wait and come back later," Conleth said.

"We need to talk to her. If it were your brother, you'd want to know sooner rather than later. It will only bring more harm to wait."

Conleth followed her through the throng of children, their enthusiastic greetings settling like stones in his chest. He slowed his pace, matching Trinity's stride.

As they approached Gwen, her smile broadened. "Conleth. Trinity. Have you come to play with us?" Gwen's smile faltered, and her shoulders went rigid.

"Rough morning with the kids?" Conleth asked, tucking away his phone and lifting his chin in Taran's direction. Taran looked weary; a deep crease etched between his brows. She peeled a beanbag off his arm.

"You'll see when it's your turn." Taran's eyes glimmered as he tossed a beanbag back toward the children. Laughter burst out around them. "How about you, Trinity? Care to play?"

Trinity tilted her head. "I don't think I know this game. Sorry."

"It's called bag and tag. I can teach you. The kids love it." Gwen moved away, but Trinity raised a hand to stop her. "Perhaps another time. I need to speak with you. It's about your brother."

"Oh?" Gwen's gaze darted toward Taran before finding Trinity again. Taran fetched a water bottle, pressed it into Gwen's hands, and studied them both.

"We visited Crag's Cliff this morning to see Aluk," Conleth said.

Gwen glanced at Taran. He pressed his lips in a tight line before their eyes glazed over at the same time. Trinity hurried to speak. "I tried to speak with your brother."

"What do you mean you *tried*?" Gwen's eyes narrowed. Taran grabbed her elbow gently, guiding her toward the shade where water bottles and scattered T-shirts lay beneath a tree.

"I didn't mean to alarm you, but I thought you had a right to know," Trinity said.

She took a deep breath, not knowing any other way to say it. "The man I met today had your brother's body, but he went by the name *Asigwani*."

Gwen's eyes widened as she met Taran's, the deep red flash of his dragon lighting his gaze. Taran rubbed soothing circles on Gwen's arm as she spoke. "Had I known you intended to meet my brother, I would have warned you. One of the ohunko possessed my brother.

Asigwani is the Great Hunter's chosen guardian of the wolf tribe. The wolf spirit tried to possess me and Peter...." Her voice trailed off, and Taran finished. "He traded his life for hers with the ohunko. As long as it stays trapped in Peter, it can't harm others."

Nausea rolled through Trinity in waves. She focused on the water bottles, unable to meet Gwen's eyes. "I'm sorry for your loss, Gwen. As an only child, I can't imagine what it is like to lose a sibling. Especially one who sacrificed themselves to protect you. He's locked away to keep Asigwani from possessing anyone else or causing trouble in this new form on the mountain?"

"He is. Some days are better than others. Perhaps Aluk will allow you to visit when Peter can speak with you," Gwen said.

"I doubt that's possible."

"I'm sure Conleth can persuade him, or next time I go, perhaps it would be best we visit together if you really wish to speak with him," Gwen said.

Peter chose this. Walked into that prison willing to keep Asigwani contained. The hikers hadn't had a choice, but what about the others?

Trinity pulled out her phone, her fingers hovering over the screen. Guardians. Plural. Hidden across the mountain.

"Your offer is kind," Trinity glanced over at Conleth. His gaze held a quiet understanding. "But..." The words snagged on her tongue. Conleth lowered his chin. Taking a deep breath, she met Gwen's gaze. "Peter is no longer there."

Gwen looked at Taran.

"He's gone," Taran said softly.

Gwen's eyes squeezed shut. Her hand found Taran's arm.

He pulled Gwen close, his mouth near her ear. She collapsed into him like she'd been waiting for permission to break. His hand settled on the back of her head.

Trinity's grip tightened around her phone. Cedric was still missing. They hadn't found the hiker. Dragons lived on the mountain.

She couldn't afford to fall apart now.

The first two needed to be settled before she faced her fate.

Swiping tears from her eyes, Gwen turned towards Trinity. "Since Peter can't tell you, I will."

Levi, the boy from the arcade, bounded over, concern creasing his face. Gwen waved, her smile snapping into place. He waved back and took off to rejoin the game.

Gwen's smile faded the moment he turned away. "Peter worked with the hunters. He scouted and helped set the traps to take the spirits from our people, but the spirits trapped inside the crystal shards can burn out. Unlike the shadow spirits trapped here, once burned out, they're gone."

"Peter burned through one too many and became ill," Conleth said.

"Hollowing," Trinity murmured. She'd seen the scans of spirit signatures dimming like dying stars, the crystalline residue unstable. Volatile, even.

"He would have died." Gwen said.

Trinity's heart lurched. "Do you want someone else to step in with the youth? You could take a moment. Just for yourself?"

Gwen didn't answer right away.

Trinity's hand rose toward Gwen's shoulder, then fell back to her side.

"No. I knew it would happen. I hoped... Well, I didn't expect it this soon," Gwen said.

Trinity's skin prickled. Gwen's gift pulsed against the restraint of her arm cuffs. It shouldn't have been detectable. Yet, the hum of the cuffs tickled her senses.

"You spoke with him. Did Conleth tell you about the hunter's attack back in March?" Gwen asked.

"I'm afraid that hasn't come up in our conversations yet." Trinity searched and found Conleth not far from her, holding out water to a young girl looking flushed. His head turned, and his gaze locked with hers, heat sparking in her belly.

"We've had a lot of things to sort through," Conleth said.

She hadn't meant to stare, but now he stood within reach. He hadn't touched her, but the space between them had vanished.

"Last week, I flew Gwen up to see him after that last big storm hit and felled the trees blocking the pass up the mountain. I sensed Peter weakening." Taran said, his face etched with a grief that mirrored Gwen's.

Trinity fixed her gaze on the children playing in the distance. Conleth took her hand, entwining their fingers. The touch jolted through her fingertips. She squeezed Conleth's hand tighter, drawing strength from his silent support.

"Did he say anything else? Tell you anything?" Taran directed the question at Conleth.

Trinity answered before Conleth. "No. I was hoping to learn more about the hunters. Anything that might lead us to Cedric. Or the missing hiker. Before anyone else is harmed."

"Hunters." Taran's eyes sparked deep red. "They are ruthless mercenaries hired by a power-hungry bastard who wants to exploit our gifts for his own gain."

"Did Peter ever mention names? Or perhaps any hidden locations? Anything to help me find Cedric?" she asked.

"He mentioned the hunters. I knew them too well. It's why I came to the mountain." Gwen's gaze locked on Taran for a moment before she continued. "I wanted to save my brother. Cedric... he adopted me, and Peter tried to watch over me, protect me."

"You know Cedric? Why didn't you say something yesterday?" Trinity stepped forward, her gaze sharpening.

"Because I told her not to," Taran interjected. "How are we to know your true intentions?"

"How am I to know you're not lying?" Trinity crossed her arms.

Conleth rested his hand on her shoulder.

"My mother gave me to Cedric. My stepfather—Peter's father—was not a kind man. When he discovered what I was..." Gwen hesitated, voice softening. "Cedric told everyone I was his daughter. We moved around a lot."

"You came here with him?" Trinity asked.

"No, Cedric had several places, compounds, that he kept locked down and secure. I always stayed inside the compound. Then there were the scout houses." Gwen blinked. "Peter stayed in several of them, but before we found him, he was holed up in the old ranger station above town."

Cedric, compounds, scout houses.

Trinity pulled out her phone and swiped to create notes.

Was Cedric involved with this organized network, or had he gone off the grid and undercover?

Cold sweat prickled her skin. This "power-hungry bastard" Taran mentioned was exploiting shifters; it was her job to help protect them.

Finding Cedric needed to become her primary objective.

Finding Cedric might lead her to more answers.

"Are there children involved too?" Her initial plan — a discreet investigation into the missing hiker, into Cedric's disappearance — would become broader if Cedric involved children.

Were they shifter children? What if he adopted them hoping they would attract shifter spirits? Trinity's pulse sped like a humming-bird.

"I'm the only one he wanted," Gwen said, crossing her arms and her eyes going vacant again.

"Because you're special." Trinity's gaze fell to Gwen's arm cuffs. "Or do you think there are more?"

"We've been to all the places. No one else was there," Taran added. "The hunters squatted at the clinic in town before we opened it again."

Gwen gripped Taran's arm tightly. "They wouldn't all have stayed there. There was a place, a cabin Peter mentioned, that they used sometimes. If I couldn't find him, I was to go there next. "He called it a 'puddle-pad' in case things got too hot; they'd go there to cool off. It's somewhere near Sentinel Peak, but I don't remember where."

"A puddle-pad," Trinity murmured, the name rolling off her tongue like a secret code. Could it be a safe house?

Her pulse quickened. A cabin. Then doubt crept in. How many false leads had she followed already?

"There are dozens of cabins around Sentinel Peak," Conleth said, scratching his chin.

The vastness of the search area swallowed her fragile hope whole.

"I didn't think about that place until now." Gwen stepped back, gaze drifting to the youth gathering near the tree. Water bottles passed from hand to hand, laughter low and tired.

"I'll call Rourke and Sia, "Taran said, placing his hand in his pocket. "Between the rangers and the enforcers, we'll find the place."

"It's near water." Gwen murmured, tracking the kids as they dropped into the shade. "Each site had a code name."

Trinity moved further away from the children, not sure if their hearing excelled like the shifter males around them.

Taran looked at Conleth, who nodded in silent agreement.

"No, not all of us can read minds," Trinity huffed, holding her phone, waiting for more information to give them more of a lead.

Conleth grinned at her, his eyes twinkling. "There's a small lake near Sentinel Peak on the edge of the ancient life tree."

"More of a pond," Taran added grimly. "I can have my guys search. Later tonight we can fly overhead and see what is out there. It's posted, so there shouldn't be anyone in those parts, but it's worth looking." He leaned in and whispered. "It seems our respite is over, unless you want to have Arden take over with the kids today." He pressed a kiss on Gwen's forehead.

Concern passed across Gwen's face as she shook her head.

"I need to check in at the clinic." Conleth stated he still required additional staff for the medical facility in town, yet she barely registered him.

Trinity's gaze lingered on the children gathering around Gwen. Her chest tightened with a strange ache. She shoved the thought aside before it could take root. Dangerous. This could not happen. *Would not happen.*

She pulled back her shoulders, stared out at the mountain, lush with trees and looming high into the clouds.

Inside her, a pressure twisted like a lock opening, and she closed her eyes. Whispers brushed against her conscience, like a mother soothing a child or a lover beckoning to the other softly.

Whatever it was, it startled her.

Trinity's eyes snapped open.

"What is it?" Conleth asked. "Are you all right?"

Those amber eyes darkened, those thick lashes lowered, and her heart skipped a beat. Oh yes, Conleth Vasumen would become her doom.

"I suppose having gotten up before the sun this morning, I need a nap as well." Why else would her mind take her down imaginary paths?

Conleth's lips curved up, his eyes glinting as he took her hand and led her back inside the lodge. "You can nap while I check in at the clinic."

His touch comforted and terrified her, confusion stirring between her heart and mind. Was she allowing feelings to develop and cloud her judgement?

She checked her phone again, then forced herself to put it away. Part of her wanted to curl up in that comfortable bed upstairs, but her fingers drummed restlessly against her thigh. Somewhere out there, Cedric was waiting.

Inside, she stole several glances at Conleth. She admired his unwavering focus and quiet competence.

He paused before the elevator. "My dragon is fighting me on this, but I think it's best if you rest. It hates being away from you, even for a minute, let alone a few hours."

"I'm a grown woman. I don't need someone watching over me all the time."

"It helps me focus on what I need to do while away from you, knowing you're safe. I'll arrange for someone to bring lunch, and if you need anything, Ben is here."

Conleth held up his hand before she could argue. "We're a tight-knit group, and not everyone is like Gwen. She was an outsider, and now we have many entering the mountain."

Trinity sighed and nodded.

"Get some rest, *Uhana*."

Conleth hooked a finger under her chin. "We're a team."

His hooded gaze lingered on her mouth. "You and me. We will figure this out, but you must keep an open mind."

His lips brushed her temple, feather-light.

She stepped back into the elevator. The doors slid shut.

An open mind. What an odd thing to say.

Thirteen

SWEAT BEADED ON CONLETH'S forehead. Though the mountain air was cool, it did little to temper the heat rising from within. His dragon spirit had grown unrelenting these past few days, making his blood run hotter than usual. His muscles ached from hours of hacking through the wilderness, refusing to showcase any of his dragon strengths should they encounter outsiders. For the past two days, they'd been searching the trails, investigating abandoned cabins thanks to Gwen's faint memory and tearful recollection. But there was a scent here, although faint amidst the woods and his mate. His dragon spirit twitched in his chest. A fragile flame fueled by the desperation in Trinity's eyes.

Was this a desperate gamble, a place made up as part of his brother's scavenger hunt, or the key to unraveling more proof for Trinity to convict Cedric and dismiss his disappearance?

He didn't have an answer. Only the weight of Trinity's hope pressing against his chest. Conleth glanced back, catching a flash of her dark jacket through the underbrush. She moved purposefully. She scanned the trail ahead. Unlike him, she seemed unfazed by the trek, her movements sure and light. Even exhausted, her determination burned bright.

Aluk's voice echoed in his mind, another trail, another maybe. Even he didn't know this place. Conleth glanced at Trinity, her stride steady despite the bramble. She trusted this lead. He wished he could.

She paused, waiting for him to catch up. "Anything?"

Conleth shook his head, wiping a bead of sweat from his brow. His thoughts had caused him to lag behind.

"Not yet. But the trail seems to lead towards the clearing up ahead. The cabin isn't much farther." He winked, trying to erase the worry etched on her face.

They continued their trek, the air growing cooler and stiller as they neared the clearing. Above them, the clouds gathered, pregnant with rain. Each gust of wind that whipped through the trees carried away precious remnants of the scent. Conleth quickened his pace, glancing back at Trinity with a grin. "Looks like we're in for a race against the storm. You think you can keep up, agent?"

Clouds hovered above with the promise of a new downpour.

"You underestimate my ability to keep up, dragon?" She darted past him, a mischievous smile on her lips.

Conleth let her dart ahead, inhaling for scents beyond the storm. A spark lit in her eyes at the discovery. He couldn't afford to share it with the clearing so close.

As the trees thinned, the air shifted. A small log house slouched among the pines. Its rough-hewn logs, darkened with age, roof heavy with moss.

Trinity's eyes widened, gaze snagging on the single window beneath the eaves, its pane opaque.

Her smile wavered. Conleth's skin prickled, his dragon restless beneath. Then a low, distant rumble came, echoing through the mountains like a warning.

Trinity's smile vanished. The cheerful chirping of birds halted. Only the mournful sigh of the wind through the pines dared to break the sudden stillness.

Conleth's eyes narrowed, his gaze scanning the clearing.

"Please tell me it's because of your dragon."

Conleth wrapped a protective arm around Trinity's tense shoulders. "We're not far from the clearing," he said, his dragon spirit flaring in his chest. "There's a storm brewing in the distance."

Trinity rolled her eyes. "When is there not?"

He chuckled, but the approaching weather wasn't what sent a tremor through his dragon. A prickling sensation danced across his skin. He couldn't pinpoint the source, but the air itself crackled with a faint malevolent energy.

Trinity shivered, her eyes darting nervously around the clearing. "Do you... sense something too?"

Casting a glance around the clearing, Conleth searched for the source of his unease. "We need to get inside." His dragon hissed, sending out waves of dominance in warning. "Hopefully, we'll find something of use."

Trinity tucked a piece of hair behind her ear. A small, rounded ear, which defied the Fae stereotypes. His gaze lingered on her, frustration clawing at his spirit. Fae. Human. *She is our mate.* Yet, the curse, impenetrable as the mountain itself, centered on one forbidden thing: a Fae union with a shifter. His brother had already broken this law, binding himself to Gwen. The old ways no longer held sway, but if Taran truly had a Fae mate, and Trinity was indeed Fae, then perhaps the Fae queen wove this very loophole into her curse.

The first drops of rain fell from the sky.

Conleth pushed open the heavy, creaking wooden door. A wave of stale air, thick with dust and the faint scent of wood smoke and singed keratin, assaulted his senses. He stepped inside as his eyes adjusted to the dim light. It filtered in through the doorway into the cramped interior. An old woven rug graced the floor. Empty provision crates sat stacked in a corner. A cluttered workbench opposite the small fireplace held a collection of tools and several animal pelts.

Trinity joined him, her gaze sweeping the room with a mix of curiosity and apprehension.

His dragon pulsed a warning within him, the oppressive energy stronger inside the cabin. He scanned the room, his gaze falling upon a military-issued satchel hanging from a peg by the door. His hand brushed against the cold metal tucked within. He unfastened the strap and peered inside, his jaw tightening at the sight of crudely crafted silver cuffs.

"Conleth," Trinity whispered, pushing aside the rug to the trap-door beneath. This far out in the wilderness, he expected a root cellar or den beneath the cabin. But for a human or a Fae?

"What made you think to look there?"

"Why else would someone have a rug in a cabin like this if not to hide something?" she asked.

"You're something else, *Uhana*."

He waved her back, and she stepped away.

Conleth crouched by the door, reached, and paused when a choked gasp escaped Trinity's lips as she moved to the workbench. Her fingers traced the smooth surface of a large amethyst crystal nestled among a collection of vials and pouches. Recognition spasmed across her face. "Amethyst." She held it up. "They're making containment crystals."

"We found the right cabin."

Trinity's eyes darted toward him, fear and anger flooding her violet eyes. "I thought it was a geological anomaly. I... I told him about the crystal," she confessed, the blood draining from her face.

"Hey, it's okay." Her confession hit like a stone to the chest. His dragon spirit bristled inside him, demanding answers, but the storm pressed closer, cutting short his questions.

Trinity pulled out her phone, snapped photos, and then held up a crystal and examined it after putting her phone away. "No. It's not."

She wrapped up the pieces of crystal in a cloth to stuff in her pack. "My first assignment was in the artifacts department. Strange things came in all the time. My job has been to research them, find out what they do and where they came from."

"You researched the crystals," Conleth said.

"Yes, among other things. I loved my job, and the agents would often come to me and inquire about particular ones they found. They were curious about the items' values. One particular agent came often—too often. He invited me for coffee and then dinner. Late one evening, he saw the crystal. I'd had too much wine and told him what I knew about it. I woke in the storage room, crystal gone, and realized he had set me up." She twirled the crystal. "He'd been after this. Not me. Because of my naivety, I let these fall into the wrong hands."

Her hands trembled holding onto her pack. "No one believed me. No one matched his description."

"He disguised himself." A muscle ticked in his jaw.

"A glamor." Trinity's voice shook.

Who else held such knowledge within the archives?

"Most likely, it's someone within the agency."

"Cedric?"

"Cedric?" She tipped her chin and locked gazes with him. "You don't think Cedric gave the crystals to the hunters? He's been the shifter representative for decades. He wouldn't..."

"If not him, then who else?"

"Any number of people at the agency."

She glanced at the crystals.

He let her hold on to them for now. Aluk and the rest of the council would want to see them properly destroyed.

"I would have lost my job if not for my grandfather," her voice trailed off as a deafening crack of thunder echoed through the mountains, shaking the cabin.

Our mate feels responsible. Comfort her.

He wanted to offer comfort, to reassure her, but first he needed to keep her safe. "We're in this together, remember? Give me a name and I'll take care of the guy."

"You can't."

"Just give me a name," he insisted.

Outside, the trees twisted unnaturally, their trunks bending as if bracing against something unseen. A deep groan echoed from the mountain's belly.

"The punishment was mine. There's nothing you can do to him."

He growled, his chest rumbling. "Through your agency perhaps, but here, we have our own justice."

Trinity went silent.

"Trinity, that man used you. He manipulated you."

Heat surged beneath his skin, pulsing through his chest and down his arms like molten pressure. He stalked to the doorway, muscles coiled tight, and scanned the landscape. Outside, the air bit at his skin, but the dragon's fire roared hotter. The urge to shift clawed at him, scraping just beneath the surface.

He circled the cabin, boots crunching over gravel and brittle leaves. His breath came sharp, controlled, the growl lodged in his throat refusing to rise.

Movement.

A glimpse in the distance.

Conleth froze.

The dragon inside him stilled. Heat held in check by sheer will.

Rain came down in a steady stream, soaking his clothes and causing steam to rise against his skin. Trees bent like a wave forward. *Must protect.*

He rushed back into the cabin. "We need to get out of here. Now."

"What's happening? Is it the storm?" She gestured towards the window. Conleth followed her gaze, his heart pounding in his ears. The roar of displaced earth and rock filled the air, growing louder with each passing second.

Panic flooded Trinity's eyes, her hands trembling as she fumbled with her pack. His dragon surged, protective instincts roaring to life. The primal urge to shield Trinity, to fight the encroaching danger, threatened to consume him. But Conleth fought back. *No dragon. We stay here.*

Protect!

He needed a plan, not the blind rage of a beast fueling him. He slammed a cage around his dragon, keeping it from taking over.

The mudslide blocked their escape on the ground, and the storm's fury made flying with her a risk. As if the mountain heard his worries, rain lashed down in a relentless torrent. He yanked the door closed against the weather.

"What do we do?" Fear lit within her eyes, mirroring the chaos raging within Conleth's dragon spirit.

His gaze darted back to the opaque window, the mudslide now an angry churning beast, swallowing everything in its path. Soon it would open its mountainous maw for the cabin next. He sent a mental plea to his brothers, hoping at least one of them would hear his distress call. *Mudslide on the eastern side near the abandoned cabin by the old dried lake.*

"Get below," Conleth ordered, trying to hold in the terror that clawed at him. He gestured towards the trapdoor, their only escape route.

"We don't know what's down there," Trinity protested, her scent a potent mix of terror and distrust. His dragon slammed against him, snarling, needing to comfort her. But he locked the cage on it, grunting with effort. Outside, the mountain laughed at their plight, the thunderous roar of the mudslide a mocking symphony of destruction.

A strangled cry escaped Trinity's lips. Conleth's gaze snapped to the source of her distress. A dark shape developed in the far section of the cabin. The shadow twisted and writhed like a living thing before solidifying into the form of a mountain lion. Its eyes, twin pools of inky blackness, burned with unnatural intensity.

A growl rumbled in his throat. "Below. Now. I'm right behind you."

When she didn't move, Conleth glanced over at her.

Trinity's mouth worked like a fish. He grabbed her pack and chucked it down below. Conleth growled, stepping between her and the shadow. Trinity jumped down the hole, her feet hitting packed earth with a jarring thud. A sharp gasp tore his attention from the shadow.

The shadow cat growled and hissed before turning and leaping at the wall, going higher and higher, until it disappeared into the ceiling beams.

Conleth hopped through the opening, the trapdoor thumping closed behind him. The rough stone walls scraped against his shoulders as he landed in the narrow space below.

Stifling darkness pressed in on him. The temperature plummeted from the storm-warmed cabin air to the bone-chilling dampness of the underground chamber. Each breath came laden with moisture clinging to the inside of his throat like a film.

"It's so dark," she whispered, her voice drifting through the blackness. She reached out, fingers brushing against him. The space felt smaller than it seemed from above, or maybe the darkness was playing tricks. Conleth resisted the urge to take hold of her hand. Heat flared in his eyes as his dragon spirit pressed in, sharpening his vision.

"Can you see anything?" Each word emerged from her as a tiny puff of warmth swallowed by the cold.

"I have a dragon spirit. I can see in the darkness." Conleth stepped closer, and she pulled her hand away, leaving a chill from the absence of her touch.

White noise masked the prickling unease that crawled up his spine. His dragon sense became overwhelmed by the scents, the thick darkness, and her nearness. Only his hearing remained sharp.

The rhythmic patter of rain against the roof was a constant beat, but beneath it, a distinct sound snagged his attention. Above the walls groaned, and the earth churned, grinding and stirring above.

"What do you see?" She hugged herself, and the gesture tugged at him. Conleth sensed the shift in her energy before the temperature registered. His dragon flared, warmth rising instinctively wanting to shield her from whatever she'd just sensed.

His eyes burned and watered. The scent of decay hit him in waves: first the sickly sweet stench of old death, then the sharper bite of rotting flesh, underlaid with the metallic tang of dried blood and the earthy must of things left to decompose. Nausea churned in his gut, and he had to swallow hard to keep from retching.

"Something died down here."

The smell, combined with the unsettling sounds from outside and the tomb they stood in. Trinity's body tensed, her breathing shallow and rapid.

"You're safe with me, Trinity." He curled his arm around her shoulders. She leaned into him. His dragon-blood made him a furnace, and the way she melted into his heat told him how cold she'd become. "What's down here is long gone. Let me look. Stay here; it's larger down here than it seems."

He half expected her to turn and take further comfort against him, but little by little she eased away from him, the scent of fear lessening from her.

A slight tremor radiated through the ground. He strained to hear beyond the steady drip... drip... drip that echoed off the stone walls, each droplet amplified in the confined space. The storm's relentless assault on the cabin above created a muffled drumbeat, while the mountain's unsettling groans seemed to reverberate through the very bedrock beneath their feet. In the pauses between sounds, he could hear Trinity's soft breaths and the rapid flutter of her heartbeat. Or was that his pulse thundering in his ears?

She shuffled around her pack and pulled out her phone.

"Trinity, wait!"

The beam of light from her phone sliced through the darkness, illuminating the unmistakable form of a mountain lion. The harsh LED light threw grotesque shadows against the weeping walls, making the already cramped space seem to pulse and breathe. Water continued its relentless dripping, matching the frantic rhythm of Trinity's breathing.

The mountain lion's body lay twisted and lifeless inside an iron cage. Its lifeless eyes stared blankly into the beam of light.

Heat blazed through Conleth's chest and along his arms. The cold air should have hissed against his skin, steam rising in protest, but he forced the dragon's rage inward, locking the heat beneath his human exterior.

Then, a deafening crash echoed from above. The cabin shuddered under the impact, beams groaning, dust and splinters raining down like ash.

Trinity flinched. Terror flashing in her eyes, those gold flecks sparking with an unnatural intensity as she instinctively pressed closer to the wall. Immediately, she recoiled when her palm met the cold, slimy condensation coating the stone. Steadying her breath, she moved closer to the cage.

Her hand trembled as she reached for the animal through the bars.

A faint gasp escaped her lips as her fingers brushed against the metal.

Conleth lunged, grabbing her by the waist and yanking her back as the ground rumbled underneath them. "Those are iron bars."

"I...I..." she stammered, flexing the fingers of her hand as if trying to shake off the sting. Her gold and lavender eyes swirled, the colors changing like a storm rolling in to reveal her heritage.

His eyes lingered on her hand; the delicate skin stretched taut over her knuckles where the metal burned her skin. His hand hovered for a moment, the desire to touch her warring with a hesitation he couldn't explain. He settled for the gentle brush of his fingers. She sucked in a breath. Her eyes glazed with a mix of fear and pain as he took her hand to inspect it.

Conleth lifted her hand, placing a soft kiss on the back of it. Their gazes locked. Violet merged with gold. The centuries-old prophecy shared through the generations of his dragon spirit and its bloodline flashed through his mind. A Fae mate. Like Taran.

The missing key to breaking the curse.

Trinity, with her unwavering courage, and Gwen, with her fiery strength, which meant there had to be a third. For Aluk. But how was that possible?

Her phone tumbled to the ground, causing Conleth to focus once more.

"We're going to die here, aren't we?" Trinity's words came out in rapid puffs of visible breath. "We're trapped, and it's all collapsing upon us. We'll be buried in this tomb, and no one will know the truth."

"No one is going to die, *Unahu*, except for those whose souls have become lost." His spirit growled at the encroaching shadows. "There is fresh air seeping in nearby. Don't touch the bars. I'll find us a way out."

Taran? Aluk? Conleth's chest tightened. *I've found another.*

A tremor beneath the surface gave him pause. He expected to find weapons or a hunter, but not this.

Can't get to you until the slide stops. We need to keep it from reaching the town. Taran's voice filled Conleth's mind.

Until then, they remained trapped, cut off from the outside world, and it hit him with full force. The mudslide held them prisoner. Trinity was in his arms, safe, but the mountain lion's shadow spirit could return.

"Can you get him out?" Trinity stared at the dead mountain lion. She tilted her head toward the sound of his voice. "I need to touch him. Please."

Conleth listened to the growing chaos above them. The sound of the mudslide was like a relentless drumbeat of destruction. His dragon coiled, ready to spring free, not liking staying trapped. He glanced around, spotting a break in the wall. It appeared too straight for nature to have made it. Reaching for the bars of the cage, Conleth yanked it open. First, he needed to free the mountain lion; then, he would investigate the crack. It might be a way out.

"It doesn't hurt you." Trinity scuttled away. She picked up her phone. Casting light again as she moved to reach for the carcass.

"Looks like we both have our secrets," Conleth said. "Want to share the rest of yours?"

Swallowing hard, she rested her hand on the mountain lion's head. After a beat, then two, she drew away, a grimace twisting her features. "Nothing."

"What did you expect?" he asked, pulling her back away from the carcass.

Trinity met his gaze, gold swirling in her mesmerizing eyes. The color of her irises was now almost invisible, eclipsed by the intensity of her emotions. "Life," she whispered. "I wanted to see his last moments. It might have given us a clue about what happened to him."

This ability of hers... His dragon spirit rumbled in his chest, opposed to any judgement on his tongue. She was his mate. *She was Fae. Like Gwen. Like the curse...*

His brother Taran chuckled in his head. It made him growl louder, and Trinity trembled. He hadn't meant to project his thoughts that far.

"You can see into someone's life?" Conleth tensed. "Have you seen into mine?"

"No," she said, raising her light to better see his face. "You must believe me. You're the only one I can't get a read on."

Conleth let out a surprised laugh. Perhaps it was the dragon spirit within him, protecting him from the Fae's gifts. It was her people who cursed him and this mountain, after all. But a strange sense of vulnerability accompanied the relief.

"And this gift... to read others... how is it done?"

"Touch." She lifted her fingers. "Only if living cells remain. I can fuse to call their memories back. The dead surrender only their final fragments."

Conleth had watched Gwen wield her Fae-born gift before, but the idea of peeling back the mind itself tightened his chest. Awe pressed against the dread until both left him unsteady.

"And the living?"

If she could reach into a shifter's mind, no secret would remain buried.

Would she see further into his dragon spirit than it allowed him to access? His dragon rumbled a warning, but Conleth pushed back inside against the locked door his spirit kept between them.

Trinity clasped her phone, shining the light down at their feet. "As far as their minds will take me," she said with quiet confidence. The gold in her eyes reflected the power within her.

"You've seen Gwen and Aluk's pain, haven't you?"

Her eyes filled with a mixture of awe and sorrow, held his gaze in the darkness. "I don't make it a business of imposing on reading other's memories."

"But you can touch them. Just touch them?" A spike of something hot speared his gut. The thought of her touching others made his dragon irate.

"And if you kiss them?" His pulse hammered. Thoughts of Gwen and her strange gifts flashed in his memory. She could draw the spirit from a shifter. "What will it do?"

He could focus only on the impossible restraint and the craving coiling in his chest. She belonged to him. No one else.

"Umm... I've never... I'm not...."

This was unfamiliar territory for them both.

"Perhaps we should test the theory," he murmured, stepping forward until their faces were mere inches apart. His dragon spirit braced, coiled and ready.

It's just a kiss, he assured his dragon.

Then kiss her, open the bond, and then mark her.

Trinity's eyes widened, the gold glowing under his gaze. Before doubt could take hold, Conleth closed the gap, lips meeting hers in a soft, searching kiss.

A gamble. A desperate hope that physical contact might bridge the gap she claimed she was unable to cross. Sparks of surprise danced on his lips before a hint of something untangled between them. His dragon spirit tattoo warmed against his skin. He pulled away slowly; the air crackling. Her sweetness lingered on his lips.

"There," he said huskily. "Now tell me, *Unahu,* can you read me now?"

Fourteen

Trinity's breath hitched in her throat as Conleth pulled away, his touch lingering like a phantom ember on her lips. The kiss, unexpected and sweet, left her reeling. His question rang in her ears, but emotions sparked within her like a kaleidoscope.

Before she could voice her jumbled thoughts, a low rumble echoed from above. The relentless assault of the storm subsided, replaced by an eerie silence. Conleth's hand brushed against her, pins and needles jolting through her as if her gift were trying to wake her from a deep slumber.

"Nothing?" His voice grew rougher now, dragon-touched. Those darkened eyes held her captive. A slow smile curved his lips.

"Nothing from your memories," she clarified, then frowned.

"Guess that means you'll have to keep trying. You know, for science."

Heat flooded her cheeks even as she stepped back. "Absolutely not!"

His smile widened at her reaction. "What? You seemed to enjoy the research just fine a minute ago."

Her lips tingled with the memory of his kiss. Her hand twitched toward his chest, then froze. A warning hissed in her mind. Her grandfather's voice, sharp as a whip. Her stomach turned, and she stepped back, trying to reclaim her sense of control.

"There is nothing to test." *You're a disappointment, Trinity. You should have run when you saw he was a dragon shifter.* Trinity gritted her teeth.

She pushed him away again, the echo of her grandfather's prophecy coiling tighter around her. Every path curved back to the same wall, leaving her caged in her own choices. The edge waited somewhere ahead, and each step dragged her closer.

"I shouldn't have told you." Her arms wrapped tighter around herself. "Now we both have secrets that could destroy us."

"Trinity." His voice gentled. "Bargain or not, you're always safe with me."

They searched around the tomb. Trinity skirted the iron-barred cells, toes dragging on the cold stone. She pressed her shirt to her nose, gagging as the stench of decay clawed at her throat and made her stomach lurch. Her phone's light wavered, a thin cone barely illuminating the walls slick with moisture. Every shadow seemed to twitch, reaching toward her. Her chest tightened, and each step echoed, sounding too loud in the suffocating gloom.

She let the phone drop into her lap, saving the last of its battery for an emergency.

Conleth moved through the dark with uncanny ease. His dragon sense guided him through the cramped stone, every step steady where hers faltered. *Lucky dragon.*

"Sounds like the worst of it has passed."

Relief loosened her shoulders, though the air still pressed heavy. The mudslide might have ended, but the tomb of rock and earth held them fast. Someone would come eventually. At least, she prayed it would be someone. The shadow spirit of the dead mountain lion lingered in her mind, waiting. She shivered.

She jabbed her phone screen again. "There's no cell service on this cursed mountain."

Nothing. The silence thickened, unnatural, until the shadows seemed to stir. They slid along the walls, stretching long and thin, reaching like fingers. A slow chill traced her spine as if the stone itself had turned against her.

He stood too close. The air between them thinned.

Her breath caught. What if he kissed her again?

Her skin remembered heat blooming, knees weakening, and the way her thoughts scattered like ash. She hadn't meant to lean in. Hadn't meant to want.

Her fluttering pulse betrayed her.

If he asked...

Her fingers curled against her thigh as if the pressure of her grip could keep her choices from slipping through her fingers.

"My brothers know where we are. Someone will come if we don't find a way out before then."

Conleth's fingers hovered near her hair, and she dodged him. Even before his voice filled the space, she sensed the tone of his intention as though it had leaked into her veins. "I think we need to focus on getting out of here, don't you?"

Her tongue darted across her lips, tasting him again, though her chest constricted as if warning her to stop.

Let's get out of one mess at a time, shall we?

She glanced at Conleth. "Did you say something?"

Conleth stretched out his hand, brushing away cobwebs and loose stones until his fingers encountered a crack in the stone wall. His hand followed it, and a click snicked from the section as the wall swung inward, revealing a narrow dark passage. "You can use the light on your phone. Don't forget your pack."

Oh, that hadn't been what she thought she heard and dismissed it.

She stared into the black maw of the tunnel. "We don't know where that leads. It could be a dead end."

Conleth turned, a glint in his gaze. "There is only one way to find out."

He extended a hand towards her.

"This is a terrible idea." Trinity located her satchel.

"As it is to stay here." He kept his hand held out.

Given the option of staying buried in this tomb or the passage, she stepped past him into the tunnel.

To her surprise, Conleth stepped into the cell. Bending low, he picked up the large, stiff cat and carried it. "He deserves to have a proper burial."

"How do you even know it's a shifter? Could be just a cougar." Admiration churned with a strange mixture of emotions.

"That look ordinary to you?" Conleth asked, the gleam in his red eyes deadly.

"... No, but they usually shift back when they die. Why hasn't he?" Trinity asked.

"Unless the Fae are behind this," Conleth grunted as he followed her to the tunnel opening. "The shadow spirit when we entered the cabin was most likely his. Once we are out of this tomb, whatever has him trapped in this form will release its hold."

"I see."

He blamed the Fae. She let the words pass, but they scraped.

She held the proof of the crystals and the photos she'd taken before the storm. "Are you sure? Are hunters normally associated with the Fae?"

It swallowed them whole, leaving the faint glow of her phone light and a growing sense of unease that hung between them.

Hunters are human, but they used Fae-blood and their gifts to aid the hunt.

Her foot caught on a loose stone. She flailed, gripping the wall for balance. A spark of heat pricked along her skin; she knew he was watching, every nerve alert under his gaze.

"My dragon doesn't like it when you're afraid. It wants to hunt whatever threatens you. Let me go ahead before I lose the choice."

A ripple of awareness skimmed across her skin. He sensed her fear, and that truth buzzed in her chest like static, impossible to ignore.

The tunnel pressed in from all sides, forcing them into single file. Her phone cast shadows that twisted along the stone like reaching fingers, but some shadows appeared to move independently. They retreated from the light in unnatural directions. Trying to avoid them, she scraped her arms against the damp walls, making her wince.

Conleth hoisted the feline beast onto his broad shoulders, the stench of decay oppressive.

Trinity pressed against the wall, tensing as he walked ahead. The tunnel seemed to stretch on endlessly.

"Do you sense anything up ahead?"

"Mountain air. Rain-washed earth. We're getting closer to the surface."

With his tall height, Conleth had to hunch over the dead mountain lion several times when the tunnel inclined.

"Stay close to me." His body was like a shield. Trinity clung to the back of his jeans. Water seeped from the walls, soaking her sleeves. Goosebumps prickled her arms, and a shiver raced down her spine as the chill sank into her muscles.

"Save your light unless you need it."

They walked for longer than Trinity cared to keep track. How long had they been underground? What horrors awaited them when they reached the end? The tunnel mouth opened, and they climbed out between the large jutting rocks.

A faint ripple washed over her skin, like a breeze, but lighter. Inside the tunnel, she hadn't noticed the change in the air. But now that she stood clear of the tunnel's mouth, the splash of the gentle rain was like mist against her skin. Like a cool embrace after the harsh darkness.

Trinity took a deep breath, filling her lungs with the crisp, clean air.

The storm clouds had thinned, revealing a bruised gray sky that wept a light rain.

In the not-so-far distance, the once lush forest floor was a churning sea of mud, with uprooted trees like fallen giants marring the landscape. Conleth rested the mountain lion carcass on the rocky slope, the body ripped, the muscles contracting. Trinity rushed toward it, her heart pounding in her chest. Desperation propelled her forward. But Conleth stepped in her way, his hand firm on her shoulder.

She gasped as the large feline's body relaxed, stretched in its dead form, and took the shape of a short man with gray-streaked black hair.

"Go ahead." Conleth got out of her way.

Trinity crouched near the body as Conleth closed the man's eyes. She inhaled slowly, grounding herself before placing a hand on his chest. The gesture was familiar, practiced, but this time it yielded nothing. No flicker of memory. No final breath. Just silence pressing back against her reach. The darkness simply refused, and a void filled her.

"Trinity?"

"I'm sorry. He's too far gone to share." She bit her lip, gazing at the destruction in the distance.

"Thank you for trying."

She watched as Conleth laid the body back at the edge of the tunnel, sadness etched on his face. He kneeled beside the lifeless form, a silent prayer passing between his lips. "He was the last of his bloodline," Conleth murmured. "We must be careful. His spirit will follow him until he reaches the Great Hunter's Forest."

Loss washed over her. Not just the death, but the end of a bloodline, the snuffing out of one of the Great Hunter's gifts.

As if summoned by Conleth's prayer, the clouds above them parted, casting an enormous shadow over the clearing. A low growl echoed through the woods. Conleth rose and moved toward her. A deep rumble came from his chest. Before Trinity could react, the shadow emerged from the woods, taking the shape of a mountain lion. Its eyes, like black coal, fixed on her.

It crouched, tail slowly swishing. Her legs grew shaky. "Conleth?"

"Run!" Conleth hurled himself forward, claws slicing through the air. Dirt and leaves erupted around him as his body collided with smoke turned solid mass. The spectral beast hardened, black and snarling, and Conleth's arms locked around it, dragging it to the ground.

"Go!" Conleth roared as he rolled with the shadow cat on the rocky terrain.

Trinity bolted, boots pounding against the wet earth. Wind lashed her face, the storm clawing at her as she spotted the lean-to ahead.

She ducked beneath it, breath ragged, fingers fumbling against cold metal. Snowmobiles. Mud or snow, what difference did it make? If Conleth couldn't shift with her, this was their only shot.

She glanced back.

Conleth circled with the shadow, its smoky form slipping and re-forming, trying to flank him.

Trinity threw herself onto one machine, hands shaking as she searched for the start button.

No key.

Her pulse slammed against her ribs, breath coming in short bursts. She gripped the handlebars tighter, willing the machine to start, willing herself not to fall apart.

The cat snarled, low and guttural. Conleth answered with a roar that shook the trees.

Trinity's fingers fumbled through the compartments, breath shallow, hands slick with sweat. No key. Just a first aid kit and a foil blanket.

She stared at the blanket, envisioning wrapping the shadow tight and warming it to death. Her lungs cinched tight, preventing her from laughing. She forced herself to move.

Another roar split the air. A scream followed, high-pitched, slicing through her nerves.

She jolted. Scrambled off the first snowmobile. Lunged toward the second.

A dark green pack clung to the side, its edges frayed. Her pulse kicked. That number. She knew it.

She yanked the pack free. The straps bit into her fingers.

A shadow fell across her, blotting out the sun.

"Is it..."

The hair on her neck lifted, a thousand tiny needles dancing across her skin.

She glanced toward Conleth. His chest heaved, breath ragged. Storm clouds churned above.

The shadow beneath Conleth buckled, then unraveled into smoke.

The air snapped cold. Trinity blinked. The smoke solidified, revealing the silhouette of a man standing several feet away.

Broad shoulders. Thick neck. Mud smeared across torn clothes. Gashes split his chest, still bleeding, the wounds raw. His skin held a sickly gray sheen, like something half-shifted, half-wild.

"Trinity!"

The man leaped up as the earth rippled under their feet. The forest moaned, and rocks shifted. The sound of cracking and breaking of the trees caught her breath in her throat.

She couldn't breathe. His eyes locked onto hers. Black as polished onyx, they glinted with feral intelligence.

Her stomach dropped.

His hair, matted, and wild, stood in jagged tufts like a crown of thorns.

"Get away from her!" Conleth growled.

Trinity turned, heart hammering, just as a massive tree crashed down between them.

The man lunged, yanking her from the lean-to. Her scream vanished into the roar of falling branches.

He slammed her against the wood, breath hot and sour. His smile twisted, a cruel slash across his face.

Conleth... where was he?

The wind howled. Branches snapped in the distance. Cold dread crawled up her spine.

"He warned you I would come," he rasped.

Her legs refused to move. Breath stalled in her throat as her gaze darted around him, searching for Conleth.

"And you are?" She forced out, barely a whisper. Her throat cinched tight, trapping the scream behind it.

His smile widened. Amusement replaced his cold, predatory glint. "I have waited for you. I know who you are, Fae."

He placed a fist to his chest. "I, *Pezi*," he declared, his voice thick with a strange power, "will be the one to free us from your evil."

Her breath caught. She knew that face. She'd seen his photo.

"You're the missing hiker," she whispered.

"That man no longer exists. I am the last you will see."

"I'm here to help you," she whispered, cold sweeping through her limbs.

"You dare return to this mountain? Do you think your dragon can protect you from destiny?"

He lunged. Fingers clamped around her throat.

She clawed at his grip, nails scraping flesh. Her lungs burned. Vision blurred. Her chest thrashed against the pressure.

The stench filled her nose. Sweat, mud, and something fouler.

"Your death is but a price," he rasped.

Her body arched. Her gift surged. Light fractured behind her eyes. Not Pezi's memories or the hikers. Something older. Ancient.

Her heart pounded in her ears like war drums. Her vision faded. The world unraveled.

Bare feet sliced through sharp grass. She didn't have much time before *Agasga* noticed she was gone. Her chest burned with each breath.

Down the rows of beanstalks, she darted, the ceremonial fires flickering beyond the forest's edge. Drums and rattles shook the air, summoning the spirits who would mark the boys' coming of age to become warriors.

In the distance, the mountain rumbled. It shook the earth under her feet, causing her to stumble. She fell between the rows; pain inflamed from her ankle.

"*Kwatako!*"

Fire blazed from the sky, hot, angry. It sent sparks to burn the trees, and the drums stopped.

"*Kwatoko!*"

"Run!" she heard. "The spirit guardians attack us!"

In the sky, the great winged beast wheeled against the moon's silver face, its shadow cutting across the ground below. Air caught in her throat. Her fingers dug into the beanstalk's rough bark, her other hand bunching the fabric of her skirt until her knuckles went white.

Behind her, growls rumbled through the darkness. Men crashed through the crop rows, boots pounding earth. A woman's scream cut short with a wet crunch of bone.

She couldn't run. She'd never get away. She gulped for air and sank the length of the stalk to the dirt at her feet. Two hands caught her before she collapsed. She flinched, but the voice in her ear was familiar.

"I have got you, *Unahu*. No harm will come to you."

He swept her in his arms and dashed between the stalks. Ceremonial colors painted his warm, sweat-slick flesh. Under her touch, the black mark of his dragon moved along his arm, a comforting anchor

By the time they reached the end of the field, smoke billowed, and fire swept across the crops. He spun in a tight circle, head jerking left then right, before bolting toward the treeline that bordered the clearing's southern edge. The pulse in her throat hammered against her skin as three dark shapes emerged from the roiling smoke, eyes burning like coals in the haze. "Guardians."

Slowly, *Kwatoko* eased her away from him, his hands firm but gentle as he steadied her against a tree and set her on her feet. She clung to him, fingers digging into his arm. He rested her hand on the tree to support her. "No. *Kwatoko!*"

"I cannot protect you this way. I must shift to fight. It's our best chance."

She trembled. "Why? What has caused this?"

Kwatoko placed his hand on her cheek. Warmth spread down her neck, and for a moment she allowed her eyes to flutter with the comforting touch of her lover. Through the smoke, the earth trembled again. The spirit guardians, three men, shifting into a wolf, a bear, and a mountain lion posed in wait.

In the sky above, the great firebird roared and cried out, lighting the night with flashes of its fiery breath. Kwatoko lowered his head. "They've taken my brother's mate. I won't let them take you, too."

Flames curled along his arms, golden and fierce. His body stretched, wings unfurling, feathers glowing like molten fire. His eyes blazed, heat rippling through the surrounding air.

She fell back as the ripple seized through the ground. In his spirit form, Kwatoko spread out his wings and challenged the guardians. He released his fire, and the guardians retreated. Shouts erupted from the shadows. Wood splintered and cracked as hulking shapes tore through the huts. The ground trembled under pounding paws, low growls vibrating through the smoke as the bears charged forward.

Yet, amidst the chaos, hope flared, a great comfort. Each time his gaze swept over her, a surge of warmth flowed in her veins. He struck out with his massive, scaled tail, sweeping away the wolf and several bears. He snorted, sparks shooting from his nose.

Suddenly a gust of *Kwatoko's* wings sent her flying back, and she curled against a tree. She rolled and struggled to get up. She had to keep them from harming *Kwatoko*!

"He had nothing to do with this. Leave him be!"

The spectral predator glided forward, eyes like molten coal fixed on her. She stumbled backward, chest tightening. "Please stop this!"

The massive feline pounced. Claws tore into her.

A scream ripped from Trinity's throat. Raw. Jagged. Endless. Her voice fractured, scraping the air until it barely sounded human.

Her ears rang. Conleth's shout pierced the haze, distant and warped, like it came through water. She blinked. Once. Twice. Then the lean-to was gone.

"Now, you see," he rasped. "You must die."

"Trinity!" Conleth shouted.

Flames reflected in his eyes, rivers of fire spilling down the mountainside.

She clawed at the man's hands as he wrapped a rope around her neck.

Conleth roared. He rounded the lean-to and slammed into the attacker. They tumbled, limbs tangled, striking first.

Trinity dropped to the ground, fingers tearing at the rope. Her breath came in broken gasps. Black dots swarmed her vision, threatening to take her under.

She twisted, thrashed, but his grip held firm. Each movement met an unyielding force, something more than human.

Panic clawed at her chest. Her lungs collapsed inward. The edges of the world blurred.

Through the haze, she thought she saw Conleth toss the man aside.

He rushed to her, yanked the rope free.

Her throat seized. Breath dragged its way out in ragged bursts. Heat streaked her cheeks.

Conleth cupped her jaw, tilting her head.

"Breathe, *Unahu*. Breathe."

Her lungs convulsed. Her chest rose in uneven jerks. She shoved at him, fingers trembling. He stumbled back.

Conleth turned toward the retreating figure.

The man's body rippled. Bones cracked. Limbs stretched.

A mountain lion burst forward, muscles stretching beneath tawny fur.

Conleth charged, boots pounding against the forest floor.

He halted at the tree line, chest heaving, and threw back his head.

His roar split the air.

Another answered. Distant. Unmistakable.

"Trinity."

His voice cut through the haze.

She pushed herself upright. Breath hitched. Tears streaked her cheeks. Her lungs fought for air.

Conleth dropped beside her, one arm wrapping around her waist, the other steadying her shoulder. "I thought I lost you."

The ground trembled. Wind whipped around them.

Above, an enormous black dragon descended.

Trinity sagged against him, her legs folding beneath her. Without Conleth's hold, she would've collapsed again.

"Don't move your neck. It's Aluk," Conleth said, kissing her forehead, and Trinity went slack against him. *You're safe. I will allow no one to harm you.*

Where had she heard that before?

Fifteen

CONLETH SAT ON THE edge of his bed, afraid his pacing would wake her. He breathed in. Lavender. Then iron. The faint taste of blood spread across his tongue. His dragon coiled in his chest, heat radiating along his arms. Every scrape and whisper from the hallway set his nerves on edge.

Her neck bore the dark marks of the ohunko's handprints. Hands Conleth wanted to crush for touching and trying to harm his mate.

This one had gone for her because she carried Fae blood. The Fae had cursed their kind once, nearly destroying them. His dragon didn't care if she had Fae blood, but the ohunko did.

Conleth balled his hands into fists.

Pezi hunts to redeem himself.

Conleth grunted in agreement.

Outside the room, the inaudible murmur of voices continued, and his dragon bristled.

Running the back of his finger down her cheek, her throat, he kissed her temple and whispered, "I'm right outside. I'll leave the door open in case you wake before they leave."

Outside his room, Taran crashed on the couch. Gwen leaned against him, her eyes bright and alert. Kaya, Ben's mate, arranged trays of snacks in the kitchen, while Ben poured a drink from Conleth's small wine collection.

"Where's Aluk?" Conleth asked, taking the offered glass of red wine from Ben.

"He's still out hunting with Rourke's men." Taran stretched an arm around Gwen.

"Why aren't you with them?" Conleth glared at Taran. "Isn't it your job to ensure the safety of the forest?"

"Whoa," Taran said, pulling back from Gwen. "You were out there with her. She will be alright, won't she?"

Conleth gulped down the wine. The bitter bark taste did little to calm his nerves or put his dragon spirit at ease. He sat the glass down before he crushed it.

"It's not Taran's fault." Gwen placed her palm against Taran's rigid shoulder, her fingers working small circles until his shoulders relaxed. "I should have told you about the cabin sooner."

"It's not that," Taran took her hand. "It's the missing hiker. He's the one who attacked Agent Oberlin."

Kaya paused; her hand trembled as she placed the tray on the coffee table. Her large eyes fixed on Ben. "I thought he was dead?"

"Different hiker," Ben waved away her concerns. The clink of glasses echoed like gunfire in the quiet room.

"Taran and Rourke never found this one. Apparently, he's possessed by one of the ohunko." His dragon growled low in his chest, warning him of the unseen predator lingering just beyond the walls.

"A guardian spirit," Kaya whispered. "The Great Hunter did not intend for them to linger. Unless they are like Ben?"

"Is it possible?" Gwen curled her feet up on the couch. "Another one?"

Taran grimaced. "We've encountered the other two, makes sense we would need to deal with the third."

"I don't know.... years possibly? It's impossible to say. Mountain lions don't exactly leave social cues lying around."

"As well as that may be, you're forgetting there are four guardians." Ben pointed out, refilling Conleth's empty glass.

"They were once the heart of the first tribes. They sealed their bond in oath and blood. Centuries had worn them down to whispers and shadow, their fractured minds turned hungry and wild."

"Are you saying we should suddenly be wary of you and your dragon spirit?" Conleth asked.

"I possess the most powerful ohunko of them all," Ben lifted his chin.

"And yet, we still can best you," Taran laughed at Ben.

Ben's scowl sharpened, teeth gritted, but he didn't move closer. Taran laughed, chest rising and falling, yet paused when the air between them shimmered.

"Now, boys, play nice," Gwen said.

"We sent the bear back with you know who," Taran wiggled his brows, and Gwen smacked his arm. "This isn't a fantasy story with an evil villain. We should tell her. Screw Aluk and his silly game."

"We can't." Conleth glanced back over his shoulder. "This assignment is important to Trinity. She blames herself for what the hunters did. She trusted a fellow agent with information about the crystals, and he used her to advance his own career. After that fiasco, if she finds out what we've done, it'll not only jeopardize our position, but they might reassign her off the mountain. With Cedric gone, we need her to stay. I need her here. My dragon won't allow her to go, and WE can't afford to have more PPI agents sent here."

"They'll close the mountain." Kaya took Ben's glass and sipped. "Isn't that what we want?"

"They'll close the mountain," Gwen agreed, "but I see Conleth's point. The government will flood this place with its military, take control, and make sure we're not exposed to the rest of the world. What will happen when they decide we're too dangerous to leave alone will make the ohunko seem like nothing."

"Right," Ben sank into a chair and pulled Kaya onto his lap. "Do we know why it attacked her?"

Gwen's eyes met Conleth's for a brief, intense moment. "I could tell you, but someone would need to remove my cuffs," Gwen held up her hands.

Removing the guardian spirit from the hiker was dangerous. The wolf ohunko tried to possess Gwen. The mountain lion might try the same. They would need either a crystal or another person willing to sacrifice themselves, as Peter had, to keep it trapped. Unless they risked opening the portal to the Great Hunter's Forest again.

"Not happening," Ben said.

"What did Trinity say?" Taran asked.

Conleth listened for a moment, heard her breaths, and sighed. "I don't know. We'll need to wait until she can talk. Do you think the guardian attacked her because she has Fae blood?"

"It's possible. The wolf possessed Gwen because of her ability to heighten the spirit's gifts. To be a stronger warrior," Taran said.

"The mountain lion always hunted the boundaries," Ben said, his eyes glowing with the presence of his dragon spirit. "Pezi guards against what should never again walk free."

"How does that relate to Trinity? Do we know what her gift is?" Gwen touched her arm cuffs.

Conleth cupped the back of his neck. He admired Trinity's power, but fear radiated from his dragon spirit. He couldn't shake the confusion about his place in it all. "She told me she can touch and see a person's memories, but when she lays her hand on me, the dragon burns it away. It won't let her in."

Ben sat up taller, his eyes flaring red. "Does Aluk have another set of cuffs?"

Gwen sucked in a breath, and Taran's dragon growled.

Conleth's upper lip curled up. "No one is cuffing my mate."

The dragon coiled tight in his chest, fire racing along his arms. A growl vibrated through his bones.

"You don't see it," Ben waved his hand toward Gwen. "If her abilities are like this one, she can reach into what we were before the Great Hunter gifted us. She could unravel everything that binds us to our spirits. That's why the guardians will keep hunting her."

Taran's face hardened. Ben hit a nerve. His cavalier comment rankled Conleth, too. The words came from Ben's dragon, ancient laws and the vow to protect their clan, but it got under his skin and angered Taran.

"We don't know that." Taran growled, standing abruptly, towering over Ben. "If you don't shut up, your death will be the next thing we'll discuss."

Gwen grabbed Taran by the hand, and she got to her feet. "Taran, stop."

Conleth nodded, looking straight at Ben, and propelled his thoughts to his brother. *She can see into your memories,* while he said, "This isn't helping."

Taran whistled low under his breath.

"What?" Ben demanded, glancing between them. His eyes narrowed.

"It could be her Fae blood," Gwen rubbed her arms again, "Or is it possible she's linked to one of the bloodlines in the tribes?"

"Either way, we have to stop the ohunko from possessing her," Taran said, tugging Gwen closer, placing his arm around her shoulders. "That's enough for tonight. My mate can barely stand, and we're not doing anyone good stumbling around in the dark. Sia's got two men coming. One will stay at the elevator and the other will park outside your door. We'll wait for word from Aluk and start fresh in the morning."

Conleth turned the key, the metal biting into his palm. The door shivered under his grip; the hinges groaned like old bones. His dragon thrummed beneath his ribs, coiling tight, warmth making the shadows stretch and quiver in the lamplight.

He trusted his brothers, but this didn't sit well with his dragon. This wasn't enough. They were missing something. They needed a better strategy. And how much longer could they send Trinity on a hunt to discover the truth about her assignment?

Instead of the couch, he stretched out on the bed beside Trinity, her thick lashes lying against pale cheeks. *We almost lost her,* his dragon spirit said. *I failed, swore to let nothing harm her. I failed once, and I almost failed again. The ohunko will come for her again. We must mark her to protect her.*

Pain radiated through his body, a deep ache as if an old wound festered. And maybe one did, for his dragon spirit couldn't contain it anymore. To lose her would be to lose his dragon spirit. Neither of them wanted to live without their mate.

He pressed his hand lightly over hers. Dragon fire racing down his tongue, coiling in his chest with a low, warning thrum. *Mark her.*

Conleth held back, the muscle in his jaw clenching with frustration, letting his dragon's fire simmer rather than blaze. He couldn't. Not without her knowing. *You must.*

He needed her to wake first, to ask her permission. His dragon grumbled, but both their patience was running out. Another sunrise without her feeling the mate bond would drive him insane. She needed to understand why her soul called to his.

Sixteen

Conleth hesitated outside the bedroom door. Movement scraped across the floor inside. He knocked once, softly.

The door opened before he could push it.

"Conleth." Her face went pale.

His dragon stirred at the sight of her, drawn to the exhaustion rolling off her in waves.

When her body sagged, he stepped forward on instinct, catching her before she fell.

"Trinity," he breathed, crossing the room in two strides. "You shouldn't have gotten out of bed yet."

Pain swept across her face before she masked it with that stubborn set of her jaw. The sharp light in her violet eyes made him pause. Her hair lay limp over her shoulders, and shadows clung to the skin beneath her eyes. She wasn't yielding to the pain.

Mark her. Help her heal faster.

He searched her face for the tremor she tried to hide.

Trinity met his gaze, a spark igniting in the depths of violet. "I'm fine," she insisted. "You can call off the watchdogs."

He didn't believe her.

"Alright, but first let me look at you." He nodded toward the bed. "Sit."

Her gaze held his for a heartbeat. Violet eyes blazing before she sighed and complied, settling on the edge of the mattress. Conleth kept his touch gentle as he checked for injuries. Each brush of his hand created a small twitch in response. His dragon spirit hummed beneath his skin, wanting to ease her discomfort with his closeness. The vibration inside him carried an aftertaste of smoke and iron, like a long-cold hearth.

She flinched, and his rational mind blamed the guards outside. His dragon knew better, tasting the memory choking her before he did.

"Your throat will ache and take a few more days to heal." *Offer to heal her faster*, his dragon spirit pressed. "Does it still hurt to speak?"

She touched her throat. "The lemon balm drops have been a great help, thank you."

"Whenever you are ready to talk about it, Aluk has questions, and I think we should discuss what happened beneath the cabin, too." The kiss, the attack they all tangled together, and protectiveness overwhelmed him. *Mark. Her.*

"Are you offering to be my therapist now, too?"

"I can feel your apprehension at the mention of Aluk, and if you want Sia's men to go away from guarding my suite. They need to know why he attacked you."

Trinity shuddered, her hands going up to her throat.

"Like a cherished member of our community. They're here to protect you." He captured her hands, pulled them down, and held them in his, noticing the ice coldness of her fingers. He misunderstood her actions for fear of the guards rather than the memory of the man attacking her.

"He said..." She blinked; her lower lip sucked in as she bit it.

"What did he say to you?"

Her eyes met his. "He said—"

Tears flowed down her face. "He said my destiny is to die, that I should have stayed off the mountain. He was going to kill me...again."

Again. A violent shudder rippled through him. His chest tightened as if the beast inside tried to retreat. "Explain, please."

Trinity glanced around. She pointed to her phone on the bedside table. Conleth retrieved it and held it out toward her. Opening the app, she handed it back to him. "I wrote it out. I didn't want to forget a detail, not that I could," she whispered.

Conleth read the report on her phone, his insides freezing. This wasn't right. He saw flashes between her words of firelight, scales, and the smell of burning fur. His dragon spirit opened the memories, letting them bleed through the text into his mind.

One image snagged him, running through tall stalks and fire in the sky. Too distant, yet sharp, like a shard of glass buried deep under his skin.

She recalled the vivid details of a memory from her encounter, but not the mountain cat's perspective. Hers? "This is written as if..."

This shouldn't have been possible. The grief rising from his dragon wasn't sympathy for another's pain. The sound of bones breaking and the knowledge that they had once been his own rose from memory.

"I know." She clasped her hands together. "I've never gone into a memory and been part of it. What do you think this means? I sent it to my grandfather, but he hasn't responded yet."

She'd sent it to her grandfather. Was this meant as an agent's report or a granddaughter's warning? Panic bubbled inside him, but he forced himself to finish reading.

He grasped at the dragon spirit retreating, shame flooding him. He handed her back her phone, rocking back on his heels. "I always knew this went deeper. The council of elders could risk no one going against their wishes. It's no wonder the Fae queen cursed us."

Tell me I'm wrong. Tell me the fates of our people and lost mates did not go beyond our alpha. His dragon spirit retreated further inside him. He ached for a different fate, and deep down, Conleth understood his dragon could not refute him because Conleth was right. He and Trinity were part of this wretched curse.

Mark her. Stop the ohunko from touching what is ours.

The past had taught him to be careful, to keep his distance. But looking into Trinity's frightened eyes, he saw his own terror mirrored there, and all his careful walls crumbled. "The ohunko are the chosen ones. The Great Hunter gave them special abilities beyond those of regular shifters. Instead of allowing you into his memories, Pezi showed you one from the past."

"Not my past," Trinity whispered. "It was… I was someone else. He showed me her death, but from a long time ago. I wasn't even alive then."

A chilling silence enveloped the room.

"No, that's not how it works. Animal spirits live beyond the warrior in their bloodlines, but not so with the shadow spirits. Their bloodline is gone. Pezi showed you someone from my line, a mate from generations back." He paused, his face darkening. "I think you saw the day everything went wrong. The rebellion that started this whole curse."

A sob tore from Trinity's throat. "So, then it's true."

Her hands clutched at her chest, and her eyes glimmered with tears. "It's my destiny to die."

Conleth's world tilted. His grip on her hand tightened. "No, Trinity." Cold fury ignited within him. "You're my mate, and I will protect you or die with you." He burned with a fierce love, but beneath the surface, in the place where his dragon spirit resided, consuming terror took root. He would not lose her. Not when he found her. *Not again.*

Her eyes widened. "It was your dragon, wasn't it? The one I saw in the vision?"

"It's in the past." He quickly masked his spirit's fear from shining through to her.

"What makes you think you can stop my fate from happening?" she rasped.

His gaze dropped to the pulse point on her wrist. Hope throbbed in the vast desperation of his dragon spirit. He traced a finger down her arm, feeling the warmth of her skin against his. The pull of his dragon rushed within him. His desire, a deep-rooted instinct to claim, protect, drew heat at the tip of his tongue.

Her breath hitched as his touch lingered. Was it fear, or something more? He dared to hope. "In your vision, did you have a mark on your wrist?"

She frowned, lost in thought, her gaze cast down. "No. I don't know. I don't think so."

"May I mark you?" He waited, his heart pounding, for her response.

Just do it, his dragon hissed.

Her gaze met his, filled with a mixture of fear and longing that matched the swirl in his chest.

"My brothers," he said, the consequences heavy on his tongue. "They are not known for their patience. They wait for me to bring you to speak with them. The mark..." He trailed off, tracing a finger over her wrist in an invisible design. "It's a binding promise."

But she hesitated. The fear in her eyes tore through him like a dagger. He needed her trust, her certainty.

"It will protect you." He needed her answer. A refusal would not damage his dragon. It would destroy him should she reject him.

"Let me give you this protection. Please," he said, the urgency in his tone undeniable, but a sincerity that laid bare the depth of his soul tempered it. He wanted to shield her, yes, but he wanted her to understand the extent of what she meant to him.

She drew a shaky breath. Slowly, she lifted her wrist, and with a small trembling nod, she surrendered.

Joy rushed along with a profound sense of gratitude. Conleth lifted her wrist, the delicate bones trembling slightly beneath his touch. Her eyes were a storm of emotions, most of which he couldn't quite decipher, and neither could his dragon spirit. Within himself, longing and acceptance pulsed from his dragon.

Heat flooded his tongue. Conleth dipped his head, his tongue grazing the designated spot on her wrist. A hiss escaped her lips. He tightened his grip instinctively, not wanting her to jerk away as he branded his mark upon her.

Conleth licked the mark after he finished, using his saliva to heal the burn. His eyes never left Trinity's face, searching for any sign of regret. Her cheeks flushed, her eyes turned dark purple with swirls of gold, and her lips parted as large tears dripped down her cheeks.

"Trinity."

"This makes me your mate." Her voice, when it came, was a mere breath. Deep crimson flooded her cheeks. Conleth stepped closer to her, keeping her from getting up and escaping him. "It lets anyone who sees the mark know you are my mate, but it's a promise, like an engagement until I claim you and seal the bond."

Her eyes darted around the room. "You can't want this. Me."

Was that her only objection? It came too late. She bore his mark. Conleth cupped her face, his thumb brushing away a stray tear with a tenderness that surprised him.

"I've wanted you since the day you walked into my clinic, Trinity. You can't tell me you don't feel this fire between us. Did you honestly believe I could simply leave after that kiss? That I could pretend you don't belong with me? You're my mate."

"No," she rose to her feet. He allowed her to push him back; a chasm opened between them. His dragon roared in protest within him. "There will be no claiming. You understand?"

He stared at her, the echo of the growl still lingering in the air. "I understand."

"I let you mark me to protect me, that's all," she said, her tone flat.

He didn't believe it, not by the wash of turmoil in her eyes. His dragon paced, snarling with impatience. He waited this long for a mate. What was a little longer? *We could lose her before we claim her!*

His hands clenched at his sides. She needed to come to him willingly, not because the mountain left her no choice. He wanted her to see the man who would set the world on fire for her, not just the one standing between her and it.

"I can wait, *Uhana,*" he said, aching with every word. "I have waited this long."

"And I shall die; perhaps even this will set my destiny in motion if it hasn't been evoked from the moment I saw your dragon," she whispered with chilling finality.

Despair crashed over him. His dragon spirit threatened to drown beneath it. To lose her, to lose them both, was a fate he couldn't bear. He pushed the anguish away, refusing to let her glimpse how deep it went.

"We will face this destiny together." A vise wrapped around his heart. "Whatever you're afraid of, we'll face it together. There is still so much for us to uncover about each other and the curse binding us.

The elders are gone, and the council did not oppose Taran and Gwen. Have no fear of our union."

He leaned closer, searching her eyes. "You feel this too, don't you? This pull between us?"

Then his lips brushed against hers, feather-light.

Trinity's breath hitched, her heart hammering against his chest. Then, hesitantly at first, she met his kiss. Soft and yielding, yet beneath the gentleness, a spark awaited to ignite. He deepened the kiss, a slow dance to an age-old melody. He tasted the lingering fear and the nascent trust blooming between them. Each touch, each brush of lips was a promise. Safety. Belonging. He chased away any doubts from his dragon spirit. Fate wouldn't dictate their path. He wouldn't make the same mistakes as his ancestors. No one was taking his mate away. Ever.

Finally, he pulled away, his forehead resting against hers. Her eyes fluttered open, wet with tears. Another tear escaped, tracing a glistening path down her cheek. He brushed it away with a tenderness that surprised even him.

"And the mark? What happens when we don't complete the bond, and you claim me?"

The question struck him like a physical blow. His dragon stilled inside him, and his soul suddenly chilled. "The mark will fade," he forced the words out, each one pained. "And my spirit will leave me." His dragon roared in his head at the possibility she might reject him.

"Then we are both doomed."

His dragon writhed in his gut, mirroring the turmoil gripping him. "So, it would seem."

Conleth had to tread carefully, but fear of rejection from his dragon spirit, of pushing her further away, threatened to paralyze him. "The mark will keep you safe. The ancient guardians honor the old ways; they will see it and accept our bond, even without the claiming."

Seventeen

THE STERILE WHITE OF the clinic at the lodge was a stark contrast to the earthy tones of wood beams, stonework, and warm walls of the other resort areas. Conleth and Trinity stood side by side, their hands clasped tightly. A dull ache came from the mark on her wrist, reminding her of Conleth's protection. Her gut twisted, knotted in several ways. She allowed him to mark her. Protection. But if she allowed him to claim her. Death.

Inside the clinic, Aluk awaited. His casual attire from earlier was replaced by a dark, almost military-style jacket. The tailored black pants completed the outfit, giving him the aura of authority of the mountain dragon alpha. Trinity recognized grief from his memories in his dark, gleaming eyes as he clasped his hands behind his back.

A faint antiseptic smell hung in the air, mingling with the lingering scent of pine from outside. Trinity scrunched her nose against the potent scent.

"Thanks for coming down and meeting here." Aluk's gaze flickered between Conleth and Trinity, his expression grave. "They found the hiker who attacked Agent Oberlin."

Trinity's grip tightened on Conleth's hand. Her heart sped as panic grew in her chest. "You found him? Where?"

"Off the trail outside the village." Aluk stepped back, waving for Conleth to go ahead of him. "A local discovered the boy a few hours ago. Sia and his men brought the body here. Taran is on his way."

Inside the examination room, a white sheet covered a human form lying on the examination table. The figure's unnatural stillness chilled her to the bone. The body drew her gaze as her mind raced. A sharp pain shot through her neck, a jolt of awareness that pulled her focus back to her own body. Her hand flew instinctively to the tender spot.

"Body... he's dead," she whispered, her voice barely audible.

Conleth squeezed her hand, offering silent support. "I assume the cause of death is heart failure?"

"You tell me," Aluk said, his eyes glued on Trinity in an unsettling way. "Does the body match the others?"

Conleth released Trinity. He pulled down the sheet, revealing the man's face and pale, almost chalk-white skin. She watched him intently, searching for any sign of reassurance. But he gazed at the body, filled with strange intensity. The warmth in his amber irises was gone, replaced by the fiery red of his dragon.

"Is that him?" Aluk asked in his commanding tone, wanting an answer. "Is that the one who attacked you?"

Tearing her gaze away from Conleth, she looked at the man's face. Her throat tightened with recognition, and black spots appeared before her eyes. She took a deep breath through her nose, feeling suffocated.

Conleth reached over and touched her cheek. "Breathe, Uhana. It's him. The *ohunko* is gone."

Trinity's knees threatened to buckle at the revelation of the man's identity. Conleth's arm curled around her waist, anchoring her.

The figure on the table was no longer the malevolent presence she remembered, emptied of the spirit that haunted him. Still, the memory of those cold, dead eyes boring into hers twisted her stomach. Nausea surged, muscles coiling as her body screamed to flee.

"Are you going to touch him?" Aluk asked.

Goosebumps ran along her flesh at the thought of touching him. Trinity swallowed. "I..." His words finally registered, and betrayal, thick and hot, threatened to smother her.

She could almost hear his pleading explanation in her head. *We need to know everything.*

She glanced back and forth between the two men. The trust she gave him shattered. She'd guarded his secret; she hadn't included it in any of her reports and protected his family's inheritance. She'd let him mark her.

"We have no secrets among brothers." Aluk shrugged.

She clutched her wrist where his mark suddenly stung like a branding iron.

"I told Taran." Conleth's confirmation hit like a dagger to her heart. He'd told Taran, and now, it seemed, the entire mountain would know.

Conleth's hand closed around her marked wrist, nuzzling away her other hand. His touch was warm. She flinched, her free hand grasping his arm. Anger and betrayal swirled inside her, sinking deeper by the second. "*Uhuna,*" he murmured, as if he could feel her hurt and confusion. His mark pulsed against her skin. His gaze held hers, a silent plea swirling in the bronze depths.

"I've hurt you by sharing this. That was not my intention." His voice turned into a balm for her frayed nerves. "But you're mine; you're one of us now. There can be no secrets between us. Aluk is your alpha, and he's family. We look after and protect each other."

She pulled her wrist from his hold. His thumb grazed against the mark, shooting sparks through her. Tingling sensations exploded from her core. "I trusted you."

And she still wanted to, despite his actions. Even as anger gnawed at her, a part of her recognized his intentions were pure.

"I promised to protect you. This is my way of keeping you safe," Conleth said.

As she met his gaze, doubts weighed on her.

"We need answers. I suggest we start here," Aluk said, getting back to the matter of the dead hiker. "It will also answer a few of my questions and address Ben's concerns," Aluk said, authority and reasoning in his words. But his reassuring presence couldn't overpower the primal need to flee that still gripped her.

Trinity's gaze locked on the lifeless man sprawled across the table. Not the monster who had terrified her. Not anymore.

Just a body.

Just a victim.

Her fingers curled against the edge of the table, knuckles white.

Someone had loved this person. Someone would want answers.

Heat stirred beneath Trinity's skin. The familiar ache of her gift rising.

The ohunko had hollowed him out and stolen his will to live.

What else lingered in the body's silence?

Every second she delayed, she risked losing the opportunity to find out.

Trinity curled her fingers into a fist, then released them. Conleth's hand settled on her shoulder. "It's okay if you can't, but like Aluk said, it might give us important information."

"No pressure, right?" she whispered.

Aluk's chin dipped, his gaze steady. Those eyes assessed her, judged her, and stripped away her bravado. Once her grandfather discovered she'd compromised her position here, he would demote her again. She couldn't go back into the archives at the PPI headquarters. Her choices led to this assignment on the mountain or shame to her family. Without her grandfather's protection, she was a target for the hunters as much as the shifter bloods.

Conleth pulled down the sheet more. Trinity closed her eyes. She took a deep breath trying to settle the blow from Conleth's betrayal. She thought at the time she could trust Conleth. When would she ever learn?

Opening her eyes, Conleth nodded at her. His softened gaze sent flutters through her stomach. His gaze softened, and she turned away. The familiar warmth in his gaze was dangerous to her emotional well-being.

The moment her fingertips brushed the fabric, a jolt of energy coursed through her, followed by an unexpected scent of lavender and eucalyptus. The distinctive aromatherapy blend from the resort's spa. Beneath the pleasant fragrance lurked a dark and hungry sensation, causing her skin to crawl.

The dizzying rush pulled her under.

Her vision blurred, then sharpened as she stood inside a sleek, modern spa. The scent grew stronger, thick with malevolent anticipation as the ohunko's hunger pulsed through the connection.

A woman lay motionless on the massage table, her face set in cold determination. Blonde hair spilled across one shoulder. Around her, the room shimmered with heat. The woman rolled over with lethal grace. Claws erupted from her fingertips as she pounced. The man's body convulsed, his scream dying in his throat as his horror-filled eyes burned into her mind.

"Shawn!" Trinity shouted. But the vision faded. She blinked, trying to regain the images, but the vision was gone. Yet, the dread in the pit of her stomach remained.

"What did you see?" Aluk demanded.

Her mind tried to catch up with the images. That woman. She'd seen her before. The lingering scent of lavender and eucalyptus filled her nostrils, the spa's distinctive blend with a taint of something dark and predatory.

"Trinity?" Conleth touched her arm. The spark from the contact rebooted her brain to catch up.

She spun around, looking at Conleth. "Shawn." The name burst out of her, a strangled cry. Then she looked at Aluk. "I saw Shawn."

"He's in danger." When both men looked at her oddly, she threw up her hands. "Shawn!" Explanations were useless. Time stretched and warped, each second an eternity.

"I saw it." Her heart hammered in her chest.

"The coffee shop. The woman in the coffee shop! She had claws." Trinity's gaze locked onto Conleth. "You're a medic. Help him."

Aluk crossed his arms, skepticism clear in his eyes. "I thought you said her gift was looking into someone's memories."

Trinity huffed, a breathless, nervous laugh. "It is. That's what I saw." Then her laughter died, replaced by a chilling dread. "The hiker's dead. The woman." Her blood went cold. "Pezi," she muttered, the *ohunko's* name slipping from her lips. She asked Conleth, "Have you seen Shawn? How bad is he?"

"I haven't tended to anyone here except you." Conleth's brows crashed together. "It must be the *ohunko*. Its essence hasn't completely left the body. What if it possessed a woman after the hiker?"

Aluk walked out into the waiting area. Trinity hurried after him, her pulse pounding in a frantic rhythm. Shawn got hurt. They needed to get to him, but Aluk picked up a phone, hit a few buttons, and said, "Alpha Aluk. I want to speak with Shawn."

Fear and desperation warred within her. Why was he making a phone call? If Conleth hadn't seen Shawn yet, they still had time to save him! They need to get to him. She moved, about to take off past Aluk when she heard.

"Shawn."

Trinity froze upon hearing Aluk say Shawn's name.

Conleth moved to her side, his hand finding hers, but it couldn't quell the storm beating inside her. They had to help Shawn.

"You are healthy and whole?" Aluk's gaze drilled into her, a cold, assessing stare. "Very good. Thank you for answering my call. Return to your client."

Trinity's heart sank. Desperation tightened around her throat.

Aluk ended the call and turned to her. "That's a good trick, Agent Oberlin. Are you going to tell us what you really saw?"

"You want to know what I saw? Fine. I'll tell you exactly what I witnessed."

Conleth's fallen expression only fueled it into a white-hot flame.

Trinity lifted her chin, her throat aching as she said, "I saw a woman. A beautiful woman with copper-colored skin, dark flowing hair, and sparkling honey-gold eyes. She was laughing and running, begging you to follow her."

The images hadn't faded. Heat still licked her skin.

Aluk's expression hardened, darkness filling his eyes.

"Trinity," Conleth said, his warning a mere whisper in the maelstrom of her triumph.

She spun on Conleth. "No."

Her gaze locked onto his, daring him to challenge her. "You asked me what I saw, and I'm telling you."

They still didn't believe her.

"You share everything with your brothers, right? This woman, she was your mate."

Her eyes darted to Aluk. They wouldn't listen unless she made them. "It's your fault. She wanted to leave you. And your dragon doesn't even want you anymore."

"Trinity," Conleth snarled, attempting to silence her. The truth was out, and instantly she knew she'd crossed a line. But she didn't care. He didn't believe her before, but he would now.

Aluk held up his hand, his eyes flashing between human and dragon. "She's right, but perhaps her gift isn't as good as you think."

Trinity rolled her shoulders back. She couldn't let another person get hurt. "I know what I saw," she insisted. "A woman attacked Shawn at the spa while he gave her a massage. She had claws. The ohunko is here! We need to save Shawn."

When both men stood and gawked at her, she realized how crazy she must sound.

"You spoke to Shawn. You're sure it was him?" A lump formed in her throat as disbelief washed over their faces. Aluk's jaw clenched, and he nodded.

"Trinity, it didn't happen," Conleth said. "I would have told you if I treated someone who was attacked, especially if it was the ohunko."

Why couldn't she see anything? She stared at her hands, turning them over, as if she might find the answer written on her palms. The visions had always come when she needed them most. What was different now?

If the vision came from the past, then Shawn was hurt or dead. They were running toward something that had already happened. Her gaze kept snagging on the vibrant crimson. It had the thick, metallic tang of a fresh wound, not the faint, dried scent of history.

Her throat constricted, cutting off air. The truth slammed into her like a shut door. The wound wasn't old. *Not the past.*

Trinity's gaze snapped up. She stared at both Conleth and Aluk as the icy dread of reality seeped in. What if she hadn't seen the past? "It hasn't happened yet."

Conleth's eyes widened, but Aluk didn't even blink.

"We need to get there now!" Trinity bolted toward the door, her heart racing along with her. Each heartbeat felt like another second stolen from Shawn's life.

Adrenaline pushed Trinity forward, her legs pumping like pistons. Conleth and Aluk followed close behind, their footsteps echoing down the hall. Every passing second made her stomach plummet further. The spa loomed ahead, its tranquil lights casting long shadows at the entrance.

She barreled through the entrance. The Zen fountain continued its gentle trickle, aromatherapy candles flickered undisturbed, but Trinity's arrival shattered the tranquility. Behind the reception desk, a young woman with perfect nails and a bored expression glanced up with mild annoyance.

"Can I help you with something?" The receptionist asked.

Trinity grabbed the edge of the counter. "Where's Shawn? I need to see him. Now."

"He works here, gives massages?" Trinity didn't have time to play games. Her blood pounded with the vision propelling her onward.

The receptionist blinked, her perfectly arched eyebrows shooting up. "Uh, sure. Let me check the schedule..." Her voice trailed off as she tapped away at the computer screen.

Conleth and Aluk caught up to her, the air changing with their presence behind her. The receptionist's eyes widened as they stepped into the waiting area. Conleth moved to stand beside Trinity, placing his hand at the small of her back. "Is he with someone?"

The woman nodded frantically, her eyes darting between the three of them.

"Tell us what room he's in," Conleth pressed.

The receptionist's lips trembled slightly. "I can't just—."

"It's an emergency." Trinity cut her off.

They had no time to spare.

The receptionist's gaze lifted past Trinity to the massive figure looming behind Trinity. Aluk's low growl rumbled through the room like distant thunder. The receptionist swallowed hard, her eyes widening as she pressed back into her chair.

"He's got someone in room four right now," she stammered. "But... Alpha... the client is.... an outsider."

Trinity took off towards the designated room. Conleth and Aluk at her heels. Reaching the door, she flung it open.

Towels lay strewn across the floor, a massage table overturned, and in the center of it all, Shawn. The masseuse's eyes were dull with pain. His arm lay at an unnatural angle, and a deep gash on his forehead oozed blood. A wave of nausea washed over Trinity, nearly taking her to her knees. She'd wasted too much time trying to prove herself, and now she'd truly seen the past.

Conleth's voice cut through to her. "He's alive."

Her head snapped up as movement tugged at the edge of her vision. At the far end of the room, a woman stood motionless, framed not by sunlight but by the harsh fluorescent glare bleeding in from the hallway. Her bohemian dress hung loose around her, the light carving her into a stark silhouette.

Cold, calculating eyes met Trinity's. The woman from the coffee shop, the one from her vision. A shaky gasp escaped Trinity's throat.

Black eyes gleaming with predatory intelligence fixed on Trinity. Slowly, the woman raised her hands. A guttural, inhuman growl came from her. Violent tremors seized her frame. Her body snapped taut, convulsing as if electricity surged through her. She writhed, fighting against invisible restraints. The woman's face contorted in agony while some internal battle raged within her.

She let out a strangled gasp, then pulled back her shoulders and lifted her chin.

Trinity took a step back. Whoever the woman had been was gone, and the ohunko now inhabited her body.

"I knew that you would come, *wiyoya*." The woman, the ohunko's voice, carried an odd mixture of resignation and pain. "You are not the only one who sees."

"Leave her!" Aluk commanded.

"No. Wait." Conleth growled. "We must protect the human. She's innocent."

The ohunko's borrowed face twisted with anguish. "Innocent..." it whispered, then its expression hardened. "A vessel, a tool. They come and beg for the filling of their souls and have no blessing upon their blood." But its voice cracked on the words, as if fighting itself.

Silently, Conleth moved closer to her. He clasped her wrist and tugged her toward him.

The woman, her painted lips sneered at them. "Your mark means nothing, dragon. It will not stop what is to come."

A blast of coldness filled Trinity.

"And what is that?" Aluk demanded.

"*She* has been waiting for you." A cruel smile stretched across its painted lips. The ohunko walked up to Aluk. His eyes narrowed. A low growl rumbled in his chest.

Her lips curving up, her hips swaying. She placed a finger against Aluk's face. "Soon this will all be over, and our heritage restored."

The woman turned, her gaze piercing Trinity with a malice so pure it was almost tangible. Her dark gaze went to Conleth next, a promise of destruction in its onyx depths. "Your punishment will also be hers."

The ohunko-possessed woman lunged forward, her fingers extended into dark, razor-sharp claws. Trinity froze. Everything inside her seized, a cold pressure tightening behind her eyes. The air itself seemed to hum, thrumming against her skin like a command she couldn't resist. Her body refused to move.

Trinity screamed as the woman aimed her claws toward her.

Conleth roared as he lunged at the ohunko. But the Pezi was a blur, its movements fluid and deadly. With a sickening thud, Conleth flew across the room and crashed into the wall.

Aluk grappled with the Pezi. Her strength was beyond that of a human. They wrestled, a brutal dance of blows and parries. The massage table toppled over in the chaos.

Conleth flung himself toward Shawn, taking the brunt of the falling table to shield the injured man. He groaned, shoving away the table. Shawn lay unconscious on the floor.

"Trinity, get out of here," Conleth shouted.

Sound fell away, leaving a sudden, terrifying hush. Trinity's gaze snagged on the dark, spreading stain on Conleth's shirt, right where the corner of the table had struck his ribs. He clamped his free hand over the wound, his jaw tight, wrapping a hand around his waist to put pressure on it.

The sight of his blood made her stomach pitch. The wound should have been hers. Her fault. His ribs ached where the creature had struck him, a reminder of how close it had come to tearing through her instead.

"I can't. It's like I'm frozen!" Trinity, the cold in her veins holding her in a vise, wrestled against her paralysis. A strangled sob forced its way out. Her body shook, useless, with the frantic need to run. "Take Shawn and go."

The woman's attention snapped to Trinity, and a line of ice flooded her spine. "You will die," the ohunko promised, her voice a flat, hollow thing.

Trinity met the woman's cold, dead eyes. A strange calm washed over her. The lingering questions about Conleth didn't matter now. She might not trust him, but she couldn't watch him die. She couldn't live without him.

The ohunko renewed its attack, shoving Aluk against the wall. The window glass behind the curtains shattered at his back. His eyes flared a brilliant warning red.

The ohunko drove its claws toward Trinity's heart, then jerked to a halt. For a single, terrifying heartbeat, a glimmer of anguish crossed the possessed woman's eyes.

"Forgive me," the woman whispered, the sound not hers. "But I cannot fail them again."

Aluk delivered a powerful punch, connecting with the ohunko's jaw, sending the woman's body reeling. Before it could recover, Conleth slammed into her from behind. The ohunko snarled, its eyes blazing with hatred.

"I am still your Alpha," Aluk commanded. "You will bring harm to no one."

The ohunko's coal-black eyes swirled like ink and bled from her eyes. Black tears streamed down her cheeks. Trinity twisted in frustration and gained an inch as inside her something cracked, broke, and warmth flooded back into her bones. A raw, untamed energy ignited fire and hummed in her veins.

Tremors wracked the woman's possessed body. With a surge of strength, she pushed Conleth away. Gasping for breath, she rose to her feet, her eyes swirling gray rather than black.

"Help me." The woman pleaded, desperate and terrified. "It... it doesn't want to hurt her. It's fighting itself, but it thinks..."

The woman lunged at the window. With a desperate cry, she threw herself through the shattered glass, disappearing into the cool night air.

Aluk dove for her, but in the deafening silence, the sickening thud of her body hitting the ground pierced Trinity's consciousness. Aluk stood at the window, his fingers biting into the sill.

Nausea rushed through her, and her vision blurred at the edges. Conleth grabbed her and pulled her into his embrace. "Are you all right, *Uhana*?"

She sank against him, relying on his strength when the wetness of his blood soaked into her back. The warmth spread through the fabric. For a dizzy second, she could still see him falling, still fee herself frozen while he bled for her. The ache in her chest deepened.

She jerked away from him. "You're hurt."

"It's just a scratch."

But she didn't believe him and glanced over at Aluk for support.

"Ben is on his way," Aluk announced, still holding the windowsill and staring down. His back was rigid. Trinity trembled as the feeling returned to her limbs.

Aluk turned and looked at them; pain etched across his features. His eyes were bright red and blazed with his dragon spirit. He stalked over, kneeling by Shawn, and swept him up in his arms. "I'll take him to the clinic and wait for you there." Aluk stared at Conleth for a long minute. His eyes glazed, and he nodded before leaving.

Slowly, she turned, holding onto him for support. Her legs wobbled. "We need to get you to the clinic. I know basic first aid."

Conleth smirked, his hand reaching for the bottom of his shirt, and lifted to show her. "It's already healing." She brushed her fingers over the long gash on his ribs. Conleth sucked in a breath. "We should still get this cleaned up, and Shawn needs help."

"Aluk can tend to him as easily as I," Conleth let his shirt fall and pulled her closer. Trinity rested her head against Conleth's chest. His hand brushed through her hair. "I've never been so scared in my life."

"I thought you said this mark protected me?" she whispered. "I couldn't move. I was frozen." Anger, frustration, and fear sent moisture to her eyes. "And now a woman is dead."

Eighteen

THE MORNING SUN CAST long, distorted shadows across the sheet draped over the woman's body. There were no marks. There never were. On the stainless-steel table, a white sheet covered the latest victim of the shadow spirits. Each death circled closer to him. The ohunko had made another attempt at Trinity.

They had to move her. Get her away from the resort, away from the innocents who had no defense. The ohunko tracked her. When one host body burned out, it would look for another. Every guest, every oblivious employee, was a waiting, vulnerable target.

Conleth entered his office, where Trinity sat at his desk, the blue glow of the monitor deepening the shadows under her eyes. Her fingers tapped on the keyboard. "Are you sure we should have brought the body here?"

"It's the closet we've got to a proper hospital, short of driving to Frostwood. The resort's little clinic isn't equipped for this kind of thing."

Conleth moved to the window, letting his gaze drift to the distant horizon.

The night before burned behind his eyes, a mark that would not fade. His ribs throbbed where the ohunko's claws had struck him. The wounds had healed to nothing more than pink lines across his skin.

Every throb reminded him how close the ohunko had come to tearing through her instead.

"But you don't have anyone else to help you here?" Trinity pointed out, taking him back to their first encounter.

"Rourke is sending someone to assist me here at Aluk's request." It was about time. He'd been trying to find help since the seasons changed and residents migrated back to their family homes during the snow thaw.

She closed the laptop with a decisive snap. "Perhaps I'll go check on Shawn again."

Trinity's constant worry over Shawn bit deeper than the claw marks on Conleth's side. She'd hovered after the attack and cleaning his wounds as they healed. She kept her distance while Aluk worked on Shawn. Now she paced like an anxious family member, waiting for news. Aluk snapped the bone back with a sharp crack. Conleth bandaged the claw marks, his hands steady though his pulse betrayed him. The head injury stayed stubborn, and that worried him more than he'd admit. The rest would heal in a day or two, but until then, Shawn remained in a deep, healing sleep.

"*Uhuna*, he's the same as he was when you checked on him an hour ago."

Trinity's persistent checks on Shawn had his jaw locking until his molars ached. Every time she leaned over the bed, his dragon pressed against his ribs, snarling for space.

"I know that." She headed for the door.

Conleth stepped into her path before he could think better of it. The roar under his sternum, had nothing to do with logic and everything to do with his mate hovering over another man. He forced it down before she saw the change in his eyes.

Last night, Aluk had handled the worst of it, taking the woman's body to the clinic in Sentinel Peak, and Ben reported the incident. At least that spared Conleth the agony of breaking the news to her family himself.

Ben could handle those conversations going forward.

Trinity was Conleth's priority now, but this latest death demanded a price. News of the death would spread like blood in water, calling predators from beyond the mountains.

Could he and his brothers protect them from the government, from hunters, from the shadow spirits? The guardians meant to protect them had turned.

What would happen when the government sent more agents to interfere with their way of life? How many more Fae moved unseen among humans, circling closer every day?

Heat filled his veins from his dragon spirit.

"Talk to me, Trinity. You're upset after the attack. Having to record it in a report probably didn't help in reliving it. What can I do to help you?"

"Nothing. I think you've helped enough. Thank you." She tried again to step around him.

He placed a hand on her stomach, stopping her. "You're either avoiding me, or you have a romantic interest in my patient down the hall."

"Shawn?" She leaned back, a defensive posture taking over her stance. "I barely know him."

Conleth's eyes narrowed. "Are you attracted to him, *Uhuna?* Do you want him?"

A short, nervous laugh escaped her. "Of course not."

The sound wavered, thin as paper, her heart thudding too hard against her ribs. He was too close. Too much. "Why would I want a mountain lion when I've got a dragon? And the mark to prove it?" She held up her wrist, the mark a brand against her pale skin.

"Then why are you avoiding me?" He smelled the anxiety plaguing her. What wasn't she telling him?

"I'm not avoiding you."

He lowered his chin, forcing his dragon back. "You're lying," he countered softly. "My dragon spirit can feel the turmoil raging inside you."

"The only one lying is you." She stepped closer, close enough for the heat of her pulse to brush against his chest. Fury rolled off her in waves. Fear threaded through it. A tremor hitched her breath. "You're the one who said this mark would protect me. Instead, it put us all in danger."

He caught the scent and answered wrong, mistaking fear for rejection, and the sound rumbling in his chest wasn't human.

"Targeting a dragon's mate is a serious crime. For an ancient guardian to attack you with my mark means the shadows have tainted them beyond redemption. The ohunko could have manipulated the vision to lure you there, and we walked right into its trap."

Trinity blinked. "I know what I witnessed, and it happened. I've never seen the future before. If I hadn't...." The unspeakable horror of that possibility etched itself deep in her eyes.

Conleth stared back, fighting the instinctive urge to comfort her.

"I thought we were too late," she said.

"It was waiting for us. As soon as it sensed us coming, it attacked," he explained. "The ohunko used your gift against you. With the ohunko's essence still on the body, but the spirit still alive, it sensed you tap into the memory. It showed you only what it wanted you to see."

"No," she whispered.

Conleth placed his hands on her waist. Her skin cooled beneath his palms, but his pulse surged hot. His dragon spirit pressed hard against his ribs, urging him to carry her somewhere the world couldn't reach. He clenched his jaw, forcing breath through his teeth.

"You suspected this and said nothing to me?"

"You barely gave us time to make a plan before you took off. Would you have listened?" He closed his eyes, shoving his dragon into the metal cage to keep the spirit trapped for a while. Unlike his brothers, he spent years learning to handle his dragon spirit, least he reveal his true nature while serving in the military.

"This is my fault. I just wanted to save him." Tears welled up in her eyes. "I was so mad Aluk didn't believe me."

"Don't take it personally, *Uhuna*. As you pointed out to him, he and his dragon are not in sync; he doesn't trust anyone." He tried to reassure her, to make her understand his part in it, to ease her guilt. However, she'd only made it worse by throwing Aluk's memories, his pain, at him. Aluk restrained his dragon spirit from rising and lashing out. The pain, like aftershocks, showed in his brother's blood-red eyes of his dragon.

"I can't believe you shared my gift with your brothers without asking me," she said, directing his thoughts another way.

"Tell me how I can make this right?" When he told his brother about Gwen's gift and the Fae mates' connection with the curse, he didn't intend for them to expose the knowledge. His fingers tightened on her waist. "I'll do anything but let you leave me."

"Conleth." Trinity pressed her hands to his chest. "You accused me of being attracted to Shawn. This thing between us isn't the same. A trick of fate. I might find you more appealing than him.

"A lot more," he said.

"Yes," she laughed. "I'm not your fated mate. I can feel the pull, the yearning your dragon is projecting, but it's a phantom. We come from different worlds, with different destinies. I have a mission, a purpose that transcends personal feelings. I hope to fulfill it before I die."

Fear built in her gaze, stirring like thick sludge in his stomach.

"You're not going to die." His dragon spirit thrummed in his veins. "Not while I have breath in my body and my dragon spirit in my soul. We're going to figure this out. When you touch me, can you see or feel anything?"

He moved her hand to his face, holding her palm against his cheek. She stared at him, her violet eyes flecked with gold. A long moment passed as her brow furrowed deeper.

"Nothing." Her grip on his face loosened, and she pulled away.

He tightened his hold on her hand.

"No visions. What about feelings?" he pressed, knowing her answer could cause the death of him and send his dragon back into the shadows.

Trinity froze, her gaze darting to his and then back to her hand held to his face. A glint of annoyance hinted across her features. "Conleth, stop this."

"Close your eyes," he urged. "Listen to my heartbeat. Inhale my scent, *Unahu*. Can you honestly tell me you feel nothing for me? No connection?"

His heart pounded in his ears, a drumbeat echoing from within his dragon spirit's memories. If she felt nothing, if she was truly opposed to their bond, his world would shatter. His dragon spirit roared in his mind. Because if she severed what they had, he knew he wouldn't survive.

Trinity closed her eyes, tilting her head back. She searched for the past dragon spirit kept locked down. The years he spent conforming to the outside world, learning their way to heal, and hiding his true nature. *Why couldn't she feel the fire of the bond?* He held his breath, every muscle in his body rigid. *Feel it, Trinity. You are ours. You are mine.*

The mark of his dragon tattoo twitched at the brush of her gift. The bond thrummed between them, an undeniable chord vibrating only in him. He sensed her inheritance, tugging at him, gliding over his chest.

She wants to feel something. She wants to connect with us. Claim her.

Her hand, still clasped in his, grew scalding, almost painful.

Trinity opened her eyes.

"I feel... nothing," she whispered.

The beast inside him roared. *Impossible. A lie.*

Conleth's grip tightened. "And when I do this, tell me you feel nothing."

He needed her to stop building fragile walls against him. She might not recognize him with her gifts, but he knew one way to spark their connection. He leaned forward, brushing his lips to hers in a soft kiss. Trinity responded with a hesitant kiss in return, her lips parting in invitation.

Conleth drank in the sweetness of her breath, the subtle salt on her lips. Touch and scent fused, silencing the beast inside him, dissolving his every worry into a tide of pure, warm feeling. His heart thundered, perfectly matching the frantic race of her pulse. This stillness... This woman... She was slowly, overwhelmingly, the reason he breathed.

A sharp rap on the door jolted her. Conleth pulled back. Trinity's breath came in ragged gasps. He spun toward the interruption.

Rourke filled the doorway. His lips curled in a smirk as he glanced between them.

Beside him, a tall woman with a confident air studied them with curious eyes.

"This is Evelyn. Our pack midwife," Rourke said, stepping to the side to give her more space.

The heat of their shared moment evaporated. Conleth glanced at Evelyn, but Trinity recovered first. She stepped toward the woman and extended her hand. "Nice to meet you, Evelyn. I'm Trinity Oberlin."

"Agent Oberlin is our acting shifter representative," Rourke said to Evelyn. "She's from the PPI division of the government." Rourke clapped a hand on Trinity's shoulder. "The man you're tending would be in far worse shape without her."

A growl escaped Conleth's lips. Rourke slid his hand away from Trinity.

Evelyn's brow furrowed. She took Trinity's hand. "We're glad you're here."

Conleth's gaze met the woman's as she shook hands with Trinity. Evelyn struck him as a strong woman, with a fire in her eyes that belied her gentle demeanor. When he took her hand next, she went straight to business. "Alpha Blackwood mentioned adding a birthing center in return for assistance here at the clinic?"

"I'm open to that. Some sections are still in need of remodeling. They remain closed off for now, but we can discuss that addition. I appreciate you extending your service here to help our people."

Another pair of capable hands eased the pressure. Traveling between the resort and clinic grew overwhelming as more residents returned to town. Evelyn's expertise and compassion became an invaluable asset, a gift he couldn't afford to lose.

"I've sent word for two others to assist you here, including one of my guys in technology to take charge of your reception area. Sia is sending a member from his pack that will need some training, and

I've sent word among the council." Rourke said, "I apologize for not prioritizing this place sooner."

Having a dedicated team would allow him to focus on what he did best, while also giving him the opportunity to spend more time with Trinity. "You are now, and that's what matters."

Conleth's gaze landed on Trinity, her pink cheeks adorable. Her frosty white strands of hair falling out of her perfectly coiled bun.

"Let me show you around," Conleth said. He needed Evelyn familiarized with the clinic before he got called back to the resort. He had more human patients these days than mountain residents.

Trinity's eyes gleamed as she smiled at the woman. "I don't know my way around this place, but I can introduce you to Shawn. He's resting in the room down the hall."

Evelyn glanced at Rourke; upon his nod, she turned back to Trinity. "That would be great."

Trinity led her down the hall toward Shawn's room.

Conleth stayed back a moment with Rourke. "Aluk put you up to this. I've been inquiring about help for weeks. Luckily, no one until now has needed to take advantage of the empty beds."

Rourke scratched his beard. "The council is scrambling trying to decide among us Alphas, but Aluk has the authority and put them in their place. It's been a long time since he's come down from the mountain. Perhaps he will reclaim his place at the head of the council."

It also meant a shift in the power dynamics. Especially once they broke the curse plagued upon them by their ancestors.

"Perhaps." Conleth didn't want to keep the wolf alpha from returning to his duties at the police station, but he needed to ask. "Any word on the *ohunko*?"

"Not yet," Rourke said, grimacing. "If it's hunting your mate like Aluk thinks, then it's waiting for the right moment. You need to keep an eye on her. Take her into the mountains, away from everyone until this is resolved."

He paused, dropping his voice to avoid anyone else listening beyond them. "All these death reports of outsiders will bring more trouble to us, you know?"

"I understand." Conleth walked Rourke out and headed down the hall. The idea of taking Trinity to the mountain tempted him. She stood in the doorway to Shawn's room, and he came up behind her, slipped an arm around her, and leaned close to her ear. "See, you felt something, didn't you?"

She stiffened, turning in his embrace. "More than I wish, but we can't ever... let you claim me... it can't happen." A sharp pain shot through him.

"But that... can." Trinity turned away again. Her big smile returned as Conleth looked over her shoulder at Evelyn sitting at the side of the bed with Shawn.

"You saw something when you shook her hand?" Conleth asked, curiosity pulling his voice low so Shawn wouldn't hear him.

"They are fated," she said, her grin collapsing into a frown. "I wish I didn't see the future, only the past."

"But why?" Conleth stepped back, and she moved out of the doorway, pressing herself against the wall so the others couldn't see.

"It's a gift," he said, almost reverent. "Those two might not have found each other if this had played out any other way. Do you know how rare it is to find your fated mate?"

Her gaze, glossy with unshed tears, clung to his. "With you, there can be nothing beyond this moment," she whispered. "I have to finish my assignment ... I have to find Cedric."

Evelyn stepped out of the room. "Beta Vasumen, I'm ready for the rest of the tour."

"Perhaps I'll check on your other patient. The one who no longer requires assistance." Trinity turned on her heel. Evelyn looked at him confused.

Her scent lingered in the air. The memory of her near-death clawed at him. He couldn't let her walk into danger again. The shadows would have to get through him first.

"Trinity, wait and I'll come with you when I've finished showing Evelyn around," he said, torn between going after her or assisting Evelyn while his dragon hissed. *Claim.*

But first, he needed her to trust him.

Nineteen

Hours later, silence blanketed the clinic, broken only by the soft tick of the clock in Conleth's office. Trinity sat by the window, her gaze lost in the fading daylight. She had sent an updated report hours ago, failing to include what she knew about the Vasumen family and their dragon heritage. She owed that much to Conleth. Staring at the mark on her wrist, she leaned her head back and closed her eyes. *He will bring you doom.*

Then why did she want him to claim her? Their last kiss lingered, searing deeper than desire. It had touched her very soul, every fiber of her being still humming with it. She swore she could sense his nearness even now, and as he moved deeper inside the clinic, an invisible cord tugged her to follow.

But she had come here to find Cedric. The ohunko wouldn't stop until it ended her. Was this what her grandfather meant about her doom? All this time she had assumed the dragon would end her. She pressed her fingers to her throat, a shiver crawling up as she remembered Pezi's hands, cold and unyielding, trying to strangle her.

Her phone was in her satchel. She should have called her grandfather, but she couldn't bring herself to hear the disappointment in his voice. She was a tracker. She found people. Except the gift that always led her to them turned on her. And now she was lost without it.

With no witnesses, nothing of his to go on, and her gift reversed, her assignment had just become more complicated. And what trail she found to Cedric had gone cold.

The ohunko kept her distracted from picking up anything new. But she remembered she still had the crystals from the cabin. They were still in her satchel she'd brought along when they left the resort. Thank goodness it hadn't gotten lost when they escaped the underground tomb in the mudslide. She grabbed it from the floor near Conleth's desk and searched for it until she found the cloth. On her knees, she unwrapped the crystals. They winked at her, the opaque chips like oblong diamonds. The rainbow of colors glinted in the fading light from the window.

The crystals pulsed faintly, their edges catching the light. Raw energy shimmered between them, a trap waiting to be sprung.

Trinity recognized the signs. She had studied enough, so she knew she could hold even an ohunko with the right stone.

A long shot, but her only shot.

She placed each crystal carefully, forming a rough circle on the desk. As she worked, a tingling sensation spread through her fingertips, forging a connection to the stones. Power, pure and potent, surged. Circumstances hadn't broken her. She endured. She survived. And now, she would fight.

With a deep breath, she placed her hands in the center of the crystals, fingertips connected to each one. A soft glow emanated from the stones, growing brighter with each passing second. A subtle hum filled the room, vibrations resonating through her body.

A sharp gasp escaped her lips as hot, rippling power surged through her. It unlocked her core, cracking her open from the inside out. Agony and ecstasy warred within her. Her mate mark burned, searing red against her flesh. Fire blazed in her eyes as an overwhelming connection flowed through her veins.

The space before her disappeared. Evelyn stood in an unfamiliar room, listening intently. Another blink brought the crystals back into focus around her hands. Unlike a vision, the burning sensation behind her eyes slowly faded.

Unahu?

The word echoed in her mind. Trinity pressed the heels of her hands to her eyes. Was she imagining it, or had Conleth's voice truly slipped into her thoughts?

She stared down at the crystals again. She knew they amplified the gifts of her people and trapped the spirits of the shifter-bloods. Could they strengthen the connection between mates?

A sudden jolt of adrenaline spiked her pulse. She picked up the larger crystal, bound with thin leather laces, and laid it in her palm, waiting for her blood to sing or her eyes to burn. When nothing happened, she dismissed it, blaming the initial shock of the crystals being together.

But this one. The big one glinted with raw power. She tied it around her neck, tucking the crystal under her blouse. It pulsed, and a deep warmth spread through her blood. An idea formed, but Conleth would return soon. She hadn't thought this through.

He had brought her here to draw the ohunko away from the resort, away from everyone who didn't belong in its path. Even at the clinic, the town surrounded her. No one was safe as long as the ohunko hunted her. She had to lure it out, face it, and trap it before it could strike again.

Urgency propelled her. Trinity gathered the crystals, planning to figure it out as she went. Her grandfather taught her that most targets returned home or to a place of origin. The fur. The campground.

She needed to reach the ohunko before it attacked another innocent person. The spirit needed a host to fulfill its deadly quest.

The crystal against her skin hummed with a different message, urging her toward the darkest part of the mountain forest, the ancient burial grounds.

"I will," she promised. "I'll bury you all there once I save more people from harm."

Trinity moved through the clinic quietly, her senses razor-sharp. The crystal's presence amplified everything, including the crushing need to return to Conleth's side. She forced herself forward, knowing that leaving him could save his life.

Or destroy them both.

Twenty

The halls remained quiet except for soft voices drifting from Shawn's room. Evelyn sat beside his bed, their heads bent together in intimate conversation. Her heart squeezed painfully. It hadn't taken them long to find each other, had it?

Trinity moved through the corridor toward the side exit, holding her breath as her pulse hammered in time with her heart.

The antiseptic in this part of the clinic failed to mask Conleth and his deep woods and ash scent. She breathed in deeply, having memories that sent a tingle of sensation over her body. The mark on her wrist throbbed. She needed to get out, to escape before she spun toward him instead of the door.

Conleth's voice drew her like a moth to a flame, and her pulse hitched. He stood in the main examination room. Through the doorway, the soft overhead light illuminated a couple. She edged closer, the desperate need to see him one more time.

Trinity pressed herself against the doorway, peering through the crack. A young boy, barely older than a toddler, sat on the exam table. His mother explained about her child's night terrors and unexpected fever. She kept an arm around her child, the pitch of her voice revealing her worry.

"There have been reports of a child receiving his spirit animal before the ceremony. Is it possible a shadow spirit is haunting our son?"

"He's too young," Conleth assured the couple. "The boy who received his spirit animal inherited after his father passed recently. Did either of you have night terrors?"

A man's voice acknowledged, "I did, but not until my teens, right before I received my wolf."

Conleth moved, and Trinity lost sight of the whimpering boy.

"That's why we thought maybe it might be a shadow spirit or our son's spirit animal blessing him early," the woman said, the fear and excitement in her voice twisted Trinity's gut.

Uhuna.

That voice. Conleth's voice in her head, spooked her. Trinity stepped back abruptly. If the parents of that little boy thought a shadow spirit was after their son, her chest tightened. She touched a hand to her throat. She needed to ensure that no one else got hurt. Dropping her hand, she headed further down the corridor. Relief washed over her when no one noticed her exiting the building.

The night air felt crisp, carrying the scent of baked goods and grilled meat from the local restaurants. A bittersweet nostalgia struck Trinity as she drove to the campground. The retreating sun cast an ethereal glow over the landscape, painting the sky in hues of orange and purple. She should wait until morning, but by then the ohunko would retreat into darkness again. Shadow spirits thrived in the night.

Everything inside her screamed to turn back, to wait for Conleth. An ache formed in her chest this far away from him. By the time she reached the campground and her campsite, the sun had dipped past the trees. She parked her Rover in the designated area of her site. A chill brushed over her skin, unrelated to the evening's crisp temperature.

Trinity pulled out her cellphone and sent a text to Conleth. It was time for her to leave, time for him to let her do her job. While tightening the laces on her shoes, she collected her thoughts.

The satchel filled with crystals slid beneath the seat. One of them pulsed faintly.

The one she needed.

Morning would have been safer. She should have waited.

The logical part of her mind screamed, but the ohunko needed shadows without a form, and darkness. Every passing minute gave the ohunko greater strength to travel and seek her. With a deep breath, she stepped out of the Rover, the crunch of gravel beneath her feet echoing in the stillness of the empty campsites around her. All except one.

She still needed to hit send on her text to Conleth, how quickly he'd carved a place in her thoughts. Was it the mark or the crystal hanging around her neck? Either way, the urge to scrap this reckless idea and run back to him pulled at her. She'd never been this tethered to anyone. His voice curled through her mind, soft and unmistakable. She blinked hard. No. That couldn't be. Only blood-linked shifters—or fated mates—shared thoughts like that.

Trinity shook her head, trying to keep her wits about her. She shouldn't have let him mark her. *Weak, Trinity.* She bit her lip, knowing he might not receive her text with the bad cell reception here. Her finger paused over a heart emoji, but she didn't want to give him false hope. What did it matter if she told him how much she cared for him?

Once this ended, she wouldn't see him again. She told herself that, even if her chest ached at the thought. Better than making a fool of herself. She'd done that once before, trusted where she shouldn't. She wouldn't do it again.

"It will only make matters worse," she muttered, slipping her phone back into her pocket. Her fingers brushed the crystal resting in the hollow of her chest. She drew a breath, willing it to stir, to prove the pull came from the crystal and not Conleth's mark dragging her back to him.

No reaction.

The crystal lay cold against her skin. Crystals needed a living essence to awaken them, like that of an animal spirit. This crystal remained untouched. Whatever the hunters had planned for it, they'd been saving it for something more powerful than her.

Lucky for her.

The air was crisp, a clean thing, carrying the scent of pine needles and damp earth. A faint wood smoke hung in the air. Trinity reached for a jacket and pulled it on before shutting the door. Someone had moved the picnic table and made a fire recently; the ashes carried a heavy wood scent. She approached the scared tree, pressing her palm to the old wound. Her fingers tingled, but not even a stray hair sparked a memory.

"Be careful," a voice called from the far side of the site. "The bark is sharp. My boy cut his finger on it a few days ago."

Twenty-One

Trinity spun as a man strode over from the neighboring site. Not the same one she glimpsed earlier. This man had claimed the spot with a hulking RV that loomed behind him. Dark hair slicked back over his ears, and his voice carried an easy warmth that jarred against the set of his face. The nose had mended crooked after a break, and scars scored his cheeks, the kind left by old violence that never fully faded.

Of all the campsites, the only one beside hers held another tent. When she'd selected this site, she'd tried to get the one furthest away from people. Since the ohunko left its mark on the tree, Trinity assumed it marked its territory. It would return, or she would have to track its scratches deeper into the woods. Her gaze slid to the man watching her, and a chill pressed close. If the spirit struck, would it sink claws into her or him?

"Thanks for the heads up," she replied, keeping her tone neutral despite the tug twisting at her stomach. "I'll be careful."

She opened the back of her Rover. Supplies from her last trip still filled the space, minus the ruined tent. She folded the seats flat and spread her sleeping bag across.

From the corner of her eye, she caught the man at his campfire. Sparks jumped against the dark while his gaze slid toward her. Their sites pressed too close for her liking. His gaze fell upon the crystal swinging from her neck. Heat prickled under her skin. The shiver that followed ran deep, as if the mountain breathed down her spine.

"You need help setting up your campsite? It's kind of late for pitching a tent." He was closer than she'd realized, abandoning his campfire to stand several feet from her. The soft glow of the flames licked to gain momentum in the fire pit behind him.

Trinity's hands hovered over her blanket, contemplating what to do. She couldn't afford complications. Her plan was ice-thin at best, and this stranger's presence added a new layer of risk. She needed to play this safe, but *safe* wasn't a word she used to ease her twisting stomach. No one was s*afe* until the ohunko no longer hunted her. She'd either be dead, or off this mountain, but the tug for her to return to Conleth told her the latter wasn't an option. And the first didn't appeal to her either.

"No need. I'm sleeping here tonight. Just trying to be comfortable," she said, willing him to turn back to his own site.

Heat flared across the mark on her wrist, sharp enough to drag a breath from her lips. The only protection she wanted came from the bond, and the man who had branded her with his mark.

She couldn't risk pulling others into this. Yet, the campground hummed with more life than she'd expected. For a Tuesday, tents and campers lingered. Shouldn't they have cleared out by now?

She exhaled hard, dropping her chin, and fought to steady the fire racing through her veins. Anger and frustration tangled inside her, hot enough to leave her trembling.

"You're welcome to join us tonight. We've got a campfire, and my buddies got fresh venison steaks grilling over the fire and plenty of beer." The man hung out near the back of her Rover, getting a good view of her rear end.

A growl erupted in her mind. She twisted, glancing about. *Was that the ohunko?* She dug her fist into the blanket.

"You okay?" the man asked, looking in the same direction before his gaze landed back on her chest. She fought the urge to roll her eyes at his lack of decorum.

"Did you hear that?"

He tilted his head. "There's nothing out here but us."

Her stomach twisted. She couldn't decide which threatened her more—the man looming before her or Pezi waiting in the dark. Training or not, she couldn't ignore his size or the way his lewd gaze scraped across her skin. She should move, strike, but a far worse evil out there would find her soon enough.

Get back to the clinic now.

She needed to stop hearing Conleth in her head. Careful to ensure the man didn't see her movements, Trinity slipped the crystal from around her neck and slid it into the inside breast pocket of her jacket before crawling out of the Rover. She breathed a sigh of relief when the man backed away.

"Venison? Beer? What do you say?" He squinted for a moment. His smile fell.

Her whole body urged her to run. Every nerve flared in protest at his nearness. The pull inside her wrenched tighter, and she clenched her teeth until her jaw ached.

She glanced at the growing darkness. *Turn back around, Trinity.* Being alone made her a target. The ohunko might deem her vulnerable and seek her out faster. But she was alert. Her senses attuned, tracking the unnatural presence that clung to the evil spirit who stalked her.

"I didn't think this campground allowed alcohol," she said, closing and locking up her Rover.

The man grinned and shrugged. "Not many campers on this side of the park. You don't have to worry about rangers. What do you say?"

"Sounds tempting." Caution still gnawed at her. An invisible string lassoed around her heart and tugged her to step back. *Come back to me, Uhuna.*

Her mark warmed to the touch. She tugged down her coat sleeve to keep it covered. Even the crystal warmed, resting between her breasts. Trinity glanced around the darkening campground once more, ignoring the voice in her head and blocking the burning sensation of her skin.

The woods pressed in, swallowing the last threads of daylight. If the guardian shadow spirit wanted her, it would not wait long. She prayed the men in the RV kept asleep when the ohunko came hunting.

She should have planned better, thought of bystanders before walking straight into danger.

Yes, now climb back in your Rover and get out of there. Don't make me come after you.

Her grandfather used to shake his head, calling her stubborn with a grimace. She'd prove him right. She always did.

Ignoring the voice in her head, she said, "All right, I'll join you."

She stepped into the circle of firelight. Heat licked her shins, while smoke curled through the air, stinging her eyes. Flames leaped against the men's faces, carving them into lines of orange and shadow. Faces marked with creases that deepened when they laughed. Their ease hummed like an old song, but beneath it, tension coiled tight, the kind that made her pulse skip. One predator recognizing another.

The third sat across the fire. Younger, though not the boy the stranger had called him. His gaze hooked onto her and held. It dragged over her in a slow sweep, bold as a hand pressed too low on her spine.

Her teeth clenched. The fire's heat was nothing compared to the crawl of his stare along her skin.

Another growl, louder this time, vibrated inside her mind. Trinity winced and pressed her arm against her side, not wanting to reveal the mark stinging under the cloth of her jacket. "You gentlemen been here long?"

The men exchanged a brief, imperceptible glance before turning their attention to her. "Little over a week," one of them replied, his eyebrows frowning. "Why?"

"Just curious." They must have slipped in after she left with Conleth. Three men camping longer than a weekend. Why? Did they know it was illegal to hunt in a state forest? She tried to get information first, keeping her tone even. "Seen anything unusual around here?"

"Maybe we should ask you that." The youngest lifted his hand, bandaged fingers catching the firelight. "Never saw a cat scratch a tree that deep."

They are nothing compared to the claws of a dragon. Her stomach twisted sharply, the invisible lasso tugging harder, and she wrapped her arms around her waist, prepared for a physical yank that didn't come. She bit her lip, waiting for the sensation and the voice to pass. Once she captured the ancient guardian's spirit, the crystal would fill with the guardian's shadow spirit and stop projecting her guilt and other feelings for Conleth into her own thoughts and physical sensations.

"The park ranger said the same person had that site all season. That's you, right?" The bearded man beside the younger one leaned forward, his black whiskers darkening in the shadows. "What about you?"

Grateful for the distraction of her traitorous body, she said, "It is. My job takes me back and forth. I can't explain the claw marks. I assumed, like most cats, the wild ones need a scratching post."

"Oh, lady, you have no idea about the wildlife around here," Black Beard chuckled. The man who invited her over eyed her chest again.

Instinctively, she pressed her hand over her heart, feeling the bump of the crystal inside her jacket. "And you have? I am fascinated to hear about your experiences."

"Get the lady a beer, Paul," Black Beard said. "She's gonna need one for the stories we've got."

Trinity dropped into a camp chair within arm's reach of the boyish one, the firelight sharpening the hunger in his gaze. He passed her the open container, and she tried not to wrinkle her nose at the offensive smell. Her heart was a steady beat, thumping faster. Another whisper floated through her mind. *Last time I'm going to ask, Uhuna. Get in your Rover and return to the clinic.*

Yet, a stubborn determination held her in place, or maybe disbelief. They had not fully mated. She couldn't hear him. She knew shifter psychology. Yet, it was almost as if her blood boiled with his anger, flooded with his worry, making it harder to ignore. What if that were Conleth? And as he said, fate had brought them together. Her heart stopped for the longest few beats of her life. When it started again, she sucked in a breath. Conleth and she had a connection. *He will be your doom.* This time it wasn't Conleth's voice in her head, but her grandfather's. She swallowed hard, focusing on the conversation, trying to give her mind the space needed to plan her next move.

A forced smile crept across her lips as she took the tiniest of sips from the proffered drink. Perhaps she could put them at ease, and they would be more inclined to share information once their guards lowered.

True to their word, they shared their venison with her, the meat tender and flavorful. Baked potatoes wrapped in foil and cooked over the embers provided a full meal. The men ate and drank heartily, their laughter echoing through the night. The younger man leaned towards her, taking her empty plate away. "You eat like a bird," he commented with a grin.

Paul, the one who had first spoken to her, leaned back in his chair, his eyes scanning the darkness beyond the firelight. "You're new to this whole camping thing, aren't you?"

"Something like that." She clasped her hands together, unsure what to do with them now that she'd handed over her plate and sat the drink on the ground by her chair.

"Well, let me tell you, there's nothing quite like sleeping under the stars," Paul continued, his gaze drifting towards the sky. "It's a different world out here. A world where you can truly appreciate the beauty and the danger."

"I suppose it is, isn't it?" she said.

"Can't see the stars if you sleep in your vehicle," the young man leaned close to her. "Probably safer that way. You're not afraid of bears, are you?"

"Only the black ones," she laughed with the confession. "They blend into the night."

Paul chuckled, his eyes glinting with a strange light from the fire. "Speaking of bears," he said, taking a darker tone. "There's a story about one that haunts these woods." The campfire crackled, casting eerie shadows across the clearing. Two of the men leaned in. The flickering flames illuminated their faces.

"They say it's a ghost bear," the younger man chimed in.

"Some say it's just a legend, but those who've seen it... well, they don't talk much afterwards," Paul paused, waiting for a reaction. Had she not encountered an ancient guardian spirit out to kill her these past several days, she might have been frightened. For their sakes, she made a frightful face.

"It's said to have red eyes that glow like embers in the dark, and claws as sharp as razor blades," Black Beard said, sending a chill to her bones. Peter as the wolf, the mountain lion that wanted to end her, and if Black Beard spoke true, a bear ohunko still prowled the mountain. Her stomach knotted. Would it find her next?

It's gone. I'm coming. And deep down, she wished he would, the tug inside her becoming almost unbearable.

"Like the marks on the tree over there." The younger man reached for her hands. She jerked them back, rubbing her palms together to shake off a sudden chill.

Her eyes met their unreadable, demanding gaze. Every expectant glance pressed like heat against her skin, waiting to see if she would confirm what they already suspected.

"Those are bear claws?" she asked, even though she knew better.

"They like to mark their territory," Paul leaned forward, his elbows on his thighs. The firelight illuminated his grizzled face. Trinity got to her feet, shoulders stiff, pulse skipping as she edged away from them.

"Don't worry," Black Beard said, his voice softening in a chilling way. "We'll keep an eye on you tonight. Make sure you're safe." By the intensity in his gaze, she doubted that keeping her safe was his main intention.

"We're hunters," the younger man declared, standing up beside her.

"I gathered. Did you shoot the deer we had for supper tonight?" she asked, trying to be polite as she planned to make an exit.

He snickered, and Paul rose to his feet. "I did, but that's not what he's talking about." Paul stared at her. "Go sleep it off, Scout." Paul waved the younger man toward the RV, his gaze still on Trinity.

Almost there.

"Perhaps I should call it a night, too. Thank you for sharing with me this evening," Trinity said, her stomach churning. She moved away, wanting to put as much distance between herself and these men as possible.

Scout's hand clamped around hers, his grip shockingly strong. Her adrenaline spiked. Trinity pressed her other hand over his, stopping him from shoving up her sleeve.

A vision yanked her under.

Darkness spun. The moment ripped away. Scout slipped out the RV's back ramp and tore through her Rover while the other two pinned her, their rough hands searching, demanding the crystal. They dragged her to the scarred tree and tied her there, bait for the animal spirit they believed had carved those gouges. Greed flared inside Scout, hot and ravenous.

"We'll get a hefty price for a strong, gifted spirit animal," he said.

Then the vision shattered. Trinity blinked hard as the world snapped back into focus. Nausea climbed her throat, bile burning.

"I've never seen eyes as pretty as yours," Scout said.

Her heart raced. She took off in a run and slammed straight into Black Beard. Stumbling back, a deafening roar erupted in her head. The sound shook her to her core. Black Beard looked up with confusion etched on his face. The darkness above them shifted to pitch black. Slowly, it took shape, and Trinity inhaled sharply. A massive dragon flew overhead, its dark scales glinting in the moonlight.

She stumbled backward, fingers pressed against her chest, heartbeat hammering. Spinning on her heel, she darted for another path, but Paul moved first. His large hands closed around her arms, firm, stopping her in an instant.

"Running off? The night's just getting started, and we have some unfinished business, pretty lady," he sneered, his grip tightening. She struggled against his ironclad hold, her breath coming in ragged gasps.

Paul's eyes darted towards her neck. Shoving her hand away, he reached beneath her jacket. His fingers closed on empty air. A brief flash of surprise darkened his face, replaced by narrow eyes. "Where is it?" He grabbed her other arm again and gave her a shake. "Where's the crystal?"

"W-what crystal?" Her fingers twitched, and she resisted checking her pocket.

"The one I saw around your neck before you hid it. Where is it?" Paul sneered.

"That's none of your business." Straining against his grip, she raised her knee, but Paul expected the move, their knees colliding as he blocked the blow.

"That's a special type of crystal. Hard to come by," Black Beard said, the words rumbling from deep in his chest, curling like smoke around them.

Scout bolted from the shadows, nose to the sky, fur bristling as the wind carried a distant scent.

Black Beard, grabbed her arms, pulling them behind her back, as Paul let go. She tried to kick him and stomp on Blackbeard's toes with her feet, but the man was built like a bear. He shook her and said, "Keep it up and I'll knock you silly."

Trinity stilled, narrowing her eyes at Paul.

"Now, answer the man." Black Beard yanked back on her arms, and Trinity breathed hard through her nose at the jolt of pain.

"You can tell me where it is or I can find it myself," Paul said, his hands nearing the pockets of her jacket. Trinity sucked in a breath as Paul plunged his hand into a pocket. Coming out empty-handed, he swore. She bit her lip, the pain keeping her focused. She needed to keep them from unzipping her jacket.

"Where is the crystal? Where did you get it?" Black Beard's hot breath against her ear made her turn her face away.

She peered up, hoping to see more signs of the dragon flying overhead. Where had he gone? She needed to stall them. "I know exactly where it is, and I plan to use it. I suspect we're both in the same profession." Or she hoped they'd believe she was.

"This is our territory. We claimed it first," Scout informed her.

Paul's hands moved down, patting her waist, down her hips to the pockets of her hiking pants. He pulled out her keys, and her heart seized. He tossed the keys to Scout. "Go check her vehicle. She probably locked it in there."

The pit of Trinity's stomach fell. They had no intention of letting her go. Scout's vision made that much clearer. They wanted the crystal. Her fingers itched to check, to make sure Paul didn't spot it, but the rest of the crystals lay waiting in the Rover. She tightened her grip, heart hammering, and forced herself to move casually, though every glance at him set her nerves on edge.

Not wanting to make a fuss over her keys and draw their attention more to where she stashed the other crystals, Trinity said, "Apparently this isn't your territory."

The rising panic swelled like a tide ready to take her under.

"As you said, I have this site reserved for the entire season. I was here first. However, I don't see why we can't work something out." He spread his hands, a faint edge in his eyes betraying impatience.

The mention of the reservation caught the attention of the other two hunters. They froze, shoulders taut, eyes flicking to one another before settling back on her. Trinity's stomach tightened. Shadows swallowed their faces. One man blocked the firelight, leaving her guessing at the expressions behind the darkness.

Black Beard huffed from behind her. "How do we know she's not working for him?"

Who were they talking about? Where had Conleth gone? She needed to stop Scout from searching her vehicle and to keep him from discovering the crystals before anyone else got hurt. Especially her.

I will protect you. His words, not hers.

"And who might that be?" she asked. Darkness deepened and blocked the moonlight, causing dread to grab her lungs. Then, the roar echoed through the night; it vibrated to her core. Followed by the faintest voice shouting, "Trinity!"

Her lungs shrank. The dragon circled overhead, drawing closer. He exposed his existence, and soon, others would know his family's secret. They'd hunt him as Pezi hunted her. She needed to keep the hunters distracted.

"If she's not one of Cedric's, then where did she come from?" Black Beard asked.

Cedric. Yes. This might work. She forced a calm exterior. "If you know Cedric, perhaps you might know where I can find him?"

Scout lurched sideways, words tumbling under his breath about always being ordered around. He lifted his head, lips twisting into a sloppy grin. "No one wants to find him," Scout mumbled thickly. "He's probably dead, like the rest of his crew."

Paul ripped the keys back from his hands and barked a sharp order, silencing Scout. "Grab your rifle and keep an eye on the sky."

Surely, they didn't think they could shoot a dragon out of the sky. Paul weighed the keys in his hand.

Trinity's mind raced. "Are you certain? I hoped to join him."

Scout vanished into the RV. A moment later, the door slammed open with a crack that jolted her pulse. He stepped out gripping a rifle, metal gleaming in the firelight.

"Remember what I told you!" Black Beard shouted, then muttered under his breath, "He'll chase that shadow until it turns on him. I should have had him grab another rifle."

Of course, that's why they lingered, unhurried. To them, it was nothing more than a shadow spirit.

Air snagged in her throat, her chest tightening as panic clawed through her ribs. This wasn't in the vision. Had she shifted the outcome somehow? Or overlooked something vital?

"No, I've got a knife in my boot," Paul said, pulling up his pant leg and retrieving said hunting knife. "Let Scout have his fun. I'll search the vehicle while you take care of her."

"I say we tie her to the tree and lure us a powerful spirit. Cedric already has a woman who can trap spirits," Black Beard said.

"Does he have someone who knows how to cut the crystal into pendants?" She swallowed the urge to say more. Not with Scout's bloody future still burning behind her eyes.

They're hunters; you need to get away from them.

"Normally, one of Cedric's men meets me, but they didn't show. If what you say is true, and they're dead. Cedric owes me for the new batch of crystals I have for him. Unless, of course, you gentlemen wish to make the same deal with me." She looked up. No sight of a dragon overhead.

"No deal." Paul used the tip of his knife to lift a tendril of her hair that had fallen around her face. "Turn over the crystals, and we will give you a chance to make replacements. Refuse, and you won't get that chance."

Once they had all the crystals, they wouldn't need her anymore.

Trinity slammed her head back. Black Beard's hold loosened, and she swung her arms out to disarm Paul. The knife flew sideways as she darted away. Black Beard lunged for her, his beefy arms wrapping around her waist as he tackled her. Paul kicked around on the ground trying to find his knife. "I'm done playing games. Tie her to the tree."

Black Beard hauled her to her feet. She blinked as a large hunting knife pressed against her throat. A flash of fury intertwined with her fear. The invisible lasso inside her yanked hard, distracting her from noticing where the knife came from as Black Beard forced her to walk to the tree. She dragged her feet, and the blade cut into her skin. "Get me some rope."

Black Beard shoved her against the tree. The bark bit into her cheek.

Paul headed toward her Rover when a twig snapped in the darkness. Neither man acknowledged it. *Don't be a dragon*, she chanted in her head. *Don't let them see your dragon.* Hugging the tree, she bit her lip as Black Beard searched her jacket pockets a second time. She pressed tighter against the bark trying to keep him from reaching her hidden pocket.

A growl echoed through the woods, a low, menacing rumble. Trinity's breath caught in her throat as she spotted the pack of wolves emerging from the shadows, their eyes glinting in the moonlight. Tears of relief slipped from her eyes. Conleth was here. The tug ceased in her chest; her lungs filled with air. "Conleth!"

The men froze, their heads turning toward the wolves. Conleth stepped out from behind the wolves, his imposing figure naked and bathed in the ethereal glow of the moonlight. His eyes met hers, those red orbs glowing in the darkness and promising his impending wrath.

Trinity lashed back with her heel. Her boot cracked against Black Beard's knee. He grunted, the sound folding into a sickening crunch as he buckled behind her.

"There's one out in the woods. Make sure you find him!" She tore herself from the tree, her body trembling so hard her knees nearly gave. Black Beard lay sprawled in the dirt, face twisted with rage as his hand clawed for her.

A massive wolf crashed into him, slamming him flat. Snarls ripped through the night as the beast bared its teeth inches from his throat.

Trinity edged backward, breath shallow, eyes locked on the glint of those fangs.

Paul sprawled in the dirt, groaning, while two wolves prowled in tight arcs around him. Their eyes gleamed, never leaving their target.

One of them slowed. Muscles rippled beneath its pelt, bones grinding and reshaping with a wet crack. The air thickened with the sound of the shift.

Trinity turned her face aside, heat rushing up her neck. She didn't need to see the details of a man emerging from the beast. She'd already seen enough.

When she risked a glance, the wolf was gone.

Broad-shouldered, Trace stood in its place. The same man who had stepped from the trees by the creek.

"Are you hurt?" A deep voice cut through the chaos. Conleth. He stood in front of her Rover, a few yards away. Tall. Strong. A beautiful specimen of a man. Seeing him was a balm to her soul. Her entire body lit up like fireworks.

"I'm fine." Trinity tried to catch her breath. Her heart pounded in her ears, a rhythm echoing the adrenaline still coursing through her veins. She wanted to run to him, bury her face in his chest and feel his powerful arms around her, but Conleth stared at her. His body stiffened as she approached.

His eyes, usually warm and comforting, were hard and distant. The spirit tattoo over his heart pulsed fiery red, like his eyes.

The mark on her wrist burned in response.

Twenty-Two

SHE HAD DONE IT again. She had put herself in danger.

Conleth watched Trinity as she stood among the subdued hunters, her body trembling slightly despite her apparent composure. The angry red mark on her wrist pulsed. It was like a beacon to his dragon spirit, guiding him to find her.

He admired her stubborn grit, but tonight she had pushed too far. Reckless. Dangerously close to foolish. The PPI had no business sending her out here alone.

Mine.

The word throbbed through him like fire in his blood. His dragon writhed beneath his skin, a storm of fury tangled with raw relief.

As he looked at her, his jaw clenched. His hands balled into fists, the urge to storm over and claim her, to protect her, heating his blood. Conleth's gaze fixed on her. A low growl rumbled in his chest, sending Trace walking in the opposite direction from Trinity.

Conleth waited for her to come to him. His dragon thrummed with approval, energy building under his skin. He straightened, pulling back his shoulders. The urge to snatch her close and drag her out of this cursed place burned through his overworked muscles.

He lowered his chin; his eyes locked on her and her alone. Her damp cheeks and wide eyes were killing him as she stopped just out of reach.

Her body went rigid as if bracing for impact. Slowly, her gaze lifted and met his. "You followed me."

"There is nowhere you can go that I can't find you."

Her gaze fell, and her lips turned down. The hitch in her breath stung him.

The ancient guardian spirit still attacked her, with his mark on her. It didn't honor the old ways. He should have suspected as much. The longer the lost spirits remained trapped in the shadows, the more they forgot their purpose, their heritage.

He pledged her to be his mate. If it wouldn't acknowledge his mark, it would have to honor his claim.

"This place isn't safe for you." Rourke was right when he said it earlier at the clinic. With the ohunko hunting her, she was a magnet for trouble. A moth to a flame.

And he was tired of being a fireman.

Conleth grabbed her arm, muscles coiling with the urge to lift her from the ground and shove her out of reach of those men. Her fear and stubborn defiance hammered through him, pounding like twin drums in his chest. He felt every pulse, every tremor, as if he were living inside her skin.

"Let's go," he ground out, teeth clenched.

Trinity planted her feet, her jaw set. "I can't. I must help take care of this."

Around him, the air crackled with tension. Those moments when he tasted the desperation of her fear made him close to losing control. "Trace and the others can handle it. Two enforcers went after the third guy. This is their territory, *Unahu*, let them do their job."

"But it's my job." She huffed at him. "I'm the PPI agent who was present during the arrest."

"I'm sure they'll be happy to let you do the paperwork," Conleth leveled his stare with hers. "But for now, we're leaving."

If he didn't get her out now, the dragon would claw its way free again, a wildfire coiling under his skin. Every fiber of him screamed with one thought: protect her. Claim her.

She could hold his gaze for as long as she wanted. He wasn't backing down.

"You don't have clothes on," she said.

A bitter smile crept across his lips. The memory of her denying his need to claim her festered like a wound. The need pulsed with every beat of his heart. "I don't need them for where we're going."

Her eyes widened, straining through the storm of violet. Gold flickered at the edge of her vision, almost swallowed by the chaos. "I might have clothes in my vehicle. You flew here. We can take my Rover back to the clinic."

"Get your satchel and what you can fit in it," he said, noting the possessive undercurrent from his dragon. "I'm not taking you back to the clinic."

Panic slammed into her chest, her breath quick and shallow. Go with him? No, not the clinic. Not the resort. She had to stay here. The ohunko would come for her. Better her than anyone else.

A strange pull played with her logic. She wanted to trust him, to believe in the possibility of a future beyond her assignment. But her grandfather's voice, ingrained in her since childhood, reminded her of her destiny. She kept her gaze fixed on a point beyond his shoulder. "Where do you think you're taking me?"

"High on the mountain. You'll be safe there."

She wanted to believe him, but safety wasn't the only thing important here. She wanted a life, one that involved purpose and fulfillment. But her heart also whispered of a different path, a finality she couldn't escape. She'd met the dragon. She'd meet fate. "You can't hide me away forever."

"And I can't let you keep running away to get yourself killed, either!"

"No one asked you to do that." Her eyes narrowed at him as she crossed her arms.

"Your life is with me now, *Unahu*. My dragon is on the verge of losing control again. I won't have a choice if you don't let me take you somewhere safe. The beast within me will take over."

The flashing in his eyes made little zings flutter in her stomach. "I lose track of my mission when you're around. You'll be my doom, and I can't bear to have something happen to you because of me. I need to focus. Do you understand?"

"I think I do," Conleth said.

"Somewhere else then. A place where we can talk and figure this out, not some mountain perch where the altitude is too high to breathe." She guessed he had a nest or lair up there. Most mountain men had cabins. She could manage that for a night or two.

Conleth studied her, eyes dark with concern, admiration threading through the intensity. After a long pause, he nodded. "All right."

Her chest didn't immediately loosen.

"All right?"

"If you refuse to go up the mountain with me, I'll find another place," he said, both a promise, and a threat laced into his words.

Her mind raced through every detail the hunters had shared. Each mark, each story, each warning drew her closer to finding Cedric.

Assuming he still lived.

The ohunko prowled nearby. She sensed its presence pressing like a shadow on her thoughts.

"One of them took my Rover keys."

A low growl rumbled in his chest, and his eyes flashed an angry red. "Which one?"

Trinity swallowed hard, a knot forming in her stomach. Her fingers twitched as she sized up Paul. If this turned into a standoff, she wouldn't stand a chance. "The older one."

"Even better reason for you to come up the mountain with me."

His eyes never left hers. Heat surged through her veins like fire licking under her skin. Her wrist burned, the mark glowing faintly beneath the fabric. She grasped, clutching her arm, heart pounding in protest. Her body trembled with a need she didn't wish to acknowledge. Not here. Not when she endangered them both.

"One of the hunters took Agent Oberlin's keys. Retrieve them, would you?" Conleth asked as a wolf shifter jogged past them, giving them a thumbs up before heading toward the parked vehicle. The hunters slid into the back seat. Several other men shifted and disappeared into the woods.

"You don't have to keep doing that. It's not like we're partners."

She tilted her chin, meeting his smoldering gaze. The thought of spending the night out here with him made her pulse spike, hot and impossible to ignore. It made no sense, yet it did. She closed her eyes, fists tightening at her sides. *Not again.*

Conleth took her wrist, traced her mark with his thumb. "You're right. We're much more than that, *Unahu.*"

A cold ripple rode down her spine, like a blade drawn slow. It curled beneath her skin, awakening a hunger she didn't recognize. Primal. Hers? Trinity pulled her hand away, breaking the connection. "Don't call me that. Whatever it means. Stop."

The night closed in on them. On her.

"*Unahu* means mate. You are my mate, Trinity. When you left, the distance between us drove my dragon mad. Until we are fully bound, you can't go this far away."

His words struck like an arrow, slipping past the walls she had built. A part of her wanted to lean into them, to surrender to the pull inside her that kept tugging her toward him. But behind that pull waited the doom her grandfather had warned her about. If she let go, there would be no stopping the fall.

The abyss yawned beneath her, dark and endless. Her stomach knotted and churned as if trying to climb out of her body. Instinct screamed at her to stop, but there was no ground left to brace against, no place to anchor herself.

Cold coiled in her stomach, sharp and insistent. She couldn't afford to blink, not with the ohunko prowling, not when every instinct screamed that Cedric might already be gone. Still, the work wasn't finished. Trusting her heart over her head had cost her once before.

And now... she slid down the same slope.

A dull ache bloomed beneath her ribs. Too quickly, Conleth had become like air; every breath threaded with him. Heat flared low in her belly, and for a moment she hated herself for it. Logic clawed at her, warning her to stay guarded, but her body trembled, longing for the magnetic pull of him.

First, she had loose ends to tie. Cedric could be dead, or worse, still out there. Her hands itched to move, to act, to make a plan. Failing now wasn't just her failure. Her grandfather's standing, her reputation, everything she had worked for, all balanced on her choices.

Conleth's red eyes had lost their fire, the glow of his dragon spirit had turned into a whisper beneath the surface. She searched the darkening forest for any signs of the runaway hiker or Pezi lurking about.

The moon cast eerie shadows, distorting the landscape, but nothing took shape or whispered in her mind.

"We can't stay here all night. There's a ranger station within a few miles of here. We can spend the night there."

"But you just said…" She searched for the right words. "I thought you understood."

His face blurred into the dark, expression hidden, but the silence between them spoke louder than words. "If you won't let me fly you there, then give me a minute to retrieve your keys, because I'm driving."

"You don't have any clothes on!" she hissed.

"Have it your way," he shrugged. "Flying it is."

Twenty-Three

THE RANGER STATION LOOMED large in the fading twilight, a stark contrast against the surrounding wilderness. His dragon form unraveled in a shimmer of heat and light, leaving behind the man. As they neared, awe prickled across her skin. Her mind buzzed with ideas, each one more daring than the last. Conleth's bare feet padded softly on the stone path.

The station lay in shadow, lit only by the faint glow spilling from one window. Trinity bit her lip as they entered. The heavy wooden door creaked on its hinges. The scent of pine and old wood filled the musty interior. A fireplace dominated one wall, the hearth cold and empty.

Conleth moved inside, all coiled strength and quiet control. Trinity couldn't look away as he crossed the room, eyes sweeping across every shadow. The crack of wood hitting the hearth made her flinch. Steam rose from his hand as fire ignited beneath his palm, creating smoke and flames that cast dancing shadows on the log walls. "Get warm."

He left her in the room while he disappeared down the hall.

Trinity moved closer to the fire. She raked her fingers through her hair, untangling more than just knots. Her pulse hadn't settled since soaring on Conleth's back, the wind slicing past, the ground a blur beneath them. His dragon form still haunted her thoughts. Breathtaking. Terrifying. Maybe it was the altitude. Maybe it was him.

Conleth returned, dumping two bedrolls at his feet, spreading them out beside her. The soft glow of the fire reflected off his wide shoulders and toned muscles down his arms. Trinity's gaze darted away, landing on the bedrolls.

"Are you hungry? We keep some dried food here for emergencies."

She shook her head, keeping her gaze on the bedrolls. Her chest constricted picturing what might have happened if Conleth and the wolf shifters hadn't arrived when they did.

Her hand slipped into the pocket of her jacket, locating the crystal. Still safe. Thoughts of them getting their hands on it sent a chill through her. Once they took care of the ohunko she'd find a way to ensure no more crystals fell in the wrong hands.

The agency trusted Cedric. Would her grandfather or any of the others believe her if she reported what Gwen and the hunters had seen? Naming Gwen meant exposing her crimes and her Fae blood. She had to find another way to uncover the truth, one that didn't drag Gwen, or herself, into the light.

Unless the agency's officials dismissed her as delusional. Her every move risked deepening the shame already clinging to her name. One misstep, and her career, her reputation—her life could unravel. No one would step in. Not for her. And yet, if they believed her, this would mean exposing an infection within the agency, a truth dangerous enough to fracture their foundation. What could drive a trusted agent to trade loyalty for the black market of shifter spirits?

Conleth moved towards the bedrolls, and Trinity's thoughts scattered like leaves in the wind. His muscles flexed beneath bronze skin, the firelight painting him in gold. Heat bloomed in her cheeks, and she glanced away. He didn't seem to notice. He arranged a makeshift pillow from a pile of blankets.

With the fire casting a warm glow, the ranger station became more of a haven than a refuge for them. Conleth held a wrapped blanket around his waist and lowered onto the bedroll. Trinity peeked out from beneath her eyelashes. Conleth tugged on her hand. "Kick off your shoes, *Unahu.*"

Trinity sank beside him, pulse fluttering as the scent of smoke and sweat curled around her. She tugged off her boots, trying not to notice the way the firelight glided on his skin in bronze. When their eyes met, his amber gaze softened, the intensity of his dragon spirit ebbing like a tide. Heat bloomed inside her. For the first time since arriving on the mountain, she didn't feel the need to look over her shoulder.

That scared her more than anything.

He reached out, his fingers gentle as they brushed against her ankle. With a tenderness that surprised her, he massaged her feet. She tilted her head, bewildered. "Conleth."

The pressure sank into her muscles, kneading away the tension of the day. She closed her eyes, letting the sensation wash over her.

"You're tired," he murmured. "You shouldn't have tried going out alone. If not for letting me mark you, I might never have found you in time, and those hunters..." His growl deepened, eyes flashing red.

She swallowed, muscles heavy, nerves pulsing with fatigue.

"Let's not do this," she murmured, the weight of exhaustion pressing behind her eyes. She'd rushed in without thinking, reckless, and didn't need any more reminders. What kind of agent needed saving? She chewed on her bottom lip, letting silence speak for her. One wrong word, and the fragile control she'd pieced together would shatter.

"Tell me about this plan you think I may have ruined," he said, tracing patterns on her foot with his thumb.

Her heart skipped a beat. She hadn't realized how much his presence would ease the ache inside her. In this moment, with him taking care of her, she reached a new decision. One that if she died, she wouldn't regret. "I went back to my campsite to wait for the *ohunko*. It wants me. If it finds me alone, it can't hurt anyone else."

"It can hurt you."

"It threw you across a room." Trinity's heart ached. She'd put him in danger. If the ohunko set more traps, she would have to stay one step ahead or die. Her pulse thudded against her ribs. "You carry a dragon spirit, and it came after you."

"The ancient guardians have lost their honor to the shadows," he admitted, his fingers pausing in their ministrations. "They don't recognize the authority of my dragon, or even the mate mark upon you."

She believed him. *Wanted* to believe him. "You believed if you marked me, I'd let you claim me."

His hand stilled, his eyes locking onto hers. "Eventually, I hoped you'd consent for me to claim you. You heard my thoughts at the campground. You can no longer deny we're fated."

"And what if we are?"

Doom. She licked her lips, ignoring the whisper of her fear.

"I can protect you, but you must consent to allow me to claim you. Become my mate fully, Trinity. No ohunko or any other shadow spirit will try to harm you."

How could she trust him? The idea of claiming—of giving herself over to him completely—was like stepping off a cliff, blind to what waited below. Yet, the ache in her chest begged her to leap. She swallowed hard, forcing the words past the knot in her throat. "I told you that can't happen."

"You feel this between us. At the campsite, you admitted it."

She had let her guard slip, leaving herself exposed. Her stomach twisted with the memory, and a spike of unease coiled low. She wasn't ready to meet the doom her grandfather's prophecy promised.

"Claiming is like marriage to shifters," she said, trying to regain her sanity.

"It's more, *Unahu*, it's an unbreakable bond for the rest of our lives. There never was and there never will be anyone else for me but you."

Her heart stuttered, and she blinked away the rising moisture in her eyes. "And if I am gone, you'll become like Aluk? Your dragon will become dark and feral inside?"

His eyes darkened to a depth she hadn't seen before. "Aluk manages to hold his spirit within; perhaps it's the strength that made him alpha, but in losing you, my spirit wouldn't go feral, it would tear out my soul and crush my heart."

His hand retreated from her foot. Trinity leaned in, breath catching as the space between them vanished. His heat curled around her, dizzying. Dangerous. She didn't want to move away. *What if they both died? If he died? In trying to protect her, would she cause his death?* He cupped her face. "You don't need to worry about me, *Unahu*. Nothing is going to happen to you. I've always got you. Have you not learned that yet?"

A tear slipped down her cheek.

"I'm going to die," she whispered.

His grip tightened, his thumb brushing away the tear.

"We all do. With life comes death, but neither of us is dying anytime soon," he promised, scooting closer, wrapping his arms around her and giving her a sense of peace and rightness she hadn't ever experienced settle inside her.

Danger still lingered. The curse threatened to crush them, but she sank against him, muscles relaxing for the first time in hours. His arms wrapped around her, and she let herself breathe, let herself love him. The walls around her heart crumbled quietly, brick by brick, in the glow of his presence.

She'd never make it off the mountain alive with Pezi hunting her and the curse chasing after them. But she'd finally found the one place she didn't mind staying forever. In his arms.

She took a breath, absorbing everything about him—the sound of his heart, the heat of his touch, his scent. Her body pressed against him, heart hammering in a rhythm she wanted to memorize. Every second counted, each inhale and heartbeat seared into her memory as if this might be the last time she felt the steady strength of his arms around her.

Her grandfather's prophecy loomed in her mind, casting an icy pall over the moment. She pushed it away and moved on top of him, straddling him. He slipped his fingers between hers and raised her hand, tugging so she leaned over him.

Trinity smiled as she kissed his lips. "Claim me."

His eyes flared red, the dragon rising behind him. For a heartbeat, the beast flickered across his face. Heat radiated from him, seeping into her skin. As he lowered their hands, his grip tightened, his touch possessive. She watched as he placed her marked wrist against the intricate dragon tattoo over his heart. "Promise me. Make me a vow."

"By moon and star, by earth and sky, we bind our souls—mine to yours. With blood and vine, our hearts entwined, a love so pure, a bond defined," she said breathlessly with a soft laugh. "Say it with me?"

"That's a Fae binding spell," he said.

"Yes, do you know it?" Few did, but her grandfather whispered those same words to her grandmother, the ones her parents shared under the moonlight. Only a few outside their people knew this vow.

Conleth called it a spell.

The knowledge thrummed through her, heavy and precious, binding her closer to him.

"My dragon does." He lowered his chin, his eyes locked with hers. The ancient words rolled off his tongue with ease. Her heart pounded, leaped, as she joined him, repeating them word for word. Her heartbeat slowed, matching the one she felt beneath her palm. The mark heated, not unpleasantly so. A gust of joy breezed through her body. He kissed her. The world narrowed to the press of his lips and the thunder of her heartbeat.

Light shimmered in the air, golden and gentle, wrapping around them as if the mountain itself bore witness to their vow.

Ceremoniously, he lifted her hand from his heart and kissed her fingers one at a time. His touch stirred her body to life. His voice replaced any lingering second thoughts or resistance inside her mind. *Mine.*

"Yours," she whispered, hearing his dragon spirit.

The world beyond their haven blurred. Wrapped in each other's arms, they breathed as one. In the silence that followed, their hearts settled. They sought solace in each other's embrace, and in the quiet aftermath, their hearts raced as one, content and bonded at last.

As dawn approached, they lay entwined, their souls still connected by an invisible thread. Conleth's dragon hummed, and for the first time in his life, contentment washed over him in overwhelming bliss.

The first rays of sunlight painted the ranger station in hues of gold and amber. Trinity stirred in his arms, her soft breaths a comforting rhythm against his chest. He adjusted his position, pulling her closer, relishing the feel of her body against him.

Taran grumbled when Conleth informed him that the ranger station near the state park was off-limits for the morning. His younger brother needed a reminder of the time when Taran and Gwen also sought refuge in this same ranger station.

Conleth's dragon went rigid, sensing a presence that didn't belong. The morning air carried an ancient scent. Strange. Cold. His spirit recoiled.

Trinity's eyes flew open, tension rippling through her frame.

Footsteps approached from the stone path outside. The doorknob turned slowly, then the door swung open, revealing a silhouette stark against the morning light.

"I told Taran. No one here until afternoon." His gaze locked onto the intruder, his body tensed, expecting a ranger to report for duty or finish their patrol shift.

Trinity placed a hand on his arm, fingers trembling, her face pale and her eyes locked on the newcomer. Gazing down, Conleth saw the catalyst of vulnerability in his mate that ignited his dragon to press forward. He inhaled, tasted the bitter alien tang of inhumanity. His senses flared, expecting the ohunko, but this presence pressed against him, deliberate and familiar in its menace.

Trinity pulled up her blanket, a futile attempt at modesty. Lifting her chin, she said, "Grandfather."

The scent of Fae hit him, sharp and ancient, around the old man. The power in the air set his teeth on edge and made his pulse tighten.

The older man stepped into the room. He appeared to be in his late forties. The Fae-bloods held on to their youth far longer than shifter bloods. A tall man, with a regal bearing that hinted at centuries of power. His piercing blue eyes scanned the room, landing on Trinity and then Conleth. Disapproval passed across his face. "I felt the moment your bond completed. I gave you time to finish your business before interrupting. How considerate of me."

"Grandfather," Trinity repeated, pulling the blanket closer around her, her cheeks flushing.

You have nothing to be ashamed of, Unahu. We are mated. He is the one intruding on us. Trinity's confusion rippled through their bond.

Conleth's nostrils flared as the old man's scent hit him again: ancient Fae magic laced with something darker that made his dragon writhe. His jaw clenched, fangs pressing against his gums; aching to drop. The dragon clawed at his skin. *Shield her.* His fists trembled, but he didn't reach for her.

Conleth took a step forward, positioning himself as a barrier. "You need to step out and allow my mate a moment."

The older man's eyes narrowed, the blue turning violet, almost like Trinity's. He ignored Conleth, his gaze fixed on the trembling woman huddled beneath their blankets. "I see you're still alive. And you've found the dragon. Well, at least you've done one thing right," he sneered.

Must protect!

Conleth tensed, ready to strike, but he held back. One wrong move with an older Fae male could spark a storm, and he wouldn't risk it. His mate already trembled.

"You'll leave now," Conleth said, stepping in front of Trinity, blocking her from her grandfather's view. "I'm Conleth Vasumen. Or as you said, 'the dragon'."

The old man frowned, silver hair cascading over his shoulders. His pale skin, almost translucent, highlighted his angular cheekbones. His strong jawline gave him an otherworldly presence. Conleth's skin prickled at the aura radiating from him. Those deep, unyielding eyes carried centuries of experience, daring him to misstep even as they fascinated him.

He moved with a grace that didn't belong to the mortal world. The surrounding air shimmered, carrying a tension that made the hairs on Conleth's arms stand on end. Every step radiated a calm power that pressed against his instincts, alerting his dragon even before he could name the threat.

This was his mate's grandfather?

Trinity scrambled to grab her clothes and wiggled under the blankets to dress.

Her grandfather stood before them in a deep green suit, adorned with intricate silver embroidery. In his hand, a cane rested beneath his palm, the curved handle covered with the small scales of a dragon's underbelly, and the rod made of dragon bone.

Dragon bone. His dragon snarled with recognition, its rage carrying echoes of an ancient betrayal Conleth didn't understand.

Fear emanated from Trinity.

Don't be afraid, Unahu. He tried to calm her while keeping his dragon contained, but this time he couldn't cage his beast.

If we shift and attack, *it will harm our mate.*

That kept his dragon at bay, though he could feel it thrashing beneath his thoughts, claws scraping at the edges of his mind. Every pulse of its impatience pressed against his temples, making it hard to focus.

Trinity's grandfather's gaze dropped to the cane, his fingers curling over the carved bone. A thin smile curved his lips, but his eyes stayed cold. "You like it? I took it from the dragon myself."

Dragon killer!

Conleth's blood chilled. His dragon surged, claws raking at the inside of his skin.

Trinity's hand anchored him, but the shiver climbing his spine betrayed the rage boiling beneath. He ground his teeth, fighting the itch of scales threatening to break through his arms.

Conleth tugged Trinity to her feet. She stood in wrinkled clothes, while his bare chest displayed the burning tattoo of his dragon spirit.

"What are you doing here?" Trinity asked, stepping in front of Conleth.

Her grandfather lifted his eyebrows. "No introduction? After all, you've *mated* him, haven't you?"

Her grandfather spat the word like it burned his tongue. Conleth stepped forward, his body sliding between Trinity and the old man with quiet finality. His shoulders locked, breath shallow, while his dragon pushed at the seam of his soul. He wouldn't allow his mate to stand within reach of this vile man.

Her palm pressed against his chest, steadying him as she edged to his side. She angled her body to shield his nudity. Conleth doubted modesty offended the Fae, but he liked that her nearness unsettled the Fae man.

"Conleth Vasumen, this is my grandfather, Aerion Oberlin, head of the PPI."

"Director?" Conleth hadn't anticipated that. A higher-up, yes, but not the head of it. Of course, it didn't surprise him to find a Fae in charge of matters concerning his people.

His dragon roared inside his head.

Aerion winced, reaching up to wiggle a finger in his ear as if he'd heard it.

"It seems someone gave me incorrect information about many things," Aerion continued as if Conleth hadn't spoken. "I received a report of another death. This time a woman. I thought it was you,

Trinity." His words cut like frost. "Instead, I find you on the floor with one of them."

His eyes narrowed. His gaze swept from Trinity to Conleth. He didn't at all appear like a man grieving or worried about the loss of his granddaughter.

The color drained from Trinity's face. "How did you find us?"

A glint of amusement twinkled in Aerion's eyes. "I placed a ward on you years ago when I first took you in. Your communication has been brief and infrequent. Then I sensed a change in you and came right away. I can see now what caused it. You've bonded with a dragon-blood."

"Ward? You never told me about any ward."

"For your own protection, I assure you. I couldn't risk losing track of you."

Get dressed! Finally, a thought from her, and it's about his lack of wearing pants.

When he's gone.

You're offending him. She grabbed a blanket from behind her and tossed it around his hips. He caught her hands, his touch feather-light but firm. Her gaze met his, stormy with unspoken fear. He smiled, trying to assure her.

"Isn't that cute? You two have a telepathic connection," Aerion said.

Conleth's dragon spirit bristled at the old Fae's smug tone. He stepped forward, shielding Trinity with his body.

"Come with me, Trinity," Aerion said. "It would seem it's up to me to clean up your mess again."

"Mess? I've been doing my job, investigating—"

"Your bonding with him changes everything, Trinity. You're no longer just a PPI agent-you've mated a shifter. That makes you a security risk, and a liability I can't afford."

Trinity's face paled. Her gaze flickered between Conleth and her grandfather.

"Didn't I warn you?" Aerion said in her silence.

Security risk? Conleth's dragon spirit snarled at the insult. She wasn't a liability. She was his mate. Under his protection. Yet, the old Fae spoke of her like a misfiring weapon, an asset to be managed rather than a person with her own choices. Conleth's right eye twitched. His dragon spirit burned behind his vision. This man had raised her, claimed to care about her, yet spoke of her like a broken tool.

"She's not going anywhere with you. Compromised or not." Conleth glared over her shoulder at Aerion. "We'll meet you at my clinic in town. You came because a woman is dead. I wouldn't want you to be disappointed."

Aerion's brows arched, as if the very air had dared to offend him.

Trinity's shoulders stiffened; her body tensed.

Conleth squeezed her wrist reassuringly. *He's not going to hurt you. I won't let him.*

"So be it." Aerion tapped his cane on the floor. "You'd best not keep me waiting. And Trinity?"

She turned her head to look at him. "Yes, grandfather?"

"I meant what I said. Nothing has changed."

Twenty-Four

THE ACHE IN HER body was nothing compared to the jolt in her chest seeing her grandfather. His presence inside the clinic sent her heart skittering. Thoughts collided in her head, each one louder than the last. Her mouth opened, then closed. Again. Too many thoughts. She didn't know where to start, and how much to divulge.

He stood with his arms behind his back and swinging his cane.

"I apologize for having kept you waiting, grandfather."

An older woman with graying hair sat in the reception area. She looked up as Trinity drew closer. "Welcome. I'm Anita. How are you?"

Anita's gaze lifted at Conleth's entrance behind Trinity, and she grinned. "Beta Vasumen, Chief Rourke sent me. Evelyn said to tell you she's currently occupied for the afternoon."

"At least that makes one of us," Conleth grumbled, having found a spare pair of cargo pants and a t-shirt at the ranger station. The cloth pulled taunt across his chest, and Trinity had to force herself to look away.

Her grandfather cleared his throat.

"The body is this way," Conleth directed them toward the far exam room down the corridor.

Trinity came to an abrupt stop.

Conleth glanced at her, and she tilted her head toward her grandfather. *We should let him go first.*

Conleth's eyes narrowed. Red flecks bled into the amber.

He's my grandfather. He's the only family I have left.

Conleth stepped back. He lifted his chin. "Last room on the right."

Her grandfather walked past them; cane tapping against the floor.

She leaned against Conleth, his muscles taut beneath her touch. He hadn't said a word, but the strain of letting her grandfather take the lead yanked on the bond between them.

Inside the room, Conleth stepped past her to the place where they had left the body. Cool air brushed her cheeks, a welcome contrast to the heat still clinging to her skin. Trinity exhaled slowly, letting the chill settle her nerves.

"A guardian spirit killed this one?" Her grandfather peered down his nose at the body.

"Yes," Conleth confirmed, holding back the sheet.

Aerion nodded, and Conleth covered the woman's face again. "Mountain lion or wolf?"

"Mountain Lion," Trinity said. "It also attacked an employee at the resort while possessing the woman."

"And you're unharmed." Aerion tapped his cane, not asking a question. He waved his hand for her to follow him out. "I assume your mate has things to occupy him? Although I don't suppose you treat many illnesses or injuries. From the lack of staff and empty rooms, I presume this is a women's clinic?"

Her grandfather's scoff at the clinic didn't surprise her. He never missed a chance to remind his staff how far they fell short of his standards. She opened her mouth to defend the clinic and Conleth, but the words caught, brittle and useless, on her tongue.

Conleth walked around the body, wrapping his arm around Trinity's shoulders. "With the mountain open to outsiders, a clinic is a necessary resource. We plan to dedicate a portion to a birthing center here for our residents, but our current midwife makes house calls."

"Cedric didn't complete the paperwork to keep the mountain closed to outsiders. Because of the circumstances, re-closing the borders might be best, don't you think, Grandfather?"

"Request noted." Aerion pulled a timepiece from inside his suit jacket. "Although our people have had to learn to adapt to blending in with the outside world for decades. I don't believe that exposing fresh blood to the mountain is beneficial. This is the third death in less than two weeks, correct?"

"Not counting the ones prior. Chief Blackwood would have reported those," Conleth said.

"I've spoken with Rourke, and other members of his team. They are aware of the situation and have regular patrols out to watch for the ohunko causing these deaths," Trinity added.

"What are you planning to do about the *ohunko*?" Aerion asked, heading for the door.

Her responsibilities clung to her like a second skin. "I've returned to the place I first sensed it but encountered spirit hunters. I planned to return there again, try to flush it out. With help." She looked at Conleth, his eyes hooded, not helping her focus on proving to her grandfather she hadn't gotten distracted and forgotten her post. "I believe it will come for me."

"Yes," Aerion said, pausing at the door.

His eyebrows rose.

Trinity took off behind him with Conleth at her heels. *Let him see himself out. We need to discuss this idea of yours.*

Trinity moved faster to follow her grandfather's retreating figure. *I need to talk to my grandfather first.*

She had a duty to her grandfather. Doomed or not, her grandfather's standing in the PPI depended on her finding Cedric. He vouched for her, putting his position on the line for her. Without him, she didn't know where she'd have ended up. Torn between her mate and duty, Trinity followed her grandfather down the hall. Conleth had his brothers, and all she ever had was her grandfather.

Near the reception area, Aerion spun the dragon bone cane in his hand, waiting for her to catch up. "Trinity, come. Surely, there is a place to find a good cup of tea in this town."

Conleth growled behind her, making her legs weaken.

"Mountaintop Bakery is on Main Street. She opened a few months ago," Anita offered, looking pleased with her recommendation. "Beta Vasumen, the funeral director from Annette Island called, their transport should arrive in the next fifteen."

Conleth scowled at the receptionist.

"Stay here and take care of it. You can meet us at the bakery when you're done." Trinity stood on her toes as she noticed her grandfather's unamused gaze. Ignoring the flutter of nerves, she kissed Conleth softly. Her lips lingered for a beat before pulling away.

Conleth grasped Trinity's hand. He lowered his chin, brushed his thumb across her knuckles and then released her. She had an hour to debrief with her grandfather. How did she know that? But she did and accepted it for what it was. "Thank you for giving me some time with my grandfather."

Conleth looked at Aerion. "I won't be long."

"I'll grab you a coffee, just the way you like it," she grinned. "Black with the tiniest hint of cream."

Conleth's brow rose. Wait. How did she know how he liked his coffee?

Like his woman, all business with a hint of sweetness.

Her lips parted, and he winked at her.

"No worries, dragon, I have no intention of taking Trinity from the mountain."

Jazz played softly on the radio, but it couldn't smooth the silence between them as the bakery drew closer. Trinity's palms grew sweaty at the prospect of spending time alone with her grandfather. She knew him well enough to know she'd disappointed him.

They found the Mountaintop Bakery at the end of Main Street, true to Anita's directions.

Its rustic wooden shelves overflowed with pastries and cakes, creating a tempting selection. Today, however, the sugary confections seemed to blur together in a dizzying kaleidoscope.

"Shall we sit by the windows?" she asked, waiting patiently for her grandfather to decide.

The bakery's large windows offered a breathtaking panoramic view of the park and the mountains beyond. He moved to the area near the windows and waited while she ordered them tea and scones. A group of people sat in the far corner, their laughter and chatter a stark contrast to the growing unease in Trinity's chest. A young woman engrossed in her laptop sat alone at one of the round tables, a half-eaten slice of lemon cake forgotten. The peaceful ambiance of the bakery slipped away as she glanced around the room. What if the ohunko followed her here? Were any of these people possibly possessed?

In less than an hour, she'd leave again to a place with few to no people. She tapped her fingers on the counter, waiting for their order. Several minutes later, she joined her grandfather. The barista was kind enough to carry the scones to their table. Seeing her grandfather in one of his many suits, she glanced down at her wrinkled blouse and tried to smooth it down. From last night to this morning, she didn't have much time for straightening her appearance.

"I'm sorry you had to come all the way out here. I would have sent another report this morning." She wrapped her hands around the mug, watching the steam rise from the peppermint tea she had ordered, hoping it would help soothe her nerves.

"You understand, I gave you one task. I chose you specifically for this task." Her grandfather lifted a small orange scone and inspected it before taking a bite. She waited, watched, and his expression didn't change. She hoped the pastries would be a welcome distraction, perhaps enough to lighten his mood. A small part of her clung to the memory of how much he enjoyed the maple ones from back home.

"I know you warned me about dragons. Perhaps doom doesn't mean my death. Conleth protects me." Inwardly, she cringed, awaiting his correction.

His eyes narrowed, with a dark glint in them. "Then you should not have allowed the beast to claim you."

"I'm a grown woman."

A snort escaped him. "A grown woman who is a sacrifice. Do you truly believe your name is a coincidence?" His voice dropped to a menacing whisper. "What do you think your name means?"

Fear, like a chilly hand, gripped her throat. "I... I don't know. You've always called me Trinity when others have called me Lena."

"Your birth mother called you Lena, a name of innocence. But you, Trinity, are third in your family's succession. Whose blood do you think sealed this curse on the shifter-bloods, child?"

Her heart stuttered along with her words. "It w-was a w-war. History t-ells us many lost their l-lives on the m-mountain that day. The shifter bloods imprisoned our queen in the mountain to prevent her from uniting with the dragon alpha. They didn't want to share the mountain, and the union would have granted us access to the land."

"Selfish beasts. They brought the curse upon themselves." Her grandfather drank his tea and went on as if sharing recent gossip. "Beasts are not intellectual beings as we are, Trinity. They're territorial and dangerous unless contained."

"These are people, grandfather," Trinity lowered her voice. "You speak of them as if they're animals." Her gaze sought the shadowed corners of the room. "No one deserves to be cut off from their heritage. And there are hunters trying to steal their gifts from the Great Hunter."

His face hardened, his eyes narrowing. "They stole from us."

"Isn't a couple of centuries of punishment enough? The shadow spirits exist because their bloodlines are dwindling. Children are born with their inherited abilities. The woman can't inherit at all."

"We did them a favor by taking away their ability to shift at birth." Her grandfather picked up his tea and drank, his voice as cold as the brew.

Heat flared in Trinity's chest.

"A favor?" she snapped. "Robbing them of their birthright?" Her voice climbed with fury. "We are no better than the hunters, Grandfather."

His eyes flashed, with a dangerous glint in them. "It is our duty to restore the balance and take back what is ours."

"At what cost?" she demanded.

"You." His reply was cold. Calculated.

Air caught in her throat. She sat back, the words knocking the breath from her lungs.

Trinity? Conleth's voice, a comforting anchor, reached out to her, but she couldn't grasp it. Couldn't hold on to anything, except her grandfather saying, *you*. Conleth, the ohunko, and her. All three of them were connected.

She stared down at her hands, wishing for the first time in her life for the ability to look into her future. Or to read Conleth's.

Aerion smiled sadly. "Three in one, Trinity. You're the door, the key, and the lock to free our queen. You must follow your destiny."

Her world fell apart.

Piece by piece, as her grandfather recited the prophecy she'd heard all her life. "Deep within the mountain she waits, sealed by an oath, bound by betrayal, and marked by a blood vow. With each pulse, she feeds from the earth, her power pulsing through the mountain, but the seal weakens. The vessel must awaken, or our people will no longer find their gifts." He paused, then added, "You are the vessel, Trinity. When the time comes, your body will open the gate, and the queen shall rise and reclaim the gifts stolen from us."

Trinity closed her eyes, the world spinning dizzily around her.

Her grandfather's voice sliced through the fog of her mind. "Perhaps I should have been blunter, but I doubted you would embrace your true mission. Forget about finding Cedric. I've assumed him dead for several weeks now, or one would hope after his failure to keep others off our mountain. It matters not; you're still alive, and now all can be righted."

A wave of nausea washed over her.

She clutched the crystal beneath her blouse.

Her grandfather's smile widened. His gaze dropped to her hand. "I see you've found some of the aetherium crystal shards on your search for Cedric. You'll give me the crystal and tell me where I can find the others."

He held out his hand.

Her heart pounded a frantic rhythm against her ribs. He thought her dead upon his arrival. Now, he wanted the crystals. A bitter laugh threatened to escape her lips.

She swallowed the laugh, pushing it down, forcing a calm facade.

She trusted him. He was her grandfather, the man who shaped her world.

Yet the truth slithered through her mind, wrapping thorns around her heart. He'd always known. Every night after the soothing cadence of his stories, his fingers would trace her cheek and whisper, "One day, my child, you shall meet a dragon, and he will be your doom. But for the rest of us, we shall rise from the ashes."

Piece by piece, the constructed walls of her composure threatened to crumble, and she held on to them for dear life. "It's my fault they fell into the hunter's hands," she choked out. "I'd like to see them delivered back to the archives personally."

"That's hardly likely since you won't be leaving this mountain." His words landed like icy daggers, piercing through her walls.

Her breath hitched. "You're taking me off the assignment? What about your position? You said...." Her voice trailed off, afraid to finish.

"I said if you failed this time, the consequences would cost me dearly. I took responsibility for you and brought you into my home. I provided you with a good life and prepared you for this day. You owe me. And if you care about that dragon of yours, you'll march up on that mountain and give yourself over to your queen before anyone else gets hurt. No one can save you or take your place."

"What does Conleth have to do with all this?"

"Does the ohunko not hunt you? Marked by a blood vow."

"You said a dragon would be my doom."

"Lucky for us, there is still time. He marked you, making it easier for the ohunko to hunt you."

"You only came because you thought I was dead."

"There will only ever be one of you, Trinity. Do you understand how important this is? How long our people have waited. How long *I've* waited?"

Her mind raced, trying to cling to the only shred of truth remaining. "You're my last living relative. I thought you cared about me. You kept me protected all this time..."

"We are of no relation, child." His lips curved in a grim frown. "Your parents live. They have sons appointed to positions within the court to make up for their only daughter's sacrifice."

The tea in her stomach soured. "My parents are alive?"

She had brothers.

Her heart constricted for the people she had never met. The ones who traded her for a better life for themselves. She'd been their only daughter. The third born into their bloodline in all those years—all those decades. Centuries.

"You're not my grandfather?"

"Come now, Trinity, have I ever treated you like anything more than my ward?"

"A ward." She was nothing more to him than a ward. They weren't blood relatives.

"I admit, your father's estate is grander than mine. It comes with having royal blood, but what the king gives he can take away." His eyes held cruel satisfaction.

"I have royal blood," she whispered, a shockwave going through her.

Aerion fixed his stare on her and held his hand out. "The crystal. Give it to me. You won't be needing it to complete your task."

Suddenly, her throat went dry. She glanced down at the half cup of tea, the warmth of the mug comforting against her trembling hands.

A wave of heat pressed in on her, threatening to consume her. She squeezed her eyes shut, trying to quell the invasion, but it only intensified. If Aerion wanted the crystal, he could take it from her lifeless body.

She opened her eyes; her gaze locked with his. Aerion curled his fingers impatiently for the crystal.

"Trinity," he coaxed, and she shook her head. To move, to speak would let down her walls as she barely held it together.

Inside her, anger simmered, not hers, but Conleth's.

Her mark grew warm against her skin.

"Very well. Keep it for now. I'll expect the others by the end of the day. That should be enough time for you to finish your affairs and say goodbye to your mate." He pulled back his hand, finishing his tea, the cruelness of his gaze still there.

A strange calm washed over her. A sense of inevitability. The words formed in her mind, a whisper echoing the cruel satisfaction in Aerion's eyes.

Say goodbye, she thought, the bitter laugh finally escaping before she could suppress it.

"If you care at all for the dragon, you'll stop letting him keep you from your destiny. It was never his place to save you. If you do not surrender your life to the queen, finding Cedric Kelly or a few dead bodies from hikers will be the least of your problems." Aerion rose.

As he turned to leave, she caught the glint of triumph in his eyes.

"Embrace your destiny and release your soul," he murmured.

A chill raced over her skin as the truth clicked into place. What he wanted from her was unthinkable, yet beneath the fear, something darker stirred. A thrill. A darker promise of purpose unlocked in her mind.

The moment he stepped out of sight, the compulsion gripped her like a vise. The walls closed in around her, the air thinning. She gulped for breath, but it barely reached her lungs.

Hot tears stung her eyes. She knew what had to be done. Not Conleth. Not fear. Not even her own heart could stop her now.

Time blurred. She hadn't heard him approaching.

Conleth crouched beside her. "What did your grandfather say to you?"

"He's not my grandfather."

Twenty-Five

THE BAKERY SWIRLED WITH patrons and chattering teens, but Conleth's gaze stayed locked on Trinity. She hunched over the small table, shoulders tight, her trembling hands betraying her. Laughter and murmurs surrounded them. Seeing her like this shredded him inside. She sat frozen, eyes flooded with tears, breath shallow. Fire lit at his fingertips.

He shook his hands to douse the flames.

The ohunko. Aerion. Anyone who had a hand in this—he would burn them all. But not now. Not yet. Right now, she needed him. That alone quelled the fire in his veins and quieted his dragon spirit's rage.

Conleth crossed the distance inside the bakery and crouched beside her. "What did your grandfather say to you?"

"He's not my grandfather."

Conleth pulled her off the chair and into his embrace. Trinity's body stiffened at first, but then she relaxed against him. His shirt muffled her sobs. He held her tightly, his chest caving with her despair.

He scanned the shop, her grandfather now nowhere in sight. Several patrons glanced away, not wanting to be caught. He narrowed his gaze and finished his search. His jaw clenched and unclenched. Trinity soaked his shirt with her tears.

"It's okay," he murmured, stroking her hair. "You're safe now."

She pulled back slightly, her eyes red and swollen.

"Where did he go?" Conleth asked.

She shook her head; her gaze lifting to his. "He left, but I don't think he'll leave the mountain until I'm dead. Then he'll come wanting to collect the crystals we found."

Conleth's blood ran cold. "I'll kill him first."

"You can't." She gripped his shirt, her gaze lowering. "It matters not anymore. If not Pezi, then they'll send someone else."

"Who?"

"Everyone just wants me to die."

"Trinity."

"Once I'm dead, you'll be safe." She took a deep breath and gazed up at him again. "I'm sorry. With my death, the queen will reign again."

"What are you talking about?" A string of curses ripped from him, each more vicious than the last.

The bakery fell silent. Whispers died, cutlery froze mid-air, and every eye turned to him. He held in the last curse on his tongue.

"Come with me. We need to go somewhere more private."

"What about your coffee?" she asked, sniffling, reaching for her mug.

"The only thing I need right now is my mate safe in my arms." If she didn't move to walk out of there with him, he would carry her out.

He didn't need her to explain her encounter with her grandfather. He read her like an open book, replaying the conversation on repeat in her head for him to hear through their connection.

His dragon spirit snarled, coiling around his chest. *We must hunt him down.*

We take care of our mate first. Conleth slid a hand along her back and led her from the bakery. Outside, the sun's heat did nothing to calm the fire beneath his skin.

Conleth placed his hand on her thigh as he drove back to the clinic. "We'll figure this out," he promised.

Back at his office, Anita offered a tight smile, her fingers fidgeting with the edge of a clipboard as the entered. The scent of lemon lingered in the air, but beneath it, Conleth caught traces of Evelyn's lavender and Shawn's pine soap. His dragon spirit stirred, restless, pressing against his ribs like a storm waiting to break. Trinity hadn't spoken since the bakery.

Inside his private quarters, she sat beside him on the couch, her body slack against his, her gaze fixed on nothing. Her sorrowful ache echoed down their bond. The vision she'd shared earlier of her death filled him like a prophecy. One he didn't plan to allow to come to pass.

We need to talk. Can you come to the clinic? He reached for his brothers, sensing Taran not far away, but something blocked Aluk's link in his mind. Conleth kissed Trinity's forehead as he leaned a little to pull out his phone. Depending on which part of the prison his brother patrolled, Aluk might not sense him trying to communicate. So, he texted Aluk and then Rourke.

Be there in ten. Taran's answer came in his mind.

His phone pinged.

On my way, Rourke messaged back.

"You told your brothers?" Her head leaned against his heart. She'd closed her eyes, her breathing shallow.

He brushed his fingers through her hair. *If I am to save her, you have to share the past with me. What don't we know?*

Conleth closed his eyes, his spirit silent, slipping further from his reach. *Why won't you tell me?*

Pain ached from his soul, blooming and burning, and he tilted his head back, bracing for it to pass.

"That bad?" Taran arrived first.

Conleth glanced at him. The fire in his veins slowly dissipated to a dull ache. His little brother's face showed concern, and rightly so.

Trinity rested against his chest, and he slid his hand down her back, not wanting her to wake her when he pulled away. Her sobbing had drained her energy.

Rourke followed closely behind Taran, his expression grim.

Conleth explained Aerion's arrival and Trinity's plan to catch the ohunko before Aerion insisted she submit to her fate.

"We can't let her do that," Taran said.

"We need to capture the ohunko and end this curse." Rourke stood, scratching the stubble on his chin. "She had one thing right about her plan. We use her as bait."

Conleth looked at Trinity, her tear-streaked face pale and drawn. "I can't put her in harm's way."

Trinity stirred against him, leaned back and said, "It's the only way."

It didn't mean he had to like it.

"You die, and Conleth dies. You become the queen's vessel, and we're cursed for eternity." Rourke paced in front of the couch. "And what's to say the ohunko doesn't come after your mate next?" He looked at Taran.

"They would have by now," Taran said.

"The wolf ohunko tried to possess her," Conleth pointed out.

"Not kill her." Taran crossed his arms.

Conleth's dragon spirit flared. *We don't capture. We kill.*

"There's no way to kill a guardian, not even a dragon has that ability," Rourke said, pulling back his hair. He stared down at Trinity, who stared right back at him. "If we use her as bait, her grandfather will think she's obeying."

"Don't call him that," Trinity said, leaning away from Conleth's chest.

Ready to share the past?

They took my mate from me once; they are not taking her away again. The guardians will face the Great Hunter for their role in helping the Fae. His dragon growled.

"My dragon says the guardians had something to do with this," Conleth said.

They will pay for their treachery. His dragon rumbled in agreement.

"Ben would know." Rourke added, pacing in front of the couch. "He's handling the woman's family at the resort and the incident."

"Would Aluk know? Did either of your dragons?" Trinity asked, her eyes bright with hope.

He wrapped his arms around her. Having her close kept his dragon spirit centered. She was as much a part of him now as his dragon spirit. Living without either of them wasn't an option.

Taran grimaced. "Aluk is currently unreachable." *He retreated to his lair.* "I'll reach out to Ben. In the meantime, what do you propose we do?"

Conleth's jaw locked, a sharp throb pulsed behind his eyes, warning of the beast rising inside him. *Protect Trinity. Find the missing hunter. Capture the ancient guardian. Keep outsiders from uncovering their secrets.*

"We haven't found the third hunter from last night. Sia and his enforcers are still out searching."

"Do you think he's possessed?" Trinity asked.

"It's a possibility," Rourke said.

"I'll go back to the campsite. It was there once; it will come again," Trinity rubbed her arms and shivered.

"Absolutely not." Conleth's chest filled with fire, and his nostrils flared. A deep rumble rippled through him.

"Conleth is right. Campers are going to pour in again for the weekend. After what happened, they'll have it taped off as a crime scene," Taran said.

Trinity squirmed in his arms. "If it needs a host, it needs people, but we can't risk it harming anyone. What if we take the trails? Where did you find the dead hikers?"

Conleth's grip tightened around Trinity. "You're not going anywhere near that place."

Rourke leaned against the edge of Conleth's desk, a thoughtful expression on his face. "That's not a bad idea." He glanced at Conleth and shrugged. "She may have something there, but how do you plan to trap it?" His gaze fell back on Trinity.

"We'll find another way," Conleth said.

The thought of her walking into danger twisted like a blade to the gut. *No! Shield her. Drag her away. Lock her in our lair and keep her safe!*

The idea of losing her to the same shadows that once stole much from his family burned within him. He wouldn't let history repeat itself. Not with her. *Mine!*

Trinity pulled out the crystal, her fingers trembling slightly. Light caught its iridescent surface, scattering tiny rainbows across her palms. Conleth's fingers itched to take the crystal from her, his chest tightening at the thought of it slipping, shattering, letting the energy inside tear free.

"This should keep it contained. Without a host, it'll be easier to capture, right?"

Rourke's eyebrows rose in surprise. "Where did you get that?"

"In the cabin during the mudslide. Although my gran — Aerion — has requested I hand over all the crystals to him. I assume they will lock the ohunko away in the prison or somewhere similar once they trap it," Trinity said.

Hunters used the crystals to rip animal spirits from his brethren. They belonged locked away in the prison, with the hunters themselves, where no one could wield them again.

"Aluk can lock it in the prison. Although the last one — "

Taran gave Rourke a sharp look. Conleth cleared his throat. He couldn't reveal the truth about Cedric and the portal to Trinity. She already bore the scars of the ohunko and her grandfather's betrayal.

"Last one?" Trinity asked.

"The wolf in Gwen's brother," Conleth supplied, quick to add. "He's possessed by the wolf ohunko."

Are we still on a scavenger hunt? Taran looked at him, frowning.

He never liked the idea. How long before Aluk got control over his dragon? As Beta, Conleth had the authority to decide in Aluk's absence.

Tell her. Yeah, eventually, he needed to tell Trinity about Cedric. But now wasn't the right time.

After this latest attack, revealing the truth might shatter her trust in him to protect her. And his mate's survival came first. After they dealt with the ohunko and Aerion, he would tell Trinity the truth about Cedric.

It should come from me, Conleth told Taran.

Taran nodded; his expression grim. "We didn't need a crystal."

Rourke shrugged, his gaze landing on the closed laptop on Conleth's desk. "It might be easier to capture it if we had one."

"Without it someone would have to sacrifice themselves," Trinity flinched at the reminder of her grandfather, the same way she did when the ohunko's name surfaced. A low growl vibrated through his chest. *Not gonna happen.*

He couldn't allow her to sacrifice herself. If she acted, it would cost her life—and his. There had to be another way, a path to keep her safe and keep the queen locked away.

"We can't afford any more deaths," Taran said.

"There won't be." Conleth's hand slid down Trinity's arm, chasing the chill from her skin. He lifted her chin with a finger, guiding her gaze to his. "No one else dies on this mountain."

His eyes burned with a promise she couldn't ignore. "No one."

Flecks of gold burst in her eyes. She licked her lips, her heart pounding in Conleth's ears. She was the bait, but he wasn't willing to sacrifice her.

"So, what then? Trinity takes a hike on the trail, lures out the ohunko, and while it's distracted with her, we capture it in the crystal, and hand it off to Aluk?" Taran asked.

The thought of his mate facing the ohunko alone filled him with dread. "We need to be absolutely sure of our next steps before we proceed."

"It's a risky plan," Rourke agreed and asked, "Will it get close to her if she's wearing the crystal?"

Trinity's hand covered the crystal.

Conleth covered her hand. "Can you sense it? Would you know she has it without seeing it?"

Rourke hesitated a moment.

Taran stared at her intently.

Then, both men shook their heads.

"That's because it's hollow," Trinity exhaled. "Only when they are filled can those with shifter blood or Fae sense the trapped spirit's essence. It won't know I have it on me. The bigger the shard, the stronger the prism to hold powerful spirits."

Cedric and the bear ohunko, came to mind. The power he had wielded through the crystal pressed against his memory. If this new ohunko matched that strength, would the smaller crystal even hold it? There seemed no other choice.

Rourke dug his phone out of his pocket and swiped it open. "I'm needed back at the station. I can't spare many more guys tonight. With Sia's men out, too. We're running low on reserves."

"Not tonight; it's too dangerous to deal with a shadow spirit when the darkness is against us. We wait until morning. We'll catch it in the window before sunrise, where it has places to skirt the sun and weaken its attack," Taran said.

Conleth nodded. The darkness would only aid the ohunko against them. He glanced at Trinity; her eyes filled with a mix of fear and determination.

"We'll wait until morning. Tonight, I plan to take my mate up the mountain." His dragon lair was the only place he could guarantee her safety.

"Morning." Trinity repeated.

"Morning. We'll meet in the parking area around five. You dragons able to haul yourselves out of your lairs by then?" Rourke said, trying to lighten the mood.

Conleth smirked, appreciating the effort.

"You focus on your tail, and I'll call in some of my patrol rangers," Taran said.

"We got this." Conleth took Trinity's hand, squeezing it for reassurance, but the downturn of her lips broadcasted her doubts.

"Come, *Unahu,* tonight you can ride me up the mountain." He winked, and her cheeks turned an adorable pink.

###

The cavern was a cathedral of stone; its ceiling lost in the shadows. Conleth pressed his hand against the wall. Pockets lit with fire, casting dancing flames against the rough walls, revealing a large, intimate space—large enough for his massive dragon to slumber when the mood struck.

To the side, a human-sized bed sat carved from rock. Dark burgundy cushions and blankets lay undisturbed, and the canopy parted for them to retire. The firelight reflected off the ancient texts on the wall, along with other carvings, that the first dragon left.

Trinity's breath caught beside him. She stood at the edge of the cavern.

"Welcome to my home away from home."

"This is your lair?" Trinity took a few more steps deeper into the cavern. "It's... amazing."

Conleth grinned, his dragon stirring with pride at her presence. "You're safe here. No one else can enter. You and I are the only ones who can see and pass the threshold."

She was the first he brought here and the last to know of its location.

While they ascended the mountain, his mate pressed against him during the flight; she likely saw little of the mountain's ridges and valleys.

Her gaze drifted to the bed, and she trailed her hand along the coverlet. "If this is the home of your dragon, then the clinic and the resort are your homes?"

He followed her with his eyes, a smile curving his mouth. "When I returned from military service, I stayed here for a few years. Hence, the bed and the books. Later, after my dragon settled, I mostly lived at the resort. As my brother's second, it fell on me to step in where he could not, and until recently, I split my time between the clinic in town and there."

She perched on the edge of the mattress, her posture cautious even in the relaxed sprawl of the firelight. Shadows played along the stone walls, and her eyes followed them warily. "Are you sure the ohunko can't come in? Even with the fire throwing shadows like that?"

He crossed to her. "No one knows this place exists but me. Not even the ohunko."

His dragon rumbled agreement.

"Your brothers don't know?"

"It's the one thing I've never shared with them." A strange satisfaction washed over him. This was his sanctuary, his bed, and now his mate in front of him. But something akin to doubt passed across her face like a shadow. Her eyes were more gold than their usual violet hue.

"Nothing will happen to you. I won't let it. Let the Fae search for another pawn in their game of revenge." That was all it was to him now — a game he no longer intended to play. His dragon exhaled in agreement, a low breath of relief that settled through his chest.

Conleth stepped closer, his heart pounding against the ink of his tattoo. She parted her knees, inviting him silently. His gaze lingered on her, lost in the subtle curve of her lips, slightly parted. He found the elastic, tugging gently until it slipped free of the coiled bun. Strands of silver tumbled in a soft cascade over her shoulders, a velvet curtain framing her face.

"My grandfather holds a powerful position among the Unseelie." She flinched and whispered. "Aerion. He's not my grandfather."

Conleth took her face in his hands. "Give yourself time. He deceived you, and what says he's still not betraying you now?"

"Because every child in the Unseelie court knows the story, only my version was slightly different." She licked her lips. "Morning will come too soon. I'd rather not spend the night discussing this."

"Good." Her position on his bed made any further discussion challenging. "Because you'll need to trust me from now on."

A silent battle of wills crackled between them.

Keep her here. She'll always be safe. His dragon whispered, sending images through his mind of Trinity tied to his bed. No wonder she refused the first time. Safety and desire tangled together, blurring every line between them.

She'll be safer when the ohunko is captured.

His chest rumbled low, a growl vibrating through him. His dragon shared his frustration, hating that she had been put in danger.

"No more talking." Trinity's eyes held a spark of mischief. She tugged at his waist, pulling him closer.

"You're not yourself right now," Conleth said.Gold swirled in her eyes, chasing out the violet. Each exhale brushed his skin. Each heartbeat tethered him tighter. The canopy drapes closed around them, leaving only the tension that coiled between them, thick and electric.

Her trembling hand traced the line of his jaw. "I'm tired of thinking. I need to feel."

She pressed closer, her lips brushing his, not demanding, but asking. He gathered her into his arms, lowering her carefully onto the bed as though she were glass and he the clumsy one at risk of breaking her.

"Reach through our bond, *Uhuna,*" he murmured, "I'm with you. Always."

Her hands slid over his shoulders. "More. I need to feel all of you.

The plea tightened in his chest. He shook his head, his forehead resting against hers. "No. Not the beast. Only me." He wanted her to know the difference, to know what she held right now was his heart.

Her palms flattened over his chest, feeling the steady beat beneath. His heartbeat slowed until it became synced with hers. He breathed her in, memorizing every detail of her scent. Cherry blossoms after the rain. The way the violet in her eyes gave way to the gold. The softness of her hair against his skin, and the way her trust wrapped around him stronger than chains.

He held her close, her nearness anchoring him and strengthening their bond.

Trinity's eyes shimmered.

The confession rose to his lips. What if speaking their truth drove her from him?

He lifted his head to speak the truth about Cedric, but Trinity's arms circled his neck, and her lips found his in a playful nip. He tried to respond slowly, to savor the connection, but her kiss crashed over him like a storm, wild and insistent. Every pent-up emotion pulsed against him, a tide he could neither hold back nor resist. Her lips parted just long enough for him to swallow the truth again, burying it for now, hoping it would not claw its way out later.

"You're mine. And I am yours. Nothing can separate us." His mouth moved to kiss her collarbone, then her neck, as she arched back, inviting him to explore. Lost in the moment, he surrendered to the desires of his mate. In the cavern's quiet, their hearts beat as one, a rhythm echoing the ancient pulse of the earth.

Twenty-Six

Trinity lay nestled against Conleth, her heart in a tumultuous sea filled with love and terror. Deep inside a fragile oasis covered in darkness called to her. A giant shadow formed, the image of a mountain lion, whispering for her to come forth. She rolled to her side, ignoring the hiss of the cat in her mind. She traced the familiar lines of Conleth's face. His firm jaw. The gentle curve of his lips. When had he become her everything?

She knew better than to trust the quiet. The ohunko stalked her still. Her pulse quickened, breath hitching as dread curled around her ribs, threatening to pull her from Conleth's side. She moved her hand to the other side of his jaw, wanting to memorize it for eternity.

A hand caught her wrist, his thumb brushing against the inside of her palm. "Can't sleep?"

"I don't know how you can," she whispered.

He rolled to his side, looking down at her through hooded lashes. He was so beautiful it made her heart ache. "I haven't. I've felt you lying restless beside me for hours. You think too much," he murmured. "Let me occupy your thoughts in other ways."

Trinity sighed as he kissed her temple, both her eyes, and worked his way to her mouth. She gasped at the fragile bond between them against the encroaching darkness.

His touch lingered, a bittersweet comfort later as she faced the coming dawn and the daunting task ahead. The climb down from Conleth's lair pressed on her chest until every breath felt heavier than the last. Not a word passed between them, the silence louder than anything either could have said. By the time they reached the base, the damp chill of the mountain clung to her skin.

Taran waited at the trailhead beside Conleth's SUV, two steaming coffees in hand.

Trinity stood looking out at the edge of the trail, the dense green wall of the forest looming ahead. A damp, earthy scent hung heavy in the morning mist.

Conleth grabbed her pack from the back seat.

She turned while he helped her slip it on. His hand brushed aside her ponytail, landing a kiss behind her ear. She bent her head and bit her lip as his arms wrapped around her one last time. "Be careful, Trinity," he said huskily. "I'll be right behind you."

A lump formed in her throat. *Just a walk through the woods. I won't be far.*

"I know," she whispered, entwining her fingers in his one last time before stepping away and entering the labyrinth of the forest. She resisted the overwhelming urge to turn and look back at him. Her heart beating in sync with his would never change.

As she walked, something tugged at her mind — a siren song promising oblivion. She rubbed her temple, thinking of the headache coming from the lack of sleep. Her body ached for Conleth's warmth again. She'd be back in his arms soon enough. But if not... she shook her head, her temples throbbing a bit more. She pressed the heels of her hands into her eyes and drew in a breath that scraped her lungs raw. For a second, the world narrowed. Then came the clink of iron in her mind, shackles snapping closed and binding her to the path the Fae had carved for her.

Unahu?

The beat of her heart slammed into her chest, and she continued to walk.

I'm fine. I'm scared.

Fear gnawed at her belly. The shifters spoke of the Great Hunter's realm waiting for them beyond death, but the Fae dissolved back into root and wind, into the pulse of the earth itself. Conleth's claim bound her to him in ways she could not unravel, threads tying together their souls. Did that make her something no longer Fae? Did it alter the ohunko's purpose?

Her chest ached with longing; an emptiness only Conleth's presence could quiet.

I'm coming in.

The invisible rope between them tugged the further she walked away.

NO! She took a deep breath. *Not yet. Stick to the plan. You can't be that close. It has to believe I'm alone.* She didn't want him to see her like this. He needed a strong mate, and so far she'd failed to do anything except need rescuing.

Conleth growled, rumbling through her mind, distant, like thunder rolling from the far edge of her conscience.

The trail stretched out before her. She forced her breathing to slow; the steady, erratic race in her pulse not helping.

Somewhere ahead, Rourke's men waited and watched, while Taran patrolled on the other side, and Conleth followed behind. Her heart screamed for her to follow the plan. But a pull, a desperate yearning, changed her mind to command her body elsewhere. With a heavy heart and a mind filled with determination, she stepped off the familiar path into the treacherous undergrowth. The invisible rope inside her tugged, but her mind decided; she hurried to put some distance between them. A mental door closed, silencing the hum of her mate's connection.

The undergrowth became a tangle of thorns and vines. "Come and get me, ancient guardian. I'm all yours," she muttered.

With a deep breath, she pushed forward, deeper into the heart of the forest. The only sounds were the crunch of leaves beneath her feet and the eerie calmness settling over her. As she ventured further, the shadows wrapped around the ancient and gnarled trees became darker. A chill brushed against her skin, contrary to the humidity in the air.

A faint whisper, like wind rustling through leaves, caught her attention. Her senses sharpened. The song pulled her deeper into the forest. The undergrowth drew thicker, the trees closer together, casting the forest floor in an eerie twilight.

The trees closed around her. The deer path she followed steepened into a slippery incline, covered in loose rocks and damp leaves. Her foot skidded on a cluster, sending her tumbling down the slope and crashing over a large boulder embedded in the mountainside.

She landed with a jarring thud, knocking her breath out of her.

Tears pooled in the corners of her eyes, and pain lanced across her back, but she refused to give in to it. Conleth's shadow loomed large in her mind, but the mental door kept any thoughts of weakness from escaping. She yanked to unlock it, but it held strong. With gritted teeth, she forced herself to rise.

The snap of a twig sent her spinning around. A figure emerged from the shadows, tall and lean, clad in hunter's garb. His eyes, gleaming in the dim light. A rifle hungover his shoulder. "Hello, pretty lady."

"Scout," she breathed, relieved. "You're alive. Did you spend the night out here? There are people worried about you. They're looking for you."

"Don't you mean looking for you?" Scout's eyes turned black. "You might have escaped the hunters, but you can't escape me."

Don't be afraid. Don't be afraid. She stopped her thoughts, fearing they would be strong enough to break through and Conleth would hear them.

"No. I can't," she whispered. Cold air scraped down her throat, coiling in her lungs like smoke. *They don't know I'm here.* She turned in place, scanning for movement. *No one's coming.* A tremor started in her legs. She forced herself to breathe, to stay upright. *Get it together. You've been through worse.*

But the thought rang hollow.

A wave of despair surged up, cold and relentless.

She bit the inside of her cheek, hard. The pain grounded her. *You're not getting out of this one.*

Scout tilted his head. His hair flopped with the movement. "You should run."

"Then you'll just catch me and prolong this for both of us," Trinity shivered, her mental door creaking open. "I don't want you harming anyone else."

Truth. She shouldn't have gone off the path. Why did she?

"It brings me no honor to do this." Scout's face contorted.

"I was their protector," he whispered, his voice cracking with genuine anguish. "But she... has too strong a hold. It must end..." His expression hardened again, eyes going black. "You must die."

He swung the rifle and leveled his aim at her chest. *Conleth.* The cold truth hit like a stone dropped into deep water. Tears welled in her eyes. The crystal burned against her skin.

Trinity? Where are you? He shouted in her mind, her heart racing again.

I'm sorry.

"Do it," she challenged, though a tremor shook through her belly. "Save your people from the curse."

She backed against the rough texture of the rocks, her knees shaking.

If you die. I die.

"I'm sorry," she whispered, as if she could erase the bond and spare him the pain. Too late. The connection rooted in her soul.

"She mustn't rise again!" The words ripped out of Scout's mouth against his will. He lowered his rifle, shaking his head hard, breath rasping. "No... that's not..."

His eyes flooded black, swallowing his humanity. "We will never go back! She will never control us again!" He raised the rifle, barrel wavering, his hands trembling with the fight inside him. "My only regret is that *he* isn't here to see the end."

Watery eyes of a young man met hers

"It's not his fault. It's not your fault. We can find another way," she said, trying to stall him.

Whatever led her here shattered.

"To protect the rest, there is no other choice." His gaze hardened, eyes catching the light with a cold glint.

"You'll kill both of us. Do you really want to hurt one of your own?"

A sudden movement above the boulder froze her blood. Her gaze snapped upward in time to see the colossal wolf emerge from the concealing foliage. A massive silhouette stood against the morning twilight. Its eyes, twin embers of malice, burned. The creature was a monstrous aberration of nature, the wolf hunched low.

Scout raised the rifle, the glint of metal caught in the faint light.

The wolf launched in a blur of muscle and bone at Scout.

Its white underbelly grazing the top of her head.

In that split second, Scout fired, the deafening crack of the gunshot echoing through the forest.

Trinity screamed.

The wolf collapsed on Scout.

With a grunt of exertion, Scout tossed the lifeless body aside. His eyes, filled with feral rage, locked onto Trinity.

A wave of nausea washed over her.

Run!

A blur of shadow lunged, and before she could scream again, icy fingers clamped around her throat. Shoved against the cold, unforgiving rock, her hands clawed at Scouts wrist, desperate to break free. His hands loosened, then tightened again as the young man wrestled for control with the ohunko possessing him.

"If I don't," he said through gritted teeth. "They'll. All. Suffer."

His grip tightened again.

Another wave of nausea hit her, and she struggled against it.

Her mate mark burned like fire.

Trinity's vision blurred at the edges as her consciousness slowly slipped away. A fleeting image flashed before her closed eyes: Taran shoving a man into a swirling portal and catching Gwen in his arms. Cedric. She recognized the man as Cedric from her briefing with the PPI.

Her heart beat too fast, fluttering like a trapped bird in her chest. Peter and Aluk lingered close to the portal, their presence tugging at her awareness. But Conleth and their bond stretched out, reaching, searching. Where was he in all of this?

The jolt wrenched her back into the present, seeing the ohunko's face as a mask of cold indifference. She blinked rapidly, trying to push back the darkness and stay alert. Betrayal, a bitter pill, coated her throat.

The ohunko leaned in close, his breath foul in her face. "There are no secrets among dragons."

Her stomach rolled, and saliva filled her mouth. Her legs weakened as she broke out in a sweat. She took small, quick breaths. If not for the tight hold around her neck, she might vomit.

No secrets between brothers. Even if he hadn't been present, he would have known about Cedric. They would have told him. He *knew*.

Fury struck her like a match. It flared hot, searing through her chest and curling deep in her gut. The rage didn't belong to her. It spread like a sickness, burning at the backs of her eyes, demanding release. A primal urge clawed at her, desperate to lash out.

I am here, mate.

The voice slid into her mind, too familiar to mistake, yet not Conleth's.

His dragon.

The beast's spirit pressed into her, filling her veins with its fire. The dragon's strength fueled her through their bond.

The crystal's cool surface bit into her palm as her fingers clenched around it. An invisible rope deep in her chest pulled taut, then recoiled like a spring.

Her heart hammered against her ribs with a sudden, desperate rhythm. She pressed harder against the stone, her body rejecting the pull toward surrender.

Another wave of nausea hit her.

She'd been so stupid! Deceived again by a man. Would she never learn?

Her stomach heaved. It would serve them both for the contents of her stomach to spill.

Mother of Earth, she should have never trusted him. By giving in, letting them use her would only serve their twisted goals.

Take from me what you need.

With a gasp that tore from her throat, Trinity fought back against the overwhelming compulsion to surrender. She pushed back against the wicked thought. The power screamed in protest as it strained against her resistance, threatening to tear her apart. *Duty first. There is no love in this line of work.* Aerion's voice flittered in her mind.

She screamed, unwilling to yield.

With a final agonizing boost from the force within her, the compulsion turned to ash.

The ohunko's face contorted in surprise, a hiss escaping as he said, "She sees. And now she dies."

His grip tightened around her throat. Sharp tips of his nails bit into her flesh.

Her lungs burned for air.

She pulled the crystal, trying to yank it off, but strength failed her.

She drew it up, touching it beneath his arm, but touching the crystal did nothing.

The ohunko shoved her harder against the rocks. Her grasp slipped from the crystal. Her lungs fought for air. She blinked. Her head filled with darkness. *Fight!!*

Trinity's fingernails scraped against the rock as she clawed for purchase. Her vision tunneled, but fury blazed brighter than the encroaching darkness.

As if he would cry. The deceiver.

She kicked out, but no matter how hard she hit Scout's body, the ohunko didn't budge. Weakness flooded her limbs, then something hot surged through her veins, steadying her trembling muscles. It didn't, however, fill her lungs with air.

Behind him, the large wolf lay. Howls filled the air.

"You don't deserve his devotion." The ohunko hissed, squeezing tighter. "He chose you when he knew the dangers your kind brings."

Trinity willed the crystal to activate, anything for it to incapacitate Scout.

The ohunko sneered. "You have to separate me from the body to capture the spirit, but I'm stronger."

Her vision filled with black dots. Her grip slipped from the crystal. She dug her nails into his arms.

Wingbeats sounded overhead.

She keened, trying to scream, her heart lurching as her mark burned. Aerion's intense stare rising from memory. His sad smile, and whatever spells he placed on her, unfurled inside her.

No, she whispered in her mind. *Stay away.*

We're one, mate, and this time, they will not separate us. The dragon's voice came out of the darkness, closing in on her.

"Not so fast, chosen one," the ohunko hissed, its grip tightening around her throat. She fought for breath.

"He must watch. His tears to blend with your blood." Scout's eyes widened, blood draining from his face. "That's not me talking," he whispered.

Abruptly, the pressure on her windpipe eased, and she collapsed to the ground, gasping for air. Her lungs burned as she struggled to draw in enough oxygen.

When her vision cleared, she saw Scout's body convulse.

"I can't fight anymore," he gasped.

His voice deepened, becoming less human. "Enough hesitation."

Muscles rippled and shifted beneath Scout's skin as he morphed into a monstrous-looking cat. A low growl rumbled from its chest. The mountain lion, sleek and deadly, launched itself at her with terrifying speed. The animal's teeth snapped at her neck, and she rolled, trying to evade the lethal strike. With a thud, the mountain lion landed, its sharp teeth sinking into her arm. Searing pain shot through her limb as if the arm had been cleaved in two. For a heart-stopping moment, her mind flashed, and she saw the end. Its claws extended, piercing into her side.

Then, as suddenly as it began, the mountain lion was gone.

She lay panting; her injured arm throbbing with agony.

The roar of a dragon echoed through the forest, shaking her to her core.

A hiss sliced through the air.

The mountain lion landed on its feet, locking eyes with her.

The howls of wolves filled the air, coming closer.

The cat hesitated. Its gaze flickered towards the encroaching pack.

It looked above her, fear widening its gaze.

With a screech that echoed the dragon's roar, the cat turned and fled, disappearing into the dense foliage. Relief washed over Trinity as the wolves burst from the trees, a blur of black and gray fur rushing from her left.

Trinity scrambled to sit up. Quickly, she held the wound, putting pressure on the bite as dizziness and nausea plagued her.

Overhead, a large black dragon landed on the boulder, craning its neck toward her. The beast's muzzle came within an inch of hers. *Fear not, my heart. I have you.*

Trinity bit her lip to keep from crying out.

The dragon snorted, giving her a gentle nudge. Those large teeth startled her, its tongue darting out, swiping saliva over her arm.

She jerked away, and the beast drew back.

Your pain is my pain. Let me tend to you.

It turned its head, meeting her gaze with the large, familiar red glow that blinked at her.

Conleth?

Remember. We are one.

The dragon drew back its head, and she spotted the wolf Scout shot. A large black wolf lowered its head and pressed its forehead against the fallen one. In a blur of black and sounds of bones popping, the wolf shifted to become Rourke. He fell to his knees, his hands digging into the fallen wolf's fur.

Tears streamed down Rourke's face. Trinity's heart ached, the pain of her wounds forgotten by the agony etched on Rourke's face.

Trinity slumped on the ground, panting, and heaving as she fought to breathe and steady her heart. Through hooded lashes, she spotted Conleth. In all his naked glory, he landed in front of her. Fire flickered behind his gaze, but it burned with sorrow rather than fury.

"Trinity."

"Why isn't he healing?" She croaked, coughing, and pressing her mouth into her shoulder. A spike of pain shot up her clawed side.

"Are you hurt anywhere else besides the bite?" His eyes swept over her, searching for injuries.

Trinity curled in a fetal position, wrapping her arms around herself, hiding her bleeding side from him. "Help him first."

Large tears rolled down her cheeks in relief. The pain in her arm went numb as the dragon saliva worked to help her heal faster. Her hand against her side grew sticky with her blood.

Conleth's gaze swept over her again, lingering on her side.

"I don't need you," she whispered, sniffling as a fresh set of tears cascaded.

His eyes narrowed, and she stared back at him.

'Go' she mouthed.

For a moment he stared at her, causing her chest to burn.

"Conleth," Rourke called for him. Clenching his fists, Conleth's eyes dulled as he communicated with someone other than her. His jaw tightened. Another moment passed until his eyes regained sight.

He moved toward the man lying on the ground.

Don't move, Unahu. I know you are hurting.

The wolf's body shuddered. Rourke's hands trembled as he pressed them against the gaping wound. A low guttural sound escaped his lips. A mixture of sorrow and rage.

Conleth approached Rourke, laid a hand on the other man's shoulder, and Trinity grunted with the effort to move. Her ribs screamed in protest.

Help him!

The wolf's form shifted, muscles rippled, and bones popped until the familiar contours of a human emerged in place of the beast. Trinity sucked in a breath.

The man on the ground was a perfect replica of Rourke.

"It hit his heart," Rourke said, his face ashen. Shifters healed from almost any injury; a bullet in the heart wasn't one of them. Several moments later, a dazzling, ethereal creature materialized from the man's body. Its form shimmering with an otherworldly light. It stood tall and proud. A profound sense of wonder and loss washed over Trinity.

"Thank you for your gift," Rourke whispered to the wolf, who bowed and disappeared into the air.

Her chest hollowed with each breath, bringing with it a searing pain. How long would the man's family wait to receive the blessing of his warrior spirit? Without this curse, the shifters would no longer lose their spirits to the shadows. It was a blight upon the land, a thief of lives.

Desperation hit her. Trinity glanced down at the healing bite on her arm. Conleth's dragon saliva worked like a Band-Aid. She felt the skin knitting back together, but the fresh wounds from the mountain lion against her ribs coated her other hand with blood.

Her body throbbed with pain.

Gritting her teeth, she pressed her hand against the gash, willing the blood to clot. Numbness crept into her fingers as the dragon's healing power worked its way through her system like a cold drip of medication. Her blood heated and sizzled under the pressure as her body cauterized the wound. She gritted her teeth, lying there, a prisoner in her own body.

Taran emerged from the forest, his bare feet and legs exposed to Trinity's gaze. "Where is the ohunko?"

"In the body of the missing hunter," Trinity said, a mere whisper emerging from her throat. It warmed against the pain like a heating pad as her eyelids grew heavy, her body working to heal.

You went off the trail, Conleth accused, coming towards her again, his face a mask of concern.

And I should never have trusted you.

Twenty-Seven

Conleth cradled Trinity in his arms. He ignored the sting of the branches against his exposed skin as he walked through the forest and returned to his SUV. The deserted parking area contained only his vehicle and Rourke's.

He deposited her gently in the passenger seat of his SUV. She sat limp, looking away from him. "I can feel your pain."

Tears slid down her face.

Gently, he cut a slit up the side of her shirt to inspect her wound. He touched her elbow to move her arm, and she hissed, lifting her arm out of his way. "I'm sorry. It will take a day or two for these to heal."

He pulled out a bottle of water and a clean cloth. She bit her lip while he pressed the damp cloth against her side.

"They're deep enough for stitches. I've got surgical glue. I'm sorry for the pain you're going through."

"I want the dragon," she whispered.

"We share the same body fluids. Once I'm done, I'll kiss all your wounds and help speed the healing process. I promise."

Her eyes, usually filled with a spark of mischief and curiosity, became distant.

She'd gone off the trail, nearly died, and dragged his heart through hell. His hands trembled as he cleaned the wound. He kissed each slash, a battle between anger and relief as he licked the last one. "Trinity." A please for her to look at him, but she didn't.

Her body stayed stiff, her mind far away, and that hurt worse than any wound he could stitch.

Conleth held out a half-used bottle of water and medication to take away the edge of the pain. When she didn't respond, he placed the pills in her hand, and the water in the other. "You'll thank me later."

She glared at him from the corner of her eye. He buckled her in, placing a spare shirt between her side and the seatbelt, then gently closed the door on her side of the SUV. Walking around the back of the vehicle, he raked his fingers down his face. What a complete and utter failure this turned into, leaving another man dead and Trinity in danger again.

He slid into the driver's side of the SUV. She turned her gaze to the side window. The water bottle sat nestled in the cupholder, and the pills vacant from her hand.

"Talk to me. Don't shut me out. You went off the trail. It took me longer to find you. What if Ryder wasn't already here and came to your defense? I almost didn't reach you in time!"

"Ryder. That's the wolf who died." She continued to stare out the window.

"Yeah, he was Rourke's brother." His hands tightened on the steering wheel, hitting the gas far too hard and sped out of the parking lot.

Don't be reckless, his dragon growled.

A rumble vibrated from his chest. Trinity leaned further away from him. For the past hour, her thoughts had come across as a tornado of emotions through their bond, making it hard to read her. Even his dragon blocked things from him.

Silence rode with them back to town; only the hum of the tires on the road broke it occasionally. Not even the flash of pain in her eyes broke through the wall she'd built between them.

Conleth couldn't stop glancing over at her. Pale skin, bruises blooming along her neck, and eyes dulled by something deeper than exhaustion. His dragon spirit hissed at the ache throbbing inside him. Not his pain. Hers.

When her gaze dropped, and her shoulders sagged, his soul cracked. His mental shield slipped for a moment, and his dragon hissed. *The Fae compelled her. She had no choice in her actions.*

The Fae man dared to touch her—dared to twist her will. Conleth's knuckles tightened on the wheel, teeth grinding as his dragon spirit heated his blood. The need to kill burned through him.

Deal with the Fae man later; mate needs us now.

Since when do you stop at protecting what is ours?

When our mate is badly injured. First heal, then hunt.

His foot eased off the gas pedal, not wanting to push the limits of the vehicle's speed and endanger her again. It took several deep gulps to push away the desire to hunt and eliminate Aerion.

No one should ever have the right to make someone do something against their will.

"Trinity." He reached over to touch her hand.

She pulled away, her body jerking. "Don't," she whispered. "Just drive."

Conleth's throat tightened.

She knows the truth.

"You need to rest. I'll take you back up the mountain where it's safe."

"With your dragon," she asked.

"With me," he insisted, hurt that she suddenly preferred the beast to him.

I haven't kept secrets from her.

If I'd told her about Cedric, she would've left. And if she left, the council would've lost their only chance to keep the mountain safe. We'd have another war on our hands. I didn't have a choice.

Aluk had made the call, and Conleth had to follow it. He hadn't liked it, and he'd planned to tell her. He just hadn't told her soon enough.

"It would become hotter than an oven in my lair if I stayed there with you in my dragon form," he added, trying to lighten the mood.

She sighed and turned back to the window. The silence that followed became more unbearable.

"We'll go to the clinic. You can rest there, and I'll ask Sia to send someone to stand guard outside your room. If you don't want me there with you, know I'll be close by," he offered, his knuckles tightening once more around the steering wheel.

No response. Just her vacant stare, fixed on the passing trees, and the growing distance between them.

"What can I do?" The words came out rougher than he had meant. "It's not your fault. I know that."

He hadn't meant to raise his voice.

She'd scared him nearly to death this time.

Aerion's betrayal still burned in his chest, a slow smoldering ache he couldn't shake. He'd compelled Trinity to take another path. It wasn't her fault. He should have told her the truth before they sealed the mate bond. Surely, Aerion didn't want her dead.

No, he wanted her to sacrifice her soul to the queen.

She'd been the one to decide to confront the ohunko. Both their deaths meant the queen remained trapped. She willingly made that decision for them, but she fought at the end.

He growled, nostrils flaring.

She flinched, and now he was the one making it worse.

"I would pull over and let my dragon fly you to the clinic, but there are still outsiders on the mountain and the sun is fully up now."

We're going to have to talk about this. He tried to reach her through their bond.

"Can you bear with me long enough to see you safe and tended?" He glanced at her, hoping for any kind of response.

No answer. She closed her eyes and tried to shut the metal door between their bond again.

You made a decision to end us both. He sent the words through their bond. *And you think my silence is worse than that?*

She slammed the metal door between their minds, shutting him out.

"If you would prefer, I can let Evelyn assist you." He didn't want Evelyn tending her. Conleth wanted to be the one to ease her pain, to soothe her hurts. He'd lick every inch of his mate's body if it meant speeding her healing. If she'd let him.

No.

So, she hadn't closed him off entirely.

Aerion wouldn't get away with this. The Fae man was a more dangerous threat than he had first assumed. He'd raised Trinity, not as a ward, but a vessel for their cause. Now, his mate believed she—they—needed to die to save the mountain.

No other way...

Her thought, not his.

The steering wheel cracked under the pressure of his grip.

I need an enforcer or two at the clinic. Can you contact Sia? He'll need to know what happened. Conleth pushed his thoughts to Taran.

On it.

Another wave of fresh tears flooded her face. They rained down like acid in his gut. "Give me the silent treatment, but don't shut me out, *Unahu*. You need to understand there are things I couldn't tell you, not until you became my mate."

Her gaze finally shifted to him.

"Aluk wanted you to discover the truth on your own about Cedric. Would you have believed us when you first came, if we had told you? And what would happen to our people when you put it in your report?"

Her eyes widened. He had her attention.

"I was going to tell you. Last night. But it didn't seem the right time. We got distracted, and I knew you were trying to say goodbye. You were afraid. He compelled you, didn't he?"

She nodded, then looked back at the passing scenery as they came into Sentinel Peak.

He failed her, and it sank deep within him. "That's why you'd prefer Vareth, my dragon. You drew on the strength of my spirit to break the spell. You are as safe with me as you are with Vareth. Always. I wouldn't have let you out of my sight if I'd known."

She shook her head, biting her lower lip.

"Hate me if you wish. People's lives are involved. My people. And you were a stranger on our mountain. We needed to know we could trust you."

She flinched at his words. "I don't hate you."

"But I've lost your trust. I feel it. My dragon spirit is attuned to you. What is it I can do, *Unahu*, to make things right between us again?"

Twenty-Eight

TRINITY LAY IN THE sterile white hospital bed. Conleth left her one of his clean T-shirts that came almost to her knees and an extra blanket in case she wanted it. When he brought her inside, she insisted on a room at the end of the hall, a silent rebellion against the magnetic pull of his presence. Yet even here she sensed him, a subtle hum of his dragon spirit that resonated through the walls. The invisible thread keeping her tethered to him strengthened between them. No matter the distance, it would yank her back toward him.

She clung to a tissue, blowing her nose for the hundredth time. There weren't enough pillows to stack against her to replicate Conleth's warmth and solidarity. Pitching the tissue in the trash, she heard voices in the hall. A knock on the door frame followed.

"I brought tea," Evelyn said, holding up a mug. "Chamomile and dark honey."

Her smile fell flat. Trinity sensed an undercurrent of tension in Evelyn.

"Thanks," Trinity sat up, reaching for the mug. As she took a sip, her eyes drifted to the door, a sense of unease creeping over her.

"You should drink all of that. I'm not to leave until you finish every drop."

Trinity's hand trembled as she peered at the liquid in her mug. The liquid within, of a deep, inky hue, seemed too dark with a shimmer when the light hit it at a tilt.

Her grandfather, Aerion, used to say that to her often.

Evelyn's eyes held a dark, menacing glint. If Trinity didn't know better, she would think it was the ohunko. Could it have gotten here with the wolves chasing it?

A wave of doubt washed over her. Was she seeing things now that weren't there? Was her mind frayed from the ohunko's attack and playing tricks on her? But the voice in the back of her mind told her to trust her gut instinct.

"How is Shawn? Is he here with you?" she asked, hoarsely.

"Resting, as you should be." Evelyn waved her hand toward the mug. "Drink. I added some dark honey to sweeten the bitterness."

Trinity ran her tongue over her teeth. Her neck felt stiff and sore; her arm had healed, but her ribs throbbed. "How did you know to add dark honey to my tea?"

"Your mate. He wants you to rest and heal." Evelyn's voice seemed off from the last time they spoke.

Dread seeped its chill into her bones.

Trinity's mouth soured. "Conleth doesn't know what I like in my tea."

Where is Evelyn? Who had she heard speaking out in the hall?

I thought she was with you. Conleth said through their bond. His joy of her speaking to him slipped through the connection between them.

The woman in my room isn't Evelyn.

Her breath hitched, chest tightening as heat surged beneath her skin. The walls felt too close, the air too thin.

"Drink the tea, Trinity," the woman's voice cut through the static in her mind with a quiet authority that demanded obedience.

Her pulse surged, sending a stinging sensation through her mark.

"I'm not thirsty." She set the mug on the stand beside her. Swinging around her legs, she faced Evelyn, hardening her gaze. Evelyn's eyes turned an unnatural shade of blue and seemed to bore into her soul. Her insides pinched at the confirmation of her suspicions. "You can drop the disguise, Aerion."

A slow, predatory smile crept across Aerion's face, replacing the gentle facade of Evelyn. The transformation was as swift as a viper's strike, his eyes glinting with cruel satisfaction. "You paid attention to my lessons on glamor."

"You trained me too well."

"I imagined you as my own so many times, it was hard, but in the end, you were nothing but a ward. I will, however, cherish the years we had. I had no children of my own. The demands of the court did not allow time for such luxuries."

The wall lurched, angles skewing as if the room itself recoiled from him. Familiar shapes twisted.

"Don't do this." She pressed her wrist to her heart, feeling any second Conleth would come rushing through that doorway.

"You always were too trusting. You had no reason not to be, but the moment I needed you to trust me, you failed me."

Any second... *Now would be a good time, Conleth.* Heat kicked up in her veins, the echo of his spirit pressing against hers like a promise.

"Perhaps you should have treated me better." Heat flushed her cheeks, and her pulse thundered in her ears. She scanned the room looking for a weapon, but there was nothing but a bed, a tray and a few blankets.

A touch of mockery crept into Aerion's tone. "You were treated like a princess."

"I never had friends. I was alone," she said. The events of the past few days — the betrayal, the manipulation — were all part of a larger plan. Aerion had orchestrated everything, using her trust and love for him against her.

"Attachments would have only complicated things. However, I blame myself for the diabolical of the missing crystal. I under-estimated you falling for male charm."

A bitter laugh escaped her lips. "Yes, because I had so many boyfriends, you had to scare them away."

"One wasn't it? I'd hoped you'd learned your lesson."

Aerion would not control her emotions, her thoughts. She survived the crystal incident. She would live through this. As she contemplated her next move, Aerion turned his head toward the doorway, lifting his hand.

"And here comes your mate now. You've bought time. Another tactic I see you have excelled at. Too bad we'll be gone before he reaches you."

Her heart kicked into overtime as Aerion pulled a syringe from his coat pocket. "I can't have you messing up everything I've worked for, child." Aerion lunged towards her.

He aimed the syringe directly at her neck.

She scrambled backward. The rough fabric of the blankets fell from her. She yanked them up and pulled them in front of her as a shield.

The syringe pierced the thin barrier with a wet, sickening *thunk*, the tip buried deep within the soft material. Inch by inch, the world narrowed to the glint of the metal, and a cold sweat prickled her brow.

Aerion's voice, a venomous hiss, sliced through the tension. "You ungrateful child!"

His breath, hot and fetid, washed over her, causing goose-bumps to prickle along her arms. "I gave you a task. I compelled you, and you disobeyed me."

"I... I couldn't," she stammered, her gaze darting to Conleth. His body slammed against the invisible barrier of the door. A safe tactic Aerion must have placed after entering her room.

Conleth's eyes, twin embers, glowed with an intensity matching the ominous crimson of his hands.

A crackle of energy pulsed from the doorway, fire lighting between his fingers as his muscles bulged, pressing on the space to force through the Aerion's ward.

Her muscles tensed; her body prepared to spring toward Conleth. *It's warded.*

Her eyes narrowed at Aerion.

Conleth jerked back, his chest heaving as his nostrils flared. *How do I break it?*

Aerion's face contorted into a mask of fury. "Couldn't? You dare defy me? Your family will pay for your disobedience."

He yanked the blanket, and Trinity let go to avoid the sharp tip of the needle.

She rolled off the bed and hit the floor.

Jarred for a moment, she scrambled to her feet.

Aerion's eyes flamed with determination.

She darted to the bedside table, closing her hand over the teacup. With a swift movement, she hurled it at him, buying herself precious seconds to gain distance. As the mug hit the floor behind Aerion and splintered into pieces, she launched herself toward the door, hoping to escape.

The invisible wall refused to let her pass.

Conleth stepped back, reaching for her, but the ward remained between them. Scales prickled down Conleth's arms. His eyes turned red as rubies.

Flipping around, with Trinity's back against the ward, its energy zapping at her skin, she trembled. Conleth's roar echoed from behind her.

Aerion, syringe in hand, walked towards her. "You can come willing or we can do it my way. Either option leaves you with no way of escape. Unlike the ohunko, I promise to make it painless."

Trinity pressed back further against the invisible barrier. "You're a coward. You pretend to be this powerful Fae lord, and yet you fear my dragon."

I'm yours as you are mine, mate.

"And I will have even more power once our mountain source is secured. Th council chose me because I am one of the oldest and most powerful Fae alive. Unfortunately, you received little training. When your gift appeared with no coaxing, I knew you had the potential to be powerful, the type of gifts befitting a queen."

Trinity's mind raced, pieces like a puzzle falling into place. Royal blood. Powerful. She gasped. She'd been trained in everything but using her Fae gifts. All this time, she had assumed she had only one.

Their bond could be her salvation. Focusing on the intense heat emanating from Conleth, she drew from it, harnessing the power flowing through their connection. A surge of energy opened, and a sensation unlike anything she'd ever felt coursed through her.

That's it, Unahu, *take from me what you need.*

The air around her shimmered as she concentrated.

Aerion stepped closer, flicking the end of the needle. He held up his hand. His magic pushed her back against the invisible wall, holding her in place. A hungry vortex formed at her fingertips. The fire that once raged in Conleth's hands slipped through the ward and danced in Trinity. It's raw, untamed energy coursed through her veins, igniting a strength she never knew she possessed.

With a swift movement, she twisted her palm toward Aerion, unleashing a torrent of flame.

Aerion lifted his hand to plunge the needle into her as the fire engulfed him in a fiery inferno.

The crackling flames quickly swallowed his scream. His body thrashed in a sea of fire. He rolled on the ground, desperate to extinguish the flames consuming him.

Trinity froze, watching Aerion writhe in pain.

Behind her, the ward flickered and died with a 'whoosh' as Conleth rushed in to pull her back in his arms. She buried her head against shoulder. With the ward gone, the room filled with cooler air to chase out the intense heat inside.

Fire alarms sounded and lights flashed in the hallway beyond the room.

When the flames subsided, only ashes and a lingering acrid scent remained.

Trinity turned, her breath coming in ragged gasps. She raised her hands, her palms blistering. Her head spun, the buzz of Conleth's dragon spirit lingering in her mind. The power rush that had fueled her actions drained slowly.

Conleth held her tightly around the waist, preventing her legs from collapsing underneath her.

"I drew from your dragon spirit and used its fire. I... I killed him."

She survived.

Aerion was gone.

Conleth kissed the side of her head. "I told you we are a team. We are one. Did you not feel when I gave you strength to stay alive with the ohunko?" Conleth gently took her hands, examining the blistered and reddened skin. "There is nothing I wouldn't do for you, Trinity."

Her eyes welled with tears.

"I've got salve in the exam room. Your hands should heal quickly."

Already she noticed the blisters dissolving, and the heat living within her turned down like a propane stove with the burner on low.

Twenty-Nine

CONLETH HAD WATCHED IN horror as Trinity drew his fire, transforming her into a being of pure, consuming fire. He had been terrified in part, but another part of him was exhilarated. His mate, his other half, had discovered a strength and power that he hadn't known existed within her. With his dragon spirit. With him.

Now, as the adrenaline faded, fear crept in. He failed to protect her. He had been a prisoner, unable to aid her one too many times.

We gave her what she needed. Our mate is strong and powerful. It's in her blood. Conleth's dragon rumbled within him.

Conleth scooped Trinity up, cradling her in his arms. She needed medical attention, but she healed fast thanks to their bond.

"My brave girl," he murmured into her hair.

This is why the Fae want to control us. His dragon continued in his mind. *Their power comes from nature; it is strongest on this mountain because this is where our spirits dwell. The Fae deceived us. The woman wanted to control us, use us, and to protect us, the alpha made a choice to keep her contained. Once she realized her intentions were known, she cast the curse upon us. No one knew she was the queen until the warriors came and attacked us.*

The guard sent lay unconscious down the hall. Conleth sent Anita to turn off the fire alarms. Evelyn hovered over the guard. She looked up from her task as he carried Trinity from the room. "Call Trace and touch nothing in that room until he gets here."

Amid this chaos, Rourke needed time to mourn.

Anita's eyes widened. Evelyn laid a hand on the older woman's arm. "Is she well?"

"She needs rest." Trinity went limp, her body succumbing to two attacks in one day. But a well of pride filled inside him. Her power — a force of nature — was a testament to her lineage.

The realization struck him like a thunderbolt. Aerion said she had royal blood. Trinity was part of the legacy of the Fae, the third-generation female born from the same blood as the alpha's intended mate in the mountain.

Their power, rooted in the heart of this ancient mountain, connected with the animal spirits of Conleth's people.

His need to shield Trinity blinded him to the second threat until it loomed too close.

His dragon spirit withheld from him for so long.

Shame burned through him from the ancient echo of the beast he carried within. With the bond fully unlocked, Conleth's soul flooded with memory, a torrent of emotion and a vast library of the past he never knew existed.

Relief surged through him, fierce and fleeting. They had thwarted the Fae's plans. For how long?

The *ohunko* lurked in wait.

Traitors, his dragon hissed.

They needed to hurry. Leaving Trinity alone never counted as an option, not after everything she had endured. But where could he take her and trust that she would remain safe? Like the female before her, she carried the kind of power that could shackle them all again.

She won't, his dragon argued. *She is one with us. Innocent. We protect.*

Would his brothers see it that way?

As he carried Trinity away, her weight became heavier with each step. He needed to reach a place where no one could touch her. The thought sickened him, yet the old dragon fortress on Crags Cliff offered the only true safety. Their grandfather had turned it into a prison decades ago, sealing it with stone and silence, a place built for isolation and control.

He considered it again, not as a cage, but as the one stronghold where she might remain safe, yet free. A place where they could test her powers, unravel their secrets, and forge a weapon strong enough to stand against the Fae.

He looked down at Trinity, her dark lashes against pale cheeks. His dragon spirit rumbled. *She is not the enemy. She is ours to protect. Ours to love. This is why I didn't unlock the past for you. Would you have claimed our mate with this knowledge?*

Something inside him, beyond his dragon, deep in his heart, said he would. His to protect. His to love.

Then he would need to earn back her trust and become the mate she needed to keep her on the mountain. "Whatever it takes," he murmured, holding her. "I will fix what I have broken."

Starting with capturing the ohunko and eliminating the threats against them.

In the meantime, Trinity slept like the dead. Conleth could not leave her side. He watched her, his hand hovering over hers, tracing the delicate lines of her palm. He longed to apologize, to beg for forgiveness, but she needed to wake up to listen.

When her lashes finally fluttered open on the third day, a wave of relief washed over him. Her body, healed from the previous battles, was soft and warm against him. Her eyes, when they met his, held a depth of sorrow that mirrored his shared pain.

Would she reject him after all this?

He kneeled beside her bed. "I failed you."

He vowed to protect her, to be her shield against the ohunko, but he failed to identify Aerion as a threat. To see the truth from within his spirit.

The Great Hunter gave them this gift, and his pride almost prevented them from keeping her safe.

Never again, his dragon swore in his head.

Trinity's hand reached out, covering his. Her touch was gentle. "I'm glad you did."

"What?" Conleth's mind reeled.

A soft smile graced her lips, her eyes sparkling with a warmth that filled him with a sense of peace. "If you had rescued me, I would never have discovered the truth about myself. About us. I needed to face Aerion alone. I needed to dig deep within myself and find who I was, and you gave me the strength to do it."

A lump formed in his throat as he listened to her words. "Because of you, I'm no longer a victim. I have power. You shared your dragon with me. The spirit within you is a gift from the Great Hunter. He matched the spirit with yours, as fate has matched us."

Words failed him. His dragon spirit stirred, awed by the fire in her eyes, the strength in her silence.

"I'm back in your bed at the resort, aren't I?" She sat up.

His t-shirt hung loose on her frame, but it looked better on her than it ever had on him. The faint scent of pine and smoke clung to the fabric. His scent. She was here. Breathing. Alive. Crag's Cliff could wait. He wasn't ready to let her out of his sight again.

"We've been trying to wake Aluk. There's still the matter of the ohunko. Listen, *Unahu.* Once the ohunko is dealt with, I want you to stay. If you don't want to live with me, stay here. I can stay at the clinic in town. I know you still don't trust me. My dragon spirit has kept secrets from me, and I will share everything I know. But give me a chance to earn back your trust. I can't live without you."

He sucked in his breath, held it, awaiting her response.

"Nor do I." She sighed. "There are things I should have told you about Aerion."

"Time slipped from us, and he stayed too close to you. I'm sorry he proved to be more than the grandparent you believed."

Trinity nodded; the flutter of her lashes against the moisture there pained him.

"He serves on the Unseelie Court. It won't be long before they look for him and figure out what has happened. They'll send someone else out to find me, and once they discover him dead... It'll start a war, won't it?"

His smile faltered. She was right. The moment they discovered Aerion's ashes, they'd send someone else to investigate.

They won't touch her now. She's become part of us. Shifter and Fae combined. She'll be of no use to their cause.

That didn't mean they wouldn't blame his people and come after them.

No one will take her from us.

Not fate. Not the fae. No one.

"I think that war started a long time ago, *Unahu.*" He explained what his dragon told him. Trinity scooted to the end of the bed, sitting up to face him. He took her hands in his, keeping his grip gentle.

Despite being bruised and exhausted, she remained the most beautiful woman he had ever seen.

He reached for her slowly, lifting her chin with a touch that trembled more than he wanted to admit. If she pulled away, he'd let her. But she didn't.

He kissed her. Soft at first. A whisper of warmth against his lips. And when she stayed, when she leaned into him, the floodgates broke. Protect her. Keep her. Love her. Never lose her again.

He would have chuckled at his dragon spirit's constant chanting had he not been more occupied. Conleth poured everything into the kiss: his dragon's devotion, his own aching need, the promise he hadn't dared speak aloud.

She still needed to heal. Still vulnerable.

Conleth groaned, forcing himself to pull back before the fire inside him consumed them both.

"Promises are easy to make," Trinity said.

So, his dragon whispered them to her. *I swear, mate, no more secrets. I took the vows of your Fae heritage, and you allowed me to claim you through mine. We're in this together, no matter what.*

A small smile graced her lips. "I love you."

She leaned forward and kissed him again, and this time he didn't intend to stop.

Thirty

TRINITY FROZE BEFORE THE mirror, her eyes widening as energy swirled from her hands in living streams of light. The power throbbed through her veins, tethering her to the earth even as it lifted her chest with a rush of freedom. What could she unleash? What might she lose control of? Could she hold it long enough to stop the ohunko?

She turned, pulse hammering, to find Conleth watching her.

Her throat tightened. "I don't understand," she whispered. "All this time... I carried more power than I ever imagined."

"We'll find someone who can help you harness it. Arden helps the young prepare for meeting their spirit animals and in preparing for their first shifts. Perhaps he can help you."

Trinity sent a surge of gratitude through their bond. Those dark hooded eyes swept their gaze over her, affirming the deep feelings linked between them. He would die first than see her harmed. Like the mirror in their borrowed cabin, it reflected her feelings. Conleth arranged with Sia for a cabin outside the village instead of returning to his lair. Going back to his lair felt wrong, like an insult to the pack, whose alpha had helped save her. She wanted to stay close and mourn with them. "Tell me again about Ryder."

Conleth placed his hands on her arms, warding off the chill creeping there. "Rourke and Ryder are twins. They split many years ago, Ryder becoming alpha of the Avalanche Pack and Rourke of the

Sentinel Pack. Several months ago, Ryder went rogue, leaving the pack to Sia. We thought he'd gone mad. His mate said he acted paranoid and went out chasing shadows. Sia said he hunted the ohunko."

Why would a wolf shifter become rogue if he ruled the pack unless he knew he wouldn't return? Did shifters have the ability to foresee the future? To sense the impending danger?

"How long?" she didn't have to ask the rest; Conleth knew.

"Right after the thaw."

"Anything else happen?" She procrastinated, not wanting to leave the sanctuary of the cabin and its welcoming scents of orange and spice to mingle with Conleth's ash and pine. They couldn't tarry here. She didn't want to endanger others.

He tilted his head. She could almost hear him thinking. "We locked Peter away."

"And the wolf ohunko," Trinity murmured.

"Are you ready to go?"

Trinity twisted in the mirror, tucking the last strand of hair into place. The suit could wait for another day. She stepped into her field clothes: dark green pants, a fitted black shirt, and a knife strapped against her leg. She tucked her compass and the black stone Conleth gave her into her side pockets. Conleth had taught her how to temper the dragon flame, and keep it from searing her alive if she siphoned from him again. She learned quickly, yet the pulse of Fae magic inside her made her unpredictable. The stone gave her a place to direct the heat and the fire if it were to release uncontrolled from her hands again.

Conleth's hand brushed her chest, fingers catching the crystal at her throat. "Are you sure you want to wear this? I can take it."

Her hand closed over his and squeezed. "I need to do this."

The crystal pressed cool against her skin, a reminder that she had survived, but also that the ohunko still hunted her. Trust stirred inside her, fragile, edged by fear.

Conleth's eyes softened, and she wondered if he had read the thought. He let out a breath and released the crystal. "Perhaps keep it tucked in your shirt for now."

She smoothed the pendant with her palm, forcing a lightness into her tone. "Are you sure it's okay to wear this? I feel under-dressed for the occasion."

The mirror returned her reflection. So much had changed since coming to the mountain, since Aerion's truth. Power coursed through her veins, leaving her feeling more vulnerable than invincible. What if it failed her when they needed it most?

It seemed important that Ryder started acting strangely right after the wolf took over Peter and got locked up in prison. Her training taught her to look at every little detail; nothing was a coincidence. She couldn't understand the relationship between the wolf, the spirit, and her place in the curse.

"I suppose this will do." Conleth's eye glinted. "But I much prefer you in your birthday suit."

She swatted at him playfully, loving his personality coming back after all they'd been through. Her cheeks grew warm at his suggestion, but she grinned, happy to spend this moment with her mate. Life was too short to waste, she decided, especially when one's life hung in the balance of protecting others. Funny that Aerion's threat of a dragon becoming her doom would become the one thing to save her from losing her soul. Now, they had only to convince the ohunko to let her alone to live her life in peace.

The thought of a younger version of Conleth running around spread immense warmth through her core. Conleth grinned, his eyes glinting as the thought reached him through the bond.

"Too bad we need to go, or I would suggest we explore that thought further." Conleth tugged her by the waist, yanking her against his rock-hard chest.

Grief hit her hard. Sorrow pulsed through the bond, tangling with Conleth's pain. Was it his sorrow? Hers? She couldn't tell anymore. His dragon spirit gave him the gift of healing, but even that couldn't save Ryder. She leaned into him, resting her head on his shoulder. He didn't speak, just wrapped his arms around her, holding her.

She breathed in his scent once more, wanting to memorize it.

"I'm ready." She patted his chest. "We pay our respects, then the *ohunko* is going down."

Conleth's lips split into a wide-toothed grin. "Now that, I like to hear."

Thirty–One

On the far edge of Avalanche Ridge, the villagers walked along the forest trail. Leaves crunched underfoot, and the scent of pine mingled with the earthy dampness of the woods. Shadows stretched across their path, swallowed by the thickening canopy.

Trinity, Conleth, and Taran moved along the trail, their footsteps muffled by fallen leaves. Ahead, the ancient oak rose like a sentinel, its gnarled branches stretching to the sky, sprawling over the clearing. Ribbons, feathers, and small offerings clinging to the tree's limbs, left by grieving hands. At its base, stones formed a circle marking the sacred space. The wind whispered through the trees, filling the air, and an owl's distant hoot sent a shiver through Trinity.

"Are you sure it's safe to bring her?" Taran asked, keeping his voice low.

"She's not leaving my side." Conleth wrapped an arm around her, pulling her close to his warmth. "We'll pay our respects and go."

Trinity watched as several men carried and placed a wrapped body in the center of the stones, her heart heavy with sorrow. A young woman wept, her arms wrapped protectively around her rounded waist.

"He had a mate," Trinity whispered.

Taran tilted his head. "Perhaps we should go."

Trinity hesitated as Conleth gently nudged her to retreat. "There are so few here," she murmured, her gaze scanning the small gathering. Rourke, the pregnant woman, and only a dozen others gathered.

Duty rooted her to the spot. She owed it to this man the witness his final moments, and perhaps, in doing so, she could find a measure of peace, too.

"Let's not invite the ohunko here, shall we?" Taran said, holding out his hand for her to turn back. She glanced at Conleth. His chin dipped slightly, a quiet command she could not ignore, yet she lingered, eyes locked on Rourke. He held the woman by the elbow, guiding her back from the tree. Men formed a circle around the fire. Between them, flames licked the air, consuming the body until nothing remained but drifting ashes.

Conleth tugged on her hand.

Questions circled in her mind.

How would they rebuild the community?

She was still Fae, and he was still a shifter-blood. Could she use this merged power to help protect those on the mountain? Would they accept her after what her people had done?

The dark forest beyond the clearing rippled with the wind. Waiting. She didn't know how, but she *felt* it waiting. For whom? For her?

"Ben will meet us outside the resort. Gwen is with Arden inside the lodge helping with the youth," Taran said, and Trinity knew he spoke aloud for her benefit. Her mental communications reached only her mate. Unease filled her. "Are you keeping them inside because of the *ohunko*?"

Because of me? She hesitated, the question hanging unspoken in the air.

Trinity took a deep breath, calming the rising panic within her.

"There's a storm coming, see it in the distance?" Conleth pointed behind them. Darkness pooled in the forest and stretched across the sky, clouds crawling like smoke toward them.

Her stomach knotted. "I shouldn't be around people. It's going to come again."

And it would keep coming for her until they captured it like Peter and the wolf ohunko.

"You're not facing it alone again, *Unahu*." Conleth slipped his fingers between hers and tugged for her to come along. "We will capture it together."

A warm glow spread through her chest from Conleth. Yet doubt gnawed at her, a cold, insidious voice. "I don't think we can."

Tears pricked at the corners of her eyes, blurring the edges of the world. Her chest ached from the fight she'd waged, the battles she'd survived, and still, everything threatened to slip through her fingers.

Conleth's chest rumbled at her thoughts. His thumb rubbed across her knuckles in a soothing stroke. The blisters healed from her burns, and the heat evaporated from her palms.

"We're missing something. The first two were too easy," Taran said, his footsteps almost silent for a man his size as he walked behind them.

"What do you mean about the first two?" Trinity asked, forcing her mind away from the man who had tried to save her. Later, she'd ask Conleth about helping the shifter's mate.

Right now, she needed to stay alive.

"The bear was easy; Cedric already had it contained in the crystal shard that we sent through the portal with him." Conleth brought her hand up and kissed her knuckles as they entered the village. All the shop doors had closed, and no one lingered outside. She stumbled as she gawked. They weren't all at the funeral. Where could they be?

Conleth kept her upright as Taran explained the portal. "It's an opening to the realm of the dead; it's the land where we go in death and join the Great Hunter. Gwen's the only one we know of that can open it."

"There's a doorway to the dead?" She believed him, but the flicker in Conleth's eyes showed the doubt she cast there. "Are you sure it doesn't go to the Fae realm?"

Taran and Conleth walked in silence as they left the village, heading for the resort. Had they considered the portal might lead to the Unseelie realm?

The idea of spending eternity in a realm of darkness and decay made her stomach tighten. She had been born Fae, a creature of light and magic. All those lost souls, trapped, twisted, welded into this world by those with power to create and control them.

If the doorway led to their realm, it could mean grave danger for them all.

"Are there mushrooms around it?" she asked, testing the boundaries of the conversation she sensed in their heads. Conleth blocked her mentally. Yet the familiar press of his control tingled in her mind. The bond he shared with his brothers differed from the one he had with her. She would need time to understand the new dynamics between them.

"No mushrooms," Taran cleared his throat. "We've seen the hunter. The portal almost sucked in Gwen when we sent Cedric through."

Would the Fae realm have trapped Cedric if he had gone through the doorway? Would he be at their mercy, or would the Fae use him against them?

"Why not imprison him like Gwen's brother?" she asked.

"Because others would come and try to free him. Your PPI would set him loose, and he was too dangerous to our people," Conleth said.

"There would be an investigation based on the charges against him," Trinity clarified, offended at their lack of faith in the PPI to resolve the matter.

"They'd set him loose," Conleth repeated, a hint of agitation coming from him.

"And killing him would have brought your justice system upon us, but if he's alive and gone, our people stay safe," Taran said, as they came to a stop at the front of the resort. "Peter wasn't a threat; he did us a favor by taking the wolf ohunko from Gwen and hosting it to keep it contained. Crag's Cliff was once the fortress of the dragon clans; no spirit can escape it."

The thought of Cedric stepping through the mysterious doorway of the dead or even into the Fae realm didn't sit right. She understood the why, but the where could have far worse consequences later. If her gut was correct, and the Great Hunter's Forest lay within the Fae realm, they would have been better off keeping him locked in Crag's Cliff with Peter. Returning him to the wilds of the Fae realm might give the royals another tool against them if a war ever came.

There was still Pezi, the mountain lion ohunko.

She shivered, remembering the last time it had come for her.

The crystal hadn't reacted when she touched the hunter's body. Nothing. And the ohunko? It hadn't flinched either.

Was that young man doomed, just like she might be?

Her gaze drifted to the horizon, where storm clouds gathered like a warning.

She'd once thought meeting Conleth, even dying for him, seemed like a tragic fairy tale. Beautiful. Inevitable. But now, standing on this mountain, with the weight of fate pressing against her chest, it didn't feel like destiny.

She wouldn't let anyone decide her ending. Not the Fae. Not some shifter council. Not even prophecy.

Ben waved from the resort. The sight of him sent a chill through her.

His dragon spirit pulsed against the bond she shared with Conleth that made her skin prickle. His eyes, more dragon than human, gleamed in the fading light of the gathering clouds as he motioned for them to follow.

Conleth and Taran exchanged perplexed looks. They moved to a terrace away from anyone entering the resort. "What is this about?"

"The ohunko shifted," Taran cupped the back of his neck.

Ben rocked back as if someone had slapped him.

"It can shift back to Scout, though, right?" Her ribs ached remembering the way its claws pierced her.

"If it shifted," Ben crossed his arms. "It's gained its full strength."

Taran walked toward the entrance of the resort. Gwen came through the doors, frowning as he pulled her into an embrace.

Trinity recoiled, her lungs working double as her breaths became rapid and shallow. As she trembled, Conleth put his arm around her. "That's bad, isn't it?"

Ben shook his head, about to say something, when Gwen and Taran approached. Gwen touched Trinity's arm. "Hey, it's good to see you're okay."

Just the brush of Gwen's fingers on Trinity's bare arm caused her to gasp. She grabbed Gwen's hand.

"Trinity?" But Gwen's voice was distant. Conleth's voice in her head wasn't audible. One moment she stood beside him. Another, she stood in a shaded area of a clearing with Aluk. She heard her heart drumming in her ears. Gwen stood with her cuffs off, and the air rippled near her. Aluk shouted, his eyes turning red, and out of the shadows came Scout. And as suddenly as she had stepped into the vision, it yanked her out. Trinity gasped. Gwen's hand slipped from her hold.

"*Sylnaros*," Taran pulled Gwen away from Trinity.

"I'm fine. I'm good." Gwen's rounded eyes stared at her. "Why do I feel you just took something from me?"

Conleth grunted, shaking his head as if to clear it. He breathed in through his nose and out his mouth. "That was an experience."

"It just happened. I'm sorry," Trinity clung to Conleth. *Are you all right?*

I think you took me for a ride in the future.

She looked at him, searching for any signs of his displeasure, but instead, he smiled. "That was amazing."

"What's going on?" Gwen asked.

Trinity licked her dry lips. "We're going to need Aluk."

Taran's brow furrowed. "What did you see?"

Conleth pressed a hand to his forehead. "Gwen went through a portal, and Aluk and Scout stepped out from the shadows of the trees. That shouldn't have happened."

Ben scowled. "Don't ask me for help. I can't leave the resort, not with Aluk in hibernation."

Trinity's pulse spiked. "But we need him. I can't be bait again. It will not fall for it."

"It *will* come for you," Ben said.

Trinity stepped closer to Conleth. He slipped an arm around her, pressing his face to the side of hers, listening to the quick thrum of her heartbeat.

"It'll know it's a trap. We can't afford to put more people at risk," Taran muttered, rubbing his chin.

"Tell me what you need me to do?" Gwen said.

Taran kissed her temple. "I'll fill you in on the plan later."

Gwen smiled sadly at Trinity. "It's going to be okay."

Trinity got the impression that Gwen's words were a more comforting lie than a genuine belief. She would show Gwen that she could survive the ohunko, and they'd keep the curse from locking against the shifter bloods for another century. Their children deserved their inheritance.

"How do you know she's not leading you all into a trap?" Ben asked.

Heat gathered in her palms, and Conleth captured them in his. "Because I saw it, too. We go wake Aluk."

The heat dissipated in her palms at Conleth's proclamation. *Together.* Trinity grinned at him. *Together.*

Ben growled. "This isn't a good idea."

Thirty-Two

JAGGED, ALMOST ALIEN ROCK formations stretched into the darkness, punctuated by strange, bioluminescent growths that cast an ethereal glow. In the center of this subterranean cathedral, Aluk lay in his dragon form.

"He's a mountain of muscle and scales," Trinity said, and Conleth chuckled. He hoped he wouldn't have to defend his mate against Aluk's dragon if it woke angry or hungry.

Ben and Taran entered the lair hidden beneath the resort with them. Ben stood, feet apart and his arms crossed. His eyes turned a bright hue of gold as his dragon tried to reach out to their alpha.

The soft, rhythmic rise and fall of Aluk's chest was the only sound in the cavern, a low, primal heartbeat that echoed through the space.

"He won't wake. It's worse this time. I've never seen him this way," Taran said.

Conleth remembered when Aluk's mate perished, and his brother vanished into himself. The dragon had taken over, dragging him into a deep slumber. No one saw the rage. The grief. Aluk tried to bury it beneath silence, and Conleth had watched, helpless, as the strongest of them unraveled.

Trinity didn't see it. Couldn't.

Conleth had recognized the secret layers of his oldest brother's pain, and he'd dare the wrath of the dragon keeping his brother from protecting this mountain. Trinity's life now connected them all.

"I told you coming down here was pointless," Ben said.

"What's wrong with him?" Trinity asked, reaching for Conleth's hand. Aluk's dragon terrified him on a good day. The beast's scales rippled with blue and red tips on its scales. Large spikes ran along Aluk's back and head.

"He and his dragon aren't in sync," Conleth said, at Trinity's frown. *His bond weakened at the loss of their mate, but the alpha in him must protect the mountain. We might need to adjust our strategy.*

Ben growled, and Conleth's dragon spirit rose in his chest.

Taran put his hand on Ben. "She's part of the family now."

But Ben's eyes narrowed on her. "You shouldn't have brought her down here. This is dragon business."

"And she's part dragon," Conleth squeezed her hand, giving her a sense of unity and belonging. "She drew my fire within her and burned a man to ash."

Ben looked at him like he'd grown to head. "She shouldn't be down here. She's dangerous."

"To whom?" Conleth challenged, pulling Trinity closer. "Fire can't harm us."

"How do we know she can't take another's gift like that one's mate?" Ben lifted his chin toward Taran. "Perhaps we need another set of cuffs."

Conleth glared at Ben. "Or perhaps you have a death wish."

Conleth lowered his chin, his lip curling up into a snarl. Trinity placed her other hand on his arm. "No one is dying. Not today."

Conleth's eyes narrowed as his dragon spirit rose to the surface. The thought of Trinity in cuffs enraged his beast. *Protect.* Even against his family, he would.

Ben growled as Trinity took several steps toward Aluk's muzzle. He breathed out, warm air expelling through his nostrils and blowing Trinity's hair. Their dragons could reach the size of an army tank. Aluk, the size of a ship. Conleth stayed close to her back. "What are you thinking?"

She glanced over her shoulder at Conleth. "I think I know how to wake him. May I?"

I trust you. Conleth gave her a reassuring nod.

"Be our guest?" Taran answered, waving his hand toward their beast of a brother.

Ben grunted and muttered, "I hope he eats you."

A rumble came from Conleth.

Taking a deep breath, Trinity placed her palm in the center of Aluk's muzzle and closed her eyes. She drew on his spirit, searching for a memory. Her bond with Conleth opened to give her strength, and she knew they shared her sight. Conleth counted the beats. One. Two. Three. Four. Five. Six. Beads of sweat gathered on her forehead.

Trinity gasped.

The dragon's head snapped up, Aluk's eyes glowing with an eerie red light. Conleth grabbed her and yanked her back, shoving her behind him. "Watch out!"

The dragon reared up, its massive body blocking the only exit. Ben and Taran pressed against the rock. Conleth stood protectively in front of Trinity.

"Aluk!" Conleth shouted.

"Shift!" Taran yelled at the beast.

The dragon bared its teeth.

"Aluk!" Conleth's shout tore through the cavern, but his thoughts didn't reach. Mental contact with him snapped. The beast blocked him. The dragon lowered its head, nostrils flaring, eyes locked on Trinity.

Heat rolled off Aluk's dragon in waves, forcing her back a step.

Conleth's muscles coiled. His claws dug into the rocks beneath his boots. He could feel the dragon thrumming through him—ready to strike.

Trinity's heartbeat hammered against his chest.

Then he lunged forward, voice low and fierce. "We know what they did. We can't stop the ohunko without you."

A low, guttural growl rumbled from deep inside him. Goose-flesh rose along Conleth's arms, scales crawling beneath his skin as the dragon pressed to break free. His muscles twitched with the force of it, claws itching to rend, heart hammering with the beast's rage.

"There isn't room," Trinity pleaded, the sound of her heart beating loud in Conleth's ears.

Taran warned, "Eating her will curse us again."

Conleth locked his gaze with Ben, who lifted his head, leaning back and letting his eyes shift completely for his dragon to peer out. "*Wiyawakan ani aki pawit niyan opi nis wi kani mitawa aya.*"

Conleth translated for Trinity in his mind. *Do not let your mate's death be in vain; help us save the people and cleanse the land of the evil which plagues us.*

"*Piyan,*" Conleth's dragon spoke through him.

Aluk's dragon glared down at Conleth, taking the focus off Trinity. It growled again, its teeth not showing as much. The slits of its eyes absorbed into their red depths as the dragon closed its eyes and its head lowered.

Conleth remained wary, staying between Aluk's dragon and Trinity.

"Don't you—." Taran rushed forward, but Ben pulled him back.

The dragon shivered. Scales shimmered with a kaleidoscope of colors. Slowly, the dragon shifted. The humid air thickened around them. Conleth grabbed Trinity and rushed for the entrance where cool, fresh air waited. "Come on."

He steered her across the smooth rocks, cutting off her view. Heat radiated from him, pressing against her skin. The dragon inside him roared in warning, possessive and restless. Her pulse spiked at the intensity, human or Fae, and she couldn't look away.

Trinity struggled against his grip. "What's happening?"

He clasped her tight.

"Don't," he said as she squirmed. "It's too hot in there for you."

"I channeled your fire, remember?" She said, her words muffled against his shirt.

"We're not testing the theory today," he leaned out, as the air rippled with waves of heat. He closed his eyes, summoning his dragon forth enough to turn his skin to scales and become a shield for his mate. She leaned against him, fisting his shirt, and pressing her face to chest.

"What did you do to him?" he asked her.

While unable to reach Aluk through their telekinetic bond, Conleth growled in frustration.

"I invaded his dreams." She whispered. "I saw his dream as if it were a memory and told him to wake up, to act like an alpha."

Conleth sucked in a breath. "You're lucky he didn't roast you on the spot."

Trinity shrugged. "It woke him up."

Conleth chuckled.

"Where is she?" Aluk shouted, his voice echoing through the enormous cavern.

Conleth relaxed at hearing Aluk's human voice and stepped back. His scales retracted as he tucked a hair behind her ear. "The beast is most definitely awake. Stay behind me."

Aluk stood unclothed in the middle of the cavern. Days of growth covered his jaw and chin, and sleep made his hair wild. His fists clenched at his sides as he watched Conleth bring Trinity into his secret haven. "Is nothing sacred here anymore?"

"I told them this wasn't a good idea," Ben said. His gaze locked on Trinity.

"Lock her in the prison or cuff her like the other one. Her ability is more dangerous than the rest. The elders were right to forbid ties with the Fae and the outside world." Not Ben, but his dragon spirit spoke.

"What is he talking about?" Aluk looked at Conleth.

His eyes went dull, as did Ben's.

"Whatever you have to say, Ben, you say it so all can hear." Their cousin struck a chord with Taran, too. "I thought by now your dragon's prejudice would have faded against Gwen. Now that Trinity is among us, it seems to grow like a wart upon your face."

Ben turned his head to look at Taran. Rowtag, Ben's dragon, spoke. His voice deeper and harsher than Ben's, "You wanted to know what turned the ancient guardians? Nothing. The council ordered us to protect the mountain and the people, no matter what. The Fae woman would have stolen our gifts and given them to her people. She would have enslaved us, and they would have hunted us like animals once more. Each of us guardians forgot our posts. We let our human counterparts rule us. She went after what we loved most and used it to take the others down. She cursed their bloodlines to the shadows to ensure none of the Sentinels could return. Now she is weak, and we cannot let our hearts trap us under her control, nor be fooled by those with her blood."

"Trinity's no longer Fae. She shares the gifts of the dragon-bloods," Conleth said.

"Still Pezi hunts her," Rowtag said.

Right the wrong and return the guardians to the Great Hunter.

Aluk lifted his chin, his chest heaving as his eyes flashed between dragon and man.

"But you didn't help them?" Taran asked the question they'd both been thinking.

A ripple rose in Ben's chest, his spirit tattoo glowing beneath his collared shirt. "Do I not serve my alpha among you while the others are trapped in darkness with the lost ones?"

"You lost someone, too." Trinity hugged her waist, her hand pressing to her heart. The crystal she wore before the last attack from the ohunko dangled there from her neck.

Conleth no longer shielded her but kept her within reach.

"We took a vow. No mates. In return, the promise of extended life. Our duty lies in protecting our kind from the Fae. Few of us could resist the baser needs of humanity. She is the third daughter of the royal bloodline, as long as she lives, she's a threat to us all."

Trinity took a deep breath.

"Are you threatening my mate?" Conleth said, growling.

Rowtag's eyes flashed gold.

"Stand down, guardian," Aluk snarled.

"She's not a threat, Aluk. Take a sniff. She reeks of dragon; it's in her blood. Even if they tried, Conleth's dragon spirit ties her soul to his.

Aluk strolled up to her.

Trinity rolled back her shoulders.

He leaned toward her.

A loud rumble came from Conleth.

Aluk inhaled deeply. He leaned back and nodded. Lines furrowed across his brow, and his eyes turned red. "You are confined to the lower regions of the mountain, otherwise I'll lock you within Crag's Cliff, myself."

"Will you cuff me too? Like Gwen?" Trinity lifted her chin.

"That's not a bad idea," Ben said, himself again.

"Then you risk cutting off Conleth from his dragon spirit," Taran said, hovering nearest the exit.

"No, but Conleth...." Aluk grimaced. He rubbed a hand across his forehead. "She's yours."

Mine.

We have greater threats at large.

She doesn't leave your side.

Done.

"We captured the wolf guardian, locked him away, and sent the bear guardian back to the Great Hunter. Now, we need to do the same with the cat," Ben cracked his knuckles.

"*Pezi.*" Aluk grunted. "He lurks in the shadows and waits. The assassin. I see him in my dreams. His scent torments my dragon spirit."

Conleth stilled. Aluk had never mentioned dreams to them before. *He's been carrying this alone all this time.* What other struggles was his brother keeping from them?

"He won't be for long," Conleth said.

Ben blinked, his hand against his chest.

Taran bumped him on the arm. "You good."

"Haven't had that happen before," he grumbled.

Conleth exhaled, letting the tension flow out of him.

Aluk moved to sit on a rock, and Trinity turned away. Conleth strolled over to a place in the rock wall and tossed his brother a pair of shorts. "My mate doesn't need to see that."

Aluk snatched the shorts and put them on. He inclined his head toward Trinity. "If you ever invade my memories or dreams again, my dragon won't hesitate to turn you to ash."

Conleth's nostrils flared. "And mine won't hesitate to challenge yours."

Aluk growled, his chest expanding, and his hands clenched into fists.

"If she doesn't burn you both first." Taran smirked.

The 'she' in question didn't find it amusing. However, she got Taran was trying to defuse the tension between Conleth and Aluk. Trinity glanced at her hands, tempted to give them all a show of fire, and then promptly decided against it. Ben didn't need another reason to want to cuff her, and she'd known Conleth considered taking her to Crag's Cliff for protection.

"We all need to calm down and discuss why we're all down here," Taran said.

For once, Trinity couldn't agree more.

Conleth's broad shoulders slumped, but his dragon stayed close to the surface. She listened while Taran informed Aluk of what happened with the ohunko, with Trinity's grandfather, Aerion, and what his dragon shared with him of the past.

Aluk rubbed his beard, and shadows formed beneath his eyes the more he listened.

"I say we lock her in the prison. Dragon fire protects it. The Fae or the ohunko can't touch her there, and if the ohunko comes, we spring the trap and put the guards on alert," Ben said.

Trinity's gaze jumped between Ben and Conleth. Locked up? The thought of a small cell tightened her chest and made her blood chill.

No one is locking you up. Conleth assured her.

"That's your answer to everything." Taran paced around Ben to move closer to Aluk.

"Gwen's brother is in prison," Ben pointed out.

"And when her brother's body perishes, the wolf guardian shall follow the bear and the mountain lion guardians. It is for the Great Hunter to decide their fate."

"I haven't been fighting for my life to be locked away," Trinity said, stepping in front of Conleth, but he pulled her back.

"My mate stays with me," Conleth said.

"We've already established that," Taran took his side.

"The Fae will retaliate," Ben seethed. "She's caused us more trouble. Locking her away protects her and us."

Trinity struggled against Conleth's hold. "After all we've said, and you still just want to lock me away?"

Conleth held her tightly, trying to calm her. His dragon sent soothing vibes through the bond for reassurance.

"We're closer to breaking the curse than we've ever been," Taran pointed out. "Each one of us now has had mates with Fae blood."

"Not I," Ben said.

"Uncuff Gwen. We can capture the *ohunko* and toss it back into the portal for the Great Hunter to cast his judgment upon it. Leaving it here still poses a threat," Taran said, ignoring Ben, who wasn't a Vasumen brother.

Conleth tensed beside her as Aluk tilted his head, considering Taran's suggestion. What harm was it for Gwen to take off her cuffs? She hoped he would agree.

Finally, Aluk nodded.

Trinity breathed a sigh of relief. Taran's plan seemed like the best option. If Aluk and his dragon weren't in sync together, then the *ohunko* might see him as weak. She winced at Conleth's rumble in his chest. He looked at her, and a flood of love filled her from their bond.

"What says she doesn't bring another war to the mountain?"

She understood Ben wanted to protect his people, but she refused to allow them to lock her up. Going to Crag's Cliff, yes. Inside a cell. No, she had to stop the *ohunko* without giving up her freedom.

Conleth's eyes flashed with fire. "We don't know that."

"Have we become any better than the ohunkos who swore to protect our people?" Taran asked.

War would come, as surely as she lived and breathed.

How did they stop the Fae from retaliating? They wouldn't allow this mishap to go unpunished. They might try to kill Conleth to free her soul from him, but they didn't want her dead like the ohunko. Or would they, if she no longer served their purpose?

"If it's a war the Fae want, then let them come." Aluk stood; his eyes more human than dragon. "Let's take care of the mountain lion *ohunko,* first. Taran alert Rourke and have him fetch Trace and Sia."

No one moved or reacted until Aluk's brow spiked, and Conleth informed him of Rourke's brother Ryder's death.

Aluk grimaced. "Then, Trace and Sia. Taran, call Nardo in Frostwood and warn him of the impending weather, and Taran, you'll get Gwen."

Aluk's gaze locked on Trinity. "Do you have a crystal?"

How he knew she carried one didn't matter. His entire being radiated his alpha dominance.

"I do." Trinity held up the one around her neck. "The ohunko is currently in the body of a young hunter."

Aluk's eyes narrowed. "Then he's about to become the hunted."

He lifted his chin, rolling back his shoulders.

Conleth's grip relaxed around Trinity. "What do we do now?"

Thirty-Three

Dark clouds rolled over the mountain, dropping bucket loads of water from the sky in a constant downpour. They couldn't stage their plan with the mudslides threatening Sentinel Peak, and the village vulnerable below. Conleth, Taran, and Aluk took turns working with the wolf packs and the other shifters to secure their homes, while Conleth insisted Trinity remain in his lair where it was safer.

The rain had softened to a fine mist, clinging to the mountains and draping the forest in a damp haze. Days later, mud clung to her boots as she moved through the underbrush, each step squelching softly. Branches scraped against her arms, and the chill in the air seeped through her jacket, but she barely noticed. Her pulse thrummed in her ears, a steady drum of determination.

The storm had left broken branches and upturned earth in its wake. Faint splinters of wood crunched underfoot, reminders of the mountain's tantrum. She inhaled, tasting the sharp tang of wet pine and earth. Every breath sharpened her awareness. Somewhere out there, the ohunko hunted her.

Conleth's warning echoed in her mind, tugging at the edge of her thoughts. The ohunko would become more frantic with each passing day. Her stomach tightened, a coil of fear and resolve twisting together. But fear alone would not stop her. She lifted her chin, squared her shoulders, and pressed deeper into the mist.

She scanned the trees, muscles tensing, shadows shifting just beyond the veil of fog. Her grip tightened on the strap of her satchel, heart hammering with both dread and anticipation. If the ohunko came, she would meet it head-on. If the Fae dared follow, she would face them, too. Her jaw set, and the forest seemed to shrink around her, but she walked on. One step. Then another.

They followed a path into a clearing, each side lined with ancient trees, its canopy an umbrella against the mist. Trinity and Conleth stood between two colossal oaks, the trunks forming a natural frame. The air felt charged. Tension crackled like static electricity.

Her heart slammed against her ribs, refusing to settle into any normal rhythm. Somewhere beyond the veil of the forest, the ohunko lurked. Conleth's arm wrapped loosely around her shoulders, warm and solid, but the band around her lungs only tightened as they waited.

He turned to her to face him. His hand slid up her neck to cup her face. "We face this together."

"What if this doesn't work? What if it sees you and won't come?"

"It wants us both, remember?" Conleth slid his hand around her neck, drawing her closer.

Through their mate bond, his dragon curled around her frayed nerves. *Safe.*

Where are they? She didn't want to say it out loud and alert the ohunko to their position.

Rourke has taken off Gwen's cuffs. They are on their way. Conleth leaned in, pressing a kiss beneath her ear. "Relax."

Trinity's gaze drifted to the dense undergrowth, a sea of green and fog floating eerie over the forest floor. Aluk stood a few paces away, his silhouette a dark, imposing figure blending in with the width of the trees.

"*Unahu*," Conleth dipped his head to her neck, inhaling and wrapping around her waist. A flush crept up her neck and across her chest, heat pooling in places she shouldn't be thinking about right now.

They waited for the signal for Taran and Gwen to arrive. No wind or sound entered this place.

Conleth slid his hand down over her bottom and squeezed. She startled, and he chuckled. *I will have to work harder to distract you and get you to relax.*

He kissed her neck, working his way up to her jaw, to her lips. She wanted to kiss him back, her breath coming in pants, her lungs working overtime. *Breathe.*

How much longer?

He nipped her bottom lip playfully, teasing. The sound of Aluk's name slipped through her mind like a sigh, telling them to get a room. They needed the ohunko to think they'd come here to be alone.

Twigs snapped.

Trinity froze.

It's Taran and Gwen.

She took a deep breath. An unexpected soft breeze carried the scent of pine needles and damp earth, creating a momentary lull in the tension. Conleth pulled her closer, his embrace a warm, protective cocoon. In the fading light, dragon-fire had bled through the familiar amber.

His lips brushed hers, a gentle touch that belied the deadly game they played. She closed her eyes, allowing the illusion of safety to wash over her.

"Gwen, open the portal," Aluk said.

Wearing a dark hoodie and leggings, Gwen stepped out with Taran behind her.

Conleth's hand touched the small of Trinity's back. The gentle touch did nothing to ease her tightening muscles or her heart from racing. *He won't hurt you this time.*

I know.

A surge of power emanated from Aluk, expanding outward. The forest seemed to hold its breath as the shadows grew darker. "Find the ohunko, *Pezi*. Send him to me," Aluk commanded.

The surrounding shadows stirred, peeling from trees, bushes, and rocks. Wolves, mountain lions, and bears formed and dissolved just as abruptly to their task.

Gwen moved closer to the arch of two trees. Taran lingered behind her, sentinel-like.

Aluk stood opposite Gwen, dressed like a lumberjack in his plaid shirt and jeans with that long beard and glowing red eyes.

Trinity glanced around the forest, scanning for any sign of movement.

Aluk paced, scales rippling down his arms and disappearing.

She stepped back, her body instinctively reacting to the waves of dominance that flowed from him. Perhaps calling out an ancient guardian wasn't wise. What if Aluk's dragon became too aggressive? Would it provoke the ohunko and make it even more dangerous?

"If you want the ohunko to come, brother, you need to tone it down," Conleth said.

Trinity bit her lip, unable to look away from the crimson fire in his eyes, the coiled power in his stance.

"If it's still in the human, it might take a while," Taran said, standing like a sentinel at the forest edge. "I've tracked enough lost souls through these woods to know the shadow spirits don't give up their hosts easily."

Aluk snarled as he paced around them.

Conleth took her hand and squeezed her fingers, sending little zings of comfort to her core.

An hour passed, and Gwen straightened from leaning against a tree. "I feel them."

"Wolves," Taran whispered over the rustling of leaves.

Aluk and Conleth both tilted up their heads, inhaling deeply. Their nostrils flared at the fresh scent.

"There's a cat," Aluk growled.

A figure emerged from the shadows, cloaked in darkness. Trinity recognized Scout's tall form, but he looked different with his face painted with intricate symbols. His eyes glinted black filled with the shadow of the mountain lion spirit within him. Except for a breechclout, he stood barefoot before Aluk, but his gaze did not fail to seek Trinity. Her arms prickled with goosebumps.

Trinity forced her gaze away from Scout. Somewhere beneath the black eyes and painted symbols, a young man remained trapped.

Gwen stepped closer to the archway of trees. Her fingers flared — red, then yellow — cutting through the darkness, and tracing the seal carved into the door.

The dark glint in Scout's eyes met Aluk's with a silent challenge. The ohunko, Pezi, stepped into the clearing, his voice a low rumble. "You called for me, Alpha?"

"I'm glad to see the ancient guardians still have some respect for their alpha." Aluk pulled back his shoulders.

"I am trapped between duty and honor," the ohunko said, his voice breaking slightly. "I remember... I serve to protect, not destroy. She breeds from the enemy." His gaze passed from Conleth and Aluk to meet her gaze.

An uncontrollable shiver ran down her spine.

The air crackled as Gwen whispered, *"Nimitqwa Ktelo."*

Trinity latched onto Conleth's arm as an ethereal mirror rippled into view between the arched trees. Her breath came in ragged gasps as the tension in the clearing thickened. Conleth growled, trying to push her behind him, but Trinity locked her knees, refusing to move.

Scout's eyes, gleaming with a predatory light, fixed on Aluk.

The ohunko planted one foot behind the other.

Trinity stared at the shimmering portal.

The energy emanating from it resonated with her, a pull so powerful it felt like a magnet drawing her in. She took a step closer, fear trickling from the back of her mind.

Conleth's grip tightened on her hand, his fingers digging into her skin. *Stay back!*

Trinity's feet moved forward. Stop. She couldn't. The portal hummed through her bones, a siren call she couldn't name.

Conleth's dragon pressed against their bond, but her hand was already reaching toward the shimmering veil. Just one step closer. Her fingers stretched toward it.

Trinity no!

He jolted her out of her trance.

Trinity pulled her hand from Conleth and stepped back from the portal.

"Your work here is done, ancient one. Return through to the Great Hunter." Aluk gestured toward the portal.

Scout's lips curled into a sneer. "It was you who placed me on this quest, great one."

"You ordered my mate killed?" Each word a venomous dart. Conleth's low growl vibrated through her, his dragon edging closer to the surface. Goosebumps rushed up her arm. Trinity pressed against Conleth, her palm flat against his chest, but his skin was already scorching. The first ripple of scales erupted down his arms and neck.

Aluk's gaze met Conleth's. His shoulders stiffened, then his eyes flashed dangerously between red and dark."I did not."

The ohunko's laughter echoed through the clearing. "I never thought the day would come for an alpha to lie."

Aluk lunged forward, grabbing Scout by the throat. Scout's body stiffened, his eyes wide and swirling with darkness.

"Speak, guardian," Aluk growled, low and menacing. "What do you mean I commanded you on this quest?"

"Not you, but the dragon within you, the true alpha. The one who tossed his own mate into the heart of the mountain and commanded each of us to protect our people and keep the Fae from stealing our gifts. I will not return to the Great Hunter, having failed my quest."

She sensed a trap closing in around them.

Wait before you act. Don't trust the ohunko. *He's trying to save himself.* Trinity pleaded with Conleth to keep him from shifting to attack his brother.

"He wouldn't have done that," Taran growled, his eyes more red than dark.

"I can't hold it open much longer." Gwen groaned, her hands slipping down, the portal wavering. Its shimmering surface grew unstable.

If the portal closed, they'd lose their opportunity to be rid of the *ohunko.*

"A little while longer. Please," Trinity pleaded, wishing she had a way to help Gwen.

Aluk's chest expanded and rumbled. "We are not repeating the past. I did not command you to harm the mate of my brother."

"No," Trinity placed her hand against her throat. Her gaze flew to Conleth. "But I know who may have."

Conleth curled his lip. "Aerion."

Aluk tilted his head. "It would take a powerful Fae to glamor themselves as a dragon and compel the guardians."

Scout's jaw slackened.

"He's a Fae elder. He tricked you." Trinity took a cautious step toward Scout. Her eyes locked on his boyish face. "They tricked me, too. They want to use me to gain power and suppress your people. And you've been helping them. The Great Hunter sent you to protect your people. Your bloodline is going extinct. This is your chance to make it right. You don't have to hurt me. Conleth and I have mated. They can't use me anymore in their plans. You see, there doesn't have to be bloodshed."

She took another step closer.

Conleth growled from behind her.

Scout regarded her with a contemptuous sneer. "Says the Fae female who will bring death to us all."

Conleth snarled. "Touch my mate, and you die."

"Without my quest, I have no purpose." Scout looked over at Trinity. His lost look stirred an all-too-familiar hurt within her. Until she reached the mountain, all she had cared about was finding Cedric. All along she'd been a pawn, like the ohunko.

"Your purpose is to protect our people," Aluk reminded the ohunko. "If you want to restore your honor, you'll release the young man whose body you hold and return to the Great Hunter to join the other guardians."

Scout's face contorted, his eyes wild, darting between Aluk and the portal.

Aluk released his grip. "The choice is yours, Pezi."

Scout gasped for air, struggling to regain his breath.

"Time is running out." Taran moved closer to Gwen, his jaw tight as she groaned under the strain of holding the portal open. Trinity's gaze darted between Scout and the portal. It wavered and sweat poured down Gwen's face.

Scout's hand clamped down on her arm. "I cannot rest if I fail again."

She shoved against him, but his lips collided with hers.

Conleth wrenched her from his grasp as he lunged at the ohunko.

Scout's body crumpled to the ground with a thud.

Trinity stumbled backward. What happened? The ohunko slithered under her skin, cold and invading. Her mate mark burned. She touched her head as the spirit filled her mind. Her breath came in short, ragged gasps as her thoughts became muddled. Her mate bond with Conleth became faint. A dense fog swirled around in her head. The spirit filled her, took control of her body as Trinity stared into the thick mist rolling towards her. Bile rose in her throat. The bitterness of it gagged her.

Conleth knelt by the body, but Aluk moved forward. He hauled Scout to his feet, dragging him to the portal.

"He's gone." Conleth turned. "Trinity."

I'm going to face the Great Hunter, and you're going with me. I shall not fail. A cold and commanding voice echoed in her head, blocking her mate bond with Conleth. The spirit's presence drowned out her scream.

Conleth's eyes widened as she moved toward the portal, unable to control her body—like a puppet on invisible strings. *Why are you doing this? They compelled you. I know what that feels like.*

A cruel smirk spread across the cat's face in her mind's eye. *Because I'm doing it to you right now.* The voice in her head intensified. *If I merge with your soul, then you shall never come back. But the mountain needs blood and tears, and I shall not go without completing my quest.*

Pezi, the *ohunko,* clawed deeper into her mind, trying to consume her from the inside out. She threw up a shield, blocking the spirit from her core. A ring of fire surrounded her soul in response. The cold spread toward her mate bond, reaching for Conleth, but she shoved back with everything she had. "Trinity," Conleth said again, his voice a low growl.

"She's mine now," the ohunko taunted.

"The Cat has her. It's in my mate!" Conleth roared.

Trinity! His desperate cry filled her mind.

You want me dead, then face me like a warrior. Don't try to possess me! She pushed back in crowding against the cat to gain control.

Conleth struggled to hold her, his muscles straining against the *ohunko's* attempts to twist free.

I will face you here, where the others may not interfere. The cat prowled around her, its onyx eyes glinting in the dark recesses of her mind.

Taran and Aluk rushed forward, and Aluk grabbed Trinity's leg as she kicked out at him. Her screams echoed through her mind. *I'm not going through that portal!*

Conleth's grip tightened; he snarled as fire circled the mountain lion, causing it to jump back away from her. *I've waited a long time,* Conleth's dragon spirit growled. Vareth filled her mind, too. *You will never take my mate away again!*

"Hurt it, you hurt Trinity," she heard Aluk say with a grunt as her foot landed against his gut. Pain split through her skull. Her temples pounded. Her awareness bounced between her mind and her body. *You can't kick an alpha!*

The ohunko inside her hissed.

"Whatever you do, Trinity, fight. Don't let it enter your soul," Conleth's voice reached her from outside.

A sharp pain pricked the center of her mind. The cat crouched and then disappeared. Trinity spun in a circle, heart hammering, then froze. A man stood among the flames. The same symbols covered his body as Scout's body. His short dark hair spiked, and in his grasp was a bow with a loaded arrow.

"Fight." Conleth said into her ear.

You'll kill us both, she said to the ancient warrior.

Not if you give me your soul, chosen one. Together, *we will be the most powerful guardian of all.*

"You should have stayed in your world," the ohunko said, his eyes swirling between darkness and blue. "I had almost forgotten what I am until you woke me from my post."

Pezi raised his bow and aimed the arrow at Trinity's heart.

She heard Gwen saying, "Close off your soul. It's like closing your mind off. Put a shield around it and don't let it touch you."

Yeah, she'd done that. Fire leapt from her core.

"Shut the portal," Conleth shouted.

She tried to concentrate, to pull from their bond, but his dragon spirit drew nearer. She could still feel Conleth's arms around her and other hands restraining her body.

The ohunko hissed at Conleth in Trinity's voice, "Touch her and I dive for her soul. It's a shame, really. She's filled with incredible power. She would have made a strong mate."

Conleth growled. "Give her back to me."

Unahu, fight. Don't let it take you. Use what you need to force it out. His voice, or maybe his dragon's, pleaded.

"She can't," the ohunko said mockingly, pulling back his arm.

There was nowhere for her to retreat. No place in her mind to escape.

Conleth, she whispered.

A large dark shadow with red eyes landed alongside her.

A glimmer of hope appeared as Gwen said, "No, but I can."

I've got you, Unahu. Focus on that shield.

Trinity's body acted of its own accord, kicking and squirming.

"Cease!" Aluk commanded. Her body stilled. The ohunko trapped her consciousness deep in her mind. She watched the arrow release, a tiny speck against the vastness of the sky.

Dark wings enclosed around her, shrouding her in darkness.

"Carry her closer to the portal. Careful, don't touch it," Gwen's voice called out. The sensation of being carried made her stomach lurch, or was her mind floating?

"No," Trinity shouted. "NO!"

Conleth's dragon raised its head above her. *Forgive me, mate, for I was weak without you, but never again.*

Suddenly, someone whispered to her. Chanting. Words muffled. The ohunko shouted. The call of a warrior. Heat blazed above her. Conleth's dragon spirit released its fury upon the *ohunko* in her mind as Trinity's body jerked. The cold sucked out of her. The scent of flesh burning, of ash, made her stomach heave. When the stream of fire ceased, she breathed, coughed, and choked. As she vomited, a pair of muscular arms cradled her. Trinity moaned, blinking as things came back into focus.

The portal shimmered and stabilized.

Beyond the portal, a lush, primeval forest stretched out. A magnificent creature fell and rolled, transforming in one fluid motion into a man. Raven hair adorned with feathers, chest marked with glowing symbols. A primal cry tore from his lips as he sprinted toward them. Gwen's hand moved. The portal vanished.

Trinity's legs gave out, and Conleth caught her.

I've got you, Unahu. I'm never letting you go.

She'd kept her shield up. Her soul was still intact. *I'm safe.*

Tears of joy sprang to her eyes. *It's gone.*

Slowly, Conleth's dragon spirit retreated, leaving their bond open for the overflowing sensations of love and belonging between them.

Gwen collapsed against Taran, her breath coming in ragged gasps.

"We did it," Gwen said, breathlessly. "Are you okay?"

Trinity closed her eyes, waited a moment, then opened them. Her hands shook. "You don't know how good it feels to have that cat out of my head. Thank you."

A shudder ran through her. "I can still feel where it tried to claw into my soul," she whispered.

Conleth's arms tightened around her. "You're safe now. It's gone."

"But for how long?" Her gaze lingered on the spot where the portal had been. "That's the Unseelie realm…"

Conleth showered the top of her head with gentle kisses. The pressure and spinning in her head had finally ceased, but her heart hammered on. After a moment, she steadied herself and slipped out of his embrace. Her gaze found Aluk. He stood with his back to them, his dragon's low growl vibrating through the forest.

"Where's the body?" Taran asked.

Trinity looked down. There was no sign of Scout. A collective gasp swept through the group as they scanned the area. Aluk turned around, a leather cord dangling from his hand. He opened his fingers, revealing a broken crystal.

Trinity's knees felt weak. "What is that?"

Gwen's face paled. "Is that what I think it is?"

"How can that be?" Taran asked.

"I don't think that portal is what you think it is." Trinity pressed her hand against her temple. She shared a vivid image of a forest with twisted trees. Their branches reached towards the sky like skeletal fingers. The air held a cold, eerie mist, and the ground displayed strange, glowing mushrooms.

"That's your Great Hunter's Forest, but I know that forest," Trinity said, looking at Conleth.

Conleth's eyebrows furrowed. "What do you mean you know that forest?"

Conleth opened their bond, and Trinity closed it. She might not be right. For their sake, she wanted to be wrong.

Trinity hesitated, unsure how to explain. "In a book in Aerion's library. The Fae call it Mist Forest. I can't be positive without the book, but I think you opened a doorway to the Unseelie realm. It would explain why I felt pulled to enter it."

Trinity's hands went cold. If the Unseelie had ties to the shifter bloodlines... She looked from the broken crystal to Conleth. In the Unseelie realm, shifters were nothing more than animals. Her throat tightened. "They escaped," she whispered. "Your animal spirits escaped from *them*."

She heard the growl of Conleth's dragon in her mind. Did it sense her thoughts? She reached through their bond. The dragon didn't know. Yet, a lingering sense of one who did hovered just beyond her grasp.

"Can you prove that?" Aluk's eyes flashed with his dragon's presence. His tone carried an authority that was not entirely his own.

"Not without returning to Aerion's estate," she admitted. "We might find it in the PPI library, but I don't know if I can go back there."

Aerion's estate sat on the northern edge of the Endless Mountains, right outside shifter territory. She might have a small window of time to return before anyone discovered his death. Several members of his household staff were human, which might work to her advantage. It was safer than relying on the PPI, at least until she could confirm it was truly safe to go back.

"Your place is here with me," Conleth said, opening the mate bond wider, pushing his love and acceptance to anchor her.

She pressed her hand to his chest. "Always."

Aluk clutched his hand back around the broken crystal. He closed his eyes, taking several deep breaths. When he opened them again, he said, "Taran, take your mate to Rourke and get the cuffs back on. Alert him of the new threat."

"Aren't we going to find Scout?" Trinity asked as Conleth led her past his brother. Her arm brushed Aluk's, his gaze on something in the forest. Trinity staggered as the vision vanished. She bit her lip, fighting a gasp clawing its way up. The images burned behind her eyes, vivid and insistent. She blinked hard, forcing herself to breathe.

"What is it?" Conleth asked.

Trinity's breath caught as her mind kept flashing the image of a beautiful woman with vivid green eyes. When Conleth's eyes grew round, his scales slipped back under his skin, she realized she'd unknowingly shared it through their bond.

"We can't deal with anymore threats right now," she said, pressing her face against his chest. "I nearly lost myself there, Conleth. I need …"

She couldn't finish the sentence, but she needed him, needed to feel safe and alive.

"Leave the hunter to me." Aluk's intense glare landed upon her. "Take your mate and go."

He warned her about evading his memories, but did the future count?

"We should go home and enjoy the time we have before they discover what's happened."

Aluk stalked off into the woods, pulling off his shirt as he went.

"Do you think he'll find him?"

Conleth's gaze lingered on her. "You need time to heal," he said murmured. "Everything else can wait."

"Can it?" Trinity glanced back toward where Aluk had disappeared into the woods. "Scout's still out there; we may have opened a door to our enemies; and I just had a vision involving Aluk."

"One crisis at a time, *Unahu*. Right now, you need to recover from nearly having your soul torn apart."

Trinity opened her mouth to argue, but exhaustion pulled at her like a heavy blanket. The adrenaline from the fight fled her, leaving her feeling hollow and shaky. Maybe he was right. Maybe she needed to be whole before she could face whatever came next.

Conleth must have sensed her internal surrender.

"Trinity," Conleth said gently. "Resort, lair, or clinic."

"No Crag's Cliff?"

"Is that where you want to go?"

"Lair." She didn't need luxury, just walls thick enough to keep the world out. Somewhere she could breathe. A place where she could explore her new gifts and this emerging connection with her mate. "I need to feel like myself again before we face whatever comes next."

Also by S.E. Lower

<u>Warrior's Mark: Dragons</u>

Marked by Loyalty (Novella)

Marked by a Vow

Marked by an Oath

Marked by a Curse

About the author

S.E. Lower writes urban fantasy, paranormal romance, and epic fantasy, bringing readers into worlds filled with magic, hidden realms, and supernatural intrigue. Whether it's dragon shifters, fae, or the forces of darkness and destiny, her stories are packed with immersive adventure. When I'm not writing, she loves thrifting for hidden gems, walking through the woods, and spending time with her kiddos and husband traveling open roads and looking for her next adventure.